Also by Paulette Stout

Novels

Love, Only Better: Bold Journeys Book 1

What We Never Say: Bold Journeys Book 2

What We Give Away: Bold Journeys Book 4 (March 2025)

A Million Ways: Stories of Motherhood (Anthology)

Short Stories

All About Kyle

Ho Ho Hanukkah: A Kyle and Rebecca Holiday Story

The Breakup

What Eyes Can't See

A Novel | Bold Journeys Book Three

Paulette Stout

Media Goddess Inc.

FIRST EDITION

Edited by Miranda Darrow.

Cover designed by Rena Violet

ISBN 978-1-7366371-7-3 (eBook Edition)

ISBN 978-1-7366371-8-0 (Paperback Edition)

Library of Congress Control Number: 2023914524

Published by Media Goddess Inc., 241 Arlington Street #814, Acton, MA 01720

Visit paulettestout.com for author information.

For those seeking to belong, know you've found a home.

Author's Note

Growing up in Manhattan, I was surrounded by professional people of all genders and ethnicities. When reading women's fiction, however, I don't often see that rich diversity reflected on the page. In writing my books, I include diverse characters that span races, religions, gender identities, and economic backgrounds. Why? Because that's the world we live in.

After writing the side character Barbara Washington for two novels, I knew she deserved a book of her own. She's a talented, Black professional who embodies so many of the amazing qualities I found in the women surrounding me growing up. And while I can draw on my personal experiences of otherness and exclusion as a bi-racial woman of color (Hispanic/Jewish), I'm not Black.

So I committed myself to getting Barbara's story right.

I interviewed Black women and women of color to learn about their lived experiences in our society. I consulted books that explored the experiences of Black women in the workplace, including The Memo: What Women of Color Need to Know to Secure a Seat at the Table by Minda Harts, and You Don't Look Like a Lawyer by Tsedale M. Melaku. Additionally, I had amazing Black women read many rounds of my manuscript, each providing insight, depth, and texture to Barbara's journey. Finally, I respectfully listened in Black social spaces to hear real-time concerns, frustrations, joys, and banter. I then infused these invaluable lessons into the book.

Words cannot express how indebted I am to my sensitivity readers: Dr. Shirley Knowles, Michelle Quarles, J. D., and Melany Barrett for their commitment to helping me bring Barbara's story to the page. Hearing them express how meaningful it was to open a book and see someone like them on the page confirmed for me that we got the book right.

If you read the story and feel seen, I'm so glad.

If you read the story and feel overwhelmed, questioning whether the Black experiences portrayed in the book actually happen, I invite you to sit with those emotions and press on. It's the expectation society places on women of color, and especially Black women, every day for a lifetime.

Paulette

Chapter 1

BARBARA

Waves lapped the hem of my nightgown, the wet sand seeping through from hours of sitting. The fabric floated in a moment of blissful weightlessness before the undertow sucked the magic away. Just like my life.

It was my wedding day, only I wasn't the bride. Not anymore. Joe, my ex-groom, was off bedding someone new. No doubt the owner of the red thong. I found it moments before I saw her wearing my fiancée in the bed we'd shared for three years. My fairytale world shattered by dental floss masquerading as underwear.

Another wave rolled in, this one chillier. No two were alike. Some caressed like bath water, sharing gifts from the ocean floor. Others were icy, as the dark depths reluctantly crashed to the surface. A reminder that the cold truth is always there. Lurking. Same as my discovery about Joe.

The signs were there, despite my willful blinders. Joe's wandering eye in social situations. His whistling after evening business dinners. His lack of disappointment when I had to work late. Both our jobs were demanding. I was on track to make General Counsel at my company at age 31, a huge accomplishment for anyone, let alone the only Black woman on the legal team. My mistake was thinking Joe understood and supported me. He knew the sacrifices success demanded.

Or so I thought.

A whopping misstep in a life founded on precision. Not that I had much choice. My dad, a famed lawyer himself, expected perfection. As did the rest of our high-achieving family. Failure was unthinkable in the Washington household. Its rare occurrence received blank stares like you were speaking a foreign language, and was easily dismissed as an outlier. Our norm was excellence.

Perfect grades from kindergarten through college.

Passing the bar exam on the first try.

Getting the dream job.

Meeting the ideal guy. A smart, accomplished, driven Black man even my dad liked. Instead of buying him off, as he'd attempted with my past boyfriends he didn't like, they became fast friends. Dad took my breakup with Joe almost harder than I had.

Until now.

Until today.

I rubbed my arms, building up friction to warm myself. But the chill penetrated my bones so deep, I feared it'd stay forever. I inched backward, the sand sticking to my pruned fingers as the morning sun peeked over the horizon.

It was a beautiful day.

My wedding pictures would have been glorious.

The reality hit me like a two-ton weight.

My miscalculation of scheduling a non-refundable destination wedding backfired in epic fashion. I had a ceremony with no groom. But I refused to invest any more time, equity, and love in a man unwilling to return those gifts. Our breakup was inevitable. The accelerated timeline turned into a merciful parting gift to myself.

Meanwhile, giving the event reservation to my best friend Rebecca made perfect sense. It saved me from shopping for a present (not that I mind shopping, as long as there's a concierge involved), but it also meant my painstaking preparations would go to someone I loved. The no-frills courthouse ceremony Rebecca had planned at Manhattan City Hall wasn't hard to top. Her finances were always tight. The plan was logical to a fault.

Too bad my damaged psyche refused to play along.

The idea of my breakup with Joe was so new. Until the thong, our destinies were intertwined. I moved into his brownstone on New York's Upper West Side and we immediately became a power couple. He joined me on legal outings and golf trips. I was his plus-one on client junkets to Cancun, Puerto Rico, and Aspen. Visions of our future life crystallized. Until it vanished behind a wall of writhing flesh I couldn't unsee.

Another wave washed in, foam fizzing as the water receded. I wiggled my toes in the sand, willing myself to feel less abandoned. My mom's absence hit worst at times like these. She'd been gone nearly 14 years, yet each morning I awoke hoping her cancer had been a bad dream.

Mom, I need you today. I don't know how I'll manage to be there for Rebecca.

My eyelids drifted closed to listen for her. Instead, my dad's voice rang through. *Suck it up. You're a Washington.*

Could I do it?

Stand at the altar on my wedding day—as Maid of Honor?

"There you are," Rebecca said, walking barefoot in the damp sand. Her long curly locks and ankle-length maxi dress blew in the salty breeze.

I attempted a smile, but tears trailed down my face as they had for hours.

"Oh, honey," Rebecca's tender expression said it all. She sat to give me a tight arm squeeze, her warmth a surprising welcome.

"I knew this was a bad idea. Let's skip the ceremony."

"Oh no—"

"We have all the City Hall paperwork done. We can lounge in the sun and have a quiet day."

My back stiffened. "Forget it. Your parents are here, his parents are here, and I bought a Valentino dress straight out of Milan and it will be worn."

She eyeballed me, uncertain. "You sure?"

"Definitely," I said, almost believing it myself. "I even skipped my trademark stilettos. Christian Louboutin and sand don't mix."

Rebecca slapped her heart. "Yet another sacrifice you've made for me."

"I'll add that to the tally."

Rebecca's expression grew serious. "I can't help but feel this is my fault. I never should have introduced you to Joe. But he was so charming and confident…"

"That he was." My chin sagged to my crossed forearms, the ocean's swells mirroring my tears. "I fell hard and blew by all the red lights flashing caution."

A tsunami rolled in, drenching our clothes and sending us yelping away. Yet another wake-up call that my dream was over.

Rebecca flicked her arms dry. "You'll find someone new. And he'll be better. Look what happened to me. Ethan dumped me and I met Kyle. The same will absolutely happen to you. Probably when you least expect it."

I wanted to believe my friend's earnest prediction. "Promise me I'll meet a good man and everything will be okay?"

"I promise." She pulled me close. "You're strong and smart and own your future. It'll be magical. Your next Mr. Right could be anywhere. Even here on this island."

Our attention drifted to a dude sleeping on the lounge chair behind us, his state somewhere between drunk and dead. Our gazes met and Rebecca shrugged.

"Okay, maybe he's not here at this moment, but he's out there. Besides, you're an amazing woman who can define herself, with or without a man."

I linked her arm. "Forget my troubles. We're here to celebrate a match that worked—yours. And, thanks to me, we both smell like kelp. I'd say some bathing is in order."

"You sure? I was serious about postponing."

I bumped her shoulder. "Today is your wedding day. Let's make it amazing."

"I love you. You know that?" Rebecca said.

"I do."

We stumbled up the beach chatting while our wet gowns tangled between our legs, launching us into a fit of giggles. She headed back to her cabana and I struggled along in the sand toward mine. Rebecca was right. My future was bright and I was determined to begin living again.

While I fought with my nightgown, a shirtless guy jogged by. With suntanned skin, brown curly hair, and a sexy-as-hell snake tattoo circling his torso, he was a bad boy who looked deliciously good.

He shot me a smile as he passed, our eyes connecting for the briefest of moments. Once lost, his absence hurt. I whipped my body around to watch his retreating form jog down the beach.

"My lord is that man gorgeous." I said to no one, but he must have heard. He began jogging backwards with a wide grin.

Shit.

"Back at 'cha, lovely."

I turned to hide my heated face, but my ankles tangled in my dress and I toppled over on the beach like a mermaid caught in a net.

"Oof!" I grunted. My shoulder took the brunt, but I got a mouthful of sand, the ground up shells sticking to my tongue. I spit them out, then wiggled an arm free to swipe away the rest.

"You okay?" My Adonis yelled.

Mortified was more like it.

Still gathering breath and detangling from my twisted dress, I didn't answer. He drew closer, kneeling by my side where his manly scent only made matters worse.

"Are you hurt?" he asked.

"Only my pride..." I admitted, wiping my face clear of sand as best I could. Damn, he was even more gorgeous up close. Hazel eyes and lean, powerfully solid muscles that flexed as he squatted. Snowy skin peeked out from where his shorts slipped at his waist. Not that I was looking.

"Here." He extended his hand to help me and we both rose to our feet. I'm tall at 5'10" and he was still taller. I wobbled, dizzy, but he caught me.

"You okay?" he asked studying me, worried. Having a man be concerned for me was a welcome change and I was ashamed to admit how much I'd missed it. I did my best to recover, standing up tall.

"You're a menace, you know," I said.

His eyebrows shot up. "Me? I never touched—"

"You can't parade around with that gorgeous body and expect women not to fall over. Christ, that tattoo alone is knee-melting." I busied myself with wiping sand off my arms while he burst out into a delicious, rolling laugh.

"You always this direct?"

"Yes. It's one of my most redeeming qualities."

He smiled at that. "What's your name?"

"Barbara."

"I'm Sebastian. Apologies that my unbelievable hotness was an inconvenience."

"It wasn't entirely inconvenient," I whispered, hoping he didn't hear, though he probably did.

Sebastian watched me with an expression I couldn't place. Like he was deciding whether to be flattered, insulted, or devour me with his lusty eyes.

We stood, unspeaking. Probably because neither of us knew what to say or do. A gust of wind blew my long hair in my face. By the time I cleared it away, the mood had shifted.

"Glad you're okay. I'll go put a shirt on. You know, to protect public safety?" He hiked a thumb in the direction he was running.

"You do that."

"Sure you don't need help to your cabana?"

"Positive, but thanks anyway."

I stood my ground and waited for him to leave first.

He resumed his jog, turning back to smile and wave goodbye. I shooed him away with both hands and heard his delicious laugh mix with the ocean breeze as he ran into the distance.

Back in the suite, I checked my phone. A few work emails. I skimmed the subject lines for anything urgent but resisted the urge to read any fully. They were going to announce the General Counsel decision on Monday, meaning my life was about to change. It was a promotion I deserved and had interviewed for. Any jitters I had about landing the role I'd "temporarily" held for two years evaporated after the resounding Board support that flowed in following my interview. While it wasn't officially mine, I'd more than earned it. With my now ex out of the picture, I could dive into my new job with no apologies. Work distractions would normally be welcome, but not today. I needed this vacation to be a vacation. I closed the app and deleted the daily "forgive me" texts from Joe.

He had to be joking. Once a cheater, always a cheater. I deserved better. How many times had my mom proclaimed she'd smack my dad with a baseball bat if he ever cheated? Enough that he knew better. She said it kept him in line and that I should never accept a lesser standard of fidelity from whomever I chose to marry. Mom was looking down on me and I needed to make her proud. Forgiveness was one thing. Stupidity was earned.

While toweling off from my shower, a gentle rap sounded at the door. Leslie, the final member of our college-bestie trio, stood smirking into the peephole.

"You going to open up?"

"I'm naked."

"Nothing I haven't seen before!" Leslie joked, as I opened the door enough for her to squeeze in.

"Where were you all night? I called and texted. I even walked around to the ocean side and saw your room was empty."

It figures. An accomplished investigative reporter, Leslie's detective instincts were always on high alert. But then they had to be when you're navigating the seedy underbelly of New York City to chase stories.

"I was on the beach watching the waves. I kept expecting one of them to wash enlightenment over me, but no dice." I padded into the bathroom, half closing the door to slip on a pink satin bathrobe.

"It'll take time." Leslie called through the door. "You've come so far in the last month, absorbing it all, moving out..."

"Don't remind me. I never expected to be back home living with my dad. When did I become a screwup?" I exited, heading to the mini fridge for a bottle of water. I offered one to Leslie, but she shook it off.

"There are many words to describe you, but screwup isn't one of them. You're the least screwed up person any of us know. This is a setback, for sure. But you're an amazing woman. You'll get through i t."

I sipped my water, then replaced the cap. "Normally I'd agree with you, but it's hard to be optimistic right now."

"Don't force it. Live in the moment and feel what comes. Be pissed off. Be sad. Whatever, it's okay."

Leslie had a point. My whole life was spent with my head down, barreling ahead toward the next goal. Controlling my outward emotions, I always presented a logical mind, never exposing the true toll unwavering perfection took on me. Professional hair, perfect wardrobe, taking on more assignments at work without complaint. Never responding to slights or passive-aggressive insults from colleagues or bosses. I was expected to dazzle in every social situation. My parents made it crystal clear: I had to be twice as good as my white peers to get as far. Yet I didn't want to get as far. I wanted to blow them away, outpacing everyone else until they were panting heaps left in my dust. I envisioned myself scaling a summit and looking back down, laughing while my cape snapped in the breeze. Consistently striving for that high bar left no time for pity parties.

I'm long overdue.

But my best friend's wedding day couldn't be shittier timing.

"I promise to 'feel,' but today, I'll settle for faking my way through."

"That works." Leslie said. "Hey, it won't all be misery. I hear the gal who planned this shindig spared no expense."

"She didn't. Thank heavens for that!"

"We're on a gorgeous island, the sun is out, the water is a color I've only seen in commercials..."

"And at least we don't have to wear the bubblegum pink dresses Rebecca was stuck in at Kyle's sister's wedding. You see those pictures?" I shuddered.

"Tragic. I'll never do that to you." Leslie's pocket buzzed. "Oh, shit. I have to get ready. I set an alarm, so I didn't lose track of time."

Leslie squeezed my satiny shoulders. "You can do this. You are the best-friend-ever to gift them this day. You're a generous, loving person. You deserve every happiness, and I'm so sorry today didn't work out as planned."

I kissed her cheek. "Scoot. I'll see you soon."

The moment she left, I flopped on the bed. *Feel what I'm feeling? Was that even allowed?* If I did that, I'd be rocking in a corner, hugging my knees. There was no time for that. And I refused to look mopey in Rebecca's pictures. Like it or not, I had to put on a brave face for a few more hours. Then the weekend was mine. Maybe a dose of Rebecca and Kyle's undying love was just the balm I needed to soothe my broken heart.

Chapter 2

SEBASTIAN

The glow of my cellphone faded as I slipped through the sliding door to my cabana. Dripping from my dip in the ocean after running, I ignored it en route to the bathroom. I blotted my face with a hand towel before doing a quick sweep around my body. Even after five days here, I still half expected the ocean's turquoise to tint the white terry. But the color was real, even if this getaway wasn't.

A week entirely to myself with no responsibilities? What a gift. I'd leave for the day and return to find the room neat as a pin. It was a luxurious life I could totally get used to, if not for the eye-popping price tag. Well, less pricey than it might've been. A big wedding canceled a block of rooms, forcing the resort to heavily discount their primo accommodations. My travel deal alert, the one I always ignored, finally came through. The price was too tempting to pass up given my week's break between jobs. My new position started Monday, but until then my time was my own.

I hadn't taken a vacation alone since... actually, this was my first one ever. Staycations were more my thing after a financially lean upbringing. All we could typically afford was to cram our meager belongings into a rental car for a budget getaway to my aunt's in the Poconos. But leaving meant missing out on the neighborhood action. I'd come back and my friends would shake their heads and say, "you had to be there."

For once, being away felt right. I had a sizable raise heading my way. Combined with years of scrimping, it was time to stop pretending I couldn't afford it. We lived off scrambled eggs and ramen for so long, my current bank balance had since become hard to absorb. I kept thinking I'd blow it and end up like Mom, trading food stamps for cash to buy me shoes. Some days, the luxury of eggs was a pipe dream. Even after Mom found steady work, we lived much the same. Fortunes flipped in an instant.

How many in my Lower East Side neighborhood thought they'd finally made it when their champagne bubble popped? Folks would whisper on street corners, placing bets on when it'd all come crashing down.

Yeah. Best to keep my expensive tastes at bay.

Buffing my head dry, I peeked at my phone.

God damn it.

I pantomimed throwing my cell against the wall before exhaling a cleansing breath.

Okay. Better.

I activated voice dialing. "Call Mom."

"Calling Mom." The device parroted.

It rang less than once before she answered. "Oh, thank God. Where were you?"

"You know exactly where I am. On vacation. And I don't need a neighborhood news report three times a day. I'm trying to unplug, remember?"

"Never mind that. Guess who was waiting for me outside of work today? Guess. You'll never guess…" From her tone, it sounded like I wouldn't want to hear the answer.

"Um." I wasn't in the mood to play guessing games when a glorious breakfast spread awaited me. Good thing I got my impatience from her. I opened the mini fridge for a courtesy bottle of water.

"Never mind, I'll tell you. Dante."

"For the love of God. What now?"

"He stood there holding court like he owned the place."

A huge gossip, my mom knew everyone in our neighborhood. Plus, her job at the Department of Motor Vehicles made her the early warning system for every marriage, divorce, and DWI in our Lower East Side community. And in Dante's case, a release from prison. I gave up years ago trying to get Dante to straighten up. He acted big until his butt landed back behind bars. He thought Mo's protection would keep him safe, but that was near impossible for a jamoke like Dante.

Unlike him, I'd stayed clean since my last stint in juvy at 16. I quit being a knucklehead in time for my juvenile record to remain sealed. It beat having an adult rap sheet shadowing me at every turn like Dante's. The moment he got out of jail, he came nosing around me for scraps. Being flat broke after prison was one of those times.

Regardless, Dante and his latest mess would wait until after my getaway.

"Mom, it's hard to relax when you call constantly."

"This is different. Dante will…"

"…not annoy me while I'm away on a tropical island. You're right."

I read her mind, though, and she wasn't entirely wrong to be worried. Dante straddled the fence between harmless pest and dangerous thug. The uncertainty kept us on edge. But I was under Mo's protection, and it'd been years since Dante posed a genuine threat to me. Mom was stuck navigating off fumes from my former li fe.

"I think you need a vacation of your own."

I heard her stiffen. "Don't crack wise to me. You're not too big to fit across my knee."

I burst out laughing. "C'mon. Your head is a foot shy of my chin. Let this spanking fantasy go."

"The garden rake! I could—"

"Enough. I'll see you in a few days. And no more calls. Even we need boundaries."

After a quick shower, I dressed and headed to the breakfast buffet. I loaded my plate with cheese, fruit, granola, bacon, and a toasted bagel before finding a seat on the veranda. I could almost tell the time by the temperature of the sea breeze caressing my skin. The heat was mild now, but in a few hours would sizzle just enough to make me want to try cooking an egg on the pavement. For now, resort workers busied themselves in morning routines. They washed, vacuumed, and rolled carts stacked with folding chairs to the beach to set up for the daily slate of weddings. A couple's retreat in the marriage business meant every day was wedding day. Like at the North Pole with 24/7 Christmas.

I popped a grape in my mouth and leaned back to take it all in. Meanwhile, harried diners at the next tables rushed their breakfasts. Either that or they sat smitten with their tablemates, ignoring their meals entirely. Most were getting married themselves, had just gotten married, or were present to witness someone else's nuptials, as I did each day. Staged on public beaches, strangers' weddings offered loads of entertainment with zero obligation.

As the only child of a single mother, I had obligations to spare. Mom needed more diversions. She had the community garden in our Manhattan neighborhood, but that wasn't enough to keep her mind off me. I loved her, but her attention bordered on smothering.

I swatted a fly away from my plate before grabbing an orange cube of cheese, the creamy tang erupting as I chewed. My going-away party popped to mind. A fun night, but I had a pit in my stomach the whole time, wondering if I'd made the right decision to leave. Being in-house counsel was great, except for all the paper pushing and order taking. I craved a role with authority. One freeing me to lead a team, create a vision, and see it through. I had to leave to do that.

When I dreamed of making it and changing the world, being a lawyer seemed a glamorous choice. All those smart people who showed up to juvenile hall with shiny leather briefcases, talking about the law? I wanted to be like them.

Fancy clothes.

Clients looking to you as an expert.

Yelling "objection" in court.

Yeah, I got the legal bug bad and never looked back.

With my new job looming, I wondered if this would finally be the place where I could make a difference? Where I could touch real people's lives and make them better. Was that even possible in corporate law? Did I need to try criminal defense, or leave law entirely?

My chest tightened just thinking of quitting the only passion I'd ever known. Well, since dropping my gang, that is. All the more reason for me to continue to improve lives. I got my second chance at life and had no intention of blowing up the career I'd built over 14 years. Being the top legal officer at a company gave me the power to create meaningful policies that did good in the world. Or at least, avoided screwing it up worse.

I finished breakfast and cuffed my linen pants to stroll on the beach. I never tired of watching waves, hearing gulls, or sifting toasty, white sand between my toes. When snorkeling the other day, the colorful tropical fish and coral made the underwater world sing with magic. It's no wonder people got married here. The experience promised adventure and love.

At that, my mind went straight to Barbara. She sat there for hours, looking completely lost. I half expected her to stride into the water and never emerge. Something was wrong in Barbara's world. No one looks that hopeless without a reason. But I knew better than anyone that tomorrow was one good decision away. It was never too late to start down a new path, no matter how dark it seemed.

A glint of metal caught my eye in the sand. I reached down to find a gold earring with a dangling crystal drop. I pocketed it to return to the customer service desk, imagining some poor slob losing a wedding ring.

Being surrounded by weddings made me wonder what my future held. I'd been so busy with work and Mom that dating hadn't been a priority. At least not seriously. Perhaps that was another thing about my life that was about to change.

Chapter 3

Barbara

The bridal cabana's sheer curtains billowed enough for me to discreetly view the staging I planned for myself. Harps played ethereal music as guests navigated the beach runner to the shoreline ceremony location. Fifty white wooden folding chairs arced in rows around the flowered trellis at the center. The elevated dais platform ensured all guests would have a good view of the proceedings, performed by a non-denominational officiant. Joe and I shared the same Christian faith, but it worked perfectly when swapping the ceremony for two non-practicing Jews.

Rebecca exited the bathroom, smoothing her wedding dress, and my heart skipped a beat. Her olive skin glowed in an off-the-shoulder gown with a sweetheart neckline. Simple elegance, with no appliqués, lace, or beading. The perfect dress for a gal who usually wore black everything paired with a menagerie of cute shoes. A comb with silk roses swept her dark hair back on one side, the rest hung loose in perfectly formed ringlets past her shoulders. Her deep brown eyes shined bright.

"This is really happening," Rebecca said.

"Yup it is!" Leslie said.

"Ready muñeca?" Her dad offered his elbow, using her pet nickname that meant "doll" in Spanish.

"Yes. Definitely."

A photographer popped in to take a few candid shots of bridal prep. As we shifted around the suite, my mind drifted back to our many fun adventures.

Jumping in the Trevi fountain in Rome.

Countless picnics in Central Park.

Soggy shoulders from crying through life's tragedies.

Today would be another milestone we'd remember forever.

Yet, standing here as a bystander to the wedding I planned for myself, my mouth turned to paste. Rebecca and Kyle deserved a special day, but the pit in my stomach was a tangible reminder of my wedding that wasn't. As much as I wished otherwise, I hadn't finished mourning the future I'd lost.

My life's script went to plan until now. Joe's betrayal, a red, angry blemish on my resume. It was a blessing, I knew. But having that whopper left my world spinning off its axis. Would there be more? Or would my new promotion on Monday restore my Washington mojo?

I hoped it would, but hope wasn't a plan.

The event coordinator tapped her watch, so we moved out onto the patio as the music changed to the wedding processional. The number of non-invited onlookers surprised me, but then, the shared beach was open to everyone. A handsome man leaned against a pole in linen slacks and a white shirt. He toasted me as I passed. Was it? Yes, the jogger from the beach. His shoulder length wavy hair, goatee, and hazel eyes made me tingle all over again. Now cleaned up, you'd never suspect a huge snake tattoo hid beneath. Which was the real man? This version, or the rebel runner?

I stared too long, and he smiled, sending heat shooting up to my face.

Crap, am I'm blushing? Twice in one day. I better get my shit together.

Taking my place in front of Leslie, all eyes searched the aisle for the main attraction. The processional music shifted as Rebecca appeared. Every guest rose, oohing and whispering as they snapped smartphone pictures. I'd never seen Rebecca more radiant. Her broad smile and sparkling eyes focused on her special man. She'd found a great guy. Someone who loved her and sacrificed himself on more than one occasion to keep her happy and safe. They were truly meant to be. They'd be riding that black motorcycle of his until they turned eighty. You could just tell. Their fairytale was beginning and I had a front-row se at.

They exchanged vows and sealed the ceremony by Kyle shattering a glass underfoot, the sole remnant of the Jewish ceremony tradition. Watching them kiss, the true meaning of marriage weighed heavy on me. The permanence. The undying love. The bond needed to build a lasting partnership. Rebecca and Kyle shared it. Joe and I never did. Not really.

My parents popped to mind. I wanted that undying bond so desperately I projected it onto my papier-mâché relationship with Joe.

When he proposed, I smiled so big I believed it myself. But was I more excited about the accomplishment than the man? Proof I could be successful and have a strong Black man at my side, without ever pausing long enough to question whether he was the right one? Perhaps. Watching this ceremony and knowing Kyle and Rebecca as I did cemented one thing for me.

Joe did us both a huge favor.

We weren't soulmates and would've ended badly. Best that we never got married. I wanted the same love as Rebecca. The same undying commitment of Mom and Dad. Until then, I'd focus on work. Dig in to succeed, without any guilt about whether my star shone brighter than Joe's.

Goal set, I linked arms with the best man and marched back up the aisle. Time to celebrate.

Chapter 4

SEBASTIAN

The sunset blazed the sky with shades of blood orange, fading to gray as night fell. I sat sipping a mixed drink at the bar, which gradually filled with couples lost in love. Watching them, it was impossible not to believe that love conquered all.

Drink empty and waitstaff occupied, I strode to the bar for another. The long strip of glossy bamboo hosted a sole drinker. A woman sipping a glass of white wine at the end. She wore a white dress, her long dark hair mussed as if she'd been dancing.

Was it?

Yes.

Barbara.

My beauty from the beach. Though she looked far more content than when I'd seen her earlier that morning. Something about her had changed. Us crossing paths for the third time in one day tallied too many cosmic coincidences to ignore.

I sidled over. "We meet again."

Her brown eyes sized me up. I could tell she was torn between indifference and curiosity. We'd had a moment earlier, and I wondered if she remembered. Or, if I imagined it. Lucky for me, her curiosity won out.

"Where's your bride?" Barbara said, motioning to the chair next to her.

"Don't have one."

"No?"

"I'm the thrifty traveler who buys the left-over suites when big weddings cancel."

Barbara winced, taking a sip of wine to recover.

Too close to home? Maybe she knew the bride who canceled? Either that or my wallet-conscience living sounded lame.

"We met this morning. Not sure if you remember."

"Hard to forget a man who made me face plant in sand."

"Yeah, well, for the record, I'm not a menace. Not anymore, at least."

"That remains to be seen." Barbara flashed me a look that made it look like she wanted to find out.

My pulse spiked at her gauntlet, but I played it off and waved for the bartender instead. She approached while tightening her waist apron.

"Need a refill?"

"Yes, I'll have another Sea Breeze. Can I get you another glass of wine?"

"Not just yet." A small smile crept up to Barbara's eyes.

"Something amusing?"

"I rarely see men drinking pink drinks without apologizing."

"I never apologize for who I am, let alone what I drink."

She turned to me. "That's the most amazing thing I've heard in a long time. I'll toast to that."

I raised the glass placed before me but pulled back. "Whom am I toasting with? Full name."

She smiled. "Barbara Washington."

"Sebastian Kingsbury."

We clinked.

"So what brings you here so deep in thought, Barbara Washington? It's how you began your day as well."

"Sorry? I don't follow." Barbara's brows furrowed.

"On the beach. This morning. I was out for an early run, but you looked to have been there for hours."

She sat back, taking me in. "You noticed?"

"Hard not to notice someone so lovely." Sebastian said. "Excuse me, didn't mean to flirt. Your husband—"

"I'm not married," she raised her bare ring finger, smirking. My moves were rusty as hell, and likely didn't go unnoticed.

"Oh. Here, attending a wedding, then?"

"For my best friend. They have a deep and passionate love. The stuff out of movies. It almost makes you believe it's possible." Barbara spoke into her wineglass before taking a sip.

"There's a story there." Sebastian said.

"Yes. There is." She met my gaze for the first time. Her dark skin glowed in the candlelight, but the curve of her back showed she carried a deep hurt.

"Tell me," I said.

"Are you always this forward?" Barbara parroted my question to her from earlier in the day.

"Pretty much."

"I am too, but not about personal things. But since I don't know you, and you can't use my words against me in a court of law, maybe I'll make an exception."

"Be careful. I'm a lawyer," I said.

"Really? Me too. What do you practice?"

"Corporate law. I'm about to start my first gig as General Counsel."

"I am as well. We should toast to that. Two hot shots on the rise." Our glasses clinked.

"Tell me about what you do." I sipped my straw, letting my spiked fruit juice work its magic. *Why was I so nervous?*

Barbara halted me with her hand. "Not tonight, counselor. I don't want to talk shop. That okay?"

I sat back. "Of course. Hard not to jump into legal mode, comparing notes and resumes..."

"Why is that?" She asked.

"I guess it's our way of justifying the effort and expense. Like our loans get lowered with every retelling."

"Or we're trying to prove ourselves worthy of someone's time. Like we're worth talking to..." Her voice trailed off.

"That's our cue for story time. Come on. Out with it." I took a long sip and shifted closer to listen to Barbara's tale. A soul-crushing one that would leave any normal person a wreck hiding in a dark room. Catching her ex cheating and gifting the wedding to her friend. But here she was, living her dream day through another. The pictures, permanent reminders of Barbara's canceled wedding. The loss hollowed my chest, triggering lost memories of my own. Of my childhood, maybe I was six or seven. I'd stare out my bedroom window day after day, wondering whether any of the men passing by four flights below might be my dad. None ever were. Before I could walk, my father vanished after a typical disagreement with Mom. I kept thinking he'd return, but he never did. Gone, just like Barbara's wedding day.

"You're an amazing friend," I said after she finished.

"Thank you. When I woke up this morning, I feared I'd made a terrible mistake. But after seeing how happy they were, how happy their families were, I knew I'd made the right decision. They deserved a wedding to remember. I was glad I could help make that happen."

I raised my glass. "Here's to fairytale weddings. May we all have one."

We clinked and each downed the last of our drinks.

"I'll take that wine now, if the offer still stands," Barbara said.

"I'll do you one better. Have dinner with me. Your wedding was early and you must be hungry."

"I'd like that. Even though you prefer girlie drinks."

I stood, taking Barbara's hand to help her stand before leaning to whisper. "There are a lot of girlie things I prefer. But let's eat first."

Barbara feigned being shocked, but her amused smile gave her away. "I've missed this."

"What? Eating dinner?"

"Being relaxed. Being me. I feel so 'on' all the time. It's exhausting."

Barbara linked my arm for the short walk to the Blue Oyster Club across the resort. It was the restaurant I liked best and she hadn't been on the island long enough to have a preference.

We dined over the next two hours, drinking, laughing, and having a surprising lot in common. Both from Manhattan. Both lawyers. Both having one parent now, though Barbara's life sounded like a dream compared to mine. That was, until her mother tragically passed away her first year of college.

Our conversation flowed until settling into a comfortable silence. Neither of us rushed to fill the void. It was the thing I loved best about gardening with my mom. We could be together, yet independent in our thoughts. Remarkable how Barbara and I achieved this ease within hours.

My attention drifted to the patio, where couples swayed to the house band. Whispering. Each duo in a world unto themselves. Barbara watched them, an eager restlessness settling over her.

I stood, offering my hand. "Care to dance?"

She hesitated for a millisecond. It must be weird to be on a date at the location and day you were destined to marry another. Lucky for me, she placed her hand in mine and I wove us through the tables to the dance floor.

I wrapped my arms around her, settling my cheek against hers as we began an easy sway to the island ballad. Her floral perfume, intoxicating.

"I love that you dance. So many men don't." Barbara said.

"I'm a bundle of surprises."

She pulled away, eyes tracking my face like she was committing it to memory. "I don't know what to make of you, Mr. Kingsbury."

"Is that good or bad?"

"I haven't decided yet."

Yet. Yet meant there was a future after this dance. Maybe after tonight. She was the most amazing surprise of my time on the island, and I wasn't ready for it to end. Not by a long shot.

I held her close as another song started.

Barbara's hand caressed my back. "So, what's next?"

"What do you want to be next?"

"I don't know. Part of me wants to peek under that delicious linen shirt of yours. But rational Barbara says that's a spectacularly bad idea."

"Who's being direct now?" I teased.

"That's who I am. Take it or leave it."

"I'll take it."

I nuzzled into the deep kiss I'd longed for since seeing her sitting on the beach 16 hours earlier. Her fingertips left a trail of electricity behind as she explored my torso.

Wet and wanting, our kiss accelerated, our breaths growing labored until a throat clearing dropped us back to earth.

Our server.

He stood aside, waiting, and I had half a mind to thrash the guy for his interruption. Barbara's eyes remained closed, her mouth puckered into a ruby pout I wanted to devour.

"I'm so sorry, but we're cleaning up for the night. I'm sure you want to settle the check?"

Break his neck is more like it...

"Cabana 12. Thanks."

By the time I turned back, the magic had evaporated. I probably should have said my good night, but I had no intention of letting her go so easily.

I took Barbara's hand and guided us out of the restaurant, onto a paved garden path. White spotlights illuminated the prickly barks of each towering palm tree we passed.

Every fiber of my being wanted this woman in my bed. Well, except the single thread warning to go slow. She's been through hell today, and a one-night stand would likely shatter her completely.

But who said it'd end after tonight?

Why couldn't it be more? We lived in the same city...

"Where are we going?" Barbara asked.

"Would it be presumptuous of me to say Cabana 12?"

"A little." She tugged my arm to stop us where the paths crossed. Left led to my room, right would take us to the beach. I knew where I wanted to go, but it wasn't about me. The last thing she needed was for someone to treat her as selfishly as her shitty ex.

"Sorry. You're such a wonderful surprise. I got carried away."

"Do you mind if we take a walk instead?"

"Sure. Whatever you want." I kissed her hand and set out for the beach, but she stopped me again.

"What? No fight? No shaming?" She asked.

"You said…"

"Yeah, but you listened. Thank you."

"You're welcome. Come on."

The waves grew louder as we approached the shoreline, the rising moon rippling in its surface, making a path I longed to follow. Walking to the moon. Wouldn't that be an amazing end to my unexpected day?

Barbara released my hand to approach the lapping ocean. Slipping off her shoes, she wiggled her toes in the sopping sand until the sea rolled in for a hello kiss.

"This is where I found you," I said.

Barbara answered, her gaze transfixed on the moon. "Was I lost?"

"You looked it, yes. Like you wished you could become one with the water and float away."

"You got all that from watching me sit on the beach?"

I shrugged.

She turned. "What else have you learned?"

"That you're an amazing woman. Loving and generous, and always trying to do the right thing. But you're beginning to question that philosophy."

Barbara opened her mouth to retort but closed it. We'd spent one evening together, yet I bet I understood her better than her ex.

If he had, he wouldn't have been chasing tail all over Manhattan. Sometimes strangers are the safest place for inner secrets.

"Sounds like I'm close," I said.

"Maybe in your spare time you can open a fortunetelling booth in Times Square."

"I might do that."

"So, Mister Swami, what comes next for me? If I were to do the unexpected thing, what would that be?"

I strolled to her side, and she lifted her chin for a kiss. But I stopped, near enough to feel her breath on my face. "Let's have an adventure, you and me. Tomorrow, let's get a car and explore the island. Take whatever comes our way and do the unexpected. Are you up for that, Ms. Washington? Are you in for an adventure?"

Her eyebrow pulsed. I could tell she wasn't used to backing down. You didn't earn your way to the top like she did by avoiding risk.

Yet this was a risk for me, too. Given my history, I'm slow to trust. No good ever comes from divulging a past neatly sealed away in juvenile records. But something told me Barbara was worth risking rejection. The worst she'd say was no, and I'd be no worse off. If I didn't try, I'd forever wonder what could have been with my island beauty. The mischief in her expression lifted my hopes.

"Okay, mystery man. I'm in. I'm in for an adventure."

Chapter 5

Barbara

After Sebastian walked me back to my room, we savored a luscious kiss that sent me sprinting for a cold shower. I immediately regretted not following him to Cabana 12. But my nagging conscience won out. I'm not Joe.

How many times had I ignored Joe licking his lips at cocktail parties? What would that say about me if I hopped into bed with a guy I met hours earlier on the day I was supposed to be married to someone else? My gal-pals on the other side of the island would tell me to go have some fun. That I deserved it. That I spent too much time with my head buried in work. But I had to be true to myself.

Following the law to right wrongs pulsed through my veins. A birthright, so to speak. Who would I be if I slipped off script with Sebastian? Trusting my heart last time only left it broken.

I dried off, hopped into bed, and the next thing I knew, seagulls were squawking. My eyes fluttered open to find morning sun streaming through the windows.

It wasn't a dream. I'm still here on the island and having a day of adventure with Sebastian. Anticipation tingled at the thought of him, as did lingering regret at not having the passionate night our idyllic evening demanded. But that would have ended our time together. We'd awake and likely never see each other again. This way, there was unfinished business between us. I hadn't planned it this way, but it worked in my favor. I flipped up the covers to get ready.

Though, was I really up for the unexpected? Me? Sensible Barbara? Ever at the ready with a list of consequences. Would I be able to ignore the judge in my brain and embrace a day of adventure? I'd soon find out.

I answered a few texts, one from Leslie saying I was okay and wishing her a safe return to New York. Another from my brother Brian in Boston, always a worrier. And last from my Aunt Evelyn, the best stand-in for Mom I could imagine. Always ready with the wisdom I needed to course correct. I sent her a heart emoji and nothing else. She returned two.

What would my mom say about Sebastian? How would she counsel me to proceed?

A gust blew the curtains clear of my open window, exposing the sun sparkling off the ocean's surface outside. Beckoning me to come out and play.

I exhaled my relief.

Thanks, Mom. I like him, too.

Migrating to the bathroom mirror, I wasn't the least bit surprised by my mop of hair. Salty tropical breezes hadn't done wonders for my top-shelf extensions. If I didn't figure something out, I'd arrive looking like the "before" picture in a shampoo commercial. How would Sebastian react to a disheveled playmate? I know how Joe would react. He'd toss a passive aggressive comment my way, causing an immediate about-face for more hair product.

How had I survived with Joe for so long? A trance was lifted, leaving me free to register all the negative experiences I'd been storing up in my brain. With Sebastian's easy bearing, I couldn't imagine him behaving like Joe. But then again, he was a man. And I barely knew him.

Yet, it was undeniable that in one night, we'd forged a different kind of intimacy. An intimacy of kindred spirits navigating life on similar paths. His ability to size me up so exactly made me feel heard in a way I only now realized I'd been desperately missing. But if I didn't get going, there would be no day of adventure at all.

After ten wardrobe changes and an exhaustive hair styling session, I emerged into the cabana courtyard looking "effortless" casual. Sebastian stood waiting, looking the rogue with his wavy hair, scruffy goatee, and blue Hawaiian shirt covered in white palms. With shorts and leather flip-flops, no way he spent 90 minutes grooming. His effortless casual was likely the genuine article.

"Good morning," he smiled. "I got us some coffee for the road. I also packed us a few snacks until we can find a place to eat breakfast."

"What an under-achiever. I bet you already went for a run." I smiled, accepting my hot paper cup. "And thank you, by the way. Very thoughtful."

"I'm nothing if not thoughtful. You look beautiful." Sebastian's whisper tickled my ear.

"Thank you. I feel beautiful, and you look just as fetching."

"Fetching? Are we a reader of English period romance?" he asked.

"Yes, but I never realized it had wormed its way into my vocabulary!"

We settled into Sebastian's rental car, a convertible Chrysler Sebring, making me glad I'd tucked a headscarf in my day pack. It'd help keep my hair from getting stuck in my lip gloss.

The winding road took us along the lush island coast, where low tide waves were reversing course. Sea birds pierced the ocean's surface, each alighting with a wiggling prize of silver fish. Nature was amazing to behold in all its ecosystems. Shrimp eat the debris, fish eat the shrimp, birds devour the fish, and so it goes. There's always someone stronger and more predatory waiting to gobble you up.

What's the matter with you? I'm on vacation with a gorgeous guy and my mind found a dark underbelly to a natural ecosystem. I needed this day of adventure more than I thought.

"So," Sebastian began. "Our day has rules."

"Wasn't today about having no rules?" I held my long strands of hair in a fist to keep them from whipping in my face as we drove.

"We must counter our instincts. If our gut says no, yes it must be."

"I'm not sure I like these rules."

"Then you must love them." Sebastian reached over and squeezed my hand.

Energy radiated up my arm, jolting my senses to attention. Yes. Today was about living, not thinking. And did I ever need to quit thinking.

"Okay. Today, I'll say yes when my instincts say no. Nothing dangerous, though. Right?"

"That remains to be seen," He winked.

We ate a quick breakfast in a sunny roadside cafe perched atop a cliff. My instincts said to skip the pancakes, so I ate three. Ever a water drinker, coffee it was, and I savored every aromatic drop. Maybe letting go wouldn't be so hard after all.

By early afternoon, we'd waded in the crashing surf—getting our clothes soaked, bought goofy souvenirs, and said no to a zip-line since both of us wanted to do it. That left us strolling down a bustling retail district when we passed a braiding salon.

"Aren't these something?" The braided models in the pictures were mesmerizing. Each had a distinct pattern of interlacing braids. Some long and thick, some woven with electric pink hair for accents, others wound around the scalp like a crown before dangling down the back in a cascade of finely braided perfection.

"You like?" Sebastian smiled.

"It's pretty cool, don't you think? I see women proudly wearing braids on the subway sometimes and I get so jealous. They're proud of their Black heritage and want everyone to know it."

"You're not proud of your Black heritage?"

"It's hard to when my parents were relentless about fitting in. Look like everyone else. Prove my worth. Work twice as hard—and never let them see you sweat. Be so amazing they forget you're Black and give you what's rightly yours."

"Wow. No pressure?"

"Yeah. None whatsoever."

I shook my head. "I can't believe I just said that out loud. To a white guy."

"In my defense, I'm pretty tan right now." He pulsed his head toward the salon. "So about the braids..."

"No. No way. Oh my God I couldn't ever." I backpedaled from the shop window.

"Hold on now, young lady. That's not what today is all about." Sebastian grabbed my hand and pulled me back.

"That's easy for you to say. What have you done so far that countered your instincts?"

Sebastian leaned in for a deep kiss. As our mouths became one, I melted into his urgent embrace. My heart pounded so loud he must have heard it. But I didn't care. I didn't care we were blocking the sidewalk, or whether people were looking. I dropped my purse on the ground, so my fingers were free to explore the firm muscles of his arms. After forever and an instant, he gently pulled away.

"What countered my instincts? I didn't drag you back to Cabana 12 the moment I saw you."

My legs buckled, but he caught me. Our eyes absorbing the other. This guy was hitting every note of the Barbara symphony like a virtuoso, saying just the right thing at every moment.

I braved a glance at the salon window. That was a bridge too far. And had implications far beyond today. It had implications for my new career as General Counsel. My dad would flip his lid and he wouldn't be wrong to do so. Braids were a no-no in our household, saying yes filled me with angst I wanted no part of on this vacation.

"I'm calling a substitution."

"Whoa, now. What's that about?"

"I'm substituting one adventurous act for another."

Sebastian released me to cross his arms over his chest. "I'm listening."

"Let's find a secluded beach. I'll make it worth your while."

"Will you now?" His face lit up.

I bit my bottom lip and swore I saw him swallow hard.

Without saying another word, he snatched my hand and led us back to the car. Twenty minutes later, directions in hand, we were speeding down a windy road toward a cliff. We descended an endless flight of creaky wooden stairs, holding a picnic blanket from the trunk and a bottle of Champagne.

Once down on the sand, I took off running.

"Hey! Wait up!" He yelled.

I giggled, gasping for breath as I turned the point, and found a cliff overhang that completely obscured us from above. I turned right and left and the beach was deserted. That's when I did the unthinkable.

I pulled the string of my halter dress loose and let it drop to the sand. Only a skimpy pair of bikini-cut panties remained.

"Holy shit!" Sebastian said. "You weren't kidding about making it worth my while."

I sauntered over. "Let's make it count."

I cupped his head and pulled him down to my mouth. Our tongues urgent, roaming with abandon. This day of indulgence left me lifting my leg to pull his growing hardness closer.

"In the ocean." I whispered.

He stripped while I shimmied out of my underwear. Then he retrieved protection out of his wallet.

"You sure?" he asked.

I walked closer, took the wrapper out of his hand and bit it open to slide it onto his hardness.

"Let's go." I led him into the warm ocean, deep until I was bobbing and he was standing when he pulled me close.

His hands smoothed over the surface of my skin, making me quiver like liquid. When he swam closer for a kiss, I surged up, wrapping my arms around his neck, and my legs around his waist. His hands rested on my sides where his thumbs caressed the undersides of my breasts.

Then he was in me, filling the void Joe left behind. The void I never thought would heal, yet here I was. Making love in the ocean with my island Adonis. My arms slinked around his broad shoulders. His hazel eyes and tender heart were everything I wanted in a man. Knowing he respected my "no" the night before made me want him all the more.

"Oh my God, Sebastian." I moaned. He angled me perfectly, using the buoyancy of the water to hit my spot and sending pleasure racing around my body.

My voice choked in my throat as heat consumed me, flushing my face and making me arch deliciously into him further. The water only heightened the ethereal sensations, making me wonder why I'd never made love in the ocean before.

Sebastian followed soon after with a cry of his own, which sent a few nearby gulls rocketing skyward.

The birds soared into the heavens, the puffy clouds now tinged with a pink kiss of early sunset. I imagined them watching us from above. Two people, lost in passion, bare for the world to see. Bare to each other inside and out. Emotionally. Spiritually. Connected. We floated on the surface, his fingers tickling the palm of my hand.

"Can I take you to dinner when we get back to New York?" He asked.

I burst out laughing, flipping to splash him. "You better do a hell of a lot more than that!"

"Good. It'd be criminal to not see you after today."

He swam over for a deep kiss, then we let the waves float us to shore.

We popped our champagne, then dissolved into each other's arms again.

Sebastian was definitely someone I wanted to get used to.

Chapter 6

SEBASTIAN

My early flight home meant that I didn't get to see Barbara before I left. Our magical day fresh on my mind, we vowed to connect when back in the City. She was special, no doubt. So much so, I'd forgotten I was starting a new job tomorrow. And I hadn't yet submitted the employee paperwork they sent. After a week of sunshine and romance, I had zero desire to sit cooped up in my tiny apartment filling out DocuSign forms.

A few more hours to savor the trip wouldn't hurt anyone.

I dropped my duffel in my living room and slipped on grimy work clothes en route to our community garden. My plot at GreenGrows was right next to my mom's, and through the iron fence, I could see her on her hands and knees weeding the rich soil. The same position she'd been in for as long as I could remember. During lean times, the vegetables and berries she grew in the vacant-lot-turned-urban-farm were often the only thing keeping us fed until the food stamps replenished.

I'd be forever grateful for the sacrifices Mom made for me, which rendered her constant drumbeat for me to move away a non-starter.

As I unlatched the black gate, I heard a familiar voice.

"Hey, Uncle Sebastian!"

I turned to find my childhood friend Mo's son, Mo Junior, holding his great-uncle's hand. Judge Peña. That old man busted my balls over school and was now pouncing on the next generation.

I trotted across the street and mussed Junior's brown hair. "Heading home?"

"Homework." The poor kid looked about as thrilled as I was. I spied the judge.

"Take it easy on him, will ya?"

"Never." Judge Peña chuckled. I knew what was coming next. Long since retired, he got his jollies from asking me the same question every damn time we passed each other on the street.

"Still a lawyer?" He asked.

"Yes, Judge. Junior, tell your pop hello?"

The boy nodded and tugged his great-uncle's hand to keep walking.

I crossed back, and through the squeaky gate, clanking the lever in place behind me. Earphones in, Mom didn't hear my exchange with the judge or notice my arrival until I planted a soft kiss on her weathered cheek.

She slapped her chest. "Lord, you scared me to death!"

"We both know I've done worse."

She attempted to stand, but her legs cramped.

"Damn these knees."

"No need to get up." I dropped to ground level.

Her ever-watchful eye went to work. "I haven't seen you this tan since that summer you lived at the youth center pool."

"Good times." I rummaged for a hand trowel in the five-gallon pail I used to store my gardening tools.

"You could have called. Let me know you landed in one piece."

"Mom. When an adult man goes on vacation, he doesn't talk to his mother every two hours."

"You do!" She jammed a gloved finger in my chest that sent clumps of soil tumbling to the ground. "Answer me when I call. You're all I've got. One fancy trip and I've got to make appointments to talk to my own son."

"Is that what you think?"

"No," she pouted. "But you still should have called."

I nudged her out of the way to take over her weeding. She pressed on her thighs to stand, then took a seat on the wooden bench I installed near her plot for that very purpose. She slipped off her gloves in a huff.

The air hung heavy and humid for April, almost muffling the bird tweets echoing off the surrounding buildings. Mom closed her eyes to listen, her agitation settling.

"Don't you want to hear about my trip?"

I filled her in on the locations, answering every detailed question she asked, where I went and what I ate and saw. Her relentless inquisition showed how much she needed a vacation of her own. Something more exciting than going to visit her sister in the

Poconos. Maybe I'd think of a place to take her over Christmas. That'd give me a buffer period to get established at work.

"You're leaving something out." She narrowed her gaze. "You didn't call me for two days. TWO DAYS. The only time you ignore me like that is when a woman is involved."

Damn her mom-ESP.

I pursed my lips, taking my frustration out on the tangled weeds. Ignoring her was my only chance. Maybe her mind would swirl to something more exciting than my love life. But she had already dug in with her arms crossed and an "out with it" expression.

I tossed the trowel down. "Her name is Barbara. She's amazing and lives here in the City."

"So when are you—"

"Hopefully soon. We haven't made any plans."

Satisfied, Mom returned to her work. I let her be and shifted to my overgrown plot. After weeding the invasive grasses that arrived from who-knows-where, I filled the birdbath and pinched off the flowers on the strawberry plants I'd recently planted. The carrot sprouts needed thinning to leave space for the remaining ones to grow. When the sun dipped behind the buildings, shadows crept across the garden. I gathered my tools in the bucket and stored them in the communal storage shed. It often surprised me that more equipment didn't go missing. But then, our neighbors had eyes like hawks. Perpetrators didn't stay hidden for long in our community unless one's life expectancy improved by playing ignorant. Either way, everyone knew who did it.

"I'm heading out. You staying?" I asked.

She removed an earbud. "A bit longer. Oh, I almost forgot. Dante stopped by yesterday asking for you."

"Okay...."

"What do you mean 'okay?' He's trouble. I keep telling you: You've got to get out of here. Move away. Why won't you? It's not safe for you here anymore."

"It's perfectly safe."

"No, it's not. Not with all these old friends of yours passing in and out of prison like it's a turnstile. Mo's protection only goes so far."

There she was wrong. While I led a small-time crew as a teen, handling business as a legal minor to protect the kingpins, Mo was the kingpin now. No one crossed him or anyone under his protection. Least of all me. Mo and I were like brothers. My old reputation, combined with our close ties, left me untouchable. Hell, the only one who'd do anything was Mo himself, and that wasn't happening.

"You're overreacting. Dante is harmless, at least to me. You know that."

But I couldn't say more without digging into affairs she had no business knowing about. Even after all this time.

"They know what you do and presume you're loaded. Please, don't go getting mixed up with Dante again. He'll drag you down if you let him."

"I won't."

She sighed. "Nothing good will happen for you if you stay living here. It never does. You'll get dragged down and everything we've worked for would have been for nothing."

I pulled Mom into a hug, resting my chin on her head. "Quit trying to get rid of me. I'm not going anywhere. If bad things were going to happen, they would have happened by now. Besides, if anyone should leave, it's you."

"Me? Why?"

"You've got your time in. You could retire and go live somewhere you could garden year-round."

"What am I? A Rockefeller? Retire. Ha!" she blasted, pushing me away. "Hell will freeze over before I leave. They need me. I'm the only reason that damn branch of the DMV wasn't closed with all the others. Can you imagine Mr. Gonzalez dragging his walker over to Greenwich Street?

"Mr. Gonzalez has no business driving. He broke the fire hydrant in front of Nikki's salon." I pointed to where the flood nearly wrecked the business of a community favorite.

Mom dismissed the resulting damage and flooding with a wave.

"So it's settled. You're not leaving and neither am I."

"I never should have let you go to law school."

Back in my apartment, I dug into the paperwork I'd ignored all week. As I clicked and filled in the forms, doubt crept in. Starting over meant meeting people. Answering questions. Avoiding land mines that could jeopardize who I am today versus who I used to be.

My eye drifted over to the TV stand and the picture of three boys there. Fresh faced and invincible, we posed at the youth center, tongues out, gang signs flashing before we even knew what they meant. We were maybe eight? I met Mo and Dante the summer before and we were glued together from then until I was cuffed in the back of a police car en route to juvy. Staring at my job papers, it now felt like I was the one abandoning them.

I went to school, got a job, and found a calling.

Mo sat tall while Dante was stuck on a conveyor belt that would lead him back to prison.

Yet, my new persona smacked of a con. People at work looked at me and didn't know that growing up, my belly was empty more than full. They didn't know I couch surfed the neighborhood for years when Mom worked nights, or that I was one chain-link fence away from ending up like Dante.

Law was my ticket out of a life full of empty fridges, torn clothes, and a hammer pulse every time a cop car cruised by. Once out of juvy, mom put her foot down. It was like I had a mother on every street corner, and she was a handful on her own. She enlisted every adult for miles to keep me off the corner.

"Go on now. Get home," they'd say. "Stay on that corner too long and you'll grow roots." Over time, neighbors morphed from meddlesome to loving. They became family, people whose lives I'd witnessed and wanted to remain connected to. Kids I knew who now had kids of their own. People whose prison terms were printed on their destinies like the tattoos they wore across their foreheads. Some reformed and thrived, but most didn't. Now, the thought of leaving a community that'd been my everything reeked of cowardice. There were good people here. I refused to be yet another guy to "make it," then turn tail.

But there had to be a way to "make it" and feel better about myself at the end of the day. I needed more than another corporate hide to hang on my wall. The conquests were ringing hollow. I wanted to help people, real people, not cigar-smoking millionaires. Mom had more pride about her role at the DMV than I did as the incoming General Counsel for Xervo. It was the top legal job for my new company, reigning over legal staff in six countries. It was a big job and I needed to get my head out of my ass. I made the choice. Like it or not, it was happening. I pulled up the next batch of forms, clicking to digitally sign each.

The monotony left my mind free to daydream about Barbara. The caress of her lips on mine left me craving more. She was a rare find, and I couldn't wait to see her again. Time would tell if her longing simmered as hot as mine.

Chapter 7

BARBARA

My Uber pulled up to the curb in front of my building. Saul, the doorman since I was in high school, scurried around back to meet the opening trunk. He took one look and went to fetch the luggage cart.

Completing my digital transaction with a tip, I emerged as Saul returned.

"Miss Barbara! Have a good time on your vacation?"

"I did, thanks. You'll send the bags up?" I was already walking into the building.

"Yes, Miss. Right away."

I removed my sunglasses so my eyes could adjust to the interior lighting. A honey glow reflected off the inlaid wooden paneling of the lobby, lining the cream marble floors toward the elevator.

The arrow indicator slowly arced its way from the tenth floor to the ground floor. Walking into this building filled me with a mix of warmth and regret. It was a happy place to grow up but moving back home screamed failure. The same defeat my dad never let cross the threshold, moved in via a truckload of U-Haul boxes. They not only stacked in my bedroom, but in my brother Brian's as well. Like an adult, he was off on his own living in Boston. I'd have to figure something out soon or Dad would get used to having me home and make leaving difficult.

Loving, but imposing, Dad usually got his way. In work, life—and with me. How could I be so strong with everyone, but snap like a cheap pair of stilettos with my dad? At work, I laid them all to waste. They'd take one look at me and underestimate the Black girl. Maybe it was time for me to up my game with Dad as well.

The elevator door opened, and I pressed our floor—12A. It was really the 13th floor, but pre-war apartments like ours skipped the bad-luck number and went straight to 14. Our odd-numbered floor might have been the only reason they let a Black family move into the building at the time. Few others wanted to live in an unlucky apartment, which made ours unusually large and the mirror of our one neighbor's.

A hand slid into the gap to reverse the elevator door before it closed completely. My fellow 12A neighbor, Mrs. Finkle. Now 78, she lived alone since her husband died twenty years earlier. I remembered going to the Jewish funeral and wondering where all the flowers were. I later learned about the quick-burial custom, which made the historical masking scent of flowers unnecessary. Such a fascinating faith. I ended up taking a class on Judaism in college.

Mrs. Finkle was busy rummaging in her purse when the door fully opened. She took one look at me, and reflexively halted. For a millisecond, her eyes darted sideways, before plastering on a smile that didn't read true.

She didn't recognize me. My heart sank that a woman I'd known my whole life looked visibly uncomfortable in my presence.

"You okay, Mrs. Finkle?" I asked.

She inspected me, and her expression changed.

"My! Barbara! It is you." She shuffled in and faced forward. "You seem to visit a lot lately. Your father well?"

"Yes, busy as ever."

"He's an important man. Always worked too hard, if you ask me. I know your mother worried about him. Good he has you to look out for him, though."

Her buttery-soft hand patted my arm.

Guilt bubbled in me, but there was no point in me explaining the last month of my life to my elderly neighbor. How it was Dad helping me, not the other way around. To do so would taint our family reputation with failure, and I had no intention of doing that. Save face at all costs.

The door opened, and Mrs. Finkle exited. "Have a nice evening, dear. Tell your father hello."

"I will. Take care." I watched her shuffle away before turning to open my door.

Our apartment looked shockingly grand compared to the small cabana I'd been in for days. Our entryway opened into a large living room at the center of the apartment, with all rooms exiting into it along both sides like the hub it was. A huge oriental carpet covered the entire 30-foot space, from the sitting area near the door to the green leather sectional in front of their never-used fireplace at the far wall. The ornate carved mantel with leaves and filigrees held our family pictures, flanked on either side by two curtained windows standing guard like sentries.

I glanced into the kitchen to the left, but it was empty. "Dad?"

I navigated into the room and noticed his book bent open on the sofa. His study door was closed, as always.

Unless the door was ajar, he was not to be disturbed. Which was just as well. The squeak and rumble of the luggage cart signaled Saul's arrival.

After tipping Saul, I lugged my bags into my bedroom on the right, rolling them one by one through the connected bathroom into my brother's room. With him living in Boston, it'd become my temporary closet.

Now was as good a time as any to pick my work outfit for tomorrow. I rummaged through six wardrobe boxes of suits, but all paled compared to the navy silk one I saw in W Magazine on the plane ride home.

I checked my watch. I knew I'd never sleep if I didn't buy that damn suit to wear to work. The last thing I needed was to arrive groggy to Morning Meeting on the biggest day of my career. I navigated to the favorites in my phone, pressing Amelia, my Bergdorf Goodman concierge. Within minutes, I'd ordered my navy suit and a darling pair of Saint Laurent blue silk stilettos to match.

Amelia would have it steamed and messengered to me by 8 p.m. tonight.

Now I could breathe easy. Moments like this were why I tipped Amelia well at holiday time. It also saved me from wandering around the store being shadowed by security. Their necks craned to observe everything I touched. I shuddered at the memory and returned to unpacking.

After transferring my clothes into the wardrobe boxes, I returned to my bedroom. The one unchanged since childhood. The walls were still pink, and the white Queen Anne furniture with gold trim remained annoyingly in good condition. My parents donated the matching canopy bed to charity when I turned 16. That's when I got upgraded to a queen-sized mattress. Small blessings. Coming home to a twin would've made this move more humiliating than it already was.

I undressed, tucked my hair into a terry cap, then a shower cap, before hopping into the shower. After dressing, I was midway across the living room to the kitchen when my dad stepped out of his study, grasping his chest.

"Good God. Didn't realize you were home."

"Your study was closed..."

"Yes, of course." He waved, remembering his own protocol. "How was the wedding? Evelyn said it went well, so I skipped calling."

I planted a kiss on his cheek. "I'm fine, Dad. The wedding was beautiful, and I had an unexpected adventure of my own."

The corners of my mouth curled into a smile, so I flattened them. But not before Dad noticed.

"You met someone," he said.

"I did. He's completely unlike anyone I've ever known. Well, not completely. He's a lawyer."

His countenance softened. "Really? He from around here?"

"He lives…" I stopped before admitting it was Alphabet City. Dad always forbade us from going into that neighborhood. I presumed he was exaggerating the danger and sneaked over to a bar during college and was stunned to find pockets worse than he described. I'd no clue what it was like now or why Sebastian still lived there.

"Where?"

"Here in the City. Not exactly sure where," I lied.

He nodded, satisfied, and returned to his book on the sofa.

Hiding my face, I made for the kitchen. "I'll make us some dinner. I picked up some interesting spices on the trip."

Anything to take my mind off work tomorrow. And Sebastian.

Chapter 8

Barbara

The subway train the next morning wove along the tracks, gently jostling its crammed cargo of passengers. Bodies pressed together, the air hung heavy with warring grooming fragrances: florals, musks, and BO from those who seemed to think soap was optional. I squeezed down the car between travelers, getting a whiff of someone drinking a Grande double cappuccino with hazelnut. I'd know the scent anywhere. It was Joe's caffeine beverage of choice. He'd walk in with his nutty indulgence, and hand me a cup of black coffee, chiding me for not having something more elaborate. Wasn't I worth it?

Ironic. I was worth better coffee, but not his fidelity. I blinked the thought away and continued down the car. If I didn't get to "my door" before the stop, I'd be stuck behind the crush of bodies squeezing out like toothpaste escaping a tube.

I side-stepped between two men, accidentally stepping on someone's foot.

"Excuse m—" I started, but the guy cut me off.

"Watch it!" The man snapped, before eyeballing me and rolling his eyes.

Like his pasty bald head was anything to write home about?

I ignored his angry Mr. Potato Head eyes and moved along to the pole near my preferred door. A woman standing there made space. She wore a yellow blouse and black slacks beneath braids that coiled around her head like a crown. She caught me staring and smiled. It was the first smile of my otherwise hostile commute.

As much as I relished my choice to skip the braids for a romp in the ocean, inside I knew the truth: I feared getting braids more than having sex with Sebastian. And while I'd always wanted them, I wasn't convinced the world wanted me to wear them. Or more specifically, the corporate world, who still viewed Black women in braids as trouble. A woman who proudly owned her Blackness and her space at the table? We'd long since been labeled "angry." A thinly veiled "othering." Someone to be tolerated, but not fully seen or included.

As much as I loved the stylistic statement, Dad's words of caution about braids were a powerful deterrent. *Your career will suffer.* The last thing I needed was for colleagues to view me as unprofessional after building my reputation on being a commensurate pro. The dependable one. The person who had the answers when others didn't. Trust would be everything in the role I was about to start. As much as I hated my cowardice, I'd never regret choosing the safer path.

Mind elsewhere, I mis-timed my exit and got stuck jostling for position out of the car. The bad juju was strong today. Maybe I should cross the platform and hop a train back downtown? Tempting, but that's not who I am. I'm the same Barbara Washington who nailed my interview for General Counsel. I deserved this promotion.

As the crowd shimmied up the stairs, I peeked at my phone. There were six emails from my boss, each sounding more urgent than the last. *Shit.* Suddenly, unplugging seemed like a catastrophically bad idea.

I hurried the three blocks to my office building on Lexington Avenue and took the elevator to the 34th floor. When the doors opened, my boss's hulking 6'4" frame hogged the reception area. Mr. Barr leaned on the white enameled desk Yvonne called home. She was a Black woman in her early 60s who'd been with him forever. She traveled with Mr. Barr through his two prior companies, always keeping his offices running. She deserved sainthood for that kind of longevity. Or free health care for the battle scars.

I hadn't seen my boss linger at reception for more than a quick handshake with arriving clients. A former lacrosse player in his youth, he looked the part. Graying blond hair and a trim frame that towered over everyone. He kept fit in adult leagues, a fact he let no one forget. The sport was as foreign to me as his perpetually nasty attitude. It made me wonder if he was born with his sharp edge, or honed it on purpose. I pictured him sharpening it on a millstone in a musty suburban basement. And despite his aged frat boy looks, the tiny gaps in his teeth gave him a predatory vibe.

He shot me a frosty glance before resuming his conversation.

Guess I was next on the menu.

I approached the gallows. "Good morning."

He did a faux double take. "Ms. Washington. You saw fit to join us today."

What was that supposed to mean? It was only 8:00 a.m. Sure, I usually arrived by 7:00, but that was not mandatory. Since when had he adopted the "to be on time is to be late" mantra?

"My brief vacation was very enjoyable. Thanks for asking," I said.

He bristled at the change in topic. He knew workers needed time off, and even bragged about benefits at investor meetings. But he couldn't help rapid-firing off emails while you were away in case you checked. When you didn't, he "volunteered" staff for lame assignments that made you regret taking vacation. I was about to learn what sort of retribution he'd cooked up for me over the weekend.

"We need to talk. Walk with me." He started toward his office, darting glares at me along the way.

"Is something the matter?" I asked.

"I tried to reach you. For days. The board chair insisted we introduce the new General Counsel to staff today before the board meeting tomorrow."

My stomach dropped through the floor. I wasn't ready to address a crowd of colleagues fresh off my island adventure. Damn my stupid email blackout. If I'd only known, I could have prepared remarks.

"Well, I'll just have to do the best I can on short notice."

We entered his office, and he closed the sturdy wooden door behind us with a click. "I'm sorry, Washington. The board urged me to look for someone from outside the company."

His words swirled around me like a cloud, not quite registering.

I'm sorry.

The board urged me.

Someone from outside the company?

My spine went limp, my leather briefcase slipping through my loose fingers onto the floor. It toppled sideways. Just like my career.

"I didn't get it?" I said out loud to myself. However, Mr. Barr took it as a conversation starter.

"You were a strong candidate but—"

"I was the best candidate. Still am. I don't understand. I thought this role was mine. I've earned it."

"Washington, please—"

"I've busted my ass for this company. You know more than anyone that I've been General Counsel by proxy for two years. Meanwhile, Randall was off God knows where. This is wrong."

"Look," he said, walking close to don a syrupy grandpa voice. "Your time will come. There'll be other opportunities."

"When? There's nowhere for me to grow. You just passed me over and gave our top legal position to a person who knows nothing about how our company operates. You promised. You said—"

"I made no promises," he lied, blood blushing his face. "This was not my decision to make. I had influence, of course, but the board overruled me. In the end, I answer to them."

I'd officially entered a parallel universe. I got two emails from board members saying how impressed they were by my stellar interview. The choice was down to me and Elizabeth Chen, another qualified internal candidate. Though to be fair, I had more experience, instincts, and moxie than my rival had in her pinky. Plus, the staff liked me way better than Chen. Evidently, none of that mattered to those in power. They skipped us both—two capable women—for a shiny new object.

I hated that the decision was finalized before I could plead my case. "Did they say why they chose the other candidate?"

"There were many factors. The new GC brings more experience with venture capital, mergers, and a few other intangibles. In the end, they felt more comfortable going with him."

Him?

"Intangibles?"

"Yes."

"Such as?"

"I'm not getting into this."

"Is being a man one of them? He definitely has that over me," I said.

This was a load of crap, and he knew it.

"Give us some credit. We're not that superficial." Mr. Barr moved to his chair and sat to open a drawer and rummage. But I wasn't letting him off this easily. I'd worked too hard and deserved more of an explanation.

I leaned on his glossy wooden desk with both arms. "I handled two acquisitions for us, nearly single-handedly since Cooper's wife had surgery and we hadn't yet hired Chen."

He continued to open file drawers, disconnecting from our conversation. No wonder he wanted to tell me over the phone. Cowardice was his go-to instinct. But glimpsing my reflection on the shiny surface below made me wonder if my new boss's "intangibles" were way more superficial than he was letting on.

"Marshall." I yelled to get his attention. "I just want to understand where I fell short. M&A can't be it. They never even brought it up in my interview."

He slammed a drawer shut with such force, I jumped back.

"Drop it. What's done is done. He's been hired. The man is here to be introduced and I expect you to make the best of it. I know you're disappointed, maybe even insulted. But it's time for you to slap on a brave face and move on. Let's make a good impression."

He stood and, with two strides, crossed the room and exited, leaving the door wide open behind him. I teetered, jaw clenched at his outburst, facing his empty chair.

How could I go play nice with the man who stole my promotion out from under me? I wonder if he even knew? General Counsel jobs didn't grow on trees. Meeting him would be super awkward, especially since I'd had zero time to process.

I bent to retrieve my dropped briefcase, then turned toward the door where a stream of employees was filing by for Morning Meeting. I was nearly at the hall when Chen walked by. She took one look at my dour expression and began smirking. She was obviously elated that if she didn't get the job, at least I hadn't either.

But who got it?

"Figured it was you," Chen whispered under her breath.

I wasn't sure I could speak without crying. Typically, Chen and I barely exchanged a word outside of meetings. She'd picked the worst moment to become chatty.

"Any idea who it is?" she asked.

"I guess we're both about to find out." I hastened my pace and darted away from her through one of the open doors to the boardroom. Its partition walls were retracted to expand the room size to fit the few hundred assembled. The rest of our global offices would join via video conference. A production crew frantically finalized last-minute preparations for the simulcast, fussing with audio boards, laptops, and black wires.

The empty stage with a podium awaited the big announcement, looking as eager as my churning insides. For one last time, I imagined myself up on stage. Beaming at the crowd and saying what an honor it'd been to be selected as the company's first female General Counsel.

Tall staffers filled in ahead of me, so I wove my way through the crowd to where I could better see the presenters. If I didn't get the job, I damn well wanted a good look at the guy who did.

Minutes later, Mr. Barr tapped the mic. "Good morning, everyone. Good morning. Thanks for joining us for this very special company meeting. As you know, when our General Counsel, Randall Fischer, decided to officially retire, it created an opening for a new leader. Before I introduce him, I want to thank our interim General Counsel, Barbara Washington, for so ably filling in while the permanent search was underway."

He paused to clap, directing all eyes to my location and gesturing for staff to join in.

My face burned, but I smiled and waved. No need for a scene. What an insensitive prick to draw attention to my moment of shame, packaging it as a triumph. A sleazy showman. All he needed was a red suit and a circus tent. Guess that made me a clown for believing in him.

When the claps subsided, he resumed.

"We did a thorough search and have selected a stellar person to lead our legal team forward. He comes to us, bringing a wealth of experience in corporate law, mergers and acquisitions, and compliance, having been the Chief Compliance Officer and Deputy General Counsel at his old company. I'm pleased to introduce our new General Counsel, Sebastian Kingsbury."

Sebastian Kingsbury?

Claps thundered while the room spun. I sought the solidness of the wall behind me while I gagged for breath. Sebastian? My Sebastian? I clasped a hand over my mouth to keep my soul cries within. How could this be happening? First Joe's betrayal, then this? Losing my job to a man who made me feel worthy and alive?

I had to get out. But seeing him rekindled the steamy lust of our last kiss in my cabana. It had lingered on my lips long after he returned to his room to pack for his flight.

Damn him, and damn me for letting my guard down so completely.

From his stunned expression as he searched for me in the crowd, there was no way he knew. He said he was starting a new job on Monday. Little did I know his new role was mine.

Chapter 9

SEBASTIAN

Hands clapped in appreciation for ... Barbara Washington? I craned my neck from my spot on the far side of the room, straining to see where everyone was looking. Sure enough, Barbara stood there looking mightily uncomfortable. Almost as lost as the moment I first saw her on the beach.

The promotion she mentioned? I'd just stolen it out from under her. How was I ever going to make this up to her? Any hopes I had of building something lasting with her vaporized in an instant.

I was so lost in thought, I almost missed my introduction. I bounded on stage, still in shock. Somehow, I managed to grasp the outstretched hand of company CEO, Marshall Barr.

"Everything okay?" he whispered while covering the mic with his hand.

Get a grip on yourself. The entire company is watching.

But I only had eyes for one person. And she was trying to fade into the wall as she made her way to an exit. It was up to me to put on a good show so no one would see her struggling.

"Yes," I stepped to the podium to address the room. "Good morning, Xervers. I'm so pleased to be here and become one of you as your new leader for the legal team. Often, 'legal' is used as a pejorative," I said with air quotes. "As in, 'ugh I have to run this through legal.'"

Laughter and nods swept the room.

"From what I understand, that's not the culture here at Xervo. Rest assured, that collaborative spirit will continue. Was that a sigh of relief I heard?"

Everyone laughed.

Okay. It's going well. Keep going.

"Let me tell you a little about myself. I'm known for leading organizations based on integrity, honesty, and staying true to company values of mutual respect. I intend to lead our organization in this same model. I value communication and transparency—as much as I can in my role, of course. My door is open, and my mind is open, too. Expect to see change, because to lead in our industry, we must always look to improve. Lift the carpet to sweep away what's hiding underneath. If we can, let's be ready for what's next when the moment of truth arrives."

I waved to the room and stepped back in deference to my CEO. Barr resumed the company agenda. Barbara had moved. I searched the faces but couldn't find my gorgeous vacation mate whose hopes I'd just crushed.

Sadly, she'd be easy to find here. I hadn't realized how non-diverse Xervo was when interviewing. I'd only seen a handful of women and relatively few people of color. After coming from a company full of passionate creators of all shapes, sizes, and ethnicities, seeing a room of mostly middle-aged white men was a trip back through time.

Not only had I joined a company like the ones my hard-working neighbors complained about, I'd stolen a job from one of the only Black people in the joint.

As the meeting adjourned, Barr approached. "I thought that went well."

"Can I have a word?" I guided us over to a quiet corner as employees fled through multiple doors.

I'd only had the job for minutes, but he hired me to be his bearer of truths. Guess the first one had arrived. "Were there any strong internal candidates on my team for this role? If so, I likely need to patch things over. Did Ms. Washington apply?"

Barr's face flashed a guilty look. "Yes, she did."

"Was there anyone else?"

"One other. Lizzy Chen. Both took the news badly, but I'm confident they'll come around in time. They're highly capable legal minds and strong assets to your team."

So good you passed them both over? The words were milliseconds from spilling out, but I held my tongue. I needed to earn his trust before pushing boundaries.

But the facts were clear. Two women. Two of the few women in the company had interviewed for the job, but he passed them both over like stale bread. Fury raged in me, that he'd dump this load of fertilizer on me minutes into my first day. I looked up as the last back-slapping men broke huddles and left the room. Like it or not, I was now one of them.

"That stinks," I said at last.

Barr chuckled, slapping my shoulder. "Get settled. I'll see you later. The board meeting is tomorrow and we have a few items to discuss."

He sauntered into the hall where he called someone's name, then barked in laughter.

The now empty room reflected my mood. Today was supposed to be a happy new beginning. Instead, I'd entered a den of complications. I stepped down from the stage and crossed halfway across the room before Barbara reappeared in a doorway like an oncoming thunderstorm.

I stopped short, lifting my hands in defense. "I didn't know. I swear I didn't—"

"Not here." She disappeared into the hall.

I followed her to what I presumed was her office and she closed the heavy door behind us. Her hand lingered on the doorknob before she turned to face me. She'd been crying. Her bloodshot eyes were framed by smudged mascara. It was subtly smeared, only noticeable if you were looking. Which I was. It killed me that I caused her misery. I'd pulled the carpet out from under the one woman I hoped to sweep off her feet.

Barbara righted her back. "Did you or did you not know where I worked when we met?" Barbara asked.

"No! I mean no, of course not. How could I? You were sitting on the beach, alone…"

"Not then! At the bar. When we were together—"

"Barbara, I swear. I had no clue where you worked or that… you'd be reporting to me."

My voice sank as the realization hit home.

I'm her boss.

I'm her boss when I want more than anything to be her lover.

I looked at her curvy form in the blue suit she texted me from the magazine, paired with the hottest set of stilettos I'd ever seen. Everything about Barbara was fucking perfect. But Barr still passed her over. What a huge insult, especially for someone as accomplished as her.

"This whole thing is bizarre," I turned away to pace to the window. It was impossible to hold eye contact with Barbara and not want to kiss her. But that would never happen again. My career choice screwed that up royally. Staring out the window, I felt as small as the ant-sized people moving 34 stories below.

Barbara sank into one of her guest chairs, looking numb. Silence settled over the room like fallout ash, our grim reality sinking in.

"I would never have applied if they mentioned the company had a strong internal candidate. I'm sick that I stole that from you."

Barbara cracked her first smile. "That makes two of us."

"I haven't seen a room that white since, well, I'm not sure when," I said.

She took the comment in, her sad expression speaking volumes. "I swear, I'm only here to fill out spots on charity golf teams. 'Washington!'" Barbara mimicked a voice I recognized as Barr's. "'I need a woman for my foursome. Washington: I need a person of color on Thursday. You'll be my fourth.' It's so humiliating. Just once I wish I could tell him to go fuck himself and find another token Black to tote around."

"That's a total HR violation. I'll do what I can to stop him," I said. "If we don't have enough diversity to fill out a golf team, we have bigger troubles."

"Thank you." Barbara's eyes nearly teared up again, my insides crumbling in response. I moved to kneel before her.

"I'll do what I can to make this right. I can't give you this role, but I can make sure you're treated with the dignity you deserve."

Barbara nodded. Even a crushing defeat like this hadn't dimmed the gold flecks in her soulful eyes.

"What I feel for you—"

"Don't..." She shifted to stare at the ceiling as tears welled.

"I've got to say this. Please."

She blew out a breath and swallowed. Staring into her eyes, we were back there on that island. Her and me. Alone on the beach, then in the ocean, then her bed. Our adventure would forever be unfinished.

"My feelings for you are real. I hoped we could be so much more. But now... Well, I've screwed that up for both of us."

A mournful expression crossed her face.

"I want more than anything to kiss you right now. But I won't and won't even ask. If we were playing our game, I'd kiss you, anyway. But our game of adventure will remain back on that island. Barbara, you're so special. You're smart, and talented and deserve better than what Xervo has done to you. What I have done to you."

Tears streaked down her face. She looked so lost and it was all my fault.

I hugged her in, and she let me, settling her head on my shoulder as I kneeled before her.

"What are we going to do?"

"We'll figure this out. We'll make it work."

"How?"

I pulled away, holding her tear-stained face in my hands. "I'm not sure."

My chest knotted. I was already battling every protective instinct I had to not sweep her into my arms, kiss her, and anoint her to the throne I'd stolen from her. Were this the streets, we'd be mortal enemies forever locking horns in battle. A winner and a loser. But it was Barbara. She deserved so much better than what happened here today. Of all the jobs in Manhattan, why did I have to choose this one?

I stood up, wiping my own dewy eyes and sniffing. "I better go. I'll check in with you later. I guess we'll have legitimate work to do together and with the rest of the team.

"I'll do my best to help." She forced a smile.

I swallowed hard as I left her sitting alone and broken in her office.

Chapter 10

BARBARA

What the hell just happened? My office looked the same, yet everything in my life had flipped upside down. My fingers clamped onto the arms of my chair as I stared blankly into the space Sebastian abandoned moments before.

Here.

At work.

Sebastian?

That he was here at all was too fantastic to contemplate. But my boss? The man who left me wanting more would now perpetually torture me, out of reach. I could still feel his eager hands cradling my face. How I wanted his kiss. I saw the longing in his eyes as well. But he was too good a man to take advantage of the situation. I didn't need to blink before knowing what Joe would have done if given the same opportunity.

But the guy I cared for more than I cared to admit was no Joe Clark. That much was infinitely clear. Sebastian was amazing and would likely make an outstanding leader for our legal team. Trouble was, the same could be said about me.

Just like with Joe, I'd been living in a fairytale. Instead of ending up as the Queen, Barr pushed me in the moat to clear the way for the King's carriage. Every sacrifice I made to prove my worth, wasted. At least if I'd known I was a glorified seat warmer, I wouldn't have gotten so attached to the dream. But who wouldn't assume in my place? My office shelves told a tale without words. A trophy collection of accomplishments. Company awards. Legal association rising star. Law school and university degrees. Pictures from winning debate tournaments, company softball leagues, golf outings, and fishing trips. I stood and crossed to my bookcase, catching my reflection in a glass frame. Forgetting, yet again, who it was the world saw.

A Black woman.

My whole life was a contortion exercise. Me trying to fit in. Be just as smart. More accomplished and degreed. Agile on any field of play or courtroom. I'd been so busy plowing ahead to become the best me imaginable that I forgot the one inescapable fact that mattered most: I was Black.

Pictures on my shelves morphed before me. Instead of groups of peers, colleagues, or fellow students—faces I knew with personalities and lives, I saw only race. In nearly every instance, I was the only person of color photographed. Many, the only woman as well. Other. Always the other.

Long before I played games with Sebastian, I was embroiled in an endless game of my own. Be me, but don't offend. Participate, but never be abrasive. Debate points, but not beyond a safe zone.

Angry labels stick and they're career killers. But what had being docile earned me? Swallowing ideas freely expressed moments later by others?

Nothing, but tire treads on my back as they drove over my body.

My cell vibrated in my pocket. *Leslie.*

"So? Did they announce your promotion?" she asked, noisy street sounds behind her.

"Oh, they announced it all right. Then introduced the man who got the job."

"The man? Wait..."

Leslie's brain whirled through the phone, processing the tragedy that was my career over the blaring traffic.

"Shit. That sucks. I'm so sorry."

"You haven't heard the worst part."

"What could be worse than that?"

"My new boss is Sebastian."

"Your hottie from this weekend? He's your boss? You can't make this stuff up."

"Lucky me, right? Lose my job and love life in one fell swoop." I flopped into my desk chair and spun.

"Did you two..."

"Yes! The best sex ever. Epic." I circled back around in my chair. "Now he's my boss." I touched my face, hoping to capture his lingering warmth.

"I don't think I've ever had to say this to you, so the words aren't quite forming in my mouth, but you better get your head on straight. Sebastian is off limits. We'll just have to find you someone else."

Trouble was, I didn't want someone else. I wanted Sebastian. He listened and made me feel alive. Challenged me to take risks and emerge stronger. And had a PhD in lovemaking. He was effectively lost to me, at least in the way I craved.

I finished up with Leslie and dug into a backlog of work. It had long been the one sustaining force in my life. Too bad it now left me depleted.

Once I crossed our apartment threshold that evening, I crumbled. Literally. Back against the door, I slid to the floor, exhausted from holding myself together.

The staff meeting with Sebastian.

The group welcome lunch.

The subway ride home and walk through the streets.

The cheery wave to our doorman.

All a facade.

More than anything, I wanted to rage. Toss tables, rip papers, scream and flail on the floor. Torching a life I'd worked hard to build would leave me with rubble. But isn't that what I already had? A steaming pile of shit after being a dedicated soldier? I played my part. Smart-lawyer girl. Smiling while I choked back tears. Saying "sure I'll work over the weekend" when really wanted to say "fuck no." Every rule my parents set before me, I followed. But here I was, the poster child for failure.

"What's going on?" Dad exited his office with a worried look on his face. "Barbara?"

He was by my side in an instant.

I leaned my head back against the door and squeezed my eyes shut. "They passed me over. I didn't get the promotion. They brought in a guy from the outside."

I braced for impact. The inquiry about what I missed. What checkbox on our list of tasks was left vacant, making this mess entirely my fault. But he said nothing.

I popped one eye open to find him mumbling to himself.

"You're not disappointed in me?"

"Of course not. I'm so sorry, Princess. You deserved that promotion. Looks like it wasn't meant to be."

He stood up, offering his hand for me to join him.

Once upright, the blood drained, leaving me dizzy. "Who are you, and what did you do with my father?"

He swatted me with his newspaper and headed to the kitchen.

"What gives? Something's not right here."

"I don't know what you're talking about." Dad reached into the cupboard and grabbed a glass that he pushed into the fridge door for ice. Cubes clanked as they tumbled in, filling it to the brim. Just as always. But nothing about this conversation was normal.

"This is the latest in a string of monumental failures for me, yet you seem unfazed. Why?"

"Tech companies like Xervo are run by boy's clubs. They don't promote Black women to senior roles. Few organizations do."

His words were a gut punch. Had he always felt this way? If so, what the hell had I been doing for the last 31 years? When I was off sacrificing and studying, working late, and skipping fun to earn my way to the top, had it all been a colossal waste of time?

"Why didn't you say anything to me? Why did you encourage me to try if you thought there was no chance for me?"

"There's always a chance, sweetheart. If anyone has the capacity to break through, it's you. It may just have to be somewhere else. You have all the skills, but now that you're this senior, the roles are fewer and the competition's more fierce."

Watching him sip his water was the first time I could remember us having a conversation like this. About the world having limits. But perhaps he'd been telling me this my whole life, and I hadn't fully understood.

Work twice as hard to get the same results.

Dress the part.

Don't let them see you struggle.

Never complain.

Volunteer for assignments others shun.

Wasn't that all coded language for "your road is harder"? Why had I never internalized the message behind the words? Because I didn't want to believe it. I chose to live in a world that rewarded hard work regardless of the package it came in. And largely, that'd been my experience. Until now. Until the rarefied air smelled like cigars.

My head snapped up in realization. "Is that why you started your own company? Because you got passed over?"

"Partly, yes. But also because, if I was going to fail, I wanted it to be on my own terms. Opening a firm gave me control over my destiny. Decades later, the company has grown. We have more partners, and the responsibility for operations is shared. My role has changed..."

I knew what he meant. I'd overheard him on partner calls, and it wasn't always pretty. Still, it was his firm. His name was first on the door. The business he built from nothing gave us a privileged life few could imagine. My road was difficult, but nowhere as hard as his. He speaks so little about work, I no longer know what he does day-to-day. I default to navigating by his fierce reputation for being a man you didn't want to cross, experiencing a lesser version of that firsthand.

I shuffled over, and he set his glass down to give me a hug. "It'll be okay. You're a Washington. You'll land on your feet and take no prisoners when you do."

"Can I choose a few? Mr. Barr? Stick him in a small cell with no sun and moldy bread?"

"Yes. One prisoner."

"This sucks, Dad."

"Yeah. It does."

Later that night, I stared at my reflection in my bedroom mirror. Locks cascaded over my shoulders as always. It looked like me, but inside everything had changed.

I wasn't a strong Black woman conquering the world. I was a pawn, getting shuffled around just like everyone else. I'd awakened from a long sleep to examine my life from afar. Up until today, I lived a preordained life. College. Law School. Job. Man. Marriage. Forever striving for the next milestone that proved my career progression. All that effort ignored the muscles needed for resilience. The bulk required to overcome setbacks with grace. Flaccid and weak, I better get flexing. But with my five-year plan blown to smithereens, I needed to formulate a new one.

My trademark approach has been to think quick and act faster. My fight-or-flight instincts perpetually activated. Opportunities might vanish if I paused long enough to breathe. Someone would steal away what was rightfully mine. I had to claim it first.

My career had always been a priority, but something shifted in me on that island. Yet, my flames with Sebastian were flickering out, leaving me drenched in darkness. I knew how fragile relationships were, and I didn't want ours over. Shallow as it may be, quitting my job seemed the logical next move. It'd free me to pick up fresh and leave the disgusting Mr. Barr behind. Why should I stay somewhere I wasn't respected? By passing me over for another, the company made its choice. Mr. Barr betrayed my trust and deserved swift consequences, just like Joe. In his case, I moved out and broke off my impending marriage. Shouldn't I cling to my tattered self-respect and send Xervo packing?

As if on cue, my cell rang. Joe's face filled the screen for his daily "I'm sorry" missive. It'd been easy to ignore the calls while fuming, and when absorbed in Rebecca's wedding—and Sebastian. But today's events left me lost, lonely, and deeply conflicted. A longing voice beat the serenade of rejection looping through my ears. My finger tapped the green answer button before I could stop myself.

"Wow. Didn't expect that." Joe's delicious, deep voice said. He'd always had a voice meant for radio. He should be introducing long, soulful interludes before jazz greats took over and your mind drifted away on the music. He'd made love to me with those intoxicating tones before we ever hit the sheets. But then, he had practice.

"You caught me at a low point." I said.

"Okay, well. I'll take what I can get. Um..." He cleared his throat, uncertain. "Hi?"

"You've been calling daily for over almost two months, and that's the best you got?" I stomped to my bed and flopped onto my stomach with a bounce.

"Yeah. When I started, I had written notes. Then I memorized them. Then I stopped hoping you'd answer."

"Well, this has been lovely, but—"

"I'm sorry. I miss you. What I did was stupid, and selfish, and cruel. Meet me for dinner. So we can talk."

I clutched the phone to my chest, tears streaming as if wrung from a drenched towel. I wiped them on my bedspread, but still more came. The irony of it, overwhelming. Once, those words might have made me reconsider. *I'm sorry. I miss you.* Those five words could very well have soothed my raging insides and lessened my uncontrollable self-loathing for ignoring the urgent warning signs of his infidelity.

How could he put me in that position? To find them joined in lust in our own bed? Once all I wanted was evidence of his shame. That, or overwhelming sorrow for blowing up our unified future. But that was then. The wedding date had come and gone. There was no going back.

So why did I long to see him?

"You still there?"

"For now."

I heard him smile.

"Have dinner. What's the harm? Two once friends breaking bread?"

Damn. My indecision gave him an opening to charm his way back. He knew he'd already won. That confidence made him a successful advertising sales executive where he worked at Sports Illustrated. And why I'd fallen for him in no time flat. I could guess his motivations for dragging me out. But what did I hope to gain? Prove my desirability? Have him hunger for me as he did Miss Red

Thong? Maybe. Was that so bad? To be chosen above others? To be loved?

"It better be somewhere good."

"It will be. I'll text you after I make a reservation. Tomorrow work?"

I lay in bed, nausea tormenting my stomach. My cheating ex wanting me somehow lessened the loneliness of sleeping in my childhood bedroom. But it was impossible to ignore that Joe's actions put me here. Rejection in every facet of my life pierced my armored exterior like punched tin. Vulnerability comes hard, but I lowered the drawbridge for Sebastian. And look where that got me. To recover, my defenses needed fortifying. I'd go to dinner, but do so with my eyes wide open. I'd let too many men get the better of me. Joe. Sebastian. Even my dad sometimes with his obsession with my success. I'd be damned if I let it happen again.

Chapter 11

Sebastian

As I approached my building after work, a familiar form leaned next to my front door. I'd know Dante anywhere. My ex-childhood friend copied his persona from watching gangsta movies. Baggy wide-legged jeans and an over-sized T-shirt covered his wall-to-wall tattoos. His pasty skin was only visible between his earlobe piercings. He'd stopped tattooing his face after placing a single black tear beneath his right eye. Though Italian, Dante had adopted Mo's Puerto Rican accent, a habit that sent people snickering behind his back. For all the show, his lame hood skills had him in and out of prison as often as I took a shower.

"Yo, King!" Dante said.

Hearing my street nickname off his lips made my stomach loop like I'd been caught shoplifting. I'd changed. Got educated and made a life. Looking at him now made me wonder for the first time if Mom was right about me still living here. Since I was, best to keep my head down and keep walking. Ignore that tug that kept gang members tethered for life. He'd lost that privilege the moment he saved himself instead of reaching his hand back to pull me over that fence.

If he had, I might be dead, in prison or sharing the street corners with him. So why, all these years later, did I still dream versions of that night when we escaped that alley together? Ran back to my number two, Mo, telling him how Dante and I almost got cuffed?

Dante lowered his sneaker off the building, tossing his trademark toothpick aside. "Where you been? I been waiting."

"Some of us have jobs? A life?" I stepped past him to the door, ignoring the outstretched hand Dante pocketed to save face.

Ever watchful, he peeked over his shoulder. Another sign of gang life: head on a swivel, looking for whomever is chasing you. Police. Rival gangs. Relatives. Snitches. Everything about Dante screamed trouble. And not the good kind.

He flicked his nose with his thumb. "So, uh, can I crash wit you?"

I stopped dead, key poised before the lock. "You're fucking joking me right now."

"Nah, no joke."

"No fucking way."

"Compadre! Por favor? See—I learned Spanish. I'm an educated man."

"Hit the library, did you?"

"Nah, the library blows at Rikers. Treat you worse than rats there. But it's better than Edgecombe. I ain't no junkie, King. Fuck that group therapy shit." Dante reached into his pocket for another toothpick.

I'd better things to do than debate the finer points of New York prisons. Plus, the longer we talked, the worse it'd be for me. If I let Dante inside, who knew how long I'd be stuck with him?

"Can't Mo hook you up?" I said, scanning the sidewalk like he'd materialize on command.

Dante stepped close, hissing through his chipped front tooth. "Mo hung me out. Why he got your back and not mine?"

Poor old Dante. He was always jealous of me and Mo being so tight, accusing us of cutting him out. We only did that once, but he didn't need to know that. Besides, all that money was long gone.

"Go ask him. I ain't your therapist. You got yours, just like I got mine. Not that you ever cared for anyone but yourself."

Dante kept his cool, unusual for a human volcano. "You know. Mo put me up to it."

Here we go...

Mo was like a brother to me back then. After I got out of juvy, I was at his house every damn day, doing homework, trying to stay out of trouble. I hated it at first, but then, it became a mission. I was hellbent not to go back to jail. Though it was a lesson Dante had yet to learn.

"Go stay at Natasha's."

"King, she's eight-months pregnant and moved to Florida."

"Yours?"

"Who the fuck knows!" he blasted before collecting himself, eyes ever darting around.

"Someone's keyed-up?"

Dante raised a fist toward my face. "Yeah? And someone's gonna catch these hands if he keeps talking shit."

I looked down at his knuckles. "That's supposed to make me want to help you?"

"Maybe you need a reminder of where you came from? Someone to take you down a peg."

"Mo'd have something to say about that."

He retracted his hands. "Fuck you."

I pushed the lobby door open and passed through. "Take care."

But before I could force the hinge closed, Dante slammed the bulletproof glass with his palm. So hard, I flinched, expecting it to shatter shards all over me.

"Don't fucking close the door in my face! You owe me."

I held the door firm against Dante's advance. "I stopped owing you a long time ago. You made your bed, lie in it. Oh wait, you can't."

"Now you're a fucking comedian?"

"No, but I'm not a Motel 6 either."

"Turn me away, and you'll regret it. I'll make sure of that."

My head dropped back. I wanted Dante gone so bad, I could taste it. A warm shower called me. But instead of rinsing off the day's stress, I'd have to power wash Dante's stink off my psyche.

I steadied my voice. "That's how you got into Rikers in the first place."

Dante's nostrils flared. "Where's the money, King? I know you have it. What's mine is mine." Dante waved his arms before gesturing forcefully to the sidewalk below. Obstacle removed, I slammed the door shut.

Blood throbbed in my ears as I walked away, more amped than I wanted to admit. After the day I'd had, I'd love nothing more than to feel the crunch of his nose under my fist. Dante's ability to drag my mind to violence that quickly scared me more than any of his bluster. The door rattled as he pounded the glass near out of the frame.

"Fuck you, King. I want my money. I know where you live. I know where you work. You think you can fucking walk away?!"

My steps echoed up the stairs I'd ascended for years. It'd been nine years since I moved out of my mom's apartment a few blocks away. Every crack in the tiny octagonal floor tiles was committed to memory. Their once-white surfaces scuffed and worn where a hundred years of shuffling feet left their mark. Focusing on the patterns helped me drown out the world. It's what I did in juvy at night, when all the kids yelled to each other from dorms bunks, refusing to sleep. On a top bunk, I'd get lost in the crisscrossing frame of the drop ceiling. Dreaming of the amazing life I'd have one day when all of this was behind me. Instead, I was back playing the same fucking game of musical chairs.

His rants grew faint, then louder again as I passed the open window on the third-floor landing. I'll give it to him. He's got a set of pipes. Though, him screaming in the street about money would make people think I had some. Which I now did, but that stash was all legit. Saved after years of working hard and eating ramen noodles.

My mistake was talking to him at all. Thinking I could be any kind of civil. Stupid. Now the dumb fuck was pissed and held a grudge like a vice. No good would come from this. As much as I loved this neighborhood and being near Mom, it made it impossible to leave my past in the past. History always repeated itself. In the case of Dante, I hoped he'd leave me be. But knowing him as I did, I'd better start looking over my shoulder.

Chapter 12

Barbara

Dressing for work the next morning, I avoided looking at my reflection. My eyes stung from crying; I didn't need to see the evidence. I smoothed on foundation, then topped it with loose powder and lipstick. By the time I looked up, I stared back. It'd have to do until I felt the part. Being fake was growing old. No wonder my childhood friends called me Superstar Barbie. There was a manufactured look to me that I'd never registered before.

My hair.

My obsession with designer fashion.

Plastering a smile on to make others comfortable and avoid awkward confrontations. To live my life meant living on a runway. Forever strutting. Staging a solo performance. But for whom?

Dark locks with copper highlights stared back at me. Hair extensions, real, but not mine. I shook the negative thoughts away and got dressed.

By the time I exited the elevators at work, my confidence had semi-returned. No menacing shoves on the subway, though I avoided my braided Nubian goddess when I saw her at the end of the car. My day was going okay so far, so I decided not to push my luck. At least, not yet.

I was unpacking my briefcase when someone knocked on my door. My heart leapt, but it was only Portia from accounting. All numbers and payables, our exchanges were strictly business. Her warm smile was a pleasant change.

"Have a minute?" Portia asked.

"Sure," I said. "Have a seat."

The beads on her long braids clacked delicately as she sat. I swore the gods were sending me Black women with braids just to shove in my face what a coward I'd been on the island.

"What can I do for you?" I asked.

"A few of us have been talking about starting an Employee Resource Group. I wanted to invite you to get involved. Maybe even as our executive sponsor?"

"I see." I wasn't opposed to the idea. But with my lost promotion, how would Mr. Barr take my involvement in an advocacy ERG for Black staffers?

"There are so few people of color here at the company, it'd be a place for employees to gather, discuss our concerns, and help educate others about why we need a healthier dialog about race."

"At work?"

"Yes, at work. Why not here?"

"Aren't we supposed to avoid discussing controversial topics in the workplace? Isn't that divisive?"

Portia's expression hardened. "We've been avoiding it for decades and it's accomplished nothing. I expected you, of all people, to understand."

"Sorry. I don't follow."

"C'mon. Yesterday? They brought in a white guy from the outside instead of giving the job to you or Lizzy Chen."

"I'm not sure it's a good time. Let me think on it?"

Portia rose in a huff. "Forget it. Given what happened to you, I assumed the need for us to stick together would be obvious. Guess not obvious enough."

"I didn't say no—"

"Didn't you, though?" Portia had a knack of saying the stuff other people considered but never said aloud. That used to be me. Actually, it was me everywhere else but work.

I pressed my lips together. She was right. I didn't want to do it. It seemed the worst time to make a stink about race. It'd make me look like a sore loser and damage whatever measure of respect I still had held with the staff.

She moved toward the opened door but stopped halfway. "I told them you'd say no. That we couldn't count on you to stand with us. Maybe that's why Mr. Barr passed you over. He didn't trust you either."

Breath left me.

She strode through the door, leaving me slumped in my chair.

How did I become the world's punching bag? The two of us rarely said two words in the years I'd worked here. Yet Portia expected me to knee-jerk and sponsor her group without a second to mull it over? If she knew me at all, she'd know I did nothing without thinking. I thought fast, sure. But I did think. I'd consider the pros and cons, the time investment, the cause, and decide. But Portia hadn't given me a reason to say yes. Her walking off in a snit made me realize I chose right.

As the day wore on, work fell into familiar routines. Meetings were humdrum and everyone treated me as they always had: with unwavering respect. There were a few glances, whispers, and false smiles. But that's to be expected since Mr. Barr had publicly blindsided me. I'd have to be patient while the dust settled, but for that, a second mug of coffee was in order.

En route to the kitchen, I saw a dolly with camera equipment roll by.

"Why all the gear?" I asked Yvonne when passing reception.

"Portrait day. Since they're all in town, and they're doing Mr. Kingsbury's picture, they're freshening up the entire C-Suite and all the board members." She answered.

I nodded.

She stared at me a bit too long. We weren't close, but then, I wasn't overly friendly with anyone in the office. Dad always encouraged me to keep things professional, ironic given the toe-curling sex I'd already had with Sebastian. But he wasn't my boss then. I smiled at the memory and Yvonne took it as a cue to lean in and whisper.

"You should have been on that wall. You deserved it. Guess they weren't ready to have someone from the motherland among their inner circle."

I learned long ago that if you're Black, you're assumed to have a shared African heritage. Our dark skin puts us in the same club. But my family hailed from Barbados, and we'd had a very different immigrant experience than American Blacks. Besides that, I never felt welcome in the club. People like Joe's sister and mother complained that I acted too white, too stuck up, and weird. They'd done everything possible to make me uncomfortable in social situations. I'd bring a covered, homemade dessert for a holiday, and Joe's sister would lift the napkin and say, "I expected you to bring Oreos."

I'd ignored more than enough digs like that. But for Xervo, I wasn't white enough to be General Counsel—or up on that wall. I tried not to make everything about race, but it was impossible to ignore the scant diversity at work. The New York office had eight underrepresented people in a staff of 300. And too few in our total workforce of 3,000.

"I'd hoped race wasn't the issue. Now I'm not so sure."

"Like it or not, it's always an issue. Especially with Mr. Barr—" Yvonne stopped herself. As his Executive Assistant, she likely got the same insulting treatment I did. Were we closer, I might risk asking.

"Hopefully, the leadership team will address representation one day." I said, watching yet another dolly roll by.

Yvonne laughed. "I won't hold my breath."

"Smart move." I resumed my coffee run, glancing toward the photo shoot set up in the conference room as my wavy-haired dreamboat came into view. He stood chatting with the photographer.

Sebastian's smile melted me like ice on a griddle. Damn him for not working someplace else. If he had, I'd be General Counsel getting my picture taken, AND would have his hotness draped over my arm. And other parts of me as well. The friend in my panties twitched in a glorious memory of his skill.

Down girl. He's your boss.

My legs started moving toward the kitchen, the wisest part of me taking charge as my mind drifted back to my vacation island. Having Sebastian around was going to be much harder than I thought.

Chapter 13

SEBASTIAN

The photoshoot presented an amazing opportunity for me to get face time with colleagues headquartered in other offices. And meeting the board in this informal way helped me better understand the political landscape of Xervo. The group seemed smart and experienced, except for our ghost of a board chair. He had a minimal social footprint which matched the guarded man I saw whispering across the room. The CFO avoided me as well, focusing his attention on Barr.

I'd have to dig-in to better understand who I could trust and who, if anyone, I needed to be cautious around. From the body language in the room, something was up. Barr did more than his fair share of low talking in corners. As the top legal officer, I'd better get a handle on his dealings before they blew up in my face.

I mentioned valuing transparency in my welcome speech, and during the various rounds of job interviews. But I already questioned whether Barr shared that outlook. I should have asked more questions about the company and its values while interviewing. The website looked spot-on, saying all the right things. However, values were lived. So far, Barr fell short.

The morning ended with a group lunch in the executive dining room, one more fossil of 40 years ago. We'd need to talk about the optics of keeping the executives so secluded from the rest of the employees. It was a far cry from the open-concept office spaces at my last two jobs. T-shirted CEOs sat in ordinary desks among everyone else. That extreme was impractical at a company the size of Xervo, but the ivory tower approach had to go. Emphasis on the ivory.

Leaders filed out, dined and tipsy, heading to the elevators. As I exited, the executive photo wall loomed large. Image after image of elder white men. My face would soon join theirs to replace my retired predecessor. He'd been gone two years, but instead of adding Barbara's photo in the interim, Randall Fischer's face filled the frame. Barbara must have cringed every time she passed this wall. They needed her, plus more, to approximate anything close to an inclusive leadership team. Each man was accomplished, but shit, they'd all been working since before I was born.

Yvonne sat at reception. Besides her, Barbara and a few others I saw on the org chart, the company and its board were as diverse as a vanilla shake. Xervo would tank itself with such monolithic thinking. Innovation required a convergence of different ideas, battling it out until the best rose to the top. If everyone had the same life experience and professional backgrounds, where would the breakthrough thinking come from?

"That went well, don't you think?" Barr paused alongside me to admire the wall.

"Quite a group of men, yes."

Barr smiled back.

I pressed my lips tight, but it was no use. My agitated thoughts flew out my mouth. "Has there been any effort to diversify the leadership team and board?"

"Bob is gay. Does that count?" He roared with laughter, slapping me on the back so hard I lurched forward.

"It's a start, but it's something we should discuss."

His chuckles subsided. "The men you met today are fine people making valuable contributions to our business."

"I'm sure they are. Absolutely. But it's my job to point out potential risks, both moral and legal ones."

"Risks?"

"If Xervo has designs to go public, or secure additional VC funding, leadership diversity is one criteria investors like to see."

He snickered, shaking his head. "I didn't take you for a social justice warrior. But I guess you wouldn't be a lawyer if you weren't worrying about nonsense."

The comment hung between us, begging for a response. But my ass would get canned if I said what I was thinking. That it sickened me to work for a guy stuck in the stone age. To be the reason qualified women lost promotions. That he ought to be taking my concerns seriously if he wanted to avoid employee litigation. Disgust brewed in my stomach, but it paled in relation to what Barbara and her colleague, Lizzy Chen, must be enduring.

"Well, back to work!" Barr smiled as he motioned with his arm for us to disburse. He probably took my silence for assent. On my second day, I wasn't in the position to hop in a phone booth and drag him into the right century. Until then, or I pried the hinges off the door to the boy's club, I'd play his game.

Navigating the maze of halls, I headed to the one place at Xervo where my skin wouldn't crawl.

"Knock, knock." I tapped on Barbara's open door. "Okay if I come in?"

Barbara looked up expectant, but then her expression changed to the one she likely flashed to opposing counsel over a negotiating table.

"That bad, huh?" I entered and closed the door behind me.

"How did it go hobnobbing with our company elite?" She crossed her arms.

"About what you'd expect. Boys being boys while I watched in horror. Pretty shameful. I'm glad you weren't there to witness it." I paced, looking up periodically as she tracked my edgy movements.

"I'm sure most men in that room were thrilled to have me gone."

Ouch. I walked into that one.

"That's not what I meant."

"What did you mean, then? Wait, scratch that. Why are you here in my office?"

"I wanted to see you." It came out more pathetic and needy than intended.

"Well here I am. Shall I get back to work? I have a new boss and I need to make a good impression." Barbara pulled herself in toward her desk.

"Don't. Please."

"Why? This is our new reality. We best adjust."

"I hate that I'm the one keeping you from what you deserve," I said.

"It's pointless to rehash this. It is what it is, as much as we wish it otherwise. Neither of us can do anything about it."

"But—"

"Stop." She held up both hands. "You have got to give me some space to process. Xervo tossed me under a semi and you keep reversing over my carcass."

She had a point. It was shitty of me to win the spoils and then complain about it to the person I defeated. But she was also the one person I longed to be with the most. After years of being alone, I felt a part of something. An "us." Silly, I know, but there was no doubt she felt it, too. How could I let that go?

"I'm sorry. I'm not sure how to handle this, here." I gestured to the office surroundings. "Have dinner with me. Away from here, we'll be able to talk."

"I can't."

"Can't or won't?"

"I have plans," she lifted her chin. Her plans were clearly a date, confirmed by the flash in her eyes. My soul died.

"If you weren't busy…"

"The answer would still be no. Christ, Sebastian! You're my boss. Don't you think that'd be a bad idea?"

"Probably."

But I can't get you out of my mind.

"Well, at least we're agreed on something." Barbara returned to her work. I stood watching the contours of her face until they relaxed. She'd tuned me out and was actually working. Her shoulders eased as the words on the page took hold. Drawing her in and away from me. Now, I wasn't only jealous of her date, I envied the damn legal brief.

I walked toward the door but paused. Barbara's beauty calling to me from across the room. Her ebony skin glowed. Her hair flowed over her shoulders like silk. Those delicate shoulders I yearned to kiss, along with the rest of her.

How could she be single?

Oh, yeah. Her cheating ex.

I prayed our work debacle didn't launch her back into the arms of the cheating man who didn't deserve her.

Chapter 14

Barbara

The moment Sebastian left, I gasped for air. Chest heaving, I covered my face in my hands. I was barely strong enough to keep myself together. I couldn't be his confidant. He'd have to cope on his own. Every ounce of me wanted to crash my mouth into his and tangle my fingers in his shaggy curls. But the time for that had passed. I was the injured party, kicked to the side.

That said, Sebastian's suspicions might be right.

Barr skipped me simply because I was a woman? And, worse, a Black woman?

Acid rose in my throat.

Could it be that simple? They wanted someone who looked like them? A crinkly man to sit with in the steam room? Round out their foursome of golf? Drink whiskey at client meetings?

My tongue reflexively cleaned itself at the thought of whiskey. Bitter acetone costing $300 a bottle. They downed it with tiny sips, swirling their glasses of ice. I didn't get it. One of many things about them I didn't get, the job being prime among them. They hadn't wanted me as the leader, yet refused to give a good reason. Instead, they patted my head like a child telling me *your time will come,* full well knowing a man clung to every ladder rung above me.

I should march into Barr's office and demand justice. But that'd be pointless. Just as pointless as working in a role with no advancement potential. Chen was in the same fix. The two of us would likely keep battling for the same table scraps, only to have another Prince Charming gallop his horse around us while we squabbled.

Everything I'd accomplished in my life meant something. Built toward a bigger, long-term goal. For the first time since forever, I saw no path forward. Who was I if not a lawyer on the rise? Why get up in the morning?

I spun my chair around to face the window. Manhattan sprawled uptown toward the horizon. My city. I had memories on nearly every street corner. Fun dinners, street fairs, galas, and museums. The green patch of Central Park lay in the middle like a leafy postage stamp. That park held a treasure trove of memories from my regular picnics with Rebecca and Leslie. We travailed through life, each helping the other overcome whatever challenges came our way.

In our friendship trio, I played the fixer. The one who swooped in to problem-solve and rescue my gal pals from whatever mess they'd gotten into. I hadn't been this lost and unsure since my mom died.

I rolled over to my desk to retrieve my phone and tapped open our group chat.

Barbara:

My world has flipped upside down.

Leslie:

What else happened?

Rebecca:

OMG, Barbara! What's wrong?

Barbara:

Can we talk?

Leslie:

Couldn't stop me.

I pressed the camera icon to launch Facetime. Moments later, their faces filled my screen. The knot in my chest eased at the sight of them.

"Sweetie, what's wrong? You've been crying?" Rebecca asked.

"I've barely stopped crying in the last 24 hours."

"Lover boy stole her promotion and is her boss." Leslie said.

"No way!" Rebecca said. Fresh off her honeymoon, I hadn't wanted to drag her down.

"So, what's the plan? You staying to fight and get what's yours, or are you going to start looking?" Leslie asked.

"I'd hoped you tell me."

The pair grimaced.

"You don't need to decide anything today. It's all new. You're a fast-action type of girl, but this time, it may be best to sit and assess. Lick your wounds before making any hasty decisions." Rebecca said.

"You have met me, right?" I hoped to avoid countering my nature.

"Listen to Rebecca. Let the dust settle and see how things go. It might normalize with Sebastian and you two can work together. If not, it'll give you more time to plan your next move."

"Can you ask for a transfer?" Rebecca asked.

"The closest office is Washington D.C. But I don't want to uproot and leave you and my family because Xervo dicked me over. There has to be a better way."

"All the more reason to hold your cards," Leslie said. "This is a punch in the gut. No doubt. Weird, since you're usually the one dishing out punishment. But you're strong, smart, and talented. I could drop you anywhere and you'd run the show in two seconds."

"Present company, notwithstanding," I said.

Leslie see-sawed her head in agreement.

ABH: Anywhere but here.

Disappointment weighed heavy. A foreign sensation growing too familiar. But I wasn't the first Washington to be underestimated, then later end up on top. Rising from the ashes, I'd blind them all and make them regret their mistake. I imagined Barr's face melting al *Raiders of the Lost Ark* before refocusing on our conversation. I had a long way to go until that pinnacle moment, and no clear road map.

After we wrapped up our call, I returned to work. The girls had a point. I hated waiting with the passion of ten thousand suns. But with no alternate plan, the best I could muster was a date with an ex I no longer wanted.

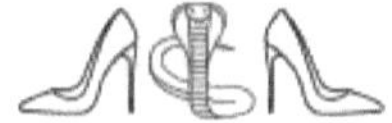

I swung home to change before meeting Joe. It was time for him to face the person he'd lost. After some mental pep-talks in my Lyft to the restaurant, I emerged from the car confident, sexy, and untouchable. He'd take one look at me and instantly regret screwing me over. My hands smoothed the black dress hugging my curves, spaghetti straps accentuating my natural gifts. I almost felt guilty.

Almost.

I grasped the glass door handle of the French restaurant Joe selected. Of course, he picked Le Petit Renard. It's where he took me on our first date and was my absolute favorite. He'd remembered that fact after talking to me only twice. Feeling heard, it didn't take Joe long to sweep me off my feet. How ironic I fell for his charms in a restaurant called The Little Fox.

One of the many mistakes I made with Joe.

In my defense, he was a prime catch. Tall, handsome as all get out, and successful by his own hard work and determination. All despite a dysfunctional upbringing with a mother and sister who excelled at manufacturing drama out of thin air. *Shit.* These were all the reasons I wanted to marry him, which made this meal a terrible idea.

I halted before reaching the hostess stand. I should leave. Right now, before seeing him. If I saw him, I could very well melt into a helpless pool and take him back. Unlikely, but a potential scenario I had to factor.

Escargot, sizzling in a pool of buttery, garlicky heaven, passed by in a puff of steam that sent my mouth watering. The vapor practically curled into a finger, tempting me to follow.

Damn him. Why did he have to pick my favorite restaurant? Not eating all day didn't help matters. Logic dictated I should stay, have a free meal, then head home. No physical contact. No kisses and caresses across the table.

I came for sustenance and nothing else.

I forced my cheeks to stretch into a smile as I approached the hostess. She guided me across the candle-lit dining room to a quiet corner, partially hidden behind a curtain. When together, we'd sit side-by-side, kissing and nuzzling between courses. Seeing him sitting there like a pot of molten chocolate in "our" booth jolted me awake. Was this part of his game? The wooing? My fingers tightened on my clutch, nearly snapping it in two. He'd likely sat in that very spot with Miss Red Thong.

Payback time.

The hostess pulled out my seat. As I lowered myself in, I took care to lean forward to offer a mounded view of cleavage before righting myself in my chair.

Joe's tongue passed across his lips, eyeing me like a buffet. "You look good enough to eat."

I flicked my napkin, placing it on my lap. "Not anymore. You saw to that."

His mask fell, leaving a sneer. "Baby, don't be like that."

"Like what? Relieved I found out before marrying a cheating ass?"

Joe leaned in. "Can we be civil? At least in public?"

"You chose the location," I spoke, doing little to lower my voice. "This is the first I've seen you since I found the owner of that red thong riding you in our bed."

"And why is that? Hmm?" He hissed. "I called. I sent flowers. I went to your dad's place. You refused to see me. I deserved better."

"I'm way too sober for this conversation." I waved, and a server rushed over.

"We'll take a bottle of *L'Espirit de Chevalier.* 2019 if you have it."

$115 a bottle. *Hey, he's paying.*

"Very good, madam." He bowed his head and withdrew.

Joe jumped in right where our conversation left off. "You didn't even give me a chance to explain. You packed up and moved so fast, it was almost like..."

Joe sat back, shaking his head.

"Almost like what?" I asked.

"Almost like you were glad. Glad we were over."

A jolt went up my spine. Thinking back, had I been relieved? That the wait was finally over? Maybe. I knew all along something was off between us but could never put my finger on what. Until his fingers were all over the "what" that'd been staring me in the face, long before I wanted to believe it. The nerve of him sitting there, guilt tripping me for ghosting him?

The server returned, opened the bottle and awaited my approval before setting a glass before Joe and disappearing.

I downed my glass before continuing, the tangy wine taking effect.

"Ignoring you was for your own protection. I had no intention of being disbarred because I hacked my fiancée and his mistress to pieces and flushed them down the toilet."

Watching him, I couldn't help remembering the last time we were here. He wore a black silk shirt that I ripped to shreds the moment we passed through our apartment door. We had a steamy intimate life. Or so I thought. Apparently, it wasn't hot enough to keep him from seeking bonus rounds with someone else.

"How long?" It was out of my mouth before my mind caught up. "How long were you seeing her?"

His dark eyes dulled in defeat. "Does it even matter?"

"It does. I've been wracking my brain trying to figure out what I did wrong. How we got so off course that you felt the need to bed someone else."

"That's the wrong question." Joe said. "What you should be asking yourself is 'why did I always put my career ahead of the man I was supposed to love? Why was I never home and fully present when he needed me?'"

Joe downed his wine and refilled his glass, ignoring my empty one.

This was a new one. Him being neglected? What about all his late nights? Had he forgotten about all the evenings I was alone wanting him?

"Why is it falling to me to be available for your needs? I have needs as well. Are we in 1950?"

"If it was 1950, you'd be home, and I'd be working. I wouldn't have to fight the phantom of your 'rising legal career.'" He air quoted before waving off the server coming to take our order.

"Your first love was, and always will be, work. How was I supposed to compete with that?"

Of all the hateful things he said, air quoting 'rising legal career' stung the worst. He had no way of knowing exactly how hurtful given my lost promotion. But I wouldn't let him get the upper hand. Not about dueling careers. His career was just as demanding, if not more so. It kept him away nights, weekends, and for week-long junket trips with customers to exotic locations. I never denied him the opportunity he needed to grow and strive. Never held him back. Why was this just coming up now? Why hadn't he made his feelings known long before he sought solace in another? *Unless...*

"She wasn't the first." I looked straight into his eyes, holding steady until he looked away. "You have been with others. Has it been all along? Were you ever faithful to me, or was this thing between us a lie all along?"

Joe sat grinding his jaw. He may be the smooth talker between us, but I'm the skilled interrogator. His expression revealed volumes without uttering a word.

"Answer me. You owe me that much."

"Yes. There were others."

"Wait..." I waved my hands, trying to flush out the flurry of questions all bombarding me at once. "If you didn't love me enough to be faithful, why propose? Why get married?"

Tension tightened my chest, squeezing out all the air and constricting my throat until my voice was a spoken sob. This conversation had quickly turned way more real than I expected.

"Look," he spread his palms wide. "I've never been exclusive. To you or anyone. I have needs. I meet my needs and move on. These women mean nothing to me and never have. You mattered. The rest, it was just sex."

A cry clogged in my throat, preventing me from swallowing. I smothered my anguish with a hand, cupping it over my mouth.

How had I not known?

I've never been exclusive. To you, or anyone.

Our entire relationship was a lie. I nearly married a narcissistic psychopath. With all he knew about me, did he really think I'd be content marrying a man who unapologetically whored around town? That I thought so little of myself to accept that behavior? If so, he knew me as little as I knew him.

I opened my mouth to speak, but no words came. I looked at Joe and saw a stranger. A stranger I almost married.

He gathered his napkin and tossed it on the table. "This was a mistake."

I nodded my agreement, staring at the candle flickering between us. All other light in our relationship, gone.

Joe stood. "I'll leave my card with the hostess. I know how much you love it here."

I met his eye.

He bent to whisper in my ear, "I've missed you, though."

I whirled on him. "How can you say that?"

"You're blowing this whole thing out of proportion. Do you know how many women I've turned down because of you? Hot ones my sister sent my way?"

"Your sis...?"

He shrugged. "She said you were too stuck up to appreciate a real brother like me. Guess she was right."

As Joe straightened to leave, I grabbed his forearm.

"If by stuck up, you mean I expect my husband not to screw every mound of cleavage walking by, then yeah. I guess I don't appreciate a 'real' brother like you." I air quoted for emphasis.

"Enjoy your empty bed." Joe pulled free, tugged his suit neat, and walked away.

When I was sure he was gone, I ran into a bathroom stall and cried.

Chapter 15

SEBASTIAN

It'd been a week and I'd done my best to dig into work and avoid Barbara as much as possible. Just knowing she was close was torture. What's worse, my legal crew was near mutiny.

Lizzy Chen and Barbara shot daggers at each other when they weren't tossing one-word answers at me. The rest of the team wasn't sure what to make of me, following the passive-aggressive example of their spurned leaders.

Together, they were doing an excellent job of pushing me out the door. Which, frankly, didn't seem like the worst idea except for my stubborn refusal to fail at my first General Counsel role.

Somewhere amidst all the mess with Barbara, resolve crystallized in me. I wanted this position. I earned the right to lead a team and leave my imprint on a company that ached for a better path.

But to make positive change, this group had to snap out of it.

I entered the conference room last and slapped my pad on the table. I remained standing.

"Can everyone hear me on the call?" I asked.

A chorus of mumbles and thumbs up signals flashed across the checkerboard of faces on the wall-mounted monitor.

"It's been a week, so that should be sufficient time for this group to adjust to my arrival. But if not, let's speak our piece and move forward. After today, I need everyone to get their heads straight and act like adults. I'll go first." I planted my feet and faced the room.

"My hiring put two of your leaders in an awkward position. We had capable women passed over for a white guy. That has to suck."

"I'll say," Barbara said, the corners of her adorable mouth curving up. A chuckle waved the team.

Progress...

"Thank you. Okay, who else? Lizzy? Any thoughts?"

"I hate people calling me Lizzy."

"What?" A chorus said in unison on screen and in the room.

"My name is Elizabeth. I prefer that. I think Mr. Barr started it, but if we could ditch the Lizzy nickname, I'd appreciate it."

"Great. Thank you, Elizabeth. Let's be honest with each other. We are a team. We're not the team you all expected going into last week, but to be effective, we need to look out for each other and be a positive example for the rest of the company."

I took my seat to be at eye level with those sitting in the room. "We have two open positions and I'd like for us to ensure our candidate pool has diverse candidates. Hire whom you think is best, but be sure you're getting a wider group of applicants from different sources. Tap trade associations of color, talk to your networks. I've also secured a budget to post on an expanded array of job boards than we've been using to date."

Everyone in the room was smiling and nodding. Except for Barbara, the one person I expected to support these efforts. I hesitated to call her out, but if I was going to treat her like any other colleague, it had to start now.

"Barbara, do you have any concerns about this approach?"

Her head snapped up. She looked in my direction but avoided eye contact. "No. It's a sound plan."

"Good. Let's turn to the formal agenda. I want to compile a list of any shortcomings we need to tighten up to protect the company and remain compliant with the law."

The meeting went better than I hoped. I identified areas to investigate and improve, from procurement to contracting, to harassment and discrimination policies. All were woefully outdated. We needed to tighten those up, or someone would sue.

As the room disbursed, Barbara remained distracted.

"Hey, do you have a minute?" I asked.

Her eyes swept the space, but no one was close. I shut the door. "You seem off today. Everything okay?"

"Yeah. I just found it ironic that you've been here a week and have made more of a stand for diversity than I had in two years."

"Why is that? It's pretty white around here. You must have noticed."

She sighed, her arms flopping into her lap. "Of course I did. But I've spent my whole life trying to fit in. I focused on earning my way, so no one could claim I got a free ride or was a less qualified hire. I try not to think about race at all, but sometimes it seems like I'm the only one."

"Race is hard to avoid. It's plain as day for everyone to see."

"I get that. But it's unfair that you as a white guy can parade around talking about race, when I'd be penalized for doing the same thing."

"Should I not point out that we can do better?"

"No, it's amazing. It's just. I never thought I could suggest those changes."

I scratched my chin. Calling bullshit on her would be rude, but... "Help me understand that."

"Barr would have accused me of starting some Selma marches and yell at me to get back to work," she whispered. "And that truth pisses me off. I should have done more."

"Take that frustration and channel it into something good. Tap those networks of yours. You must have contacts in Black professional circles who can send some rock-star candidates our way?"

She forced a wide smile that didn't convince. "I'll look into it."

A while later, Elizabeth rapped on my door. "Knock, knock."

"Come in. Close it behind you."

I was still learning who to trust around here, so private conversations were gold. My mind flashed to Dante's darting eyes, but I blinked the image away.

"Thanks for today. I can't tell you how much I hated being called 'Lizzy'. It never seemed like the right time to speak up."

"No worries. Is there anything else?"

"I've noticed some irregularities with some of our hiring practices. Specifically, how and when we choose to dismiss people. You may want to connect with HR as I've never been able to get my hands on the relevant records."

The potential that HR would hide information from the legal team sent sirens screaming in my mind. Playing cute with lawyers never ends well.

"I'll see what I can do. I'm meeting with Mr. Barr now and will raise the access issue."

"Good. Thanks." She smiled and headed out.

I grabbed my pad and followed shortly thereafter, winding down the hall and across reception to Barr's office. At all my past employers, the legal team sat among the rest of the executives. Xervo put us as far away from Barr as possible while still being on the same floor. That spoke volumes. It reminded me of my former gang, who operated at a neighborhood spot that took the cops the longest to arrive from the local precinct. They'd timed it out and sometimes double-parked box trucks to block the road and help tip the scales in our favor.

I smiled despite myself at the ingenuity, sending Yvonne waving at me from reception as I passed. I waved back and continued walking to Barr's office.

My new boss had become as annoying as Dante, who wouldn't stop calling and texting me threats. If I didn't know better, he was trying to get me angry enough to slug him in the face. Maybe I'd talk to Mo and tell him to have Dante lay the fuck off. I wish I had the same freedom with Barr.

I'd yet to figure him out, but he was shady. My boss' body language projected dirty dealings, and it was up to me to decipher what. Guys like him only shared what they wanted, a sleight of hand to keep you away from the real dirt. I hadn't picked up on it during my interview and now wondered why. Guess it was nerves. Interview questions about my background sent me into a minor tailspin.

My past was safely sealed in juvenile records. I not only didn't need to disclose it, legally, jobs were forbidden to ask until well into the interview process. No one ever did. But I still itched like a dirt bag for not pro-actively coming clean. Or from quaking inside during interviews, expecting employers to smell my past.

Mr. Kingsbury, have you ever been arrested?

How can we trust you to lead our legal team when you've been in jail?

You say you've been honest for years, but can we believe it?

Get your shit together.

Time to play grownup.

Barr was on a call as I entered but waved me in and mouthed to shut the door. Coming from an open-concept office, Xervo's doors were a luxury.

He had the usual office decor, family pictures, group shots from fishing or golf junkets. I noticed a few with Barbara's face in them. It felt weird having this glimpse into her life without her consent. It also showed how much time she spent with Barr, only to have him pass her over.

"Okay, let's get started." He said, putting his cell on the shiny desk surface. "All settled in?"

"I'm getting there."

"Good. We've got some nasty business to discuss. Our revenue is down, as is our free cash flow. With a slim pipeline of new prospects, there's no choice but to do a RIF."

Reduction in force. As in, layoffs. I hated how companies used this phrase when talking about eliminating jobs. It removed the humanity and made it easy to forget real people were affected.

"That's sad to hear. How big a hit?" I asked.

"Not too bad. Less than 30 roles impacted. We've never done a layoff before. This one is unavoidable."

I didn't want to question, but a company this size could easily come up with cost savings to retain 30 people. For some businesses, that'd equal a budget rounding error. It made me wonder if Barr had another motivation.

"Forgive me for asking, but 30 people isn't a lot. No way to save them? Cut back on the tech stack? Assess our office footprint? We've got to have underutilized real estate with so many people working remotely?"

His mood darkened. "I get that you lawyers like to over-analyze, but don't you think Finance has crunched the numbers? For fuck's sake..."

His chair squeaked as he reclined, resting his annoyed face in one hand with his finger pointing up his temple. Barr's expression showed what an asshat he thought I was.

"Yeah, of course. I just hate when workers lose their jobs."

"We all do, but it's got to happen. HR is working up a list based on employee records, so nothing for you to do yet. Every department has some dead weight, or people who just don't fit in. This is an opportunity to make our company the best it can be

.

I'd swallowed my tongue more in the last two days than I had my entire life. Dead weight? Who talks this way? Folks in my neighborhood were the ones bosses like Barr deemed expendable. People from poorer, immigrant backgrounds, without a voice. Not one of them was dead weight. Most eventually found work, but it didn't always pay as much as what they had before.

Barr's rambling drew me back. "I'll also need you to review our employment contract language to be sure we're not in violation of anything."

"Of course. Good idea." It was the first time Barr mentioned following a rule. Usually, he boasted about circumventing them, rekindling visions of his shady nature.

As I returned to my office, my instincts tingled. No doubt I was getting sucked into Barr's underhanded dealings. He said Finance ran the numbers, but something about these layoffs didn't add up.

Chapter 16

Barbara

Whatever my dad read across the living room had him totally absorbed. That, and the Wagner pulsing through the hidden speakers. Somber and ominous, this funeral music was a perfect soundtrack for my life. But if I sat here one minute longer, I'd lose my mind.

Yet watching him fascinated me. His face relaxed into complete serenity. I wondered if part of it came from working for himself. He'd didn't have to worry about losing a promotion. He already held the top spot.

A few times, he asked about me joining his firm. Usually when I was looking for a new role or wanted to stretch my legal skills. So far, he hadn't offered. Did he think me getting passed over meant I'd lost my edge?

If he thought that, he couldn't be more wrong. I did that job flawlessly for two years. The board said I was a shoo-in, until I wasn't. Should I move on? Find an organization that wanted me and would appreciate my skills?

"Daddy?"

"Hmmm?" He didn't look up from his book. Instead, he took a sip of Scotch and replaced it with a click on one of the pink marble coasters my parents brought back from Turkey. A reminder that there was a vibrant world outside of Xervo.

"Dad!"

This time he looked up, watching me over his half-moon reading glasses.

"Maybe I should come work for you? At your firm? Do you have any open roles?"

"That's not the answer."

"Why not?"

"I know your job didn't unfold as planned, but there's a better role waiting out there for you. You need to decide what you want, then focus on getting it."

I got up and hipped my hands. "Do you not think I'm good enough? Am I tainted goods or something?"

"Of course not. Sit down."

I crossed my arms, fuming.

"Go on." He soothed.

I huffed closer to him and flopped on the couch. Visions of teenage me flashed to mind. Memories of heated conversations in this very room, ones that rarely went my way. Just like this one was trending.

God, I have to get out of this apartment.

He patted my folded knee. "Princess, things at the firm... well... they're complicated right now. I wouldn't want you tangled up in the middle."

"Tangled how? What's going on?"

He rose and crossed to the bar. Dad spoke with his back to me, but I could see his pained expression in the mirrored wall. Something was up at his work. I was too absorbed in myself to notice. First the wedding, then Joe, then me moving in. Dad was always a rock of stability. It never occurred to me he had troubles of his own. He kept everything in his life so hidden. At some point, I stopped looking.

We shared a prolonged silence. I gave him space to share and could feel his inner struggle from across the room. I'd long been an adult, but our relationship had never progressed. We were forever stuck in our original roles of father and child. Him shielding me from the world's darkness. But it was time for that to change.

"You can tell me, whatever it is," I said.

"I know." He turned to face me, taking a sip. "I will. At some point, but not tonight. Okay?"

"Sure."

Dad resumed reading.

I understood his desire for silence. Quiet evenings alone had been the only good thing about Joe's late nights. Since I moved home, neither of us had enjoyed much privacy. I uncurled my legs and stood. "I'm going out."

He spared the briefest of looks over his half-moon readers and returned to his page without saying a word. But that glance spoke volumes in our private language. It meant, "Be safe. Don't embarrass the family. Remember, you're a Washington." Over time, he'd shortened the speech, sentence by sentence, until only the glance remained.

I tugged on a wardrobe change, chiding myself all the while. I knew Dad loved me, but sometimes I wondered if he cared more for the legacy I represented. How I reflected on him. Me losing the promotion no doubt lowered his opinion of me. He wouldn't say it, but that's probably why he didn't want me at his firm. The one bearing my name, too. He'd always wanted me by his side, but no mor e.

Bloom's off the rose?

I felt orphaned. Like my only purpose was to make him look good. My mother would have been able to talk some sense into him. When she died, he became a hollow husk of his former self. I'd never seen him so broken and vulnerable. His only relief was delighting in his children's accomplishments. My mounting success evolved to be a panacea for him. Sure, my brother's tech career was a comfort, but Dad's dream had always been for one of us to become a lawyer. Someone he could show off to his law firm buddies. And drag to endless golf and tennis tournaments.

"All those lessons will pay off," he'd say. We have to keep up. But I finally realized that keeping up was exhausting. A huge chunk of me just wanted off the ride.

I slipped on my new blue stilettos and headed out, waving to Saul as I passed the doorman station.

Crisp evening air welcomed me, and I tugged my blazer closed to button it. All my walks began south, toward the glowing arch of Washington Square Park. My Arc de Triomphe. As a child, I thought we owned the park and the arch, telling my schoolmates as much. It crushed me to learn we didn't. But I still claimed the pale-stone juggernaut for myself. The solidness. The strength. Just seeing it and knowing human hands made it reinforced for me that anything was possible.

A dose of that optimism would be outstanding about now.

I passed through my arch and headed west into the heart of Greenwich Village. It was a tangle of brownstones, shops, restaurants, theaters, and clubs with a rich history of independence and counter-culture rebellion. From the Hotel Albert, where Mark Twain, Salvador Dalí, Jackson Pollock, and Andy Warhol gathered, to the ground shaking riots at The Stonewall Inn, Greenwich Village had always been a fantastic place to live. A community filled with possibility.

The eclectic mix of personalities was a rejuvenating distraction from my family's rigid boundaries. When 14, I had a crush on a sidewalk musician who parked himself near the 4th Street Subway Station. I'd go out of my way to see his unkempt curly hair and hazel eyes. He'd strum passionately on his guitar, engaging passersby and smiling when they tossed money into his open case. Every afternoon, I'd stand in my school uniform watching him sing until we finally exchanged names. Evan even showed me how to play the guitar, something never allowed in my household, despite how much I begged for it.

Violin. Piano. Those were acceptable. Guitar? Never. Little did my family know it was the only instrument I could still play.

Down on Bleecker Street, I ducked down a flight of stairs and into a Greek restaurant I loved. Mediterranean food nourished the soul and the body like a warm hug. The dipping, the garlicky-feta, the fresh vegetables bursting with herb flavor. I got a table and sat swirling my Cabernet, watching the room.

Low lighting shadowed diners, draping them in mystery. Paintings from local Greek artists lined the walls, each with a gold light casting a glow over the scenes. Abstract paintings flashed color that hinted at the subject matter, sparking powerful emotions. Others showed large families crisscrossing arms as they lunged across tables to dip pita. Each character revealed their true selves. Faces gnarled in grimaces, laughter, side conversation. A gray-haired woman fed a pet peacock under the table. The chaos, both fantastical and absurd. It reminded me of the boisterous home lives of my grade school classmates, so unlike my own. After begging for a dinner invite, they'd take pity on me and say yes. More often than not, though, my parents would respectfully decline when their family's pedigree didn't me asure up.

I was only now realizing how much I craved excitement. Stepping into the world beyond the guardrails of family expectations had to be thrilling. What would it be like to wander in a forest of my own choosing? Feel the cool air and crinkle of leaves underfoot as I explored with no destination?

If only.

My food arrived, and I dug into my grilled octopus and crusty bread that I slathered with sweet butter. Next came a haddock swimming in a sauteed tomato broth with capers and lemon. Tangy, salty goodness filled my mouth as the fragrant steam flushed my senses. The colors, the scents, the lively banter from nearby tables, every face dancing in flickering candle light...this was my New York. Alive and vibrant. The only thing missing was Sebastian.

Try as I might to avoid thinking of him, he wormed his way back. Sebastian was so unlike anyone my family would approve of, yet I craved him. He represented life and passion and I wanted in. He channeled my illicit Evan strumming by the subway. But he was also my boss.

I pursed my lips before sipping my wine.

My boss.

An impossible barrier I should never cross. The last thing I needed was a reputation for sleeping my way to the top. Doors would open wide for me, but they'd be to bedrooms—not board rooms. I'd worked too hard to jeopardize everything because I failed to keep my libido in check.

While I wasn't obsessed with family reputations like my dad, I did care about being respected. Women were objectified enough without probable cause. I needed to forge my own path, and that started by staying clear of Sebastian.

Chapter 17

SEBASTIAN

A barking laugh filtered through my open office door while a few staffers passed. My fingers froze, hovering over the keyboard as if people could read my mind. But I could think of no one better to discuss the layoffs with than Barbara. She'd held the role for years and knew the team more than anyone else.

I'd always gathered leaders for these types of conversations in the past, but somehow, talking to Barbara was off-limits. But it couldn't be. I had to manage being in the same room with her and not lose my shit. We were colleagues now. It was time for me to act like it.

Just chat her.

No.

Text her.

I pulled out my phone.

Sebastian:

Mind popping by my office? I have something important to discuss.

I pressed my send arrow and waited.

Dumbass. The way I worded it was awful. She'd probably assume it was about "us" rather than work.

Typing bubbles pulsed as fast as my pounding heart. Her text reply started and stopped a hundred times, then disappeared altogether. A moment later, she stood in my doorway. All gorgeous 5'10" of her, wearing a form-hugging black suit with a hot pink shirt underneath.

"You wanted to see me, boss?" Her face sparked with curiosity.

I swallowed hard. My body responded to her like we were still naked on the beach. I'd have to have a serious chat with myself later. Apparently, it hadn't been paying attention the last week-plus as I struggled to build boundaries. Or maybe it had, and I was too far gone to notice as I scrambled over them at the first opportunity.

"Yes. Come in and shut the door."

Her eyebrows shot up as if to confirm, and I nodded. She sat across from my desk, crossed her legs, and laced her fingers around her knee. Her cleavage dangerously popped up above where her pink blouse was buttoned.

Shit. Memories of touching those mounds blinded me to all else.

"You mind leaning back? I'm having a hard time here as it is."

She looked down at her chest. "Oh! Excuse me."

"I'm trying. But damn. You're beyond gorgeous in that suit."

"Don't. Please." She squeezed her eyes shut. "You're a gift from heaven and look at us. Sitting here like we're not feeling what we're feeling. It sucks."

"One kiss. I won't tell anyone." It flew out of my mouth, my groin obviously taking charge.

She pursed her lips for a splendid minute when I thought she might take me up on my totally inappropriate request.

"We better not," she said.

"Sorry. It was shitty of me to ask." I caught her eye. "I miss you."

"I miss you, too. Now, what did you want to discuss?"

Time for business. Rolling myself into the desk, I sat straight. "There are layoffs coming. HR is working up a list of cuts without our input."

"People? Not budget?"

"Barr says they ran the numbers, and it has to be headcount."

"That's bullshit."

I shrugged. "Haven't seen any financials since I arrived. I've asked almost every day."

"Welcome to my world, counselor."

"Is he always this cryptic?" I asked.

"This is forthcoming. Usually, I'd get ambushed after the fact and be forced to scramble."

I explained my idea to present a budget option that doesn't involve losing people. Give Barr an opportunity to save a few jobs.

She smiled, shaking her head. "Please stop being so exceptional. It's as hard to resist as my cleavage."

I let the comment slide, as did she.

"We've got some consultant contracts and a few duplicative software systems. We may be able to get out of those commitments early, or restructure to recoup savings," she said.

"That's good. There are a few team-building retreats that we could cancel and do them onsite. They'll be disappointed, but it's a lot better than losing their jobs."

We scoured spreadsheets for three hours and itemized enough savings for option two, completely ignoring option one until we had to.

"You've seen these salaries before?" I asked.

"Yes. That much I had to know to manage the department."

I slid the printed sheet between us. Names and salaries. I hadn't had close contact with everyone, especially the people in the other offices. But we'd be forced to cut several to account for the same budget we'd just found.

"Our team is already lean. We can't afford to lose anyone."

"Plus, these salaries are all over the place," I said. "Even people with the same roles are markedly different. That's probably the case in every department."

"If we're lucky, our plan will avoid that. We did good."

"Yes, we did."

Silence hung between us where we sat face to face. Her perfume made me dizzy, and I had to grip my chair to stop myself from kissing her. She must have sensed it, as she stood and walked toward the door. She looked back, smiling, before exiting.

A hopeful Barbara lifted my spirits. If all went well, we might just have saved our team from Barr's clutches.

Chapter 18

SEBASTIAN

Instead of a slap on the back and praise for the solution we found to save jobs and cut waste, Barr had been scarce for a week. Every time I passed by, Yvonne said he was busy. He ignored emails and skipped the half-hour I'd reserved on his calendar to discuss the plan. When his frame strutted into my office, I was near bursting.

He dropped into my visitor chair. "You've been a pain in my ass, Kingsbury."

Barr left the door open, but the hall behind was empty.

I cleared my throat, talking low. "What'd you think of my proposal? Pretty genius, right? We found outdated tech, duplicate contracts, and more. It was more than enough to cover our department's 10 percent cut."

"You want the truth?" Barr sighed. Like discussing the livelihood of his employees was a bore.

"Of course."

"It pissed me off. HR is handling this. All your stunt accomplished was expose what a poor team player you are by ignoring direct instructions."

What planet was he on? How would saving the jobs of my workers prove I was a bad team player? Didn't it show the opposite? That I cared enough to keep them? If this guy was warm-blooded, I'd eat a subway rat.

"I expected you to appreciate the initiative. Shouldn't we all be trying to avoid layoffs? You said it before. You've never done one before, and that's admirable."

I extended the olive branch, but he wasn't buying. Instead, he flipped a manila folder on my desk.

"Your RIF list. Consider yourself lucky we didn't cleave more." Barr stood and walked out the door, leaving me staring at his deposit.

What an asshole move. I'd bet a grand he never read my alternate plan. Gave zero fucks about helping the people who worked for him keep their jobs.

The file contained one sheet of paper with an excel chart listing employee names and critical information. Only my list had a single name. Barbara's.

I clasped my head in my hands as I struggled to draw air.

How could Barr do this? Fire the best person he had, not two weeks after nearly promoting her to General Counsel? It reeked like New York in August. I'd rather quit myself. In fact...

Striding out my door, I crossed the floor and found Barr chit-chatting with Yvonne as if he hadn't just launched a fucking grenade at me. I stormed past him and into his office, where I paced until he followed me.

Once again, he left the door open. I marched over and slammed it. "You can't fire her."

"I can and I will."

"She's the best you got. It's wrong."

Barr sat eyeing me from his seat as I freaked the hell out, but I didn't give a shit at this point. Not with Barbara's job on the line.

"Chill out. Your team needs a calm leader and you're a frazzled joke."

"This is cruel. How is letting her go better than losing a few outdated systems no one uses? If you'd read my proposal—"

He waved me off. "I looked it over. Creative, but a waste of time. There's a bigger picture here. We're shaping the company for the future and need the right team and financials in place. Have a little faith that I know what the fuck I'm doing. You've been here, what? A few weeks? Know your place."

I wished to God I'd never walked through Xervo's door.

"Fire me, keep her."

"I will not. You're the leader I want, not her. Plus, that damn parachute of yours would kill me. Well done there, by the way." He opened his top drawer and tossed a mint in his mouth, chewing it with a smile. "I've got a meeting, so...."

He shrugged, lifting his arms like my protest wasted his time.

I sulked past Yvonne's desk, which was thankfully empty, and cowered in my own.

If saving the person I cared about most was out, the least I could do was give her a heads up. I texted her to come by, and she strolled in moments later. Her smiling expression fled the moment she saw me.

"What's wrong?" she asked, shutting the door.

I held out the list. "I tried."

She accepted the paper, read it, and went stiff.

"Is this real?"

"As a heart attack."

"I think I'm having one. Sebastian, didn't he look at our plan?" Barbara slumped into a chair, her knees knocking together as her arm hung limp. Still holding the page.

"He called it a creative waste of time. Told me I had to see 'the big picture.'"

"Yet another photo I'm not a part of." Barbara hugged herself. "This is so wrong."

Tears welled, and she blotted them with a sideways finger to protect her mascara. "I've done nothing but cry since I met you."

I snatched the tissue box and walked to where she sat.

"Technically, you were crying when I first saw you."

She popped one out of the box to dry her eyes, but tears flooded back. One crawled down her cheek, then paused, unsure whether to fall. It reflected the light from the window, quivering as it hung suspended. I wanted to kiss it. Bring my lips to hers and make the pain go away. I cupped her chin, lifting my thumb to wipe it off but stopped.

"I shouldn't be..." I said.

"It's okay. I need a little affection right now." She placed her hand over mine and closed her eyes.

Over her shoulder, the bookcase was mostly empty. All I had was a row of legal books and a picture of me and Mom at the garden. Barbara and I belonged there. The amazing selfie we took when window shopping on the island. It deserved to be seen and valued. So did she. Instead, Barr targeted her for elimination. And it was all my fault.

"Why did they hire me at all? They must have known about the budget gap before then. It makes no sense."

Her back curved in defeat. "Guess they didn't want the Black girl in charge."

Once loose, the words crackled with electricity. Ideas thought but never dared said aloud. The boy's club vibe of the photoshoot, lunch, and history of the executive dining room careened to form one explosive conclusion. Proof of who the company valued and who it didn't. All reinforced by Barr's offhand comments and cringe worthy innuendo.

Pretending it was a coincidence made me part of the lie. In my heart, I knew otherwise. My dormant street smarts screamed. The timing of the layoffs was suspicious as hell. If I rolled my car window down on any corner in the city to share the details, I'd get the same skeptical look my face wore now.

But there was nothing I could do to save her.

Chapter 19

BARBARA

I passed through my office door and clicked it closed.

Murmurs from colleagues filtered through the walls while the floral scent of my verbena infuser settled over me. My muscles relaxed. This was me. Familiar and right. My surroundings soothed me, every object a reminder of how hard I worked to earn my way. Study. Law school. Family. Overcoming obstacles. I'd endured too much heartache, only to be dismissed in a random layoff. I deserved better than to be left jobless by the side of the road while the bus moved on.

If only I had a dollar for every time an over-boozed colleague propositioned me at a company function in a sick attempt to live out a fetish fantasy.

"I've always wanted to be with a Black woman."

"I wanna go Black, and never go back."

"Ooh, your curvy ass is so sexy."

I hugged myself. I'd done nothing wrong, yet felt like trash. Inside I knew. I'd been pimping my values all along, participating in my own degradation.

I rounded my desk to sit as ice flooded my veins. How many more days did I have in this office? How long before the ashes of my life burned still farther to dust?

Barr had no clue how often I kept the wolves at bay with curiosity and quick action. He'd be sorry. Fuck him and that damn boy's club leadership team, threatened by the sight of a strong woman. Scratch that. A strong Black woman. Educated. Respectful, but unafraid. Why was that so threatening?

I strode toward my door to ream him out but stopped short.

I wasn't supposed to know. If I yelled at Mr. Barr, he'd know I heard from Sebastian. Then he'd be in trouble. Plus, it would prove Barr's point about me being untrustworthy and confirm the rightness of his decision to pass me over for Sebastian. In a few weeks' time, none of that would matter. At least not to me. I'd be gone, and this would all be Sebastian's mess. Part of me wanted to say good riddance. The rest wished I'd taken the initiative to leave on my own. But that would've been illogical. I was in the fast lane to becoming General Counsel until my rails led over a cliff.

What the hell was I going to do?

I hid in my office for so long, I lost track of time. I grabbed a cab and headed over to Leslie's for girl's night. After originally fighting the idea of eating in, hiding away with my two best friends was a godsend. They loved me for me, despite my dumpster fire of a life.

As I taxied down to the West Village, Manhattan's neon lights flickered on. Restaurants bustled with activity. For once, I was grateful not to be among them. Passing Abingdon Square, the block-sized juggernaut of Westbeth dominated the night sky ahead. Hundreds of apartment windows dotted the darkness like tiny teeth.

Built in the 1970s, Westbeth was a community of affordable apartments specifically for New York's artists. It offered generous living quarters with loft-sized studios. Leslie lived her entire life in the mazed hallways of Westbeth. Her parents, writers and painters respectively, moved out years ago to commune with nature in New Mexico. They swapped New York's grit for arid landscapes and Native American culture. This left Leslie with a divine duplex. Sure, she lived where she grew up, but the home was her own. I couldn't say the same.

I pushed through the lobby door, pausing by the intercom. Westbeth's gauntlet of hallways was nothing to trifle with. I'd gotten turned around too many times to count, so I fished out my cell to voice dictate.

Barbara:

I'm downstairs. If you don't want me to get lost among the art installations, you better come get me.

The "..." pulsed as Leslie texted her answer, likely forming something snarky to say.

Leslie:

Let me think about that.

Barbara:

I'm on the brink of tears...

Leslie:

OMG. I'll be right down.

While I waited, a couple walked out. They held the door for me to enter, so I slipped in. It'd only take one glance to tell I clearly didn't belong. My work suit clashed with the splattered paint-covered overalls, piercings, and colorful tattoos of the other residents. My wardrobe was designer, but not for long. I'd soon be unemployed and would have far larger problems than what Burberry was showing next season.

I turned my attention to my surroundings. The lobby sculpture was a sheet of golden honeycombed wax bent in a cone and rotating. Within it, spinning a counter direction, hung a woven nest of black, red and white wire, rope and string. Watching the "Untitled" piece reminded me I was orbiting Leslie's world now. She belonged to New York's artist community. Standing among the art and hearing the muted sounds of music renewed my understanding.

Joe's words came flooding back. *Why did I always put my career first?* Had I done that with my friends as well? Tossed them aside for a company that rejected me? I certainly hoped not, but some sober reflection wouldn't hurt.

"Sweetie, what's the matter?" Leslie approached in a drapey, off-shoulder T-shirt, leggings, and formerly white socks. Her brown hair in a lopsided topknot. So different from the crisp, preppy vibe she sported for work. She folded me into her arms. "You're crying?"

I answered with a sob, half stuck in my throat.

"I'll get you a washcloth to clean up."

I turned to the mirrored wall and gasped. "Oh my God! My mascara!"

Dark streaks ran down my face, yet my cab driver hadn't said a word.

"You'll blend in around here. Vincent on the second floor pretends he's Alice Cooper."

We looked at each other and burst out laughing. Full and rich, it flushed out the toxic energy that'd claimed me since I heard the news.

"C'mon." Leslie guided us to the elevator, taking it to the fifth floor. I trailed her through a series of glossy white identical passageways to her apartment door that she'd left ajar with a bolt.

"Aren't we trusting?" I bent to remove my shoes.

"The same families have lived here since I was born. If we had anything to steal, it'd be gone by now."

I ascended the stairs which led to an open space loft surrounding the staircase opening on all sides. It left ample room for artists' minds to wander and create, unconfined by the limitations of room size. The kitchen was to the left and partitioned areas for bedrooms were behind that. A wall of windows to the right reflected the table lamp's soft glow on the living room's eclectic mix of plush sofas, rattan tables, and Native American rugs. Beyond that was a glorious view of Manhattan.

"There you are!" Rebecca rose from her cross-legged spot on the floor to give me a kiss. "Lord! What happened?"

"Let me get that washcloth." Leslie jogged to the rear of the apartment, then returned to the kitchen to dampen the terry. "Allow me."

Warmth hit my skin, sending chills radiating down my arms. "I've missed being mothered. Boy, do I need it."

"We'll get you back to Barbara in a flash." She gently dabbed the terry under my eyes. "There. Our fashionista has returned. One Alice Cooper per building is enough." Leslie smiled.

I turned to look in a nearby mirror suspended from the ceiling by a thin cable. I looked like me, and instantly relaxed.

"My good luck has run out, girls." I flopped onto the sectional sofa.

"What do you mean?" Rebecca asked.

"I'm getting laid off."

"Wait, what?! That's ridiculous!" Leslie gestured with her arms. "You've led that place since that old guy, what's-his-name, was off retired or whatever. This makes no sense."

"So unfair." Rebecca curled up on the couch next to me.

"Thanks." I squeezed her hand. "How was the honeymoon?"

"Too short. Kyle needed to get home for a photoshoot. But don't change the subject. We're talking about you."

"For that, I'll need wine..."

"On it." Leslie grabbed an open bottle of red from the stone island in the kitchen and slid three goblet stems between her fingers.

"Teach me your balancing secret. Serving may be in my future."

Rebecca rolled her eyes. "There's nothing wrong with waiting tables, but I think we can put your law degree to better use."

"Tell that to Mr. Barr."

"Wait a minute. What about lover boy? Isn't he your boss?"

"He tried. He even offered to quit, but no dice."

"Then fuck that entire den of misogyny. You've been complaining about them for years. People get let go all the time, it sucks. But it happens. Trick is deciding what to do next."

If only I knew. I leaned forward to pour myself a glass of the fragrant red. I swirled it around, watching the legs drip down the insides to rejoin their brethren. Even the wine droplets belonged somewhere. But where did I belong? In another corporate job? Starting over in a new company was as unappealing as it came. If it wasn't, I might have looked for a role long ago. Now when I went looking, I'd lack the halo of an employed worker. Someone so in demand that they had no gaps in their resume.

How naïve I've been to think they'd pick me for General Counsel. Not only was I a woman, but I was the wrong kind of woman. My problem was not recognizing it sooner, but there was no avoiding it. They had a bird in hand and chose the bush.

Based on their expressions, my friends clearly awaited my trademark optimism and sass. And a solution. That was my role in this threesome. For once, I was too worn out to try. I emptied my glass and sat back to hug myself.

The pair exchanged glances. This was unfamiliar territory. You'd think with my disastrous life lately, they'd had enough practice.

"It may be awkward to put feelers out, but it's best to start. You must have some professional contacts you can tap?" Leslie asked.

"You're the most well-connected person we know," Rebecca said. "I'm sure between your dad and his networks, something will shake loose quickly."

"I have connections, but most are at law firms. And so many are, let's face it, just as likely to give me a shot as Mr. Barr."

"You've got to start somewhere. Don't doom yourself before you try. You're logical; make a list and work your way through." Rebecca rose to walk to the kitchen for water.

"Remember to focus on what you want out of your next role," Leslie said. "You have skills, experience, and a lot to offer. You might very well find a home in an unexpected and better place."

Why did my mind go right to Sebastian? Maybe because he felt like home. He'd quickly become my favorite place to snuggle, letting me draw on his stores of tenderness and strength. He got me on a deeper level, but that's because he did the work to dig in and understand. I loved my friends deeply, but I longed for Sebastian's energy. The free-spirited way he embraced life, despite all the hardships he'd encountered. Once he was no longer my boss, there wouldn't be any reason to stay apart.

Rebecca smiled as she reached to refill her wineglass. "You never answered the question."

"What do I want? Honestly, no one has ever asked me."

"We're asking." Leslie sat cross-legged on the floor. "Ms. Washington, do you enjoy being a lawyer?"

Leslie had her crackerjack reporter voice on and outstretched her invisible microphone. Rebecca giggled before pivoting to face me on the couch. I had an audience. But suddenly, I wanted to disappear under the sofa, alongside whatever pocket change was hiding there.

Did I still want to be a lawyer? I think so. I'd never wanted to do anything else. "Yes. I do. I love it."

"Christ, Barbara. We'll be here all night at this rate." Leslie said.

"Don't rush her." Rebecca air smacked in her direction.

"Do you want to stick with corporate law?" Leslie asked, dispensing with her pantomime to dig into the bowl of pistachios on the table.

"No" was out of my mouth in a flash. It was an instinctual reaction. All the posturing. All the otherness and masking. The lack of diversity. The zero respect for women. I could honestly say I did not enjoy corporate law. When I dreamed of becoming a lawyer, the last thing I considered was paper-shuffling at a company. Where was the impact on people's lives? I helped keep the business out of legal jeopardy, but where was the humanity in it all?

Rebecca reached to refill my glass, but I shook her off. I was onto something and needed a clear mind. If I wanted to work with people, how could I make that happen and still earn a living? I'd never seriously considered private practice, but it was worth investigating. I caught Rebecca's eye.

"How's working for yourself?" I asked.

"I couldn't love it any more. I'm finally free and have found my purpose."

After tossing corporate shackles to the side, Rebecca started her own ezine with her former MOD Magazine editor, Viraj. Their new media venture was already showing signs of success. Readers who encountered Rebecca's blog, or blockbuster series in the world-renowned fashion magazine, now flocked to *Dear Diary*. Even Leslie was involved, with her first investigation into arranged marriages going viral worldwide.

"I wouldn't be where I am if not for you," Rebecca squeezed my hand.

"It's all you, Becca. All I did was negotiate a settlement with MOD's publisher."

"Don't you see? Without your legal skills, I wouldn't have the resources to start a new business. I owe you everything."

"That was the most fun I'd had in years, doing that pro-bono for you," I said.

"Why can't you 'bono,' and get paid?" Leslie asked.

"Is that even a word?" Rebecca teased.

"You get my meaning. Barbara, there are oodles of people out there who need a champion to help them fight the big guys. There's got to be a business in there."

She had a point. Rebecca was a living example of how you could strike out on your own and forge an independent path. I could try. Instead of using side projects to fill my emotional well, it could be my full-time profession. Feel emotionally whole AND make money? If you'd asked me a week ago whether my career satisfied me, I would have said absolutely yes. It took having it yanked out from under me to wake me to the fact that it left me hollowed out. I'd just been too busy to notice. A movie reel showing my potential future flickered across my mind. I envisioned a Bat Signal searching the sky of Manhattan, drawing me to people in need so we could crush the bad guys.

It was a fun thought, and certainly better than no thought at all.

"Thanks gals. You've given me a great idea to start with." I lifted my empty goblet. "I'm ready for a refill now. And if we don't eat soon, my first lawsuit will be against you two."

Leslie and Rebecca suppressed smiles.

I was back.

Chapter 20

SEBASTIAN

Barbara didn't make it in today. I had to cover for her on a few projects, ruffling feathers and garnering some whispers from her fellow legal team leaders gathered around the table with me. I suggested they be more sensitive; anything more would've sounded defensive.

Everyone knew the deal.

It sucked to lose a promotion. Chen was taking it decently well, but her head wasn't on the chopping block. She owed her job to the woman she just insulted behind her back.

The petty culture of Xervo would take getting used to. A larger company with more seasoned professionals meant more ladder climbing and catty gossip. Hopefully, I could nip that behavior from our team. But changing the rest of the staff would require a bigger mandate than my two-week tenure commanded. For now, I'd stomached enough.

"Let's adjourn until tomorrow." I flipped my notebook closed and rose, expecting everyone to join me. Instead, they sat darting sideways glances at each other.

"What?" I asked

Elizabeth reclined in her chair, flipping a pen in a blur between two fingers. "Rumor mill has it that there are going to be layoffs."

Braeden, another lawyer, shrugged. "With Barbara out, we wondered…"

"Some rumors are true, some are false." I scratched my stubble, looking for a safe spot to stare while I lied. Their attention seared into me. But if they expected me to leak intel, they'd be sorely disappointed.

"As the legal team, we must hold confidences. We have access to the company's most sensitive information. Us gossiping undermines trust in our ability to keep quiet when needed. Am I making myself clear?"

Elizabeth rolled her eyes. "I didn't start the rumor, if that's what you're implying."

"Maybe not, but gleefully spreading the news is a bad look. Think twice next time."

I strode out of the room, not waiting for my pack of hyenas to follow. Every moment since I arrived at Xervo felt like a monumental mistake. Should I quit? It'd screw Barr and keep my brain from exploding with frustration.

I was mid-way past reception when Yvonne hailed me.

"Mr. Barr wants to see you."

Fantastic.

He was pacing, combing his blondish hair with his fingers.

"Ah, good. You're here." He slid a stack of files across his desk. "Review these profiles for the rest of the expendable workers. Tell me if you find any red flags."

"And if I do?"

"We'll figure it out."

"What about Ms. Washington? If I find a reg flag there?"

He narrowed his gaze. "You won't."

Back in my office, I started rifling through the files, each with an employee ID and picture attached. It didn't take long for a worrisome pattern to smack me across the face. For a company Xervo's size, with as little diversity as we had, the layoff list was a gut punch. I checked and only 3% of our workers were from marginalized groups. Half of Barr's "expendables" were employees of color.

Then something clicked.

I shuffled the folders around to find the ones I'd arm-twisted from human resources. The HR director kept stalling until I shot her my best "stop fucking with me look." Now I understood her reluctance. The numbers showed few candidates of color passed through the screening process to earn job interviews. And that's following their sorry attempt at recruitment. You'd think they'd realize and make active steps to fix it. Nada. It's almost like they didn't notice the neon billboard blinking in their faces.

What's worse, Xervo had an unusually high number of no-fault settled dismissals. These were one-off, negotiated separations that weren't part of larger layoffs. They expertly hid their dirty dealings with a steady turnover drip that rivaled a leaky faucet. Only this was a human-made problem.

If they barely let qualified candidates of color in the door, then cut them loose at the first opportunity, they were seriously falling short of EEOC requirements. Not only that, they were illegally discriminating. No way this would stand up in court if workers got wind of the practices. Which was probably why they guarded access to the information.

They didn't want anyone to know.

But instead of hiding the wrongdoing, why not stop it? There was no benefit to risking the company's future over some backward beliefs stuck in the Jim Crow South. They were losing great workers. The employee records showed as much. It was a senseless crusade of one small-minded frat boy.

Damn.

I'd been had, but good. But now that I knew, walking away was a no-go. Despite everyone in the neighborhood tagging me as a quitter, that wasn't me. I hadn't abandoned my friends. I saw through their false promises. Their lies of security and family. Their shortcut to a rich future of cars, jewelry, and endless partying. There was no better wake-up call than armed guards pacing outside your locked door. They'd tell you when to get up, when to eat, and when to shit. No amount of sweet talk could erase the echoes of metal bars slamming closed.

That's where Barr belonged. If I wasn't going to leave, what would I do with the information I discovered? Every path forward led to the man at the heart of it all. As an employee, I had to tread carefully. If they caught wind, they'd fire me, smile, and continue on like nothing happened. The idea of staying here made me want to puke. They hired the wrong guy for the right role. I had power. Good people worked here and deserved better. Instead of joining Barr's underworld, I'd fight for the staff. I couldn't save this latest group of wronged employees. But I could stop what Xervo did to Barbara from happening again. The hard part would be keeping this news from her.

Liar. You're already hiding who you are. What's one more secret?

I'm not hiding it. It never came up.

Besides, that's not who I am anymore. Who I was as a teen doesn't define the man I am now.

You're afraid she'd drop you like a stone if she found out. The past is calling...

Only yesterday, I found out Dante spread rumors in the neighborhood that I leave my bedroom window unlocked.

Think Barbara needs that kind of baggage right now?

Not likely.

I packed up for the day, hating myself for not being able to save her.

Chapter 21

BARBARA

The layoff announcement came two weeks later. By then, I had rehearsed my shocked expression in the mirror so many times my cheeks hurt. Fortunately for me, Mr. Barr did the deed. He looked miffed that Sebastian chose to work from home. So much so, he began griping to me about his General Counsel. Part of me wondered whether Sebastian was intentionally tanking to save my job; prompting them to fire him instead. But no such luck. My tenure at Xervo ended today. The generous severance would hopefull y suffice until I landed something new.

As I packed the last box, my every move echoed off the walls of the cavernous room, robbed of contents to muffle the sound. Empty shelves. Naked picture hangers centered within clean patches of paint where my degrees formerly hung. A desk free of legal briefs. All removed. I'd made multiple trips to the car service vehicle parked in the underground garage. Still more boxes to haul to Dad's apartment.

He stunned me with his indifference about my layoff. Not only that, Dad's obnoxious optimism made losing my dream job sound like no big deal. This from a man who'd stew for weeks if he lost at Monopoly. His bizarre reaction, coupled with his inability to maintain eye contact, didn't add up.

I was out of work for the first time and no one seemed to care.

Maybe that was my fault. I projected a fiercely independent persona when I craved a caped superhero rescue. Or at the very least, someone to point me in the right direction and tell me everything would be okay. I'd never felt less fierce, and that scared me more than anything else.

My job had always defined me, setting guardrails for my life giving me purpose. When meeting people, I introduce myself as Barbara Washington, lawyer and daughter of the great Gregory Washington. Without a title to anchor me, who was I? And did I matter?

From here on out, I'd have plenty of time to decide.

I slipped on my trench coat, leaving it open and the belt hanging. Stacking the last two boxes atop each other, I headed for the elevator. Yvonne shot me a sad look from behind her reception desk.

"Is that everything?" she said.

"Yes." I looked around the lobby, remembering it when I first arrived. Before the remodeling and fancy furnishings. It'd grown so much since I started, and I had too. Now I knew otherwise.

She rose and walked to where I stood. "You'll be fine. Smart women like you always are."

Yvonne spoke to me, but the words likely reassured herself. Staying after layoffs was no picnic, either.

"Guess we'll find out." I turned toward the elevator as she returned to her desk.

Mechanical workings echoed down the empty shaft, a void that suddenly sounded very appealing.

I shifted the weight between my arms, wondering which door would open. Which car would take me to the lobby for the very last time? I heard whispers of other people standing behind me and turned to find fellow castoffs toting their own menagerie of belongings. Some in shopping bags, others in boxes. We wore the same lost expression, unable to console or even acknowledge each other. It took me a moment to realize of the six of us waiting, five shared the same complexion. For an already non-diverse company, they couldn't afford to lose this group of talent.

Yvonne's unease came into focus. With us gone, Yvonne was the only woman of color left in the New York office. Elizabeth Chen had been missing for a week, but her status remained fuzzy. The one time I tried to reach her, I got an automatic reply directing me to Sebastian.

I watched Yvonne where she sat slumped, arms in her lap.

Then it clicked.

How did Barr choose who to dismiss? Each person toting boxes I knew to be a solid employee. Meanwhile, lesser performers remained. That's not the pecking order I would have chosen. What bullshit. Barr could keep his company and shove i t.

I pressed the call button four times with my elbow, willing one of the doors to open. Xervo wanted me gone, and I shared the sentiment.

Once crammed in the closed elevator, my frustration flew out my mouth. "This layoff stinks to high heaven. If you're okay exchanging personal information, I'd love to stay connected as I do some digging. We may have some legal options."

The sideways glances were almost as epic as the silence.

"If I find we have a valid claim, I'll need a way to contact you."

Slow nods rounded the elevator, but each waited for someone else to speak. No one wanted to be first to join the mutiny. But only crew members mutinied, and our boxed belongings and jobless selves made it clear we didn't qualify.

"Ms. Washington," Portia began. I hadn't seen her since her visit to my office asking me to sponsor her employees of color resource group. How ironic that Xervo had just purged the majority of us eligible to join.

A pang of regret rippled through me. I should have followed up, but it was too late. If I had taken it more seriously, and sooner, maybe we wouldn't be jobless castoffs.

"No offense, but I can't risk future career opportunities by suing my last employer. It makes zero sense."

Nods abandoned me to rally to her side. If we only worked on a lower floor, I'd have had my crew. But they'd already jumped ship. Once this elevator hit the lobby, we'd scatter and finding them would be difficult.

"If there's a way to hold the company accountable, you're honestly saying you wouldn't be interested?"

Portia steeled her back. "That's exactly what I'm saying. Who would hire me if I took part in something like that? We don't all have fancy law degrees and two-thousand-dollar shoes!"

Melvin, from facilities, snickered, then burst out laughing. The rest joined in.

I withered inside. Is this what everyone believed? That I was nothing but a spoiled rich kid rolling in money? I looked down at my trademark Louboutin pumps, and for the first time, shame gnawed at my psyche. They weren't two thousand, but were likely closer to that than to the price tag of the shoes they wore.

In all my years of ladder climbing, trying to fit in with those in circles I aspired to join, never once did I consider how I appeared to junior staffers. Or to those from different economic backgrounds. Wealth was something I had always admired and assumed others felt the same way. The chorus of jeers from my elevator mates made it clear I was wrong.

Mumbling and jokes continued until we hit the lobby, and they all jostled past me to exit. I stayed behind in the now empty car, my garage level button still illuminated. A Town Car waited for me below with the rest of my belongings. Yet another sign I was orbiting a different world than they were.

The last thing I saw as the doors closed was Portia flicking her head in my direction before she and Melvin shared a laugh at my expense. Apparently, they thought I could afford it.

By the time I hauled my boxes upstairs to Dad's apartment. I was sweaty and defeated. Saul offered to get the luggage cart, but I refused. I barely heard him over the mocking laughter ringing in my ears. Imagine what they'd say?

"She had a taxi and a bellhop. I had to drag them home myself on the subway."

Fuck that and fuck them.

I took one look at Saul's green uniform with gold embellishments and hated myself. I stormed into the lobby and dragged every box out of the car myself, walking each up to my apartment, one by one.

Dad's office door was open, but I headed to my room. I peeled off my blouse and slacks, then tugged on jeans and a T-shirt before crossing to the kitchen for a glass of cold water. I downed the first one, then refilled it again from the dispenser on the fridge before making my way to my dad's study.

I was halfway across the living room when his conversation stopped me dead in my tracks.

Did he just say Xervo?

I crept closer to listen to his agitated voice.

"It was not an untenable delay! The Xervo RIF was 37 people."

I'd always hated that dehumanizing word. If you plan one, man-up and own the language. We were laid off. But why was Dad talking about Xervo?

"Once they come off the books, finance said it will add 20% to Xervo's free cash flow. Yes. It matches the venture deal's contract terms. You'll get updated paperwork later today."

Venture capital? Free cash flow? My mind whirled. Xervo padded its bank account at our expense, trying to sweeten its chances for a private equity deal.

I gagged, covering my mouth and grateful I hadn't eaten since yesterday. If not, I'd have a colossal mess to clean up on the floor. Though I might still. Murdering my dad was definitely on the table.

Was he going to gain financially from me losing my job? Collateral damage in a high-stakes game of poker? We were real people, and they were destroying lives. And for what? Was that why he was so chipper about my layoff? Did it mean a windfall for him and Barr?

I approached the door, then withdrew, clenching my fists in a sorry attempt to control my anger. I stormed to a lamp and heaved it over my head. Only the strained electrical cord tethered to the outlet kept me from chucking it against the wall.

"Argh!" I held it aloft, panting, not sure what to do with myself, or it, before setting it down.

How dare he? Is this how he made his living? How he afforded our top-shelf lifestyle? Our vacations, our school tuition, the expensive clothes, and homes?

A veil lifted, objects in the room vibrated with the energy of those sacrificed to attain them. The custom upholstery. The imported curtains and rugs. The knick-knacks bought while on lavish foreign trips. I'd never given much thought to how we afforded it all. What my dad did all day to give us such a fine life. A privileged one by any measure.

I took pride in his keen legal mind, wearing it as a badge of honor. People averted their eyes when Gregory Washington passed.

"Yes, Mr. Washington."

"Right away, Mr. Washington."

"My mistake, Mr. Washington."

I'd always taken these exchanges as evidence of respect. That he wasn't a man to trifle with. Given our family reputation and his constant demands for honesty and integrity, I never suspected he played by different rules. But why bother demanding from others standards he didn't uphold himself?

Was it all a facade?

A cover to hide unsavory business practices?

Memories clogged my brain, seeking new context. Which were real, and which fantasy? If he condoned Xervo's layoffs, how many more had there been? Then I saw it. He wasn't respected; he was feared.

My skin crawled with thirty years of filth, deceit, and lies now exposed as if by black light. No shower would wash off a lifetime of dirty dealings. I'd only dry off with an Egyptian cotton towel and they'd be right back.

The walls, the ceiling, my clothes. Taint stained everything in this apartment.

Including me.

How did I not see it before?

Because you weren't looking.

I approached his study, slamming the door open with such force it smashed into the wood paneling behind.

Dad jumped in his chair, clasping his chest. "Jesus! What the...."

Then he saw my face.

He looked from it to the cell in his hand. Under his breath he whispered, "Damn."

"Yeah, 'damn.'" My lungs heaved as rational thoughts scurried for cover.

"I need to call you back." He hung up.

We stared at each other, my emotions racing so furiously words failed. He was my dad. The same person who came to ballet recitals and cheered me on at model Senate tournaments. How could the man who taught me how to safely ride a public bus now throw me under one?

"What's going on?"

"You were never meant to know," he answered.

"That's it? No 'I'm sorry for ruining your career'? I was wrong to put profit before family? Knowing isn't the problem, Dad. It's the DOING! How could you ruin everything I've worked for and look at yourself in the mirror? Why bother push me to achieve? Why the science fairs and law school lectures, if you were only going to sabotage me in the end?"

"Princess, it's not what you think. I'd never—"

"It's exactly what I think. You got me fired!"

"That's not what this is—"

"Crushing my soul, was it worth it? I thought you loved me. Guess that was another lie."

I wanted to hurt him, and it worked. He slumped forward, grasping his head in his hands.

"That phone call was privileged. I can't discuss it but need you to trust me."

Was he mad? Trust the man who lied to me and got me fired? My own father? I don't know if I could ever believe him again. Tears streamed down my face, so I turned to wipe them away.

"I'm sorry you overheard that. It's a web of nasty business. What's going on here gets a lot deeper and uglier than you can imagine. It's good you're out of there. Layoffs were happening either way, and this saves everyone at Xervo from losing their jobs."

He dismissed his betrayal, making it obvious he thought as little of me as Barr. Just a dumb woman who couldn't be trusted with the details of how business operates.

I stood mute, gagging on his office's stale air and the musky scent of his aftershave. The same one he'd worn my whole life. When Dad traveled out of town for work when I was a kid, I'd dab the cologne on my pillow at night to help me fall asleep. The smell of him soothed me. Now it made me want to vomit.

"Barr's been trying to sell the company for two years. This RIF gets his financials in a place that makes it attractive for an investor. Maybe even an acquisition. It wasn't a question of keeping everyone or losing some. It was lose some jobs, or all of them. That's how this works. The money isn't there, not anymore."

"That may be true, or it might be a convenient excuse to whitewash the staff."

It was his turn to look puzzled. "What are you talking about?"

"Nothing. Forget it. You wanted me gone, you got your wish. But then you always do."

"It's a terrible mess. Take it as an opportunity to start over. You'll land on your feet. You're a Washington." He cracked a feeble smile, trying to win me over.

I approached his desk, leaning close. "I've never been more ashamed to be a Washington in my life."

He flinched at my words. "You don't mean that."

I didn't have a chance to reply because Dad's cell rang. Its trill filled the growing emptiness between us.

Legacy meant everything to him. He pinched the bridge of his nose, temples throbbing. I could tell every fiber of his being wanted to take the call. His hand twitched. His jaw clenched from the strain.

"Answer it, Dad. Work first."

"Don't. Don't go like this."

I turned to leave, thinking he'd actually come after me. Might choose family over his beloved firm. But instead of wrapping me in his arms and apologizing, he answered the cell.

I made it out and slammed the door behind me. Hand still on the knob, I squeezed my eyes shut.

Wrong choice, Dad.

Chapter 22

BARBARA

I had to get out. Not just for the day. For good. I couldn't live in the house of a man who treated me like trash. Dad was not who I thought he was.

Moving was expensive, but I had some money saved. Plus the severance. That would have to suffice until I found a new job. No way I could make a fresh start with this toxic mess hanging over my head like my old Beyonce posters.

I grabbed my purse, slipped on a pair of sneakers, and slammed the apartment door behind me. Out on the street, I turned the corner and headed east. I had no actual destination, but Sebastian's neighborhood beckoned. He talked about his community like it was a small town. A supportive one, that helped him when his mother was at work or needed help when growing up. Contrast that to Mrs. Finkle, someone I'd known my whole life, who looked at me with fear in the elevator until she recognized me.

She hadn't seen Barbara, the person she once baked cookies with in her kitchen.

She saw a Black woman. And was afraid.

But that was my problem. I was so busy trying to fit in, I became expendable. Not feared nearly enough. Not feared like my father.

I hugged myself as I walked. There were better ways to make a living than crushing people to dust. The inner workings of dad's legal practice remained a mystery to me. But something wasn't right with him and the company he founded. At this point, it didn't matter. I wanted to get far away from him and live my own l ife.

Make my own decisions.

No more subverting my wants for others. Wherever I went next, my bosses had to know who and what they were getting. Had I sometimes swallowed my words at work to avoid making waves? Yes. And see where it got me? Walking the sidewalks of New York on a Tuesday afternoon.

I crossed University Place and headed into a cafe for coffee. People scattered about working on laptops, talking on Bluetooth headsets, and doing business. What a different lifestyle than wearing designer suits, scurrying ten steps behind my dumb boss hoping for a slot on the C-suite wall.

Be fair. You worked hard, did stellar work, and earned respect.
A lot of good it did me.

While waiting for my order, I looked around at the restaurant. Sofas lined the parameter, while dining space featured round tables with electric outlets built into the middle of each. Paired with upholstered chairs and ottomans. These folks had no intention of leaving anytime soon.

A barista called my name. She had pale, almost glowing skin, magenta dreads, and a Medusa tattoo winding up her arm.

I lifted my to-go cup with a black lid and leaned in. "Do these people stay here all day?"

"Yeah. Daytimes were so slow, so we rent tables to create a co-working space. Steady flow of coffee, eats—and income, now," she said.

"Smart. Very smart." I smiled and headed out.

There were more routes to earn a living. Resourceful ones. Like working while honoring your authentic self. I took a sip of my coffee, savoring the earthy aroma and bitter tang. To sit in a spot like that all day would be heaven. I'd always wanted to be my own boss. Maybe there was a way to make it work. Even an employer valuing me as I am would be a gigantic step up.

I sipped while walking deeper into the East Village. Three-story tenements with fire escapes lined the streets, punctuated by occasional new construction sandwiched in between like skinny pencils stretching toward the sky.

The older places had more character, though. One of the worst parts of breaking up with Joe was leaving his amazing apartment. It was a brownstone on the Upper West Side. The architectural details, the chirping birds from the street below. A homey neighborhood. I ran into more neighbors in the few years I lived there than in a lifetime of living on Fifth Avenue. Once you pass someone for decades and never exchange pleasantries, no one wants to be first to admit you don't know the other's name.

But life was more than awkward silences. I wanted joy and smiles and adventure. My two days with Sebastian seemed like a lifetime ago. But I needed that magic again. The only way I could do that was to get my own situation straight and reach back out to him when the time was right. Hopefully, he'd still be as interested in unemployed-me as he was in his island fantasy girl. He saw something special in me on one of the worst days of my life. Funny how I'd accumulated more "worst days" in the last few months than in the 10 years prior. Since my mom's passing, my existence had settled into a predictable pattern. But no more.

Joe cheating.

Being a bridesmaid on my wedding day.

Losing the promotion.

Getting fired.

Suffering Dad's betrayal.

All at the hands of men who held control over me. Voluntarily, I let these guys chart my life, decisions, finances, and happiness.

And hair.

I stopped dead in my tracks. There in front of me was a salon called Nikki's Braiding Studio. A bubblegum-pink, ground-floor storefront in one of the many tenements packed into Alphabet City. I had no recollection of passing Avenue B, but here I was. 7th Street between Avenues B and C.

Had I conjured the braiding salon out of thin air by thinking of my vacation? Back then, I caved to what my breeding and legal training suggested. Natural hair would sabotage my career. But I had no boss to offend. It was time to remove the artificial fences I'd erected around myself. What a gift that would be? A life unafraid of social or professional consequences, where I'd be free to follow my instincts.

Unbridled freedom and power.

And happiness. Lots of happiness every day.

Braiding my hair would be a masterful step in the right direction.

The door jingled as I opened it and walked through into a bright room of laughter.

White walls plastered with glamor shots of models wearing colorful, edgy braids. Oval mirrors hung in front of each of the four black leather styling chairs. Only one had a customer, getting rainbow-colored extensions braided. Purple grazed her scalp, with each braid flowing through greens, blues, and yellows and ending at a red tip. The woman's flawless copper skin glowed, setting off darkly lined eyes and brows and the deepest, nearly black eyes I'd ever seen, looking sideways at me from her chair. Her plum lipstick ranged from darker edges to a lighter pink center. With peacock-blue eye shadow, her makeup palette was nothing close to the pale neutrals my mother insisted I use. Mom's mantra had always been to look like I wasn't wearing any cosmetics at all. Be a natural beauty. But here this gal was, owning her bright colors with a breed of elegance I envied.

"Good morning," a full-bodied woman in a black smock rose from a chair.

I tore my gaze away from the customer. "Hi. I'd like some braids, please."

She pulsed an eyebrow, looking me up and down. "Do you have an appointment?"

"No, but the sign said 'walk-ins welcome.' Do you have a stylist available?"

She bent sideways to look. "So it does. That's been there so long, I'd forgotten about it."

She came closer to inspect my hair.

"May I?" she asked.

I nodded. She slipped on the reading glasses dangling around her neck on a silver chain and inspected my extensions. She rubbed them between her fingers, digging down toward my scalp. Her warm breath tickled my neck as she poked around my head. After her assessment, she slid her glasses off.

"You have an experienced stylist. Why not go there?"

Starting a new life on my own meant tending to my hair without my Aunt Evelyn's connections and my dad's meddling. If she wouldn't help me, I'd find someone who would, but I was getting braids. Today. I opened my mouth to answer, but the other stylist beat me to it.

"Nikki, quit grilling the girl. You ain't got nothing on the calendar." The young man braiding my rainbow-goddess said without looking up from his work.

The other woman sitting in the salon sipped from a pink ceramic mug, attempting to look uninterested. But I had quickly become the undisputed center attraction.

I stepped forward. "Shall we?"

Nikki motioned to the second chair, and I sat. She rolled a low stool over to talk with me. "Because of your hot fusion extensions, I can give you a range of styles using the hair you already have. Or did you want me to remove it and do something completely different? That would take many more hours, and I recommend doing that over two days." She rested a binder on my lap and flipped the cover open.

The options were mind-boggling. I did some web searches for braids after returning from vacation, but nothing serious. From the array of long braids and updos, I favored thicker braids that began at the scalp and created a mane of sorts.

"What are these called?" I pointed to a picture.

Nikki tipped the book in my lap to see, but glare from the plastic sleeve now hid the image for me. "Long box braids. We can add hair to make them longer, but if you're not used to it, best not. The additional weight tugs at the scalp and creates soreness. Instead, I can braid in some copper highlights if we need length, which we might for you. Ready to lose your Beyonce?"

I smiled. "It's been my hallmark…"

"Then let's get you a new one."

Two hours in, Nikki expertly sectioned my hair and pulled up the therapy couch. My story spilled out, from my upbringing and breakup with Joe, my island tryst with Sebastian, to the layoff, and my dad's role in it. Oohs, and aahs rounded the room, as everyone joined in a singular conversation. I entered the salon looking for braids, but ended up with a group coaching session on what my next steps should be.

"You have GOT to get away," Nikki said. "You are too damn old to be sleeping in your father's house."

"Way to insult," Ramon said, his fingers still flying in a stream of color.

"She knows what I mean. She went from living at home, to living with her girlfriend, to living with the cheater, to living at home. A woman has to stand on her own two feet. Breathe free and find her own space." Nikki bobbed her head with emphasis as she worked.

Aliceia, the resident gossip, spoke next. A Latina, with thick brown curls and large hoop earrings, leggings and sneakers. "She lost her job. Who'll give her a lease with no work?"

"She sells two pairs of shoes and she'll be all set." Nikki paused her braiding and eyed me dead in the mirror. "How much were those Fendi sneakers you're wearing?"

I spied my Domino low-tops. Tan with chocolate-colored effs interlaced head-to-toe like a Greek geometric design. "I'd rather not say."

How had we gotten back to the conversation of my damn shoes? What's everyone's obsession with footwear?

"Oh, now you HAVE to tell us," Ramon said.

"$300?" Aliceia guessed, eagerly leaning forward.

"I wish!" I instantly slapped a hand over my mouth.

I looked up to see three "spit it out" expressions waiting for a reply.

I sighed. "These were probably around $700. I don't really remember."

They gasped in unison.

"Seven hundred dollars. For sneakers?" Nikki shook her head, "mmm, mmm, mmming" to herself.

"I'm all yours for $700 sneakers." Ramon flipped his imaginary hair. His was close-cropped with ripples, glistening to perfection.

"I think your boyfriend might object." Aliceia wiggled her well-loved, Converse All-Star low tops. "Sixty bucks, and I've changed the laces twice."

"You're a lawyer running around in $700 sneakers. You'll find a place." Ramon said, before brightening. "Say, Nikki? Didn't that scrawny hooker move out of one of your units?"

"She wasn't a hooker! Stop spreading rumors." Nikki's brows knitted. "The girl had it tough enough. But yes. I do have a room. Need to do some cleaning and painting, before putting it back on the market—"

"How much?" I asked, a tingle of excitement surging through me. Could I really do it? Move out and live on my own with no job? Not only could I, I had to. There was no way I was going to learn who I was and what I wanted while living on the Washington dime. Time to cut myself off.

Nikki spied me in the mirror. As if our stylist relationship was fine, but a tenant-landlord commitment demanded closer scrutiny. That wariness made me trust her even more.

"Two pairs of sneakers a month. Can you manage that?"

"Nikki, I thought—" Ramon began, but Nikki shot him a silencing stare. I got the sense Nikki was lowballing me. But I was in no position to barter higher, having a fixed income of zero.

"I think so." For how long, I'd yet to find out. I liked Nikki's self-assured nature, independence, and respectfully outspoken way of being. Great qualities I needed myself. They also reminded me of my mom. What would she say at my life's turn? Would she approve? Probably. In fact, she might have had a hand in steering me to Nikki's door.

"It's yours then. Only two blocks from here. I've owned it since my grandmother passed it to me. Mind you, it's well past its glory days and needs work. But you've got time. You do that for me and we can skip the deposit and just do first month's rent."

Hope surged in me, lifting my spirits for the first time in ages. I'd missed it. The true me. The Barbara who commanded respect and owned her destiny. I eased back in my chair and settled into the tiny tugs of Nikki transforming me into my next self.

Chapter 23

Sebastian

"Have we had any blow back from the castoff employees?" Barr's annoying face asked from my computer screen. Working remotely wasn't far enough.

"It's too soon to tell. It's only been one day," I said. "Everyone's still reeling—those who left, and those who stayed. HR will keep a close watch on things, to see if we have any wrongful dismissal complaints or negative posts on social media."

"We're good. Stop worrying." He picked up his coffee mug and took a sip. "Not my problem" was stamped in black letters on the mug's white sides. While an odd choice for a CEO, it summed up mine.

"I wouldn't be doing my job if I didn't keep us in line with the law. Workers have rights."

"So do we. I sometimes wonder whose side you're on."

"I'm on the company's side. I have a responsibility not just to you, but to the staff and the board as well."

Barr grunted. "That may be, but I sign your checks. Best you remember that."

"While we're speaking truths, is there anything you need to tell me about how this company operates? People are whispering. We had too many people of color on that layoff list. You expect me to believe that's a coincidence?"

"Now hold on..." Barr squirmed.

"If there's something you're hiding, spit it out. It'd save us both a lot of time."

He almost looked like he wanted to come clean. Share his tale of dirty work, that I'd already been piecing together on my own. Just yesterday, I found a settlement from a Black executive who filed a wrongful dismissal case. If my suspicions were right, the company's actions could very well leave it in legal jeopardy with the people they chose to let go.

He started playing on his phone. "I'm getting pinged from facilities. What is it?" He said into the cell.

I waited, wondering if he was actually talking to anyone. Dante pulled this trick more than once at home. But the one time I tried it, I got a robocall in the middle of my fake conversation. Mom plucked the device out of my hands and dropped it straight into the toilet. I howled in protest, but it taught me an important lesson about lying. And following Dante. Too bad it wasn't good enough to keep me from following him down that alley. I'd not make the same mistake with Mr. Barr.

"I have concerns about some information I've been finding..." My tone left no doubt about the seriousness.

He covered his cell microphone with his hand. "You're our General Counsel. I'd be stupid to hide anything from you. Bring me whatever you find and we'll discuss it."

He ended the video call.

I sat back, blowing out a cleansing breath. When taking this job, I didn't realize I'd spend more time digging into its past than securing its future. It's almost like Xervo hovered in a holding pattern. Most new jobs immediately plunged me into strategic planning, contracts, compliance deadlines, and more. Here, it'd been crickets. The only planning the executive team discussed was maximizing this year's financial performance. But I still hadn't seen any budgets. Barr trusted no one, and the CFO avoided my every attempt to understand the company's fiscal outlook.

The pressure of tight budgets often led people into risky behavior they wouldn't contemplate under normal circumstances. Though Barr didn't need excuses. Debauchery came naturally. Fighting those instincts was hard and the louse didn't even try.

After work, I changed into my gardening clothes and headed to GreenGrows. My carrots needed thinning and my lettuce looked like a pest was getting into it. I also sprayed my tomato plants that were newly flowering. I tossed weeds from my plot and Mom's into a communal wheelbarrow. With low sides meant for cement, the blobs of dirt-infused roots landed with loud thuds against the paint splattered metal.

"Hey there, Sebastian!" Nikki called through the fence. The garden faced her salon, which she was locking up for the night. "Anything good?"

"Soon."

"Thanks for all the greens last year. It saved me from walking over to the store, and it tasted like sunshine!"

Nikki was a ray of sun herself. A neighborhood institution, seeing her smiling face and braided hair made me think of Barbara.

"Loquisha's rainbow your doing?"

"Ramon. I had a new customer. Just walked in. Sweetest thing. I rented her Tammy's room."

That's just like Nikki to help a perfect stranger. Her heart was as big as they came. She gave and asked little in return. We needed way more people like Nikki in the world.

"Need any microgreens and radishes? My mom's overloaded and they're like nothing you've ever eaten."

"Love some. I'm heading away for the weekend, but drop some off next week."

Nikki waved and kept walking toward her building a few blocks away. Her steps echoed off the pavement then faded into the murmurs of evening. The soft hum of traffic from the FDR drive was ever-present, like a swarm of killer bees that never arrived. Streetlights flickered on, leaving the garden puddled in blue shadow.

The air's earthy freshness intensified in evening, as if the garden's plants collectively sighed after a hard day's work.

I loved this community. People left, but I couldn't. It'd be like ripping my beating heart out of my body. It had warts, for sure. But didn't every neighborhood? I bent to return to my work, only to find Dante standing ten feet away, arms dangling limp at his sides like a zombie.

"What the fuck!" I grasped my pounding chest.

Someone oiled the gate. We'd lost our early-warning signal. Whoever did it needs to be pummeled.

"Hey, King."

"Fuck you! I heard you told everyone I'm loaded and didn't lock my fire escape window."

He flicked his nose, chuckling under his breath. "Sorry about that."

"A regular fucking laugh riot."

I eyed my pitchfork and slid its handle within reach. Never hurts to be prepared around Dante.

There I was. Labeling. Same as people did to me when I got out of juvy. The difference was Dante earned his reputation over many years, and I'd be an idiot to forget that.

He sulked closer. "What do you want me to say? I can't get those rumors out of my head. People whisperin' you cheated me. They think I'm stupid, but I'm not. At least, not about this."

"That's bullshit. And you know it."

"What I know is I should've been your boy back then. Not Mo. You left, and I got kicked to the curb. Now look at you. You're the fucking golden boy of the neighborhood and Mo's the boss. I just..."

"What?" It came out harsher than I intended. But his lies meant I was forced to sleep with my windows locked. Every damn night with no air. I've tossed, uncomfortable, ever since. It almost made me want to return to the office's chilly climate control. Almost.

"I got jealous, okay? You've got so much, and I'm fucking homeless. All I wanted was a fucking place to sleep. Where am I supposed to go?"

"And whose fault is that? It's your life, Dante. Stop screwing up and get a fucking job."

I rounded the planting bed to attack my overgrown carrots. It'd keep me facing him, so double score.

"How can I 'clean up,'" he air quoted. "I'm an ex-con with a bad rep. I can barely find a sofa to sleep on, let alone an apartment. I can't even go to the shelter. I've rolled half the people and the other half want to roll me." He sulked over to the edge of a raised bed and plopped down.

As I lay fuming at night, I played both sides of arguments with Dante. How I'd get even. I ground him to a pulp with my words, then throttled him for good measure with my fists. I ran scenarios, planning each with military precision. But in all my war gaming, sad, repentant Dante was the farthest thing from my mind. The gap left me speechless to address the pathetic man in front of me. But it was the best possible result. It meant Dante realized he was wasting his life. Had he finally hit rock bottom? Not likely. His sympathy routine was probably a sneaky way to wiggle onto my couch.

"You for real?" I sat on my heels, wiping my forehead with the back of my gloved hand. My sweat-soaked T-shirt immediately chilled in the cool night air.

"Yeah."

"Where are your boys?" I searched the garden, but there were few places to hide except for the gardening shed.

"They ain't here."

"Where are they?" I asked.

"King, they ain't here. I came to talk."

"Forgive me for not trusting the man who keeps screwing me over and crawling back." The sidewalks around the garden looked empty, save a random pedestrian. But that didn't mean he wouldn't jump me himself, tonight or any night.

I sighed in relief but kept my guard up. As contrite as he appeared, his long rap sheet proved otherwise.

"Why didn't you tell the cops on me?" Dante asked.

"When?"

"Back when we were kids."

"Truth?"

"Yeah, truth."

"Mo talked me out of it. Funny thing is, you'd probably be better off if I had. You gotta stop all this thug-bullshit and be a man."

"Thanks for that."

"Save it. You really want to change?"

"Yeah."

I scraped the shovel handle in the dirt. "Then you'll have to earn every crumb. You think I rolled out of juvy into a pile of gold? I worked fucking hard, every damn day. I couldn't quit the moment I felt disrespected by some dopey manager. Who the fuck was I? A kid working for every scrap. I had to prove to them, and myself, that I could do it. Are you up for that?"

My pulse raced just thinking of my youthful struggles. Of all the times I wanted to walk away. All the times I got laughed at in college or law school for not having the life experiences that everyone took for granted. Not having cable TV, I hadn't seen all the shows people referenced. No money meant no movies, beyond what we could rent at the library. I was always a decade behind the box office. I didn't recognize the clothing brands they wore or fad foods they ate. Every penny went to living. Over the last 15 years, I've made-up for lost time, but never felt compelled to fill every gap. Not once did classmates or colleagues ever try to know me, know my pain and suffering. No way I wanted to emulate their shallow lives.

Dante sat thinking, so I returned to my planting bed.

I ripped open a bag of manure from the stables on West 36th street. I'd approached one of the many horse-drawn carriages trotting around Manhattan and asked what they did with the manure. After the guy stopped laughing, he said nothing. So I went up to the stables and got some. Over time, they began filling the bags I left. It didn't take long until every gardener I knew wanted in. The "order" got so large, we chipped in to have a driver trot it down to us since a neighbor had a connection via her cousin. But access to free fertilizer would never have happened if I didn't ask. Just what Dante was doing now.

"If you're really ready to straighten up, I'm open to helping you. But if you so much as steal a paper clip, you're on your own. I swear…"

He looked up. "Yeah? Okay, that sounds good."

I stepped forward to shake hands, but stopped the instant he flicked his nose.

"You using?" My stern tone made it clear I expected the truth.

"You had to ask that, didn't you?"

"Quit that, then call me. We'll see if we can't find you a job. Maybe even where I work. There's got to be something you can do."

I dug my shovel into the bag and lifted a mound of manure. I dropped it on my bare planting bed where I'd soon be planting squash, cucumbers and cranberry beans. The odor was foul, but soil needs rejuvenation to sustain a harvest. As Dante exited through the gate, I hoped our conversation would be fertile ground for his future.

Chapter 24

Barbara

"Are you seriously living here?" Rebecca asked as we rounded the corner of my new block, 6th Street between Avenues C and D.

I fingered the keys in my pocket, given to me earlier by Nikki. Dim streetlights left large swaths of darkness in between as hard-working people shuffled home from work. Sebastian lived here his whole life and loved it. I'm sure I'd love it, but living on my own in Alphabet City was the scariest and most impulsive decision I'd ever made. Well, aside from sleeping with Sebastian the day after meeting him.

We passed a homeless guy, swaying as he sat in a puddle of his own urine, failing to connect a bottle of booze to his lips.

I wrinkled my nose, giving him a wide berth.

Yeah, this definitely tops my scary list.

My liquored friend was the first pin pricking the air out of my balloon of bliss. Moving here was a risky move. No one would hose off these sidewalks anytime soon. And from the look of the black petrified gum blobs plastered flat on the sidewalk, no one ever had. But clean pavement was the least of my worries.

We arrived at Nikki's building, a five-story gray stone structure with a black gate fencing in the trashcans beneath her stone steps. There was a basement apartment with bars on the window, but I hadn't yet met any of the neighbors. Though there were three teenagers sitting on the stoop earlier. They eyed me curiously, but only addressed Nikki. Like everyone, they showed her great respect and were gone by the time I left.

"Here it is!" I said, sounding more chipper than I felt.

"I've seen worse, but then, those were crack dens." Leslie joked until Rebecca elbowed her hard in the ribs.

Exhausted bulbs did their best to light our path upstairs, the peeling maroon paint doing nothing to help the cause. Their meager wattage got sucked into the walls like a black hole. I almost tripped, which I'd wager wouldn't be the last time that happened. I pressed my cell flashlight on. I didn't need to see the girls to know they were making faces at each other.

At the landing, I slid each of my three keys into the locks, working them top-to-bottom as Nikki instructed. The door opened when I turned the last key and I flipped on the entryway light. An amber pool cast onto the horrified expressions of my friends.

Rebecca sighed. "Oh sweetie. You couldn't find anyplace better?"

I walked into the living room, hoping they'd join me. "It needs work, but Nikki said the new stove is coming tomorrow. And I don't have to pay a deposit if I get it painted and rip up the carpet."

Leslie flipped the wall switch. A square glass light in the center of the ceiling tinted the walls in a brown hue. Dim but bright enough to see the ruddy stain three feet wide on the tattered avocado green carpet.

Leslie squatted next to it, looking up at me. "You'd think they would have pulled the rug when they got rid of the body."

"Is that blood?" Rebecca's stare was a mashup of curiosity and disgust.

"It's spilled punch, but Nikki couldn't get it out..." The moment the words echoed in the bare room, I knew how idiotic they sounded.

Leslie rose to inspect the other rooms. The galley kitchen reminded me of the tiny one I had at Joe's brownstone. The bathroom was standard NYC, teeny white hexagonal tiles on the floor, white subway tile on the walls, with a ceramic toothbrush holder over the sink and a towel rack missing the bar. My bedroom was empty, and hopefully under the filthy carpet, had the same wood floors running through the rest of the apartment. The ceiling paint was peeling badly from an upstairs toilet leak Nikki said was now fixed. Top to bottom, the apartment looked like a crime scene from Law & Order: Barbara's Crazy to Live Here.

Back in the living room, Rebecca spoke first.

"If this is rude, you'll forgive me. But you can afford so much better. Why are you living here?"

Truth was, I'd never been on a budget or looked at a price tag in my life. I had money saved and my severance, but cutting myself off from Dad's tainted money meant I had to be careful with mine. Until I found a new job, my bank account was flowing one way—out. My sense was, corporate America wouldn't be jumping out of their chairs to hire me as their General Counsel. What savings I had needed to last for a while, and maybe longer than I'd want. That put my champagne living on pause. For the first time in my life, I had to pay my own way, though I had no idea what that meant. It left me walking a runway blindfolded. One wrong step, and I'd tumble and land alongside my boozy friend on the corner. If being stingy with my spending avoided that tragic future, count me in.

Leslie and Rebecca looked more worried than the night we arrived in Rome and the hostel was full. That time, I whipped out daddy's credit card and we stayed a glorious night in a hotel with a private bath and two queen-sized beds. The card was for emergencies, and I figured being homeless qualified. There'd be no family bank account to bail me out this time. Hence, my murder scene lodging.

"This might seem questionable from the outside, but I'm trying to be smart about the money until I understand how much it all costs. I'm a grown ass woman and have never had to pay my own way, live alone, or find a job while unemployed. Alone they're a beast, and I'm doing them all at once. I'm going to need help. A lot. More than I've ever asked for before, so I'm apologizing in advance."

Rebecca drew me into a tight hug. "Maybe being alone isn't a good idea. Kyle and I have space—"

"Me too. Loads." Leslie said. "You would easily fit in at Westbeth—"

"Live with Alice Cooper?" I burst out laughing.

"At least you'd have a safe place to live," Leslie said.

"I'll be fine here. Really. It's a lifestyle adjustment, but I'm excited to try."

I asked for a minute alone, so the girls waited for me by the apartment door.

I attempted to see the room through their eyes. Every peel of paint and blemish cast shadows, making them look worse than during my daytime visit. Beyond the questionable stain in the living room, the place really had loads of potential. Carved moldings—badly painted, but there—bordered the ceilings and floors. The drywall was warped and chipped in spots, but spackling and fresh paint would hide those scars. This was home now. The rent was paid, and I had no choice but to make it work.

When help arrived the next day, Kyle came instead of Leslie, who was on deadline. I'd worked plenty of weekends. But the work schedules Rebecca, Kyle, and Leslie kept as self-employed entrepreneurs were a foreign concept. I'd stepped through a time vortex into the modern working world of remote work and flexible scheduling. Though looking at the ancient apartment I was renovating made the direction of time travel entirely debatable.

Scraping took hours. As did vacuuming all the walls, so the resident dirt wouldn't mix with the pale gray paint I selected. Benjamin Moore was $80 a gallon, which forced me into the executive decision to buy cheaper paint. It stung for a moment, then I remembered this was my life now. No more $1,800 shoes. If only my fellow Xervo castoffs could see me now!

I rolled the "W" pattern on the wall like I'd seen in videos, succumbing to the melodic pasty sounds of wet paint. After I applied it, the W was still clearly visible. Across the room, Kyle used a straight up and down motion, rotating the roller pole 180 degrees with each overlapping strip. I abandoned the "W" and copied Kyle's motion and immediately saw better results.

The paint flowed on smoothly, completely covering the areas we'd scraped, spackled, and sanded. While there were ancient drips too stubborn to chip off, the roller coated those with ease. The transformation was immediate. The white ceiling and clean gray walls brightened the room, forming a neutral contrast for the new white trim.

Between coats, Kyle popped up on a step stool he brought to swap the ceiling light fixture for track lighting I picked up at a store nearby. One benefit of my downtown location was the proximity to the best lighting district anywhere. Block after block of nothing but lighting stores, sandwiched along the Bowery between Delancey and Grand Streets. Even my mom shopped there for lamps, preferring it to the pricier shops uptown. Complete homemaking autonomy was delicious; every decision my own, with zero pre-clearance required from anyone else.

No negotiating with my dad or Joe about paint colors.

No asking permission to tack up a picture.

Even when I lived with Rebecca at her parents' former apartment, it was hard not to feel like a guest in my own home.

This apartment was ratty and old, but it was all mine. A smile crept across my face then fluttered down my spine. This independence thing was addictive.

"Say, Barbara," Kyle said, stepping down the ladder. "If you need living room furniture, I've got an entire suite in storage. It's yours for the asking."

"That's an amazing idea!" Rebecca said. "We're paying monthly for the storage space. I'd actually be a help."

I stared at my freshly painted room. I had a sleek aesthetic in mind. Cast-off furniture from Kyle's bachelor days might not fit the bill.

"Can you describe it?" I asked.

"The set's quality stuff. I made good money modeling and my sister Libby picked it all out. Clean lines and mostly custom ordered from Italy."

I perked up. Embracing frugal living meant I couldn't afford to look gift Italian furniture in the mouth. I'd make it work, no matter what it looked like. "That sounds great. I'm getting my old bedroom set out of storage as well. When I moved out from Rebecca to live at Joe's, I didn't need it. And there wasn't room at Dad's."

Kyle rubbed the back of his neck. "Can we get movers? My days of hauling furniture up three flights of stairs are long gone."

Movers weren't an expense I'd planned on. Joe's cousin Sam owned a moving company and gave me white-glove service when I moved in with Joe. He knew about our breakup and felt awful when he found out why his best man duties were no longer required. Maybe he'd allow me one last favor?

"Let me see what I can do. If we're lucky, I can get movers to swing by and close out both of our storage units."

By four o'clock, we'd finished painting the living room, bedroom, and kitchen. All that remained was the bathroom, which I'd tackle alone the next day. Once Rebecca and Kyle left, I scrubbed the bathroom from top to bottom with a bleach cleaner, spraying the grout and leaving it to soak. Earlier, Kyle repaired a few loose floor tiles. Once rinsed off, the bathroom sparkled. With the original fixtures, it looked modern retro.

Bright light from my new ceiling fixtures, including the one from the front foyer, completed the total transformation from the night before. I brimmed with hope. I'd yet to sleep a night here since I was crashing at Leslie's, but it was already home. My pink room at Dad's was officially ancient history or would be once I moved out.

With nothing else to do, I dove into the deadly carpet, cutting it into pieces with a box cutter to roll and leave downstairs by the trash. I'd be lugging those alone. No doorman or friend to help. As I slashed at the carpet, Barr's smug face came to mind. How often had I suffered the indignity of his snide remarks? About my work, my gender, and ethnicity? Too often to count.

I rolled up a carpet sliver and went back for more, this time thinking of my dad. If not for him, I wouldn't be slicing crime-scene carpet. His pleasantries about losing jobs to save jobs while technically true, reeked like my friend on the corner. If Dad dismissed my pain with so little thought, what worse things had he done in his 40-year career? His fierce reputation no doubt had a trail of wreckage. Couldn't he show some respect for his own daughter? No matter how hard I tried, it stung to know he sacrificed me on Barr's altar.

The deep orange foam padding beneath the carpet had completely disintegrated into a foul-smelling powder. I swept the dust together with a broom and used a dustpan to lift it into a black garbage bag. I then tied each roll with twine and slid them across the floor to prop open my front door. Grasping the twine ties, I dragged the first roll down the stairs, doing as little lifting as I could.

The front door to the street snapped open with a bang, sending the kids on the front steps diving for cover.

My face flushed hot. "Sorry! Didn't mean to do that!"

Heads popped over the stone handrails. "Shit, mama! What 'chu doing?"

I grunted, my bundle bouncing down the stairs behind me. I used the key to open the trash area and flip it in. Looking at the available space, it'd be tight. But trash pickup was Monday. At least I wouldn't inconvenience the neighbors for long.

The kids sat watching me toil, making snide remarks about how my ass was delicious. How they wanted to yank on my braids and whisper sweet nothings in my ear. Then two argued about who was a bigger man, and who'd be able to handle me better.

Finally, I'd had enough. "Not one more word about who's a bigger man. None of you are. If you were, you'd be helping instead of telling jokes."

I stormed up the steps, ignoring their mute stares. At the door, I paused. "Well? Come on. Time to help."

Each looked to the other for direction, not wanting to be first.

"You in the yellow. What's your name?"

"Manny," he said. Manny's age was hard to guess, but he equaled my height at 5'10", had dark, wavy hair in a ponytail and a scruffy nub of a goatee beneath his bottom lip.

"Come on, Manny. Bring your friends, too." I walked through the door and waited for them to follow. They sheepishly trailed me up the stairs to my apartment door, where I slid the heavy bags and carpet rolls out to them, one by one.

The boys made such quick work of it, all I had to do was sweep debris off the stairs. That went into another bag, which I tossed on top of the pile myself.

"Thank you. That was a huge help. Can I buy you pizza?"

Manny's eyes bugged out. "For real?!"

They slapped each other and did handshake moves in celebration. I handed them the $40 I had in my pocket and told them to have fun.

Before I closed the front door on them, Manny called up. "What's your name?"

I thought before answering. Never in my life had I not said my last name. Whenever someone asked, I proudly said "Barbara Washington." Always, Barbara Washington. Never just Barbara. To omit my last name would deny myself the advantage my last name meant in professional and social circles. My experience showed that when people asked your name, they were most interested in the family pedigree. If you left it out, they'd ask "Barbara what?" as if being myself wasn't enough without the family context. These boys didn't give a shit about any of that. They just wanted to know what to call me.

I rose to my full height. "I'm Barbara."

Chapter 25

Barbara

By Sunday afternoon, I stood in my apartment, amazed by how much we'd accomplished in only a few days. After swallowing my pride, I gave Joe's cousin a call and his moving company came to the rescue. Given my situation, I allowed myself this one last vestige of privilege and they swooped into action. Beefy men descended on our storage units, getting Kyle's furniture and mine. Meanwhile, Kyle, Rebecca, Leslie and I headed to my dad's in a rental van. We marched back and forth like ants, clearing out the boxes I'd stored in my brother's room before turning to my mishmash of belongings in my own. Most were clothes still packed from my move out from Joe's, so I reused wardrobe boxes and jammed the rest into suitcases and garbage bags.

Dad emerged after we entered his apartment, but we didn't exchange a word. I ushered the threesome to get started. That left me standing, hands fidgeting at my sides, struggling to suppress the emotions warring in me.

Stay composed.

Remember, you're a Washington.

I followed my training, as did he. The two of us mute while grunts and lively banter emerged from my brother's room.

My heaving chest conveyed I was angry, and that his betrayal stung.

His pursed mouth said he disapproved of my braids and "rash" behavior.

My raised chin told him he owed me an apology.

His head cock said, really? Well, you aren't getting one.

I flicked my braids over my shoulder and turned to my bedroom while he walked to his study and shut the door with a tepid click.

He emerged once. I thought he would come to his senses. But he crossed to the kitchen, where I heard a glass shatter. Then more glass shattered, as Dad pitched an epic fit.

It was the first unbridled emotion I'd ever witnessed from him. And I only heard it. Either the reality of what he'd done finally hit home, or he was pissed off to lose his robot daughter. Maybe neither. He could be angry about work, or about seeing me stuff luxury garments in black garbage bags.

Not caring, I slammed my bedroom door. That rebellion felt amazing. Slamming doors was a no-no for a Washington. It meant you lost, unable to keep cool. But he was wrong. Slamming that door liberated me. I stood up to him and didn't spontaneously combust. I was moving into an apartment all my own.

Walls freshly painted.

Furnishings arranged to perfection. Kyle totally undersold his stuff. It looked straight out of the pages of *Architectural Digest*.

His sister had expensive taste and a love for magazines and might very well have swiped the grouping from an issue. A white leather sectional hugged the corner of the living room while black glass coffee and side tables, a gray area rug, and two floor lamps appeared as if by magic. But it wasn't. Movers had to carry it all up three flights of stairs, then reassemble the pieces without instructions before I returned from my dad's.

When I arrived, I leaped for joy, kissing Sam with tears in my eyes.

He said he was glad to help, given how shitty Joe treated me. He was proud of me for moving on and I couldn't help glowing with pride. Shards of my broken life from the last many months were beginning to fuse back together. I wasn't quite there, but healing had begun.

I strolled to survey my bedroom, pausing in the doorway with my hands on the threshold. I dare not enter for fear of breaking whatever fairy trance brought my old four-poster to this foreign, yet soon to be familiar space. A walnut stained bed with side tables and two dressers to match. One lamp was broken when I unwrapped it but would manage without it for now. Seeing it all made me remember how sad I'd been to leave it behind when moving to Joe's. He wanted me—not my stuff. *Only bring clothes.* Had he known all along we wouldn't last? I should have taken that as a sign. He didn't want to move his treasures out to make space for mine. But here it was. An entire room of my belongings. I even had linens, which I'd forgotten about until Rebecca filled my small linen closet from a box packed ages ago.

I opened the narrow door to see sheets and towels neatly arranged. A bounty. I'd never been so grateful for them in my life. It must be how Sebastian lived. He savored everything from fruit to kisses. If I ever saw him again, I'd have to thank him for letting me freeload on his gem of a community.

As if on cue, my doorbell chimed.

My first visitor. I had a guess who it'd be and was happy that Nikki's smiling face greeted me through my door's peephole.

"You've got to come see!" I yanked her through the doorway.

Her eyes widened, immediately noticing the new light overhead and the hint of the living room beyond.

"Lord, girl! What have you done?" She staggered forward, clasping her heart. "Think I didn't charge you enough rent."

"I'm still hopelessly unemployed. It's all hand-me-downs or stuff out of storage."

"Hand me-downs? From who? Oprah?" Nikki took a seat on the couch, bouncing to test the firmness before leaning back to put her feet up on the coffee table. "This is very nice. Very nice."

I smiled. "I had the same reaction when I saw it."

She looked up, turning serious. "You've got something special in you. Something that makes things just fall into place like magic. But life is hard, and not all doors open to a luxury suite. Never forget that."

She was right. I still had to find a job or Nikki would be forced to toss me out. And I wouldn't have a free moving service to rescue me.

But I had time and no intention of letting that happen. Not after all our backbreaking work.

"I'd offer you something to eat, but I haven't gotten to the grocery store."

Nikki stood. "No worries. It's late, and I ate on the way home from my sister's in Westchester. I'm expecting some vegetables from a neighborhood gardener. I'll bring some by if I have extra."

I was about to ask his name but stopped. I'd asked for space, so couldn't very well go running back to Sebastian. It'd been a week, and it felt like a lifetime since he walked out my office door at Xervo. It took all my strength not to reply to his texts and calls. Then they stopped. He shouldn't have been texting in the first place, but I panicked anyway. What did it mean? Was he moving on? I told him to leave me alone, so couldn't fault him for listening. Damn his good manners.

I'd thought of him every day, and now that I lived nearby, it'd be doubly hard to avoid asking around to find his apartment. Nikki knew. She had to.

Before I did something I'd regret, I thanked Nikki and showed her out. She'd already asked me to help her refinish her place and share some ideas for freshening up the stairwell. After seeing what I'd done in only a few days, she admitted to thinking too small. I loved decorating, so of course said yes. It would get us better acquainted and satisfied the tiny corner of my heart, disappointed my apartment makeover was complete. The creativity tapped an under-used part of my brain, penned in by dictates. I loved being completely in charge. *What else could I be in charge of?*

Not twenty minutes later, the doorbell rang again. I figured it was Nikki and swooped the door open wide. But instead of Nikki, a petite woman stood wearing a rumpled cardigan and holding a foil-covered disposable roasting pan.

She beamed, her brown eyes bright. "Welcome to the neighborhood! I'm the unofficial welcoming committee. Hope you don't mind. Nikki told me someone new moved in. I figured you might be hungry."

So much appreciation fizzed in me, I wanted to hug a woman I'd hadn't yet met.

"Please, come in. I'm Barbara, by the way." I closed the door and bumped into her back as she stopped short of the living room.

She turned on me, taking me in with fresh eyes. "Barbara, you say?"

"That's right."

My odd little guest made herself at home, touring the apartment, marveling in every room until she landed in the tiny kitchen where she put the pan on the counter. I still hadn't gotten her name.

"I'd offer you something, but I have nothing. Can I get you some water....?"

"Glenora. Yes, I'd love some."

I busied myself in the kitchen. "So, what did you cook for me?"

"Baked ziti with sausage. Hopefully, you don't have allergies or are vegan..."

"I eat it all, gladly."

"Most people do. Where are you from?" Glenora asked.

"Across town. Just moved out of my dad's and Nikki was nice enough to help me out."

She walked close, looking at me with darting eyes. "You're Barbara Washington."

My smile fled. How in the hell did she know my name? Who was she? I wasn't sure whether to answer.

"Um…"

"You are. No need to say it. Look here." She slipped out her phone, opened the pictures app and scrolled to one of me from the island, holding it up for me to see.

It was my turn to be confused.

"How did you get that?"

"From my son, Sebastian."

I shrank back, leaning on the fridge door. "You're Sebastian's mom?"

"Now it makes sense. He's gone totally gaga over you. I've never seen him like this about anyone. Didn't touch a lick of dinner tonight and has been moping around for days."

She paced to the sofa and sat.

I stayed put, fearing my legs would buckle. It was impossible to ignore the significance of Sebastian's mom finding me moments after I longed to see her son. But I had to stay away from him. I first had to prove to myself I could live as an independent adult. Five seconds with Sebastian and our clothes would shed, along with all my resolve. I'd become his little plaything and give up my fledgling autonomy, struggling to take hold.

While I wanted to be with him, I needed time to discover myself. I deserved that opportunity.

"Glenora, I know you two are close, but I need you not to mention seeing me."

"Why? Did he do something wrong beside fire you?" I waited for a snort of laughter, but none came. She was dead serious.

I shifted to the sofa next to her. "I'm not sure how much he's told you about me, but I've lived a pretty sheltered life. This is my first time living alone and I have to prove to myself that I can do it. If I see him, he'll be here helping and doting on me like the Prince Charming he is. You raised a good man, by the way."

"Thank you," she said with pride.

"And while that sounds lovely, and I might kick myself for saying this out loud, it's not what I need right now. Does that make any sense?"

The logic was faulty, even to me. I wanted Sebastian so badly, I needed him to stay away.

Glenora patted my hand. "No worries. But understand, he's hurting and misses you."

"I miss him, too. He gets me like no man ever has. He deserves to be with someone who has her life together."

Glenora gestured to the room. "Looks as though you have, but what do I know? You can count on me. I won't say anything, if..."

"If?"

"You let me join you for dinner. I want to learn more about the woman who stole my son's heart."

"I'll get some plates."

Chapter 26

Sebastian

Returning to the office only soured my mood. Barbara was gone and there was a restless undercurrent as staff adjusted to the loss of so many colleagues. Beyond that, she hadn't answered my calls or texts. But then, I wasn't exactly giving her the space she'd asked for. She lost her job and her engagement in short order, and that's a lot for anyone. Her dad was probably driving her nuts with questions and demands.

Yeah. Her plate is full.

I'm being needy.

Maybe I'd just cruise by her place and see if I could catch her entering or leaving the building?

Innocent? No, but I was desperate to see her.

Bad idea. Leave her be.

Her being gone left me wrecked. My already short threshold for patience evaporated the moment I saw Barr's impish grin. I'd seen enough people killed in my community to know none of us knew how much time we had remaining. Every day was a gift, and I'd be damned to waste a single one. The longer I stayed away from

Barbara, the more permanent it became. Plus, her firing removed the ethical roadblock keeping us apart. Her silence made me wonder if she wanted me in her life. Or if she ever had.

Barbara let you hold her.

Last we touched, her heaving body trembled in my arms. I caused that. She had to know how much I cared. That I wanted to be with her and see if our future could be together. Maybe that's why she needed distance. It gave her time to figure out her next step and how, and if, I fit into those plans. It made perfect sense. The lawyer in me craved a chance to present my case. Clear and coherent, as I did in court.

I pushed away from my desk and strolled to reception. Yvonne sat typing, likely correspondence for my lazy boss. He refused to write his own emails, despite having ten fingers and a keyboard.

I rapped the counter with my knuckles, and she removed her headphones.

"What can I do for you, Mr. Kingsbury?" Yvonne said.

"Please, call me Sebastian."

"What can I do for you, Sebastian?" Yvonne smiled.

"I'm trying to find our list of employee home addresses. I'm used to having that in a central HR system, but we don't seem to have one."

"You're right. We have a Word document and we update it as employees come and go."

My hopes sank. "So, you delete staff when they leave?"

"We use version control. We can always get back to legacy employees if we need it."

Yvonne shared a SharePoint link to the document, and it was aces. I clicked into the prior version and printed a copy for safekeeping. I also printed ten years' worth of employee sheets just in case. I didn't put it past Barr to delete files if he felt threatened.

Shuffling through the historical stack, I found the name of the prior General Counsel, Randall Fischer. He was on leave for years, with a last known address in Florida. He apparently left under mysterious circumstances which no one, including Barbara, could clarify. With Barbara getting pushed aside, and Barr's loose allegiance to the truth, his revolving door of lawyers was suspicious. A conversation with Mr. Fischer could fill in some gaps in the company history. It'd also address my growing unease about their hiring and staffing practices.

I reshuffled the stack of employee contacts to find Barbara. I then opened her contact on my phone to add her in. Her profile image smiled back at me. I snapped it the day I rented the convertible. Skin glowing, Barbara had just removed the headscarf to let her hair fly loose as we drove. One of the many "opposite" instincts of our shared adventure.

Right now, my sober instinct was to give her space. Were we playing our game, I'd rush over to her apartment and take her standing against a wall.

My inner debate raged. Showing up out of the blue was a desperate move of a man who hadn't had his A-game since Barbara melted it in the sand. I needed to be that guy. The relaxed, daring charmer without a care in the world.

Before I crushed her dreams and ruined her life.

We could start fresh. Have a new adventure here, in Manhattan. It's an island, too…

Tonight. I'll head over and see if she'll talk to me.

Plan resolved, I returned to my work. But the anticipation of seeing her already had me tied in knots.

I left my apartment to find Barbara's, walking the long way around my block to avoid the judge who stood gabbing on the corner. In my current state, I'd be more likely to throttle the old guy than smile at his childish teasing. Passing the threshold between my world to hers made my pulse race like entering rival gang territory. I'd never been in a fancy apartment on Fifth Avenue. Elegant Manhattan apartments for sure, but not old money places that rejected the newly monied—regardless of how famous. Buildings like Barbara's turned down mega-millionaire musicians and actors.

You didn't just need money. You needed the right kind of money. My hopes sank. The only pedigree I could offer was the dog food. Every penny I earned came from payroll, not a trust fund. I was doing well now by most standards, but she orbited another world. It could be a deal breaker. Like showing up on her doorstep uninvited.

I composed three text messages, only to delete each and pocket my phone in disgust. If I gave Barbara a heads-up, she might turn me away. But that wasn't good enough. If we were truly over, she'd have to tell me to my face. Look me in the eye and make me believe my only choice was to move along.

My chest tightened at the prospect.

Chill out. There's still a chance.

I hoped that Xervo's hiring practices hadn't driven a wedge between us. The more I dug, the more I uncovered. Barr's sketchy ethical guardrails could send the company careening over the discriminatory cliff. Employees silently slipped away without a word or announcement. So often, the practice was an HR hallmark. If Barr wanted someone gone, they were gone in short order. Likely paid to exit quietly into the night. I'd need financials to confirm my suspicions but had no way of getting them.

Too bad I can't subpoena my boss.

Take Elizabeth Chen. Try as I might, I couldn't find her. She was my most senior direct report now that Barbara was gone, and she'd vanished. Her name was still on my org chart in the company directory, but I hadn't seen her since before the layoffs. She looked to be the latest casualty of our silent assassin, Mr. Barr. The whole situation stank like Manhattan in August and I had yet to uncover the truth.

I rounded the corner of 12th Street and Fifth Avenue and approached a chipper doorman in a green uniform with gold braiding.

"I'm here to see the Washingtons. They're apartment 12A, I believe." I did my best to sound casual. Like I belonged.

"Just a minute." He ushered me into the marble lobby where he slipped behind a black stone podium to call upstairs.

The turf war in my stomach was hard to ignore. Part nervous excitement at being an elevator ride away from Barbara. Part insecurity to come face-to-face with the wealth she'd been born into. My life in Alphabet City wasn't the high-society neighborhood she was used to. I knew every nook, cranny, and person for blocks, seeing past the warts and blemishes offensive to fresh eyes. If the two of us worked out, maybe it'd finally be time for me to take my savings and move away. Escape the crime that too often claimed innocents.

Something to consider, but first things first.

We needed to talk. Who knows? I might be getting myself excited for a future that'd never happen.

The doorman covered the receiver with his hand. "Your name, please?"

"Sebastian Kingsbury."

After confirming, he hung up. "You can go up. It's floor 12A Apartment A."

"12A -A?"

"Yes. The elevator is straight ahead."

I headed into a richly paneled car with antique brass buttons. Sure enough, there were floors numbered 12, 12A, and 14. I chuckled to myself. Whoever thought that one up was a sneaky devil. There were lots of buildings around New York without 13th floors, but I hadn't seen this particular workaround.

Her floor only had two apartments and 12A was to the left. I rang the doorbell. But instead of Barbara answering it, a stately man did. *Her dad.* A tall, solidly built guy with enough lean body mass to make you think twice. But his smooth head, expensive sweater and calm demeanor screamed power.

I stiffened, my nerves taking over.

"I'm Sebastian. Sorry to arrive unannounced, but I was hoping to see Barbara?"

"You and me both." Her dad gave me a hard look up and down before stepping aside so I could enter.

"I don't understand," I said.

"I presumed she was with you." Mr. Washington walked across a living room the size of my whole apartment and opened a wet bar. He poured himself a Scotch and took a sip before facing me. Cool as a cucumber, one hand in his pocket, the other on his cut lead glass, but the intensity behind his eyes spoke volumes. He was pissed and blamed me.

I stepped into his home, technically uninvited, and closed the door. Not sure it'd hold up in court, but I didn't have a choice. I needed intel.

"Mr. Washington, I haven't seen your daughter since before the layoffs. Why would you think she was with me?"

"Oh, I don't know. Gushing infatuation." He gave me a narrow stare before returning to his liquor pour. "You're a looker, I'll give you that. But her attention will soon drift back to where it belongs. To someone with a more suitable background."

"Excuse me?" Anger boiled over, but he'd toss me if I didn't get a lid on it. The last thing I needed was an argument with Barbara's dad in his own home. I held my arms behind my back, fingernails pressing into my palm.

"I looked you up. Raised by a single mom who could barely scrape by—"

"Wait—"

"Juvenile criminal record and a history of drug dealing, vandalism, and theft—"

"Those are sealed!" In seconds flat, he'd crawled under my skin and stabbed me with a switchblade. This must be the imposing control Barbara lived with her whole life. As much as I wanted to pound that smug face of his, that wasn't the answer. At least, not yet.

He pulsed an eyebrow before sitting but still hadn't invited me in. Was he trying to bait me? I wouldn't put it past him to provoke a confrontation only to get me hauled off by the police. If he had contacts to unseal juvenile records, then he likely had some skin in the blue game. That said, they couldn't say I broke in since he invited me up. The doorman was the witness, but whose side would he take? I stepped forward but kept my distance on the area rug by the front door. Best to have a sofa in between us. With my hands behind me, no way he could accuse me of threatening gestures.

Can't be too safe around an over-protective father...

Mr. Washington leaned forward to pick up a printed sheet of paper. "Street name 'King'. Hmm. That's clever. May I call you King?"

"Sebastian is fine, sir. I haven't gone by that in a long time."

"So you say, but maybe you've upgraded to a new hustle. You were at your last firm for several years and had an excellent record but left anyway. An eager climber? Then a few days later, you meet my daughter and her entire world implodes."

"Her ex saw to that..."

He leapt to his feet. "Joe would never lure my daughter to some godforsaken rat hole on Avenue C."

"What are you talking about?!" I took a step forward but stopped myself. The last thing I wanted was for Barbara's dad to see how desperate I was to find her. But it was likely too late for that.

He stared over half-moon glasses, looking surprised for the first time since I arrived. "You didn't know."

He said it as a statement of fact, not a question. And he was right. I crossed my arms. I wasn't giving Mr. Know-It-All any more without something in return. He had me at a disadvantage and we both knew it. I needed to shift things back in my favor. She might admire him for his achievements, but I've been around power brokers my whole life. I could spot one a million miles away. Each guarded their property with an iron fist. And that included people. From the looks of it, he thought he owned Ba rbara. Which gave me an idea.

"Can't blame her." I eyeballed his living room with disdain. "You've kept her in an ivory tower her whole life. She was bound to weave herself a ladder and climb to freedom."

It was his turn to look uncomfortable. He tried to hide it behind a slow sip of the amber liquid in his glass, but it was a stall tactic.

"It's a shame, really," I continued. "You have all this money, yet your own daughter can't stand you."

I was bluffing, but from the way his nostrils flared, I'd hit close to home. But his cool demeanor showed he was no rookie at heated negotiations.

"What's your hustle? Hmm? I'd gladly pay you whatever you want to stay away from my daughter...$50K? $100,000? Name your price."

My jaw clenched. *Now he was selling her off? Disgusting.* Then his expression changed.

To relief.

"She dumped you. Yes, that explains the lost puppy face when you arrived. Why don't you tell me why you're really here? Trying to tank the VC investment? You want a cut? I'll use my influence with Mr. Barr to send some extra 'compensation' your way. But only if you steer clear of my daughter. She's been through enough already."

VC investment? Mr. Barr? What the fuck was he talking about? And what did it all have to do with Barbara?

"Hard pass. I don't want your money."

"Then I guess we have nothing further to discuss." Mr. Washington gestured with his drink. "Stay away from Barbara, though."

"You have no control over that. If you did, she'd probably still be with her cheating ex."

Before her dad could answer, I turned to go. I half expected him to chuck his glass at my head on my way to the door. I thought we were done when he answered.

"One more thing. Don't do anything stupid to derail this investment. Rock the boat at Xervo, and you never can tell what information will shake loose." He dangled my background report by a corner, pinching it between two fingers before flinging it free. White pages fluttered to the ground, creating a sea of paper around where he stood. I swallowed hard as he stepped on the pages en route to his office. "I can print more copies."

He walked through a doorway out of sight. I swayed listening to the emptiness once filled with a family. A wife. A daughter. A son. Now, he lived alone, getting his jollies by crushing the lives of others. While I cared for his daughter, it was hard not to pity a man who valued appearances more than family.

As I waited for the elevator, his obsessively calm demeanor irritated me. How could he not raise his voice? Not yell or cackle an evil villain laugh? The absence of emotion was worse than a bruising battle. Those I could handle. But raw and honest were likely foreign concepts to a man like him.

Mr. Washington was certainly reaching, but maybe that's what rich people did. They blamed others for their own failings. I'd bet major coin Barbara moved out because of something he did. I just needed to figure out where she was and what happened.

Chapter 27

Barbara

For the second morning in a row, I awoke disoriented. Broken glass and arguing in the street below startled me at 2 a.m., then kept me on edge until falling back to sleep. It was a sharp contrast to the quiet neighborhood I came from, and to my fun evening with Glenora.

Like my mom, Glenora told me exactly what she thought with no sugarcoating. A laugh riot, mostly at my expense, Glenora combined joy with an infectious sass. Though, our conversation ground to a halt when I asked about Sebastian's childhood. I expected to hear fun stories of his exploits, but she clammed up and started fidgeting. Then, quickly changed the subject. The evasive maneuver grabbed my attention. Sebastian alluded to having it tough growing up, so that could be it. Not wanting to discuss a difficult period in their family's history with a total stranger.

I rubbed my tired eyes, then threw off my covers. The familiarity of my old dresser awaited. I put all my garments in the same place as I had them when living with Rebecca. That shortcut had me dressed and out on the street in record time.

Around me, most of my neighbors trudged west, out of the neighborhood and toward public transportation. My achy body creaked, stiff from the intense manual labor of the last several days. With every step a protest, my feet refused to walk ten minutes to Starbucks. There had to be coffee closer. I turned uptown at Avenue A and within a few blocks saw a hive of activity around a door in the middle of the block. As I approached, the smoky scent of bacon, toast, and all things breakfast wafted over. Patrons exited, immersed in their first sip of morning caffeine.

Funny how our eyes instinctively close when savoring something special. Chocolate, coffee, kisses. Keeping them open lets the magic escape.

Did Sebastian kiss with his eyes closed? I was too drunk with pleasure to imprint the memory. I thought we had more time to record personal quirks like that. Now it feels like I've lost a priceless treasure.

Stop it, Barbara. Stay on mission.

Coffee, then I have to deal with my work situation.

Once back with my steaming cup of java, I found my laptop and punched in the Wi-Fi password Nikki slipped under my door while I was out. I never gave a moment's thought to Internet service. Lucky for me, she preferred adding it as a line item to the rent than having tenants wrangle with cable installs or poke holes in the walls to rig bootleg antennas. Nikki's cash-strapped renters didn't have money to blow on fancy cable packages. And that now included me.

Hopefully not for long, though.

I opened my computer and created a spreadsheet of potential networking connections. I listed names, organizations, and roles down the left side and tried to estimate when I'd last connected with them and whether they had relationships to people who might help me. After an hour of wracking my brain and purging my phone contacts, I had a list. I then did something I'd never done in my life: I added their race and gender. Shame crept over me to see how few Black women I had in my professional circles. Portia popped to mind. What would she say if she saw this chart?

Probably a snarky insult.

But I deserved it.

I wasn't exactly flush with Black contacts, but what option did I have? The leaders in charge of staffing my past companies gravitated to their own. They'd rarely extended hiring beyond people they could see in the mirror, and when they did, underrepresented staffers tended not to last. They either left on their own or vanished one day without a word.

Then an idea chilled me.

Was my dad any better?

Sure, he founded the firm, but in the many times I'd been there—at office events and holiday parties—our family's faces were the only Black ones in the room. Why was that? He owned the damn place, or part of it. Why hadn't he done a lick to elevate Black people? Or anyone from under-represented communities? Precious few women worked there as well. I noticed it, but never brought it up.

Why would I?

We never discussed race beyond our having to be twice as good, study more, and work harder. I spent so much time acting like I fit in, I fooled myself into believing it. I went to the same schools, wore the same brands of clothing, vacationed in the same places. Why wouldn't I belong? Of my closest friends, not one was Black. When growing up, the few times there were Black kids in school, Dad would never let me have them over or allow me to have play dates at their houses. He'd always say something disparaging about their parents or that their neighborhood wasn't safe.

This all left me with a nasty idea. That Dad didn't want Black people around any more than his white colleagues did. I can't tell if he believed the biases he expressed, or whether being the go-to Black guy gave him special status. Other dark faces would create competition for diversity foursomes for golf and fishing. Was Dad ashamed of his race? Black partners roaming the halls would be walking, talking reminders of his own identity. Why risk them siphoning off attention, or worse, relegating Dad to the racial equivalent of the kids' table when he belonged on the dais?

In truth, my background and life experiences left me more culturally akin to my white colleagues than the few Black people I knew. Had my coworkers felt the same way? All were civil, but rarely invited me out for activities after work. They often admitted to assuming I wouldn't be interested. Afterward, they'd overcompensate, be super polite, and pretend I was one of the gang. But I wasn't. Not really. Deep down I'd always known. But rather than confront uncomfortable truths, I buried misgivings under a pile of excuses and pretended to lose them.

But they festered.

I huffed realization.

From my hair to my new apartment to my psyche, Nikki and her salon pals did more for me in a few hours than colleagues who knew me for years. I sat in a stylist chair among Black and brown faces who accepted me as-is, with some financial ribbing, of course. My experiences were so different from theirs, yet underneath, we shared an unspoken knowing, adding context and depth to situations white people couldn't see. The Black-lived experience spanned social classes, uniting us in ways people of other races wouldn't understand. While self-preservation demanded we blur colleague slights behind rose-colored glasses, the HD lenses we wore as Black women made their generational ignorance impossible to ignore.

How would my life change now that I had ventured beyond my elite bubble? Family expectations had dictated my choices at every turn, often countering my desires and instincts. I'd muted my inner voice for so long, it never occurred to me to let her sing. My breakup with Joe, moving out, and braiding my hair were my first baby steps of independence. My overdue rebellion made Dad so angry, he pitched a fit. Given his leadership role at the firm, he absolutely should have advocated for more diverse hiring. Yet another sad revelation about the man I'd admired more than any other. It left me questioning whether I'd been wrong about him all along.

Just as I'd been wrong about myself.

And my career prospects at Xervo.

One undeniable truth: too many Black faces stood in that elevator with me on layoff day. If I reached out to connect with them, would they answer? My bank account tapped its wrist, waiting for me to find a job. Instead, I opened my laptop to the last staff list I saved. Each had addresses, mobile, and home numbers. Portia lived in the Bronx.

I wonder...

We weren't friends, and I had nothing to say besides sorry for being such a clueless dolt. But that might be enough.

The phone rang twice before Portia's bright voice answered.

"Hello?"

"Hi. Portia. It's Barbara Washington. Do you have a moment?"

She paused, a wordless chill settling between us. "That all depends."

"I want to apologize." My mouth was suddenly so dry I couldn't speak. I reached for the remnants of my coffee, then refilled the cup from the kitchen faucet while her stony silence lingered. Finally, she took pity on me and replied.

"Go ahead."

"Thanks. I've had a lot of time to think this week, reflecting on my tenure at Xervo. I'm sorry for not making more of an effort to connect with you while we worked together. You did your part and I didn't. I'm sorry."

Portia continued her silent treatment. Her expressive face usually betrayed her thoughts, so this phone call had me at a disadvantage. Was she rocking her trademark eye roll or softening into a lovely grin? I wished we were close enough to FaceTime. This one-sided conversation was getting old quick.

"Okay, well. Great chat—"

"Hold on. You dial me up after years of being a stone-cold-bitch, say 'my bad' and expect me to flop over like a puppy?"

"No. I expected you to be human. Appreciate me taking the time to reach out and accept accountability. I should have done better."

Portia slow clapped. "Bravo. Stellar performance. Now why don't you tell me why you're really calling?"

I stared at my phone screen. What was she talking about? I'd never met anyone so hell bent on giving me crap. Why was I calling? I told her why. I was sorry for not being there for her. For not supporting her as a fellow Black professional in a company with precious few of them. For not sponsoring her ERG while I had the chance to step up as an advocate for Black employees and allies.

In our last exchange, she chided me for wanting to sue Xervo. Coming to her with a request after rejecting her countless times when she came to me. I thought I'd flipped the script by calling. But maybe I hadn't. I had an ask. Forgiveness. Grace she had no intention of giving.

"I just wanted to say sorry."

She let me digest my humble pie for a few beats. "That sounded real. Apology accepted."

"What? That's it?" I asked.

"Yes. Unless you've got a plan to hit Barr where it hurts."

"I'd love nothing more, but my solo mutiny in the elevator made it clear no one was interested."

"Oh, I'm interested. What did you have in mind?"

I had lots of ideas. Never had I thought about my Blackness more than over the last few days. Old scars resurfaced, leaving me with a tattered portrait of Xervo, slashed for every slight I'd ignored and every injustice I suffered. Mostly, for being a Black woman.

Token inclusion for junkets and events.

Two years of "temporarily" holding a role, while being denied the title and photo on the wall of whiteness.

Working late and on weekends and holidays, without so much as a thank you.

Forced to play secretary in meetings and suffer snide comments about my darker skin, like not seeing me blush, not tanning (*really?*), and having stereotypical food cravings for fried chicken. Or the time I was last to the fruit salad bowl, where mostly watermelon chunks remained. *We saved them for you.*

How many others suffered as I had? And could we link it all to the layoffs?

It was worth a try.

"We need to compile a list of everyone laid off and see if the numbers slanted toward people of color."

"Our elevator sure was. If that's any sign, we probably have a case."

"It's a start but building a case will require more concrete proof."

"Does Barr being a racist pig count? He doesn't even try to hide that."

"That's anecdotal, but if we collect enough incidents, we can show a pattern."

The phone went silent. Instead of lively conversation, ambient street sounds filtered in through my window. Cars. Construction. Cawing crows. *Had I said something wrong?*

I was about to ask if she was still there when she sniffed.

Portia was crying.

"Are you okay?" I asked.

"It's just... It was a lot to take. He was fucking relentless about how dark my skin is."

Portia's deep ebony complexion was gorgeous. Fashion magazines prized it. But did the fascination smack of tokenism? It might if I deconstructed how the models were used. Outside of that, "paper bag" toned Black models were put forth as the ideal representation of Blackness. A double-othering, putting dark-skinned Black women at the bottom of an intra-racial hierarchy. Barr obviously amused himself at Portia's expense.

I clutched the phone to my chest to collect myself.

"I'm so sorry you had to suffer through that."

"He was cruel."

"You deserve better."

"You're right. I do."

We planned to call around to current and former colleagues and compile a layoff list along with documenting Barr's insensitive statements that could prove racial retribution and wrongful dismissal. While I still had to find a job, this was the purpose beckoning me. Back when I had the power to champion my co-workers, I hadn't, neglecting the very people now hurting. I couldn't help feeling that it was my fault. While I no longer worked at Xervo, I commanded a higher power than even Barr. The law. I'd make him forever regret tossing me aside.

Chapter 28

SEBASTIAN

The backboard reverberated before a satisfying whoosh of net tickled my ears. I'd been so busy working all week, I deserved a simple distraction like shooting baskets on a breezy evening. I sweated out my frustration, lifting my mood out of the basement where it settled in like an unwanted houseguest.

Without calling and texting Barbara, nothing remained but being hyper focused on succeeding at my job. Handling Barr's garbage day after day only made it worse. Any time I asked about relevant information needed to complete projects, he'd narrow his gaze with suspicion. I hoped to turn company practices around for the better. But as long as he was in charge, ethical policies would be a pipe dream. As much as I hated to admit it, joining Xervo was a boneheaded move. Leaving now would only peg me as a job-hopper. No one would hire me then.

The civilized world wasn't aware of my dicey past. But they would the minute Barbara's dad leaked it in legal circles. That'd filter to businesses and shrivel my prospects like a parched garden.

I'd have no job and no way to support myself.

As it was, good times felt fleeting. Each time my mom and I got some breathing space, a calamity would befall us and drain the bank account. We'd be back to ramen, government cheese, and whatever sprouted out of the earth. I hadn't had money troubles for years but couldn't shake the nagging fear that I was one-misstep away from losing it all.

Working for a psycho like Barr told me to keep my head down until I could make sense of it all. Helping the people at Xervo was my priority. Someone had to monitor my dumbass boss. Barr's handling of the layoffs left me questioning whether I was cut out for the corporate world. Each company was as bad as the next, screwing workers at every turn. Why bother moving? Every company looked glorious until you signed on the dotted line and the masks slipped.

I dribbled the ball, passing from right to left through my legs before setting for a jump shot from the top of the arc. It bounced off the hoop brace, careening across the court to the far end where a heated 3-on-3 match was going on. Animated spectators cheered and heckled players, clapping as they doubled over in congratulatory laughter. The real action seemed to be on the sidelines, and it was good to see young people out having fun that didn't involve blue lights flashing.

My ball rolled past the court, where sneaker squeaks scored the game's intensity, stopping by the feet of a group of teens.

I jogged over, but a kid with a black and white jacket beat me to it. He heaved a two-handed pass, which arrived with stinging force. Only pride kept me from shaking the pain out of my hands. It'd been ages since I'd played a game as vigorous as the one they watched, a casualty of distancing myself from neighborhood friends. A few tried to keep in touch, but only Dante remained. And he wasn't exactly a prize.

"Thanks." I said, barely audible over the noise, but he simply flicked his chin in acknowledgement and returned to his seat in the bleachers.

The kid was likely about fifteen, but already had two pierced ears with stones that sparkled in the court's spotlights. Bling most families couldn't afford. Then the gate clanked, and it all came into focus.

Dante sauntered over to the group, flicking his nose with his thumb. The others rose to greet him, a sign of respect. Their eyes widened in awe of my loser friend.

I knew the feeling. Wanting so badly to fit in, you blew past all warning signs. Dante was nothing but wrong decisions. He'd lead those kids down an alley maze and leave them trapped at the first whiff of trouble. Cuffed and stuffed in the back of a squad car, their lives forever altered. Hyperventilating behind the reinforced glass, their minds would blaze with a combination of regret, fury, and revenge.

Yeah, I'd seen that movie before.

I hipped my ball and walked across to where Dante stood heads together with the alpha teen, his arm draped around the boy's shoulders.

The kid's in deep.

The intimacy of the body language showed as much. Meanwhile, envy on the other kids' faces exposed how they longed to swap places, inching closer to join Dante's audience.

Dante sensed my approach, pursing his lips when he saw me.

"Dante," I said.

"Yo, King. Now ain't a good time. I got business." Dante's toothpick dangled from the corner of his mouth as he talked. Defying gravity, that magical splinter of wood is what drew me to him in the first place. His ability to speak without it falling out had to mean he had superpowers. Too bad the only one I'd witnessed was cowardice.

Ignoring him, I addressed his protégé. "Dante ever tell you how he left me cornered in an alley when the cops came? Saved himself, but they hauled me off to juvy faster than his sorry ass hopped that fence."

The boys stiffened, but tried to play it off, unsure who to trust. They admired Dante, but my words rang true. They all had relatives betrayed and caged while ringleaders ran free. Some wore it as a badge of honor, an initiation. But prison was no joke.

Dante removed his arm from around the kid and stepped aside for me to follow, the kids watching every move.

"Don't fuck with me. Or you'll regret it." Dante struggled to suppress his anger as he low talked. "I got business for Mo."

"What happened to you straightening up? Hmm? It only ends bad."

He leaned in to whisper. "It's all I got. People know me. I leave and I got nothing. You make it sound like it's so fucking easy to get out."

"Not easy. But it's the only smart choice. All the others leave you dead, caged, or crawling these courts like a homeless rat looking for scraps."

Dante crossed his arms thinking, a foul whistle from the game stealing his attention.

That's it. Walk away...

"You're a pain in my ass, King."

"Good. Payback's a bitch." I extended my hand, and he pulled me in close for a reciprocal back thump. I spoke low into his ear. "Stop using, then come see me."

He backpedaled, then called to his would-be entourage. "I got someplace to be. Catch you later."

He pointed at his minions, then left the way he came, their focus shifting to me. I approached, lifting my foot onto the lowest bleacher seat.

"Don't be following him, or anyone in this neighborhood. They'll talk sweet, then let you take the fall so fast, you'll be crying mommy before the cell door slams shut."

"Sounds like you want us to follow you? What's the difference?"

"No. I want you to think for yourself. Live a life that won't make your heart race every time you hear a siren."

A tall kid in the second row crossed his arms defensively.

"You know I'm right. I'm not saying anything you haven't told yourself a thousand times. I'm only asking you to listen."

"I know who you are. We all do."

I tilted my chin. I wasn't about to discuss my ancient history with a 16-year-old on Mo's payroll.

"You quit. We ain't chicken like you. Papi's the leader now." He smacked his friend in the chest, who remained standing where Dante left him. Emboldened, the boy sauntered closer to me to whisper.

"I hear you're Mo's bitch," he said.

"Watch your mouth." Every nerve ending in my body flashed high alert.

"Or what?"

"Look, kid. I was all-in, just like you. Until those bars snapped shut. Then I wasn't so tough. You talk a good game out here on the court. We'll see how tough you are when locked in a cell. You might wish you made a smarter choice."

"I ain't a pussy like you."

"You mean a pussy who got smart? A pussy who went to law school and made something of himself? I make my own coin. Sounds pretty good to me."

I couldn't tell if my pitch was landing. This kid lived by a narrow code, escalating at the most minor hint of disrespect. Respect was the currency of the streets. Lives were lost over it. Limbs shattered to preserve it. But I wasn't playing by those rules anymore and had no plans to take his bait.

His expression softened, fear and uncertainty behind his eyes.

I had him.

I leaned in to whisper. "Don't be like Dante. This isn't the only way to live. You can be better."

"Papi!" One of his minions called. We both turned to see the boy shrugging "*What's up?*"

His aggression returned. "Ain't nothing wrong wit me. I'm gonna be Mo one day. He says so himself. Says he sees himself in me."

"Mo's smart. No doubt. But that doesn't mean you need to hang around waiting to take the fall."

"Fuck you. I ain't falling for nobody."

"How old are you?"

"Fuck you. I ain't telling."

"Fourteen? You're probably into the big stuff. Moving drugs, handling deals..."

The boy gulped.

Yeah. I made piles of money for my bosses until I didn't. Until I was gone and replaced. Just like he'd be. I never saw a penny until our final score. Our way of getting some of the action they kept for themselves.

"You get a cut?" I asked.

"I get mine. This ain't no fucking union." He spat on the pavement.

"Thought so."

"For a lawyer, you stupid," The boy said.

"Why's that?"

He fell back, laughing, pantomiming a slit throat before he yelled. "You trying to screw Mo. You be dead."

"Oohhhhh!" the boys sang from the bleachers. Bowing heads together to whisper to each other behind cupped hands.

No one challenged Mo and lived. And I hadn't.

Or had I?

Panic spiked up my spine.

In street terms, I might've pushed the kid to demand a piece of the action from Mo.

Fuck me.

He's a kid. Don't lose your shit.

A kid working for Mo ain't no kid. His loyalty wasn't to me. It was to the man who kept him wearing diamond earrings and living high, in more ways than one. He'd go running straight to Mo to start trouble. I had to stop this.

"I think you made a mistake…" I started.

"You the mistake."

"I was just trying to show you there's another way."

He hiked an eyebrow, smiling to reveal his metallic grin.

Fuck.

A gold tooth. I'd left before I got mine. What an idiot I'd been talking to a crew chief about leaving the life he'd committed to with blood.

The boys filed past me, a flicker of menace behind their eyes.

"Nice talk, lawyer guy."

They exited through the court as silent as if they were at a wake.

Maybe they were.

Mine.

In trying to save one teen, had I just doomed myself?

Chapter 29

Barbara

Employed me had been in high demand. But three days of reaching out to contacts left me no closer to landing a job. People who used to whisper in my ear, "if you're ever available, look me up," refused to answer my emails, calls, texts, or LinkedIn messages. Nothing was worse than a read, but ignored, DM. It was the digital equivalent of stuck toilet paper streaming down the back of your pants, with no one brave enough to tell you.

Contrast that to my work with Portia, where a clear picture emerged. Xervo and Barr, specifically, had been flagrantly abusing employees of color. It was a textbook HR lawsuit waiting to happen. And that didn't factor in the over-representation of those laid-off being from marginalized backgrounds. I should prioritize finding a job, but the more we uncovered, the harder it became to walk away.

We had a case. There was an obvious pattern from our interviews. I reached out to Elizabeth Chen, who I heard stopped coming to work around the time of our layoff. Turns out, she was "encouraged" to take a package and wanted to put the whole mess behind her. As much as we battled, there was no denying Elizabeth was quality talent. Her ousting further proved Barr favored a certain type of employee, and it didn't look like us. Our case would only grow stronger after discovery. Barr would be forced to expose his dirty secrets. He's the only CEO I'd worked for who viewed his legal team as opposing counsel. I wasn't before, but I am now. Purpose warmed me from within, refilling the empty spaces in my soul.

I'd remember this moment forever.

When I decided to make Xervo pay.

I imprinted my surroundings. My living room smelled of lavender mist mixed with minty herbal tea. Sun streamed through my sheer curtains, confirming my mother's blessing. My only hesitation was Sebastian. By suing his company, I was slamming the door on any glimmer of hope I had to reunite. He likely was at home at this very moment. Within a few blocks of where I sat. In minutes, I could be wrapped in his arms, Sebastian's lips smashing into mine...

Stop torturing yourself.

Get your head right.

I stood stretching, then bent side to side, exhaling a cleansing breath before folding forward into a downward-facing dog yoga pose. My Achilles objected, tugging gently as I stretched my ankles. I'd sat way too much lately. All the networking and phone calls. At least at Xervo, I could roam the halls. The best I managed in my tiny apartment was shuffling between rooms. Sitting would become my lifestyle once I began prepping for this case.

No wonder Randall took up running.

Randall.

Since my former boss vanished under curious circumstances, I'd had nothing but nagging questions. Barr forbade me to reach out. He claimed it would violate the agreement Xervo reached with him, but refused to share the document with me. Unable to confirm whether that was true, I let it go. Barr forever hired outside counsel, which irked me to no end. It was like he didn't trust me enough to read a simple contract. But my idiot boss was gone, as was his restriction about calling Randall.

How would he react to hearing from me? I can't imagine he'd report our conversation back to Barr. Those two didn't agree on anything. I once overheard them arguing about gravity.

I fingered one of my braids. Their slick, bumpy finish had quickly become my newest obsession.

What to do?

It'd been ages since we last spoke.

My cellphone sat on the sofa. The inanimate object zinged with a life of its own, begging me to pick it up and start down a path with no return trip. Once I called, there would only be forward.

I spoke to Mom. "Seriously? This is what you want?"

After a beat, I lifted it to search my contacts for Randall Fischer. His smiling face stared back at me.

It'd be fine. He hired me and supported me at every turn.

It's just a phone call.

I dialed and he answered after two rings.

"Barbara?

"It's been a while. I hope you don't mind me calling..." My voice telegraphed how unsure I felt about this conversation.

"Of course not. What a lovely surprise." Randall said. "How are you?"

Old Barbara would have lied and pretended everything was fine. But I wasn't old Barbara. I updated him about all that'd transpired with me and at Xervo. I then asked the one question I'd been dying to ask him for years.

"What happened? You disappeared without a word?"

He sighed. I imagined him looking out onto the waves of his beach-side home in Florida, wondering how much to share. Whether to break whatever contract he'd signed with the company, under duress, no doubt.

I kept the conversation flowing.

"From what I can piece together, your disappearance has Barr's fingerprints all over it. Other employees have quietly slipped away as well, usually people of color or women. You're the one case that doesn't seem to fit the bill. I'm trying to unravel it all and hoped you could help. Maybe shed some light on whether it's intentional..."

"It's definitely intentional," his squeaky voice dripped with sarcasm. When we first met, I'd had a hard time containing my amusement at my boss' mouse-like voice. So unexpected, coming from an experienced man in his 50s, he sounded closer to a prepubescent boy.

He continued. "All was fine until I hired you. You might recall, it happened while Barr was on a short leave after back surgery? I had you interview with the board?"

"Yes, I met with two board members."

"You passed with flying colors, so I made the offer. When he returned to find a woman in such a visible role, he was furious. Said it reflected poorly on the company and would leave us vulnerable during contract negotiations. I laughed at him and said we could do with more women and people of color at Xervo. I went as far as to share data showing how we should do more to diversify. How the company would even benefit financially. The studies leave no doubt."

I had looked into it a few times and the data was sound. More diverse staff led to better decision making and higher profits. Too bad I'd never thought about the topic before they let me go. Yet another sign of how willfully clueless I'd been. I had to thank Portia for a lot of things, but owning my business value was chief among them.

"Anyway, Marshall wouldn't listen. I brought it up to the leadership team and added it to the agenda of a board meeting. As Board Secretary, I can do that you know."

Were we in person, he might have winked. I smiled, remembering how much I enjoyed working with him.

"I can only guess how that went."

"Marshall shot me down every time."

"Did he ever say why?"

"Not in so many words. He'd bristle and make comments under his breath, many unkind and offensive. I complained to him, and later to HR. I might have become obsessed with the subject. The way we were running the company felt wrong to me. After a while, I gave up on convincing Mr. Barr and focused on our department. At least on the legal team, I could be more representative in our hiring. I met with HR to discuss strategies for broadening our candidate pool, and I'm sad to say she blinked at me, clueless. No one's that dumb, so I suspected she shared Mr. Barr's biases."

Our HR leader wasn't big on innovating her craft—or on confrontations. Two gaping holes in the quiver of an HR executive. She seemed more concerned with keeping on the right side of Barr than with advocating for staff. But Randall might be right, and her apathy ran deeper.

"Did he ever admit that's why he forced you out?" I asked.

"He didn't have to. He tried to get me to fire you, but the contract you'd negotiated made that difficult outside of a larger layoff. The budget hit would be enormous."

My soul screamed, every unanswered injustice triggering at once.

Barr never wanted me.

I wasn't his hire, a man, or white.

A triple-threat of his worst nightmares.

Deep down, I suspected this was true. But hearing it stated so plainly triggered a level of outrage I never thought myself capable. I'm a human. A person. I'd not only been loyal and hardworking, I'd been courteous to an embarrassing degree when he didn't deserve it. He benefited from the very lessons Dad drilled into me from birth.

Ignore the jabs.

Shrug off lewd remarks.

Be bigger than them and you'll soon be their boss.

Humiliating scenes pinged around my brain. Me approaching Barr, hat in hand, quaking like I stood before the emperor. Begging for access to the most basic company information I needed for my daily job. Even with deference, he doled out trust in spoonfuls.

Why had I stayed so long? He treated me so poorly. If not for the layoff, I'd still be there toiling in a District, blinded by glimmering visions of the Capitol. Of acceptance and respect. But neither ever arrived.

Randall's voice drew me back. "He tried to fire me, but I'd also had a parachute. To get around it, he kept me on payroll and removed me from the company's day-to-day operations until we came to terms on a buy-out."

I couldn't have been more wrong about Randall. I'd resented him, thinking him a slouch who ran off to sip mojitos while collecting a fat paycheck. Abandoned, his absences left me to sort out all the work with fewer headcount and no buffer between me and Barr—his hostility toward me finally making sense. Randall knew Barr didn't support diversifying company culture and hired me anyway, tanking his own career. His reality was the exact opposite of my silent accusations. All my nasty thoughts and conversations about Randall flooded back, shrinking my outrage like a wool sweater in the wash.

In days, Randall and my father swapped places in esteem. One ascending, one descending, two strangers on escalators to my heart. Randall was a white man who lost his job fighting for a Black woman. Dad intentionally tanked the career of his only daughter to make a few bucks.

Actions say a lot about a person's nature. Even Dad would agree with that. Integrity, commitment, passion. You can't see it from the outside. No clothes or family pedigree impart them from birth. Each must be earned, lessons accumulating over a lifetime of character-defining experiences.

Randall passed his test.

My father failed in epic fashion.

Me? I'd only graded an incomplete but had gained so much from losing everything. This second chance to do better was priceless. Every person fired from Xervo for being the wrong color deserved their day in court. Having Barr in charge put employees at risk. He'd continue operating as the same biased prick he'd always been unless someone stopped him.

I repositioned the cell by my ear. "We must hold Xervo accountable. I'm mounting a case. Men like Barr only take notice when hit in the wallet, and I plan to make them pay. Will you help me?"

Randall sighed. Helping me would likely violate his negotiated separation terms. Hell, he might even owe the company money.

I had the skills to tackle this alone, but chatting with Randall reminded me of the mentor I'd lost when he left.

"You know that's impossible. My heart is with you, but I can't be co-counsel or assist in any way. However, if you subpoena me, I'll have to testify."

I could hear Randall's smile. He had already helped without helping.

"I'll keep that in mind, thanks."

An easy silence fell between us. It reminded me of the countless hours we spent working side-by-side in conference rooms, papers sprawled, each in our own world. I missed that. The comfortable moments alongside someone you knew well enough to say nothing.

"For the record, I had complete confidence in you when I brought you on," Randall said. "You were clearly destined for great things."

"Thanks. I hope that's still true." I paused. "Check that. I know it is. Only, the greatness will be grander than I ever imagined."

Chapter 30

BARBARA

The dreary day reflected my mood. Rain pattered at the windowpanes as I sat on the sofa. Each drop clinging for a moment before giving way and slowly gliding down the glass. Though past 10:30 a.m., the streetlights had yet to flicker off. The sun was likely in bed with the covers pulled over its head. Maybe that's where I should be. It'd only been three weeks, but a carefree routine had already settled in, beginning with researching my case against Xervo. But if I didn't get my butt in gear, my group of clients would think they chose the wrong lawyer to represent them. Not that they had many options.

I padded to the bathroom to splash my face, then slipped on a raincoat and rubber boots for the quick dash over to the cafe. The place was buzzing when I entered. Jolanda, the gal at the counter, greeted me with a smile. She'd been courteous, but really warmed up after I came in one morning with Nikki. She does Jolanda's braids as well, and it instantly elevated my status.

"Ten forty-five. Like clockwork," Jolana said.

"Routine is essential to success." I stretched, belatedly covering a yawn. Sometimes I barely recognized myself. Sloppy clothes? Yawning like a cow in public? Doing what I wanted when I wanted? Subtract a few tense moments walking home at night, and I'd never felt more relaxed. Or more free.

This neighborhood wasn't at all what I expected. Instead of a den of despair, I found rundown buildings and resilient people. Life was a struggle, but folks didn't dwell on it. Except the ladies at the salon who teased me about my former excesses. They were genuinely curious, never nasty or jealous. My new friends were more welcoming and emotionally generous than the wealthy families who'd surrounded me my whole life. I guess when you have less, you can focus on what really matters.

Jolanda rang my order without asking, and I paid the familiar amount. I trusted that she'd know I wanted a large latte with a hazelnut shot and no foam. I'd avoided the flavor because it reminded me of Joe, but then realized it was yummy. Why deny myself something out of spite?

When it arrived, I took a glorious sip of the nutty, sweet, bitter goodness and headed toward the door, near colliding with an entering patron.

"Oh, I'm sorr—Portia?"

"Figured I'd find you here! I hope it's okay if I join the call with you in person? There's only so much 'me' time I can take."

Portia was one of nine former colleagues engaged in the case I was building. We'd had several Zoom calls over the last few days. It was clear, most were having the same luck I had finding a new job. Which was none. Being together made us feel less alone and helpless. Having her here made me realize how lonely I'd been.

I gave her shoulder a nudge. "Love the company."

Portia grabbed a coffee and we splashed back to my apartment.

I led her upstairs, ignoring her horrified gulps as she passed the holes in the walls where electrical wiring poked through with orange plastic caps.

After I painted my apartment and installed bright lighting, Nikki recognized the rest of the building for what it was: a worn-out shoe needing love. While painting contractor bids came in, electricians began upgrading the wiring for the new sconces. Instead of the hideous now, my vision danced with the space's blooming potential. Meanwhile, Portia shrank into herself to avoid touching the walls.

"When I invited myself over, I didn't think it'd end with my stabbing." Portia's head swiveled, her knuckles clenched around her purse straps as she crossed the second-floor landing.

"It's a work in progress. Just like our case. You need to look past it and see the possibilities that lie ahead."

I opened the door and stepped inside for Portia to pass. Her shoulders eased once she saw the clean, modern interior.

"I don't live in a crack den, despite the hallway decor." I tossed my keys in my purse and kicked off my wet boots. Portia followed suit, then I left our shoes on the doormat to dry.

Portia took a seat on the sofa while I rounded my desk to face her. "Since you're here, I might as well have you sign the non-disclosure form I worked up."

"Do we need that?"

"Yes. It clarifies expectations on both sides, especially about not discussing details of our case with anyone from Xervo."

"That's a tall ask. We all have friends still there."

"Which is why this is agreement is essential." I pulled the five pages out of the printer and handed them to her. "I'll give you a few minutes to read through and initial each page."

I tried not to watch her as she studied the contract. Her face was so expressive, looking her way practically invaded her private thoughts. Though her opinions don't typically stay hidden for long.

"This is some scary wording you've got here. 'Breaking this non-disclosure form leaves you financially liable for any damages done to our case.' Is that necessary?" Her inquisitive eyes peeked over the pages.

"It is. If we're to succeed, we can't have claimants leaking our strategy to the other side. There are two tables in that courtroom. If they aren't squarely with us, best not to join the suit at all."

Portia clicked the pen and began signing. "I get it. It's just... I don't want to scare people off before we start."

She'd come a long way since our faceoff in the elevator. I wondered if our new alliance was strong enough to withstand the tough days ahead. After hiding their dirty dealings for eons, Xervo wouldn't make this easy. If we didn't stick together, we'd likely fail.

"All done." Portia flapped her forms, which I took from her extended arm.

I checked to be sure she signed and initialed it in all required places, then walked over to my desk to scan her a copy. I emailed it to the address she added to the form. It was a haul down to my Alphabet City location from Portia's home in the Bronx. Knowing she put in the time and effort to come in person meant a lot.

I launched the meeting and Portia squeezed beside me so we could both be on camera. We had 100 percent attendance, with seven other faces joining our two.

"Hey everyone. I have Portia here with me. Thanks for making time again. These conversations are essential if we're to hold Xervo accountable."

A grid of people blinked back at me, most uncertain. I'd have to do my best to win them over, or we'd have no case at all.

"Portia was the first to sign the NDA, which I emailed to each of you yesterday. If you didn't get it, let me know. That will be your formal commitment to join our class action suit, and it comes with some obligations on your part."

I spent a few minutes walking everyone through the form and answering questions, including how long the case would take (no clue), what our chance for success would be (also unsure), and how much it'd cost.

"Are we paying you for this? I'm still out of work and can't swing pricey fees." Melvin sat back in his living room and crossed his arms. Murmurs of agreement rounded the attendees.

Portia reached across the desk to mute my external microphone, the green light turning red. "You better give a good answer here or we're toast."

I'd been so busy collecting information and assembling claimants that I'd completely lost sight of my role. I took a Xervo package, one I didn't want to return. My job hunt had been fruitless to date, but my heart and energies were focused on this case. All the time I was tracking was worth something. I only waived my right to sue. Nothing prevented me from representing others.

I unmuted the mic. "I'm not charging an upfront fee. I'm your lawyer, so I won't be part of any settlement we achieve together. Instead, I'll earn a percentage of the award. That way, I only get paid if we win."

Portia nodded as she processed the information, her body instinctively answering.

"That sounds fair, depending on the percentage." Melvin said.

"How much were you thinking?" Shirley asked. She'd worked in IT and was the only one of our group who'd landed work.

I'd no clue, but my mom's words echoed in my ears about valuing myself. Too often, women under-charge, insecure about owning the depth of their expertise. This case would take my full commitment, and I had bills of my own.

"Standard contingency fees are in the 30-40% range, so I'll do the lower end. Thirty percent, but again, that's only if we win."

Grumbling returned. I was losing my audience.

"That sounds like a lot," Shirley said.

"Come on, people," Portia piped in. "This is found money. None of us would earn a penny at all if she wasn't doing all the work. We just need to show up a few times when she needs us. I think that's a good deal."

I had to bottle her confidence. Too often, I took a meek approach to communicating. Almost apologizing for my existence. Had I done that all along at Xervo? Was that why Barr passed me over?

Then I remembered my call with Randall.

Barr resented me for breathing.

That was on him.

As was the blame for what he'd inflicted on all of us.

I pressed forward.

"With what we uncovered so far, it's clear there's a troubling pattern of harassment and of dismissing employees of color."

"Oh, I heard Elizabeth Chen was forced to take a package." Dalia said, a former colleague from HR. "She's pissed as hell. Can she join us?"

"If she settled with Xervo, she waived her rights as I did. So our process begins with me filing our complaint, then serving Xervo with papers. Discovery will follow, which is our chance to collect evidence on hiring practices, salaries, and the rest of the dirty business Barr has been hiding."

"They deserve every ounce of grief we can send their way," Peony said.

"Once we file our case, I'll let you all know how events proceed. But we all need to keep this quiet between us. No talking about it with anyone who works there, and get me those signed NDAs today."

All satisfied, I wrapped up the last details and hung up. I turned to Portia. "We need to talk."

"About what?" Portia paced to the couch and sat down.

"You handled every check Xervo sent out, including to employees pushed out, but kept on payroll. You're an important witness."

A worried expression came over her. It was the first time I'd seen her unsettled.

"That little shit. He set me up. I knew it was bullshit."

"Sorry, what? I'm not following."

"The checks. Every time I went to Barr for signatures, he'd roll his eyes and tell me to approve them myself using his digital signature. Can he deny responsibility if he never actually signed them?"

"Not likely. He saw the books, approved the expenses, and knew where the money was going. He's guilty as hell."

She breathed easy. "Thank goodness. I thought I'd just ruined our whole case. I was the one who had to put up with HIS nasty self. I was only doing my job."

The check connection could be key. Randall's word could be questioned. But Randall and Portia together were a dynamic duo. The payer and the payee. It was akin to nailing Al Capone with the accountant. However, I didn't want to burden Portia with knowing how critical she'd was to our case's success. I squelched my excitement and continued listening.

"Evelyn said they hired someone new for my role. That alone exposes their lie that it was for cost-saving measures."

Unfortunately for Portia, Barr was just shy of illegal. "They took your role and Peony's and combined it into one. The person is overwhelmed, but on the books they could claim it was a financial win."

Portia's jaw tightened as she folded her arms. "That's bullshit."

"Yes, and too bad for them, they replaced you and Peony with one white person. They could have kept either of you and let the other go. You both have the requisite skills. It reinforces our case for bias."

When added to the hiring practices, solid evidence was forming. Then I remembered.

Sebastian worked for the enemy.

The thought of him made my body tingle. His hazel eyes, scruffy beard and sexy as hell tattoo snaking his torso. That was all gone to me. I insisted everyone sign a form not to talk to anyone at Xervo. I couldn't violate the trust myself. But that reality gutted my insides. I'd just launched a case that put Sebastian off limits for good.

Chapter 31

SEBASTIAN

"Why don't you just call Barbara?" Mom barked at me from her kneeling position at her garden planting bed.

"She asked for space. I'm trying not to be pushy."

My nasty conversation with her dad nearly a month ago popped to mind. But despite his bribe, I wanted her more than I should admit to my mother. Our discussion became near impossible with naked images of Barbara racing through my head. Tropical sun reflecting off her wet, glistening skin like she was on fire—

"You two belong together. A nice girl like that. Sometimes girls say no because they want to be chased." Mom sat back on her haunches and gave me the stink eye.

"Since when are you so interested in my love life?"

"You need a love life for me to be interested in it."

Ouch. Dissed by a 50-year-old lady from the DMV. I must be in terrible shape. But it's not by choice. Every day I pace the halls at Xervo makes me wish I'd never crossed the threshold. Barr was a prick, doing as he pleased and making the legal hairs on my neck stand on end. He's going to cost the company a fortune if anyone takes two seconds to figure it out, and that list is growing.

Private equity firms.

The IRS.

Former employees.

Barbara.

I shook the thought out, tossing my work gloves down, but mom was staring at me looking super guilty.

"What?" I asked.

"I need to confess something. I met Barbara weeks ago. I didn't realize it was her until I was handing her a welcome casserole. She begged me not to tell you..."

"You're joking. You met her?"

"Actually, we've had lunch a few times... A few dinners, too. She's really lovely." Mom bit her bottom lip, but her cute act wasn't cutting it.

Why was everyone in the fucking world nosing around my business? Mo's minions eying me fierce from every corner, like I was a traitor. Dante's antics, now Mom? My jaw clenched so tight, my teeth cried mercy.

"You're mad. I'm sorry. But she asked me not to mention it. I didn't want to break my word to someone you care about."

"You mean the woman that has me so tied in knots, I can't sleep? That one? We talk five times a day, and you never thought to tell me?" I stood, tossing my hand trowel so hard at the ground it impaled itself up to the hilt. Her lying wasn't the worst of it. It was her playing me like a fool, probably laughing behind my back. Is that who I was now? A fucking joke to the goddamned world?

I strode away, channeling every ounce of control I had not to hack the picnic bench to bits with a shovel. As much as I tried to ignore the lure, violence still promised an intoxicating release. Punching a wall. Beating a face until bones crunched under my fists. Before studying law, my negotiations were one-sided. I win. Always. But even back then, I'd never laid hands on a woman. Not once and never would. I'd thrashed plenty of men who had, though. Starting with Dante. He punched his younger sister after she broke his Xbox. He never touched her again after I got through with him. That was a beat-down to remember...

I looked up to find Mom wringing her hands.

"I'm sorry. I didn't know what to do," she said. "But I understand why you like her. She's something else."

"Don't remind me." I was about to kneel when a flash of movement caught my attention. *Dante.* He ran around the edge of the black iron fence toward the garden gate, arriving breathless and frantic.

Dante doubled over, gulping air. "King! Oh shit! King, Mo's coming for you."

Mom.

I gave her one look and all the blood drained from her face. She knew better than most what came from tangling with Mo. If you were lucky, your family had a nice funeral and could afford flowers. Otherwise, your mangled body might never recover.

I flicked my head toward home. "Go. While there's time."

"Sebastian, no!"

"Leave. Now!"

"Come with me..." She reached her arm for me, hoping to steal me away. But we both knew there was no point. If Mo was after me, best have it over with.

I was never able to clear the air with him. Make him understand I hadn't disrespected him or threatened his illicit flow of income. But apparently suggesting his minions deserved a cut had done both.

Mom's sorrowful face said it all. *I should have moved away while I had the chance.* And then she was gone, stumbling through the gate. But instead of heading toward home, she made for Nikki's.

Fuck. I didn't want her seeing what was about to happen.

"Yo, King!" The vibrations of Mo's deep voice penetrated my bones, then ricocheted off the surrounding buildings that suddenly felt too close. Like they were watching.

Center stage in a cage. That's what Mo and I would call people trapped in a spot they couldn't escape. Guess it was my turn.

I'd never been on the receiving end of his game-day strut. An imposing man at 6'4", a combination of good food and a workout addiction kept his physique menacing. Of Puerto Rican descent, tattoos covered his deep olive skin. The words across his knuckles spoke volumes about our relationship: King 4Eva. Over time, the meaning morphed from being about me to being about his iron clad reign over the neighborhood.

An entourage of four followed him, their faces all business. They'd die for Mo, no questions asked. Part of me envied loyalty that deep. I'd had it once. Before I exchanged it for a new life. A choice I never regretted until this very moment.

Mo sauntered closer, raising a hand for his boys to keep their distance. They stopped like the well-trained soldiers they were. He snarled at Dante, who recoiled, keeping away from everyone and staring at the ground like he was out for a stroll.

"You did me wrong, King. Started a fucking rebellion. People wanting rights, and whatnot. And it's YOUR FUCKING FAULT!" Mo screamed.

I knew better than to say anything until we were out of earshot. He walked aside, and I followed.

"Is this entirely necessary?" I whispered.

"I ain't playing wit chu, man. This shit's serious."

I ran both hands through my hair before sighing. "I fucked up. I'm sorry..."

"Yeah, you fucked up. This is your shit," Mo whisper screamed, impaling each word into my chest with his beefy finger. "I can't save you. Not this time. I need a show. People waiting, whispering, wondering what I'm going to do. Bro, there's only one king, and it's me."

"Nah, that don't work for me," I said. "I was just talking to the kid. Trying to show there's another way."

"That's where you're wrong. Manny's my #1 boy. Now, he's got starry eyes. Thinking of starting his own crew. I lose him? Fuck, that takes food off my plate. That wrecks operations been flowing smooth 'til you."

"Heard he's missing."

"I got him on ice til he quits talking the bullshit he learned from you."

"I fucked up. I'm sorry. It won't happen again."

"You're damn right it won't. I love you, King. You're a brother. But this is business, and you fucked with mine."

"We had a deal."

"I kept my side. Plus, the Mo scholarship fund says different. Cuz of me, you're not one of those dumb fucks dragging around college loans like a corpse. I owe you shit. You owe me, and you're off running that fucking mouth of yours. You and your fancy lawyer-self took what's mine."

I didn't get what that last part meant, but I wasn't proud of how I'd paid for college. But that money—I'd earned it with blood, skin, and broken bones. It was mine by right. Yeah, I kept it. That money changed my life. It was my ticket out of the gang and left Mo in a power position at a young age, set to rise farther. We'd all won until now. Until I did the one thing I swore never to do.

"Looks like I'm fucked."

"Payback's a bitch." Mo had every right to be royally pissed off. Street justice wasn't kind, but it beat the alternative. Anarchy, with bodies lying everywhere as rivals warred for supremacy. I didn't need that on my head.

"This sucks," I said.

He walked away. With one flick of the wrist, his boys pounced on me like rabid dogs.

The first blow knocked me off my feet. Followed by a barrage of fists pounding my face...

If I turtled, they'd wreck my kidneys and leave me paralyzed with a broken spine. Front, left me with broken ribs and a permanently disfigured face. I'd seen those. Horrified kids pointing in the street before hiding behind their mother's legs.

But it beat the alternative.

I rolled on my back, then a blow knocked me so hard I blacked out.

When I came-to, two guys held my arms while another landed punch after punch on my stomach, chest and ribs. I kicked my spaghetti legs, trying to stand. I had to get away...

The brute force of each impact stole my shallow breath, leaving me gagging on the metallic blood pooling in my mouth. Nerve endings shot pain everywhere at once, like I didn't already know. Brain overloaded, my eyes drooped closed but sprung open as a furious face approached for the next round of punishment.

Why was I here? What had I done to earn this?

I couldn't even remember.

I coughed, choking on so much blood I couldn't speak, cry for help, or beg Mo to call them off. They had my body, but they'd never have my mind. In my head, I could escape and be anywhere. I imagined myself back on the island. Sunshine, convertible. Something good. A reminder of the life I'd chosen. Of why I was on the receiving end getting pummeled instead of dishing it out to others.

I hated that life.

The grip of my gang had squeezed me tight and wouldn't let go.

I wanted something different. To be a regular person who had a job, went home, and got to sleep early. Ordinary. Boring. I was too fucking young to waste on the streets. It smothered every dream I had of being a success. Being on one of the magazine covers, hanging on clips at newsstands. I'd be so big, my dad would come rushing back and say how proud he was of me. He'd say sorry and make sure we weren't hungry every damn night...

"Enough!" Mo yelled, and the battering stopped.

They dropped me like a rag doll in the dirt. I retched up blood, wheezing for breath that refused to come. My muscles, impossibly heavy. I couldn't flicker an eyebrow. I couldn't move my arms to wipe away the blood stinging my swollen eyes. Face planted on the ground, the faint smell of compost and earth registered. Better I should dissolve into the soil and never return. Fuse deep roots into the ground and bloom into something better. Something giving. As an enormous oak tree, I'd last for generations. Neighbors would remember me. Children would laugh in my shade.

I heard the laughter.

Voices calling me home.

Mom.

Nikki.

Barbara.

The last thing I remembered was the ocean breeze blowing hair in Barbara's laughing face.

Chapter 32

BARBARA

My eyelids drooped, drowsy, as I relaxed into the soothing scalp massage of Nikki's fingertips. I moaned with pleasure, the stress relief a godsend. Paperwork was in motion and tomorrow, Xervo would be served. If I thought my new life was hectic, it was about to amp up even higher.

And the worst part was, I couldn't warn Sebastian.

He'd take the suit as evidence I didn't want to be with him. Yet, I longed for him in a way I'd never pined for anyone else. Another sign Joe wasn't "the one." But did that mean Sebastian was? If so, I had to hope our fledgling relationship would survive being on opposite sides of the courtroom.

"Ramon. Get away from that window," Nikki said. "You've got boxes to unpack."

I cracked one eye open to see Ramon staring across the street with a worried expression.

"Dante is yelling at King. That can't be good."

"Those two are in and out of it. Leave 'em be," Nikki said.

"His mom's running our way. Damn, that woman runs fast. Good for her. What is she? Almost sixty?"

"Ramon, I swear. Mind your own damn business." Nikki barked.

"Where's the fun in that, love?" Ramon tossed his imaginary hair and sauntered into the stockroom.

"That boy is always into—"

The door burst open. Glenora entered, then slammed it shut behind her. She filled the window lookout spot Ramon abandoned moments earlier. Shrinking back, the wall shielded her body from view.

"Lord! What's wrong?" Nikki rushed to her.

Sebastian's mom trembled, mumbling incoherently.

"Calm down. Tell me." Nikki held both her shoulders, trying to get her to focus.

"Mo's coming. Sebastian told me to leave..."

"And you did right. You've no business getting between those two."

Sebastian was in danger?

"Where is he?" I yelled. Somehow, I'd risen from my styling chair and crossed the room without realizing it.

A sob clogged in my throat. What an idiot I'd been, ignoring his efforts to see me. I wanted him and he wanted me. Never had I experienced the type of palpable connection I had with Sebastian. Now he was in physical danger and needed help.

Glenora looked through me like I was a vision, turning back to Nikki, who guided her into a chair.

"I'm his mother. I should help…"

"I can't let you do that. It'd only make it worse. He'll need you after this is over. Having you in twin hospital beds does no good."

"I can't lose him. I can't." Glenora doubled in half, shoulders shaking as she wept.

"Who is Mo? What's going on?"

Ramon yanked me into the stockroom closet and slammed the door. "Girl, Mo is the law in this neighborhood. He took over years ago and never let go. I hear King got mouthy the other day, threatened to cut into Mo's business. Damn fool brought it on himself."

Words were flying, but none of them made any sense.

"Who's King? Do you mean Sebastian?"

Ramon snapped his fingers in my face. "Get. With. It. Of course. Who else?"

"Why do people call him King?"

He hard rolled his eyes. "Sweetheart. Your boy was a big-time crew leader. Years ago. Everybody knew him. But Mo's the reason he could still strut around like a fucking peacock. Untouchable. Feared. King crossed the wrong guy."

Sebastian ran a gang? I'd say Ramon had to be mistaken if not for Glenora crumbling in the next room. What little Sebastian mentioned about his past made it sound like he was one of the pack. Briefly mixed up with a rough crowd until he broke away. Youthful indiscretions long forgotten. Instead, Sebastian lied to me about who he was. Either that or was I too infatuated to add up the clues he left unspoken. Not that we'd had much time.

And if he was out there getting thumped by some kingpin, did that mean he was still involved in the seedy underworld?

I had to find out.

I ran toward the front door but froze. "Oh my God!"

Three men landed fist after fist, beating the life out of Sebastian. Each blow sent his body lurching while two thugs held him up. Blood was everywhere.

I turned away as war cries from the brutes battering him filtered through Nikki's shop window.

"We've got to do something! They're going to kill him!" I shouted, but no one flinched a muscle.

Glenora whimpered while the strong, proud Nikki—who until this moment—I'd grown to respect, ignored me completely. Instead, she whispered to Glenora that everything would be okay.

But that was a lie. Sebastian might not survive.

"We have to call the police." I pulled out my phone and started dialing.

"No!" Nikki swatted the cell out of my hand, sending it bouncing to the floor with a clatter. If not for my phone's protective case, the screen would've shattered from the force.

I scrambled for it, but Nikki grabbed my arm.

"You call the police, and everything gets worse. This ain't Fifth Avenue."

"So that's it? Sebastian dies and we cry over his grave? This is bullshit!"

"No." Nikki's finger was in my face. "You wanted to live here. This is how it is. This is our community and you'll follow our rules, or die by yours. Take your pick."

Nikki panted, splitting her attention between me and the grieving mom hunched in the corner.

"You know what? Go ahead. Call." Nikki threw up her hands. "Maybe they'll come. More likely, a car will cruise by once everyone's gone. All's well everyone! New York's Finest saved the day. Yeah, that'd accomplish nothing except piss off Mo worse."

She shook her head in disgust. Meanwhile, the beating continued out the window. Sebastian's agony on display for the world to see.

How could they live this way? I'd read news reports about slow response times in poor communities. But living that reality left me so panicked, my lungs wouldn't inflate. If the police weren't coming, it meant Sebastian was on his own.

The thought of never speaking to him again scared me more than the mob outside our window.

I made for the door, but Nikki beat me to it, slamming it shut as I tried to tug it open.

"I can't do nothing... Don't you think if I run over, they'll stop? I'd be a witness..."

"Don't be an idiot. They'll slice your throat and leave you to bleed out. Do you think Sebastian wants that?"

The metal handle dug into my fingers. Its solidness, the only thing keeping me from sinking to the floor.

The men's bloodthirsty whoops of delight caught my attention. Nikki saw me looking toward the window and blocked my view with her body.

"Don't watch. Just stand here and be strong for him."

How was doing nothing being strong? It was the antithesis of every lesson drilled into me from birth. Action mattered. Results mattered. That training left me unprepared to stand here, helpless. This would be the last time I looked away while someone suffered.

Nikki put her arm around me and walked me to the seat next to Glenora, who grabbed my hand. "When it's safe, you'll help me put the pieces back together."

If there were any pieces left.

When the mob fled, Glenora and I rushed to the dark garden while Nikki got her car. I ran ahead, my arms pumping at my sides, lungs burning as I rounded the block to the far side where the garden gate stood open. Sebastian lay in between two puddles of streetlight, making him hard to see.

Cold reality battled with hope as I ran.

He wasn't moving.

Was he alive?

I reached where he lay motionless, face down in a pool of blood and dirt.

"Sebastian! Sebastian, can you hear me?"

I rolled him gently onto his back, gasping as the amber glow landed on his disfigured, bleeding face. Eyes swollen shut, nose broken, yet the worst damage had to be hidden beneath his clothes. The energy of those blows went somewhere and the human body wasn't meant to withstand such vicious punishment.

A faint stream of air tickled the finger I put under his nose, but his chest barely rose.

He had so many injuries, I didn't know what to attend first.

Who was I kidding?

I had no clue what to do and how to help.

Nikki said to wait and we'd take him to the hospital, but I grabbed my phone and called an ambulance. Every second mattered, and I was done sitting on the sidelines.

Glenora arrived, took one look and sank to her knees. "Oh my God. Oh my God, I've lost him!"

"No!" I yelled, harsher than intended. "He's alive. He needs a doctor."

Nikki hopped out of her car and ran over, leaving her hazard lights flashing in the darkness. She crossed herself. "I'm... not sure what to..."

"I called an ambulance. Hopefully they'll come quickly. Let's try to keep his airway open. Help me roll him onto his side so he doesn't choke. I'll hold his head." I slipped my hands under his neck, blood already coagulating into a sticky film that matted his hair.

After his mouth cleared, he gasped for breath, sputtering blood. He coughed twice, then went limp.

"No, no!" I tapped his face. "Sebastian. Stay with me. Please. Fight."

If only I could press my life force into his, hold his body tight against mine like it used to be. Whole and beautiful. Salty tears ran into my mouth, so I wiped them on my shoulder, my hands still holding his head.

I thought we had time. Time to figure out our mess and be together. In my mind, I made it a certainty. Instead, I cradled his broken body, doubtful he'd live five minutes, let alone long enough to have a future. His mom wept, pawing at his arm like she'd already lost him.

It can't end this way.

I won't let it.

"I'm here," I whispered. "I'm so sorry."

I pressed my forehead to his, time stretching into an eternity. *Where is the ambulance?*

Finally, sirens cut through the tomblike stillness shrouding the garden. A white and orange ambulance parked next to the front gate, and two paramedics flipped the back door open to grab their medical bags.

They hustled over to where we sat.

"What happened?" one paramedic said, switching on a headlamp to assess Sebastian's condition. I told them what happened, but Nikki interrupted when I began to say who did it.

"For your protection and theirs," she later whispered.

Glenora rode in the ambulance while Nikki dropped me at the emergency room and said to keep her posted.

I sank into a plastic chair in the waiting room, numb to the hospital happenings around me. Would Sebastian live? Or had his vibrant spirit already left?

No. He's still here. I could feel him. His light penetrated the deep crevices of my soul that I hid from everyone else. An odd mix of guilt and worry warred within me. Guilt for cutting him off for weeks and for focusing on my personal loss when Sebastian lay on a gurney fighting for his life. Worry that his shallow breath would give out completely.

It couldn't.

Please.

Live.

Tears warmed my face, chilled from the hospital air conditioning. I marked their progress down my cheek until they fell free onto my jeans. I'd never let myself openly cry. Instinct dictated I rush to wipe them away before anyone noticed. This time, I wanted the world to see. To know how much Sebastian meant to me. How sorry I was for his perpetual misfortune. He'd escaped a path many young people never recover from. Not like the girls my dad kept me away from whose family pedigree didn't match up. The men mauling him were the real deal. Dangerous enough that his mom and Nikki barred me from trying to help.

You wanted to live here. This is how it is.

Nikki's words invaded. And as usual, she couldn't be more right. I'd been treating my time in Alphabet City like a fun vacation. A dabble on the wild side. How shameful of me? To minimize their hardship and struggle? I'd be nowhere without their good graces. After tonight, I'd never be the same.

"Miss?" a voice called.

A woman stood before me, her unfamiliar face wearing a sympathetic expression. My blood went cold.

"Oh God, is he?"

"They're working on him. But come. I was told you could help with your friend's insurance paperwork?"

She handed me a plastic bag of Sebastian's belongings, but the only thing there was a leather wallet the color of his brown curls. I shuffled over to the registration desk, finally focusing on the staffer. Blond, slim, and noticeably pretty, she wore a floral blouse and a nametag. Dixie.

How a "Dixie" landed in Manhattan, I had no clue. But I answered her intake questions, surprised by how many I knew.

His name. His age, 35, though I had to peek at his driver's license for his birth date and address. I gave her the insurance card from his blood-stained wallet. I fought off the dark omen from having something so vital to his life clutched in my hands. If I took good care, maybe that'd mean he'd need it back? He'd continue a life that needed ID, money, and a CVS frequent shopper card.

The sliding emergency room doors opened and two people entered. It was hard to tell which was the patient. Not a problem we shared.

When done, I migrated back to my seat. I sat stock still among the other fretting families who twisted tissues and impassively watched the episode of Family Feud blaring from the wall-mounted television. Each of us powerless to alter whatever fate lay ahead.

If tonight taught me anything, it was to appreciate life. Grab every opportunity and hold tight.

Be more like Joe. Follow my passions and let the world be damned.

No, not like Joe.

Like Sebastian.

Infuse my every day with hints of our island adventure. Do the opposite of what my rational brain said. I'd been trying, living at Nikki's, taking on the Xervo case; neither made a load of sense. But my gut said it'd work out. The only instinct I ignored was with Sebastian, but that would change. Once he recovered, we'd talk and figure something out. But that depended on Sebastian being okay, which was very much in doubt.

After an hour, Glenora joined me. "They've taken him for emergency surgery. I don't know exactly what for, but they said the doctor will come speak with us when she's done."

My mind whirred with potential injury scenarios. I knew nothing about which injuries were likely. My wild imagination sought relief, but WebMD only confirmed my worst fears. Sebastian wouldn't make it, and if he did, he'd have a long recovery ahead.

Glenora stared into space, clutching his phone so hard I thought she'd crack the screen worse than it already was. Sebastian was her everything. They'd been alone forever, and a part of me felt like an intrusion into their special relationship.

How different his upbringing was from my own.

Poverty and hunger made farming a necessity for his family, versus the hobby gardening he did now. What a luxury choice was. The simple act of being able to afford produce for the fridge's vegetable drawer must have seemed an impossibility at points in their lives. While on the island, Sebastian savored fruit in a way I'd never seen anyone do. Pineapple. Papaya. Mangos. He'd talk about them like they were magic, likely because he ate them so rarely growing up. Manhattan wasn't exactly a tropical climate.

Simple pleasures.

In contrast, I had unlimited pleasures, none of them cheap or adequately appreciated. Conspicuous consumption was my family's motto, fueled by our desire to fit in as a Black family in elite white spaces. The member-only clubs Dad frequented. Expensive vacations. Private schools. Legal retreats. "Look the part," Dad always said. Act like you belong. Living as I had these last weeks made my old self hard to recognize. She'd become a frivolous stranger I'd left behind.

Yet, one thing stuck in my mind since Nikki mentioned it.

"I have a question."

Glenora's watery eyes met mine.

"Someone needs to pay for what they did to him. Without the police...? I don't know what I'll do if..." Tears choked my throat before I could finish.

She pulled me in tight for a hug, stroking my head. "He's gaga for you, too. Haven't seen him this distracted since he had a crush on Melissa McKenzie in third grade. And she was nowhere as beautiful as you."

A laugh escaped as I separated to wipe my eyes. "That obvious?"

"To me at least."

"We kinda have ourselves a pickle, he and I. I probably shouldn't mention, but I'm suing the company. We'll be on opposite sides, and that gets ethically sticky."

"Something tells me you'll figure it out." Glenora patted my hands, then kept hers there. And I let her. I hadn't been this vulnerable with anyone since my mom died. Not my dad. Not my aunt or brother. There was a "right" way to behave in our family, and ugly crying wasn't in the manual. I'd missed it, though. It was the same unadulterated acceptance I got with Sebastian on the island. A measure of hope returned. I prayed his surgeon shared our optimism.

Chapter 33

SEBASTIAN

I felt like hell. Groggy with a pounding head, like waking on the wrong side of a weekend bender. I risked a swallow, but my tongue wouldn't comply. Useless, it lay in my mouth waiting for someone to splash off the sticky paste coating it like gummy flour. I wiggled my jaw and jolts of pain shot up my neck, around my head and down my spine. Then the sounds registered. Electronic beeps. And an intercom paging Dr. Somebody to some place.

I was in a hospital.

Opening my lids would confirm whatever alternate reality I'd sunk into. But they were ridiculously heavy.

How did I get to a hospital aching like I'd been worked over by...

Mo.

His boys mauled me within an inch of my life.

Who got me here?

"I can tell you're awake," Mom said.

I creaked my eyes open, but the room remained a dark blur. I blinked but couldn't focus. The bed next to me was empty, visible because the bathroom's bright light sliced the darkness through an open crack. My head weighed a million pounds, but I managed to roll it toward Mom's voice. She stood over me, her weathered hands gripping the handrail so hard her knuckles bulged.

She was scared but didn't want me to know. My stupidity, once again, forced her to be the strong one. I'd screw up, and Mom would swoop in to save me. This time, from certain death. Had to be, or she'd already be ripping me a new one.

"Can you move toward the end of the bed?" I croaked, my throat scratchy and raw. "My neck hurts too much to look up."

"You can thank your buddy Mo for that. You nearly died," Mom choked back a sob and turned away. "You had internal bleeding. It would've killed you if not for the surgery. Thank God Barbara acted quickly and called the ambulance. I couldn't stop crying long enough to do anything. She's been here with me. What an angel."

I had so many questions, but my mouth wasn't working right. "Water..."

"I'll get it." Mom reached for a cup and bent the straw to slip between my cracked lips.

Tepid water slipped down my throat. I sloshed it around using as few muscles as possible. The slightest movement pierced me with daggers of pain. I blinked it away to focus. How had Barbara gotten roped into my mess?

"Was anyone else hurt?"

"No. We're all fine. But it was terrifying. We saw the whole thing through the salon window. There was so much blood... Barbara was hysterical, trying to get to you, to stop..." her voice caught in her throat.

I reached for her hand, which she took and squeezed.

"It's okay. What hospital are we at?"

"Lennox Hill. Barbara convinced the ambulance drivers to take you here. Thought you might get faster treatment. Smart cookie, that one."

"Yeah?" My spirit lightened. At least the part that wasn't screaming in pain.

"Barbara cares for you, despite trying not to. Got that in common. The two of you are so stubborn."

I tried to pulse an eyebrow in amusement, but even that took effort.

"You didn't tell me she comes from money. It drips off her, the way she demanded answers after surgery, had your room changed when they put you in one with a guy blaring the TV. She even talked to the insurance company about the coverage. She's a keeper."

"Don't remind me." I braced my arms to sit up, but ... agony... everywhere at once. "Fuck! Fuck that kills!"

"Watch your mouth. And quit moving."

"I need pain meds."

"I kept it low given your... problem."

"I never had a problem. That was Mo."

"Hard to tell whose demons were whose. Which ghosts are the past, and which remain." Mom shot me a glance to melt lead.

Fuck. She knows something's up.

"You've been best friends since you both were teens. Why would Mo come after you? Tell me—and don't lie."

My thoughts were way too scrambled to attempt lying. But I had no intention of telling her the truth.

"Do we have to do this now?"

"Who's to say they're done? Maybe we need protection from your protection. Unless..."

Damn her instincts. "Mom. I can't. I'm all banged up..."

"Dante warned us. Why? He works for Mo."

"He feels guilty."

"For what?"

Why the fuck was she badgering me?

Because she knows you're a lying shit.

"I don't know." Pain throbbed to every nerve ending in my body. "Get me those pills. I'm not a fucking addict."

"You need to answer a few questions first."

Was someone paying her to torture me? It'd been ages since we fought, but I wasn't taking her shit. Not today. Not after Mo ground me to a pulp and left me for dead. I took one for the team, but that was too damn real. Like Mo wanted me gone, permanently.

It made no sense.

We've been square, he and I, each going our separate gangland ways. He kept my name out of the neighborhood feuds and earned my continued silence. Just as I earned his.

No good would come from digging it all up.

The money was gone...

Unless it wasn't.

Unless Dante wasn't the only one being cheated.

"I know that look," Mom said. I had completely forgotten she was there, and that we were in the middle of an argument.

"I need to piece a few things together. I honestly don't get why Mo did this. I mouthed off a little at the courts, but this is next-level damage."

Satisfied, she let it go. No one wanted to figure out what happened more than I did.

Mom slid a chair over and sat clasping her hands while I fought through a fog. Eyes closed, what little brain capacity I had shifted to Barbara. Everything I learned about her made her that much harder to resist. A lesser person would have dropped me off and scrammed. But she was special. Loyal, and I'd only known her a short while. How the hell could her ex have stepped out on someone that amazing?

Plus, she stayed with Mom. I owed her big time. I also owed Nikki for saving Barbara's life. She'd only have gotten pummeled if she ran into the middle of that shit show.

"Where's Barbara?" I asked.

"She went to get me a new sandwich." Mom said.

"Something wrong with last one?"

"Sweetie, she brought me some stinky foo-foo sandwich with brie or goat cheese. I can't eat that. Besides, she didn't mind. She would have told me."

"What are you two best friends now?"

"Yeah. I think so." Mom's voice was smiling.

I must have drifted off, because I awoke to whispers and rustling paper bags.

"Tuna, turkey, cheese, ham...nothing stinky. I got pickles, but they're on the side. I also brought coleslaw, potato salad, and macaroni salad. We didn't talk drinks, so I have water, juice, Coke, Diet Coke, ginger ale, and a Dr. Brown's Black Cherry." Barbara said.

"You are a kick! This is enough for a week!"

"Well, we may be here awhile."

We. She said we. My heart thumped in my chest and didn't ache at all.

"I call dibs on the black cherry," I said. Barbara leapt up and was at my side in an instant.

"You're awake!" Her relief was evident as she grabbed my hand and clutched it to her chest before dropping it like it burned. "Sorry, I'm... I didn't mean to..."

"I think we're past that, don't you?" I cracked a smile, and she returned one.

Adjusted to the darkness, I saw her features: her nose, her lips and those eyes still glowing. But instead of glowing in island moonlight, they reflected the light of a hospital bathroom, standing over the bed of a battered man. But I'd never been luckier.

Barbara took my hand back and squeezed tight.

"Since I almost died and all, and have a new appreciation for life, this seems like a good time to ask you to dinner."

Barbara swallowed a laugh. "You're asking me out?"

"It'd be rude to refuse my invitation."

"Would it? Okay, yes. Shall we go now? Or do you want to swing by home and change first?"

"I'll decide when I can lift my head. My people will call your people."

"You do that." Barbara loosened her grip, but I tightened mine, yanking her close.

"Thank you. For trying to save me," I said.

Her expression clouded, my walloping likely replaying in her mind. She'd not likely seen a real beat-down before, let alone of someone she cares for. I'd experienced enough to grasp how brutal they could be. Movie fights always left the faces remarkably untouched. But seeing someone's face busted to smithereens, together with blood gushing from the nose and mouth, those images stuck.

"It was awful. I'll never..." Her hand tightened as tears dammed along her lash line. I wanted to kiss them away. Kiss her pain away.

"Come here." She leaned in to kiss my battered, cracked lips. Gentle, like a promise.

"I thought I'd lost you," she whispered.

"I'm stubborn that way."

She searched my face. For what, I'm not sure. She looked like she was drinking me in. Was she surveying my bruised face or remembering it as it was before? I'd never know, but as long as she stayed by my side, I didn't care.

"I'm going to eat your mom's stinky sandwich. Best you kiss me now."

I did. Then she took a seat next to what must have been my mom's smirking self.

Barbara rustled her sandwich out of the white paper wrapper, raising her voice. "Mmmm. This is the best stinky cheese ever!"

"Blech. How can you eat that? It tastes like feet," Mom said.

"It's an acquired taste. We'll do a cheese board sometime and I'll get you eating all kinds of things you never thought you'd try."

Mom chuckled. "You're charming, but not THAT charming."

That's where Mom was wrong. Barbara was the most captivating woman I'd ever met.

Chapter 34

SEBASTIAN

Sun streamed through my hospital room's windows, escaping around where the shades gapped. Outside, the world went about its day. Morning came, people shuffled to work. At some point, I'd rejoin them.

I drifted in and out of sleep all night. At least twice, I woke from violent dreams into the stranglehold of an automatic blood pressure cuff. My dreamworld merged with the details of the attack, leaving me unsettled about which was which. I'd ask Barbara when she returned later.

That she planned to return at all liquefied my insides. Logistics overwhelmed Mom. Having Barbara take charge was a godsend. They traded jabs about stinky cheese before murmuring together for hours. Mom only did that with my aunt, and not nearly often enough. She needed more close companions and so did I.

If my brush with death taught me anything, it's that none of us know when our time is up. I'd been on autopilot for so long, I'd forgotten how to have fun. Not the reckless shit I did as a teen. Exciting adventures, like the ones I had with Barbara. Stepping outside my comfort zone to embrace new experiences. Stand for something and create change that mattered. The moment I returned to work, I'd talk to Barr. Maybe I could get him to understand why his patriarchal ways wouldn't cut it. Play my cards right, and I might convince him the whole idea was his doing. Even let him take the c redit...

On cue, my cranky boss called. I reflexively twitched to answer, which only sent stabbing pain to every extremity.

Fuck me. I need meds.

But I wasn't fast enough, and my voicemail alert chirped. All that mattered right now was calling the nurse. I had a vague memory of a controller being positioned near my left hand, so I patted the pilled cotton blanket until a smooth rubber cord pinched between my fingers. I slid it until the cool, hard plastic of the signal button arrived. I pressed, then waited.

"Someone will be right in." A staticky voice blasted from the speaker.

Moments later, a nurse walked in wearing purple scrubs covered in carrots. A smile creaked across my face. The white board on the wall over the foot of my bed had "Maybelle" written in green dry erase marker next to the RN on duty.

"Do you garden?" I asked.

"I did, love. At home. Not anymore." Her voice had an island lilt like Jerome, my barber. *Caribbean?* Her long braids were gathered into a ponytail hanging down her back. While glad to see Maybelle, I longed for Barbara instead.

"Where's home?" I asked.

"Aren't we Mr. Chatty?" She wore an amused expression as she reached to turn off the call button. "Why don't you tell me how you're feeling?

"Everything hurts."

"On a scale of one to ten—"

"37. I need medication. I know my mother made out like I'm a junkie, but smoking pot 20 years ago doesn't really qualify."

Her eyebrows shot up. "Well then, we'll see what we can do. I'm sure the doctor left a standing order, should you ask."

"Ask for what?" Barbara breezed in with an armful of flowers.

My face erupted in a smile, and it almost didn't hurt. "I was negotiating for pain meds."

"Don't let me interrupt." Barbara smiled and moved across the room to the window. God, she was beautiful. Her dark eyes shone bright, red gloss made her lips look infinitely kissable. She wore a light gray blazer, white blouse and black jeans that hugged her curves like they were made for her. Knowing her wealth, they likely had been.

I stared at Barbara so long I completely forgot Nurse Maybelle was waiting. When I turned back to her, she had a wide smirk on her face. She leaned in to whisper. "Lady friend?"

"Yeah. I think so." I whispered.

"Well, get on that," she replied, standing up and resuming her full volume. "I'll see about those meds."

Barbara looked up and smiled as the nurse exited. "How are we today? I thought about bringing you breakfast but wasn't sure if you were on a restricted diet."

"Can't say. Still waiting for rounds."

"Your color is returning. Way better than yesterday."

"I'm sorry you had to watch what happened."

"That makes two of us." Barbara turned away to fuss with the flower arrangement.

Something was off about her today. She wouldn't hold eye contact and refused to approach my bed. Was she still in shock? She was fine last night. Whatever it was left my senses tingling. Before I had time to think about it, my phone rang.

Barr again.

It might be awkward for Barbara if I talked about work in front of her, but I didn't want her to go.

"I better get that," I said, answering.

"Where the hell are you?" Barr yelled.

"I'm in the hospital. I was attacked last night and—"

"Forget that. We've got troubles."

"I'm mangled in bed, with tubes everywhere. I doubt you're worse than me."

Barbara looked up, and I mouthed, "Barr." She stiffened, then grabbed her handbag.

"I'll check back later."

"Hold on." I covered the phone with my free hand. "Don't go. This won't take long."

"Talk to him. Then let me know if you still feel the same way." She nodded toward my cell and left before I could stop her.

"Kingsbury! This is serious!"

I stared at my open door, expecting her to return.

"We've been served," Barr yelled. "A group of former employees are suing for wrongful dismissal and racial discrimination."

That got my attention.

"Guess who's representing them?" he asked.

I didn't have to guess. "Barbara..."

I said it aloud, but more to myself in utter disbelief. I was now legally forbidden from contacting the one person I wanted more than anything.

Only last night, we'd kissed. She was here by my side, chatting with Mom and acting like we had a future. Like we're together, as in a couple. Why would she do that? Torture me with longing if she was only going to disappear the next day? Her flowers caught my eye, and for the first time, I was genuinely pissed at her. Barbara couldn't delay this one fucking day? I needed her here with me, and not as opposing counsel.

Barr blathered on, but my mind was on Barbara. She re-entered my life knowing the case was coming. Then waltzed in with flowers. Why would she do that?

Because she loves you.

If she did, she'd stay away. It only reminded me of what I can't have.

Maybe she couldn't stay away?

I huffed a laugh, my contracting stomach yanking on my stitches. "Fuck!" I yelled.

"Yeah, you can say that again," Barr answered.

"Read it to me, word for word. Don't skip anything," I said.

He dictated the note out loud. All of it accurate, from what I could tell. They racially profiled and targeted the staff for the layoffs. Black employees were underrepresented overall, but overrepresented in the list of those let go. Not one word of their claim was inaccurate. And it wouldn't be. Barbara represented them.

I heard Barr toss the papers in frustration. "This is ridiculous. They have no case here, do they?"

"We both know they do. You released top performers and kept lesser ones. You claimed cost savings for the VCs but rehired nearly 40 percent of the roles. This is bad math. After discovery, they'll have the goods."

He mulled that over. "Without proof, they're sunk."

"Xervo's actions are the proof. They were fired, and their jobs were refilled with new people. The exact positions." I waited for my words to sink in. Like being confronted with the totality of his ridiculous shit would trigger latent empathy. Maybe he'd show remorse. Then do the right thing and settle.

I heard him thinking. "We have to get shredding. Tell Yvonne to get that vendor in. That firm, what's it called? Steel Mountain? They have shredding trucks—"

"We're not shredding anything. We've been served and are legally obligated to keep all relevant paperwork."

"Screw that."

"Marshall, if we're guilty, let's settle. Pay the claims and be done with it."

"Don't be an idiot. I have no intention of paying any of those people. If we did, that VC investment would dry up like that." He snapped his fingers.

"And as your legal counsel, I suggest you cut your losses. Litigation will only draw more attention. We'll get negative press coverage far outside our walls. We can be profitable and ethical. We'd just need to change—"

"If you refuse to help, I'll retain outside counsel. I'm fighting this injustice. It's a bullshit money grab, and they won't get away with it."

"It's not and they will. Firings happen all the time. But you can't kick employees out because you don't like the color of their skin. That's illegal."

Barr wasn't having it. I let him rant for a while. "Give me some credit" which he hadn't earned. "It wasn't racial at all." Wasn't it? They all had good records. Why not lose low performers? Sure, that gal from accounting had a reputation for being prickly, but she'd handled all the payments for years without any issue. No way she or Barbara should have been on the chopping block.

By the end, Barr hung up to call, of all people, Barbara's dad's firm. He'd have them take the lead and loop me in as necessary.

The thought of this case keeping me and Barbara apart for however long it lasted made me pissed as hell.

I almost died, beaten to a bloody pulp, and the only good thing that came out of it was that it brought me and Barbara back together.

If broken bones and messed up organs failed to keep me from Barbara, this damn suit wouldn't either.

The way I saw it, the only thing threatening us was my past. To put that genie back in the bottle, I'd have to talk to the person who nearly killed me. But when the time came, I'd be ready.

Chapter 35

BARBARA

I tapped my dark phone screen to check the clock. Xervo wasted no time after getting my package yesterday. I got a text from Barr saying his legal representative would contact me this morning. The last place I wanted to be when that happened was out at breakfast with my dad.

What's worse, the moment I sat down, he rose to take a call. I'd been sitting alone for almost ten minutes while shaking my head at the server to shoo him away.

No, we're not ready to order.

Yes, we're hogging the table.

Don't blame me. My loving father has become completely self-absorbed.

My dad cleared his throat to get my attention as he returned. I set my phone face up on the table. Besides the case, I'd yet to hear from Sebastian. I can't imagine what he thought of it and me. In retrospect, it was a bad idea to visit him in the hospital yesterday given what was about to hit the fan. But I had to make sure he was okay. And hopefully, steal a kiss. If not for Barr's call, I'd have one last moment to remember him by.

He probably hates me now.

Just like the man sitting across the table.

The condensation on my water made me ponder my antiperspirant. Had I put enough on? *Never let them see you sweat.* My dad's lesson flashed to mind. He didn't likely suspect in a million years that his tricks would be used against him.

I searched his face, but he'd already begun our usual wordless greeting.

My arched eyebrow said, you asked me here. You start.

His crinkled forehead said you're not going to like it.

My bored sigh and sip of water said you have two seconds to get started or I'm leaving.

"My firm has been retained to represent Xervo in its proceeding against your claim."

Dad's gaze never wavered, but my lids closed in utter disappointment.

Our game was over, and he'd lost. My soul ached that he chose duty to his firm over his allegiance to me as his daughter. Beyond being the ultimate betrayal, it was a ridiculous breach of legal ethics and the epitome of conflict of interest. Only, he didn't seem to be conflicted at all. He'd made his choice, and it wasn't me.

I gulped the stomach acid stinging my throat. "Well then, my mistake. I thought I was having breakfast with my father, not opposing counsel."

"I recused myself, of course. But I wanted to tell you in person. I owe you that."

Dad owed me a hell of a lot more than a courtesy stab in the back. Did he think this farce of a breakfast date made him noble?

I had to laugh. "After everything you've done to destroy our relationship, decimate our family and my career, you have the nerve to act like you're taking the high road?"

"Barbara, please."

"Please what? 'Please don't be upset I pushed you beyond the breaking point to become a lawyer, only to kneecap your career?' Or, 'please don't leave that man who cheated on you?' This latest one might be the best. 'Please forgive me for representing your racist boss who fires people because they're Black.' Which is it dad? Which am I forgiving you for?"

He scratched his head, eyes darting to other diners to see if anyone heard my rant. Old Barbara would have ignored what was likely a habit of his elite station. *Lower your voice. We don't want to make a scene.* But he'd long since lost that courtesy.

"Why do their opinions matter more than mine?" I asked.

"Whose?"

"The strangers in this restaurant you're so worried about impressing. Fuck them. Who the hell are they? We'll never see them again. This is your chance, Dad. Step away or we're done. I've been mistreated by too many men in my life. I won't tolerate it anymore. I deserve better, and frankly, you're better than this."

The server approached. This time, Dad waved him off, pressing his palms together against his lips.

My hopes rose. Had my words knocked some sense into him? Or was that an unreasonable ask?

"This is out of my control. I can't explain how, but I need you to understand I don't have a choice in who they represent. They allowed me this one conversation to tell you."

"They? Who are they? You're the 'they.' You own the damn place."

I stood up, tossing my napkin on the table. "I'm so glad you used our time wisely. I'll be filing for discovery."

Without another word, I left. Behind me sat a small man, apologizing to the next table for the poor behavior of his daughter. Little did they know, his actions were the ones needing an excuse. He'd learn the hard way how fierce a foe he'd insulted.

After all, I'm a Washington.

The written offer that arrived that afternoon was beyond insulting. I'd like to think, were it my dad, he wouldn't have wasted my time. I never expected Xervo to meet our settlement terms. But I had to make the effort. Despite their lame proposal, I was ethically bound to present it to the group. Hopefully, after our impromptu conference call, we'd all agree to move forward with the case.

I rolled my chair into the desk and launched the meeting. I typically requested everyone turn on their cameras so I can see reactions and kept recorded files of the conversations. One's livelihood was an emotional topic. I'd only been able to keep this group together with spit and duct tape. But our cause was just, and I had the most to lose if we failed.

Faces popped in one by one, with a variety of backgrounds. Most were at home, but a few had since landed new positions and sat in professional spaces. While happy, I had a momentary pang of longing for my old life. One where the paychecks were steady and my days more predictable. Given how emotionally invested I'd been in my career, it was easy to forget I'd been living in an illusion. Were it not, we'd all still be at Xervo instead of on a video call seeking financial compensation.

"Thanks for joining on such short notice," I said, making sure the red record button was visible. "We received a quick reply to our proposal. Their recommended terms are laughable, but I'm obligated to present them to you."

I shared my screen so they could read while I summarized. "They propose granting one year of annual salary per person paid out as follows: 25% now, and 25% per year for three subsequent years, but only if we abide by their nondisclosure requirements. If any of you mention the deal to anyone, or on social media, the agreement is voided for all. And, you'd be forced to repay the money already distributed."

They were crestfallen. While I counseled them to be prepared for a lowball response, the majority looked genuinely crushed.

"I'd never agree to that," Melvin said. "I feel like this has been a waste of time."

"It's not nothing." One woman chimed in. She'd been unable to find work, and the financial pinch was setting in.

I cut in. "We can do better. Remember, we're dealing with Barr here. Did you expect him to jump at our first request?"

Shrugs and nods waved across my screen as each remembered our former boss. Most staffers didn't work closely with the CEO. But they'd all experienced his dictatorial nature, ludicrous secrecy, and his tendency to hold grudges for the most minor infractions. Like the guy who parked in his parking spot for ten minutes one day and got demoted. None of Barr's history would justify starry-eyed fantasies of an out-of-court payday.

"If we're agreed, I'll reject their offer and move forward—"

"Hold on." Melvin interrupted. "What other options do we have?"

"We could counter, but their stunt today shows they have no intentions of making a respectable settlement. That leaves dropping the case or pressing on to trial."

"Is winning even possible? Maybe we should just move on. I've found work, as has Melinda. Some of us might want to drop out." Melvin crossed his arms. That he brought the issue up at all revealed his own mindset.

A woman named Felicity raised her hand, then unmuted. "Xervo called me and offered me my job back."

"Me too," James said. "When I said no, he offered a cash settlement of 25 grand."

"You can't be serious?!" I yelled.

"As death," he replied.

Barr crossed a major line. Communicating with claimants was beyond unethical. The judge would hear about this if we got that far.

James was in his late forties and lived with his sister. With one kid in college, dangling that kind of money in front of him must be hard to resist. He'd yet to find work himself.

Icy fear crept up my back. I expected dirty dealings, but reaching out individually to my clients trying to bribe them was a new low. Even for him. Had Barr gone rogue, or was he following directions from his legal team? It smelled like a tactic my dad would try. He'd done it more than once with my boyfriends, including when I started dating Joe. Dad would flip if he knew about Sebastian, but then I remembered. There might not be an "us" to worry about anymore.

I'd lost track of the conversation happening in front of me.

"I'm sorry. What did you say?" I asked.

"That I had to think about it. Bird in hand, you know. This could drag on for ages and..."

"Yes, but the reward would be far larger if we see it through. Remember, you're not paying anything for the effort. All I ask is for your permission—and patience."

"Say we lose. Mr. Barr's deal might be the best we get?"

"Our case is strong. After discovery, when Xervo is forced to reveal their employment information, we'll have a paper trail to match our personal experiences. That includes staff records, payroll reports, witnesses... they're not acting in good faith here. They replaced a few of you, and none of the roles they filled was with a person of color. Not one. Doesn't that bother you?"

Silence settled in as each waited for another to speak first. Portia rose to the occasion.

"What's the matter with all of you? I can't even contain myself thinking of his smug face sitting atop his ivory tower—literally—while we're out here scrambling to make a living. I want justice. This is a no brainer."

God bless Portia. I'd tipped her off about the Xervo response last night, and her head nearly blew off. Surveying the screen, I could see her former band of elevator pirates were unconvinced. They mutinied against her this time.

"I'm inclined to take his offer. I'm sorry, Ms. Washington, but I'm out. I've got bills to pay," James said.

"Wait, don't—" I started, but the exodus had already begun.

"Count me out, too. All I wanted was my job back, and that's what I can have. I'd be stupid to turn it down."

"Felicity, no. Don't you see? He's trying to break us apart." But my words failed to convince her. She had already muted to talk to someone over her shoulder. "I have to go. My son's heading to work and my granddaughter is crying."

Felicity looked way too young to have a granddaughter, but then, multi-generational households were common in the Black community. As was the mistreatment we were experiencing. But workplace bias wouldn't stop if we backed out now. I had to regain control of this call or all my efforts would be for nothing.

"Remember how it felt to walk out of the building holding our boxes? Stunned into silence while our colleagues and friends avoided eye contact? I do. I worked hard—nights, weekends, holidays. I endured his disrespect and insults in silence. His tokenism as he dragged me to events to have enough 'representation'," I air quoted. "And despite doing everything right, he cut me loose anyway. He let all of us go, thinking we were expendable because of the color of our skin."

I had their attention. *Don't lose it.*

"Sit with that. Feel the humiliation again. He pushed us out the door like we were worthless. But we have tangible value. Make them understand how much. Stand with me and proclaim your worth. Demand fair treatment. If we don't, companies like Xervo will never change. Even if we lose, we'll have made a difference. Word will spread, making other corporations think twice about mistreating employees of color, expecting us to sit back and take it.

It's outrageous, and I refuse to accept Barr's racist bullshit. We can do this, but we have to do it together. Who's with me?"

My chest heaved like I'd run a gauntlet. Which I had. I'd lived a professional life as a Black woman, withstanding slights, lewd statements, lost opportunities, tokenism, and dirty glances. I'd never admitted to myself how badly it hurt. I was too busy burying my isolation behind a smile, pretending I was fine. In my heart, I always knew I was playing a part. A role my family trained me to play like an acrobatic pet. My dad could live this lie indefinitely, but the last few months had changed me. I'm stronger and more confident in my skin than I'd ever been. I wanted the world to see how the battle scars only toughened me for this fight. How I was destined to lead this charge all along. If I didn't hold Xervo accountable, no one would.

"I'm with you." Portia said with a smile. "C'mon people? Do we want that douche bag, Mr. Barr, to get away with what he did?"

I laughed out loud, as did the others. Somehow Portia had transformed from a cranky foe to my fiercest advocate. I couldn't be more grateful.

Melvin pledged to stay, as did two more. In the end, our mighty band of nine was down to seven. Losing James and Felicity was a blow, but seven was still a significant show of force. Seven people ready to hold Xervo accountable.

Chapter 36

SEBASTIAN

These stairs are going to kill me.

After lying in bed for three days straight and fighting back from the brink of death, I'll die walking up the four flights to my apartment. Too proud, I sent Mom ahead. She'd been standing next to my open door chatting with my neighbor, Mrs. Ferrante, for what seemed like forever.

I leaned against the wall on the second floor, sweat trickling behind the bandages taped to my stomach. Hiking upstairs tired me out almost as much as resisting the urge to call Barbara. I'd started texting a few times, and swore I saw her conversation bubbles go live more than once, only to disappear. I wondered what she might have said.

Forget the suit.

I need you.

I love you.

Let's be together.

My fantasy, for sure. Her version might be all business.

I filed for discovery.

Here are our demands.

See you in court.

I refused to believe this dumb case would be the end of us. Barr remained as stubborn as ever. I even ran the numbers to show how it would likely cost less to settle, but the bastard wouldn't budge. I had to do better. Convince him not to be stupid and go to trial.

But first I had to get up the last flight of stairs.

I took a deep breath, grabbed the handrail, and pulled. With my upper torso leaning forward, my legs followed. Each step yanked at the stitches and pinched my broken ribs. With the pain killers weaned back, the time had come to suck it up.

I reached the top step and sighed, resting my sweaty, shaky body against the wall for support.

"What are you doing?" Mom raced to my side. "You'll fall and crack your head open!"

"What do you mean?"

"You're swaying."

"I am?"

Mrs. Ferrante's pity read all over her face. Luckily, she returned to her apartment.

Mom braced under my arm and lifted. "Let's get you to bed. You're so stubborn. Let me help you."

Suddenly, stepping took far less effort, and we shuffled into the apartment, past the living room and straight into my bedroom.

"I wanted to sit on the couch."

"Bed. You're lying down here, and I'll get you something to eat. We've got enough casseroles for two weeks. I've been collecting them while you were in the hospital."

She rolled her eyes at my surprise. "Everyone saw and anyone who missed it watched it on YouTube."

Fantastic. The whole fucking world knew I was smoked by Mo. I'm the carnage he needed to further tighten his grip on the neighborhood—and his crews. We were once like brothers. It boiled my blood to know I'd been demoted to a belt notch.

I shook my mom off, slid out of bed and wobbled to the bathroom. A splash of cold water jolted me awake. Funny how well that works. Resolve reflected back at me in the mirror as I went for another dip.

"Don't get any smart ideas about confronting Mo. Let it be. He'll not hassle you anytime soon. He knows we'll go to the police."

I turned off the faucet, face dripping into the sink as I braced myself with both hands. "And how would he know that?"

She folded her arms and looked away.

"Mom. What did you do?"

"What did you expect me to do? Nothing? After her boy nearly killed mine?"

Of course. She ran to Mo's mom and had it out. Once close, their friendship shattered the moment Mo and I went our separate ways. Until Mom landed back on her doorstep. I can't half blame her. I'd do the same.

I blotted my face with a hand towel. "Forget it. I'm starving. What do we have?"

After gorging on Mrs. Ferrante's stuffed shells, which my mom still swore weren't as good as hers, I already felt stronger. The diet they had me on at the hospital left me depleted. With Mrs. Ferrante's food coursing through me, I'd be on my feet in no time. Work would come next.

I sent my protesting mother away and stood listening to the silence of the apartment.

No beeping.

No intercom pages.

No blood pressure cuffs jarring me awake from the two minutes of sleep I got each night.

My bed cried for company, but my curiosity about the case won out. I limped over to the white plastic bag from the hospital and pawed through the crusty remains of my tattered clothes. Stiff and brown, you'd expect blood to have an odor. Angry flashes of my beating flashed to mind. I shuddered, then retrieved my shattered phone and tossed the rest of the contents in the trash.

No wonder Mom ran to Mo's mother. With a baseball bat, no doubt. Not that she needed it. The corners of my mouth curled up at the mental image of my feisty mother. Her resilience and grit were legendary. Just like mine used to be before blowing up on YouTube. Maybe Dante was right and I'd gone soft thinking I was better than my neighbors. *No. No way.* That was Dante's insecurity talking. His life was a sewer and he wanted company. Then again, I could be knee deep in sewage and it wouldn't register with my busted nose.

The leather sectional creaked as I lowered myself. It was my first "adult" purchase when I landed a good-paying job. The rest of the furnishings soon followed. Solid pieces meant to last. None of the cheap stuff mom hauled home from Delancey Street. Dressers that hurt my brain to put together. This shit was heavy, so I tipped the delivery guys well. Funny, they were the same stairs I struggled to climb moments earlier.

Unable to flex my abs, I managed a lopsided throw-blanket toss over my legs with one arm. I better heal quick because these injuries were killing me. The only good part is that they kept me from thinking about Barbara. I should be mad as hell about her not giving me a heads-up about the suit, but I hadn't been able to summon the outrage. Not after everything she'd been through. All I'd learned about Xervo led to one conclusion: Barr had been a major dick to his employees of color. Prime among them, Barbara.

Women like her didn't fall from trees, so I'd have to figure a way out of this mess.

Barr's messages directed me to my email, and the paperwork sent over by Washington & Associates. They included Barbara's terms for settlement and the Xervo offer the lawyers worked up. The delta between the two was laughable. I also got word that one of her clients was rehired. No clue how that happened, given that we weren't supposed to have any direct contact with them.

Every page I read made my muscles tense in anger, which sent volts of pain shooting from my newly reconstructed abdomen. Barr had a way of getting under my skin. Everything he did was wrong and for his personal gain, the consequences be damned. Mo cared more about his crew than my CEO did his.

I double clicked on an email exchange between the lead lawyer and Barr.

After hiring one person back, he gave another a settlement.

Said the hiring managers reached out on their own.

Barr had no knowledge.

Yeah right.

His sticky fingerprints were all over that negotiation.

What a dumbass.

Settling with two people only showed they shouldn't have been cut in the first place. It suggested guilt. Plus, Barbara would have grounds to claim an ethical violation for bypassing counsel to negotiate with a represented party.

She's going to crush him.

I should be worried. Instead, the thought of Barbara winning made me happier than I'd been since before Mo rearranged my organs.

Those people deserved to get paid. I only wished Barbara was included. As their lawyer, she wasn't party to this case. She'd be denied her day in court to air all the bunk she'd been forced to suffer. Knowing Barr as I did and hearing the crude remarks he made about her now that she was gone, she must have a train-load of tales to share.

But she wouldn't get that opportunity.

Nor the same contract I negotiated as incoming General Counsel. My terms covered firing without cause, but most staffers didn't have that luxury. As employees at will, the company could let them go at any time for near any reason. Almost. Discrimination was the one no-no, but Barr couldn't help himself. I hated to think anyone would lump me in with him, assuming I approved of how he operated. Given the chance, I'd cross that picket line and join the wronged.

But I couldn't. Legally. I'd risk getting sanctioned, or worse, lose my law license. I almost didn't care. When I lay in that hospital bed, the last thing I worried about was my career at Xervo. I craved a life with Barbara.

Were we together, I wouldn't be able to hide my past as well as I did at work. Up to now, I'd kept my worlds apart. *A random attack.* No one at work questioned the story. And why should they? I looked like I came from privilege. Well dressed, tall, and white. Yeah, that might signal money. But my food stamps and juvy hall pedigree said otherwise. I almost felt bad when colleagues accused me of having a silver-spoon life. I'd set them straight, then watch their faces drain. It was impossible to guess someone's history and background by looking at them. Know the obstacles they'd overcome. The sacrifices they'd made. The character that shone bright when all was dark. It's what eyes can't see.

My mind drifted to Barbara. The more I learned about her, the more I loved her. I wanted to be by her side, fighting together. Instead, we were on opposite sides, without a way to communicate without risking both our careers. Her case—and cause—were just. But they were hers. For both our sakes, I had to do my job and ensure Xervo operated in good faith. Steer clear of her entirely.

Too bad both were easier said than done.

Chapter 37

BARBARA

I massaged my neck, stiff from hours of sitting at my home desk. I'd been consumed with the case for weeks. And with the trial approaching, my life after loomed large. What came next? I'd settled into a fine routine, coming and going as I pleased. No way I was dragging myself to a new job and pretending that the last five months hadn't happened.

Every one of them had a Marshall Barr.

A douche bag who treated women like trash. I'd worked too hard and come too far to accept that degrading behavior. I'd grown. When I looked for roles before, I sought validation more than income. They proved I was worthwhile, and I wore my title like designer clothing.

The Gucci bee and interlaced G's.

The distinctive "YSL" of Yves Saint Laurent.

The trademark red sole of Christian Louboutin.

Wearing high fashion was a waste if no one recognized the label.

Sadly, I'd done the same thing: pursuing a General Counsel role like it was a holy chalice. Once hired, all would be well. But it wasn't.

I'd held the prize for two years and nothing changed. If anything, it left me feeling lost. Probably because none of it was real.

I stared down at my discount outfit, mostly picked up on Orchard Street. Forty-dollar jeans, $25 sneakers, and a T-shirt Glenora bought me that said, "This is my New York." Altogether, it was under a hundred bucks. But I felt like a million. Stronger and more invincible. My bargain finds bested designer clothes costing thousands. Funny, I'd always bought into the "clothes make the man" mantra, but it was the exact opposite.

I still appreciated their fine craftsmanship and elegance. But they no longer defined who I was. Instead of craving clothes like air, I craved life, justice, and Sebastian.

I saw him for the first time this morning. He was out running. I watched his healed body from afar, longing for what was underneath. I knew where he lived. Glenora told me. I'd walked by there nearly every day, hoping to get a glimpse of him. Maybe even steal an off-the-record kiss. Or more.

By contrast, my exercise was clinging to hope that after the Xervo mess was behind us, we could be together. Start over and have a happy life. It might be a foolish wish. But holding that fantasy was the only thing allowing me to sleep at night. When I lay in the dark, alone, afraid, and wanting.

A text from Nikki jingled.

Nikki:

Can you come down? I have paint samples and want to put that expert opinion of yours to good use.

Barbara:

Be right down.

I grabbed my keys and headed down to Nikki's apartment on the first floor. I originally wondered why she chose a ground-floor unit for herself. It couldn't be fun living so close to street noise and having bars on your windows. Then I learned. Her place also went straight through to the back, opening onto a small patio bordered by a grassy yard. It was the most grass I'd seen since moving down here. Her green patch of oasis abutted the backyard from the housing development on the next street. Their tall wooden fence gave Nikki outdoor privacy, seldom found in Manhattan without a hefty price tag. Even the brownstone I shared with Joe had fire escapes and terraces peeking over ground-floor patios. I stood down there once, and I felt like I was at the bottom of a stockpot with hungry neighbors peering in. Nikki's building had windows, but no terraces. One more surprise from a woman full of them.

Nikki's door was open with a deadbolt when I arrived, so I walked through without knocking.

"Look at these." Nikki fingered a stack of sample paint strips. "I can't decide between these yellows. But now that I'm here, I remembered that gray you have upstairs."

"It's called Dove Gray. I have a little left over if you want to paint a patch on the wall to see if you like it."

"I thought that was only something in commercials." Nikki laughed, holding her swatch to the wall, then squinting at her ceiling light. "You know, I didn't realize how dark my apartment was until seeing yours."

She was right. Her living room had beige walls, yet was perpetually dim, even with all the lights on. Good lighting, whether natural or otherwise, was one of the many niceties I took for granted until standing in Nikki's shadowy apartments. My bright apartment never failed to lift my mood or fuel optimism amid my chaos. Nikki had plenty of zest and deserved lighting to mirror her spirit.

Nikki worked wonders on the stairwell since I moved in, and had more than earned a personal home makeover experience. Starting with being able to see what we were doing.

"Maybe we do your lighting first. You'll have a better notion of what color you want to choose. If you pick a bright hue, it might scream once the room is properly lit—"

"Knock, knock!" A voice yelled. "I've got a load of greens from my mom..."

My body stiffened.

Sebastian.

What the hell was he doing here?

The man I wanted to see more than anything had just walked in. My skin pricked to attention, and I stuffed my fingers in my back jeans pockets to keep from fidgeting.

Don't freak out. He loves you and you love him. At least he used to. But does he anymore? I'd had a one-sided romance for so long, I almost forgot it took two people to make it work. After not hearing back, I feared the worst. But was he still interested? With his injuries, he hadn't exactly been in any position to date. And Glenora didn't mention him seeing anyone…

Had she done that to save my feelings?

Oh my God. He'd met someone new.

The object of my desire was ten feet away. I knew it but he didn't. That put all the pressure on me to make the right decision.

"Excuse me a minute." Nikki dropped her paint swatches on the coffee table to greet her visitor. I pictured myself knocking her out of the way and jumping into Sebastian's arms. But I hadn't earned that right. We hadn't texted in weeks, and I had no idea how he'd react to seeing me. The new me. The one suing his company and taking him to court with no warning after he'd risked his career to warn me about my layoff.

The magnetic pull to the kitchen was palpable, but my feet rooted in place. If I hid here, he'd never know. Yet, some strange kismet kept forcing my path into his. I looked up, past the cracked ceiling paint and straight to heaven.

Mom? Is this your doing?

Do you have to be so pushy?

"Let me take that from you," Nikki said from the other room.

"It's heavy…" Sebastian said, as Nikki grunted.

"Who do you think lifts all those boxes of shampoo at the salon?"

"Ramon?" The two of them broke into laughter.

Hearing his voice rocketed my longing sky high. It took me back to our time on the island. When we rode around doing the opposite of what our instincts demanded. That experience changed me. He changed me. A huge part of me now felt ready to explore whatever this thing between us was. If I let Sebastian walk out again without saying a word, I'd have failed the latest test put before me.

Do the opposite of what old Barbara would do.

I released a cleansing breath and drifted into Nikki's kitchen, where they stood chuckling. Sebastian almost dropped the head of lettuce he was tossing when he noticed me.

Confusion clouded his face. "Barbara? Oh, my God, Barbara!" Sebastian abandoned the vegetable and rushed over to me. He was about to embrace me when he halted.

His eyebrows raised in a silent question. Was it okay? Did I want to be with him and give us a chance?

I smirked, hiking an eyebrow of my own. *Yes. I'm ready. Be careful what you ask for.*

The force of his body against mine knocked away any lingering doubt. My relief soared, replaced by desire so strong my heart throbbed in my chest. Or was that his? It was impossible to tell. In that one moment, our bodies fused together in a primal coupling so intense, it could only be love, if not for the simple fact that it couldn't be. Somehow, reason didn't matter. We'd bonded over shared experiences, and I wanted more. Or at the very least, to give it a chance to work.

As Sebastian held me in his arms, a pang of doubt grabbed me. If I gave in, I'd only get hurt. I couldn't withstand a repeat of the Joe disaster. I thought I knew Joe and look what happened.

Sebastian is not Joe.

He's not a lying skunk.

God, I hope so.

His arms slid up mine to cradle my face and he pulled in for a deep kiss. It was everything. Desperate. Loving. Lusty. That kiss mended my tattered soul. Broken, lost, and rejected, I thirsted for a man who understood me so completely. It was the most irrational thing I'd ever experienced, and I hungered for more.

Nikki tsk, tsked from across the room. "You better take it outside. The heat coming off the two of you could scorch this building to the ground, and I've no intention of moving."

I separated enough to turn toward Nikki. "I'm a little starved for my island Adonis."

"You called me an Adonis?" His smile was electric.

"Don't let it go to your head."

I grabbed his hand, dragging him toward the apartment door. "Nikki, I'll get some lighting options together for you. Then we can tackle the paint. Okay?"

"Yes, yes," Nikki said. "But, Sebastian..."

We halted our escape, heads snapping back in unison.

"... be good to that girl. She deserves an honest man in her life."

They shared a quiet exchange ending with his silent nod.

"I will. I promise." Sebastian said.

"If you say so." Nikki dismissed us with a wave, chuckling to herself.

Sebastian's sober expression shifted when he looked at me. He was himself: handsome, his bright hazel eyes trained on me. All wounds healed, with only the slightest of bumps where his nose had been broken—what a gift.

I took in the man before me, wondering about his shattered past. But there'd be plenty of time for that. We both had other priorities.

The second I closed Nikki's apartment door, Sebastian's lips were on mine, slamming me into the foyer wall. He was the elixir I'd craved since leaving him at the hospital, broken and bruised. But he healed, and I took that blessing as a bright sign for our future.

He caressed my arms, his mouth busy on my neck. Then he grabbed handfuls of my ass and squeezed.

A moan escaped my mouth unbidden.

Body tingling, he whispered in my ear.

"Barbara, I..."

"Upstairs," I said, breathless.

He kissed me while smiling. "So far?"

A tingle jolted up my back. Sebastian turned me on in ways I'd thought impossible. Just talking to him got me hotter than Joe ever did. My ex's selfishness didn't end at the bedroom door. But there was nothing selfish about Sebastian. I'd lay in bed imagining us making love. He was as giving there as he was everywhere else.

I laced his fingers in mine and guided him upstairs to my apartment, pausing at the door to relish the moment. Newly living alone made Sebastian my first gentleman visitor. There was something fitting about it. That the man who saw me for me, embraced my contradictions and challenged me to be braver, would be the first man I'd get busy with on my sofa.

We entered and I let the heavy door slam behind us, our lips joined with a fury. My hands explored the contour of his shoulders.

In one swift motion, he hiked my legs around his hips, kissing my collarbone.

"I want you so bad right now," he said.

I leaned forward to whisper in his ear. "What are you waiting for?"

He took my mouth so hard we slammed into the wall. His desire only flaring mine. Clothes tangled me like a net. Dizzy with want, I didn't realize Sebastian carried me to the bedroom until he kicked the door closed behind us. I landed with a bounce at the foot of my bed for a front row view as Sebastian removed his shirt.

I imagined the sun kissed skin from our trip, but unlike then, his chest was scarred from his attack and subsequent surgery. A violent, physical reminder of how much had transpired since the first time I saw him running shirtless on the beach.

His wounds you could see; mine were hidden. Together, we'd become greater than the sum of our broken parts.

I stood and crossed to him, gently tracing his scars with my finger before feathering kisses along their trail. I spoke to them as much as him. "I'm so sorry for everything. For wasting time..."

Sebastian tilted my head up, his eyes tender. "Never say sorry again. We're together now. Let's live a life where we do what we want. And love like it's our last day."

"I'd love that."

"What else would you love?" He gathered my braids in one hand, tugging gently to guide my head back and nibble my throat.

Tingles raced to my fingertips as I released a moan.

"Oh, you like that, do you?"

"Mmmm," was all I could muster, my mind already clouded with expectation.

I scooted further onto the bed until I sat, then slipped off my shirt and pants, leaving me in a peacock blue lace bra and panties. His eyes widened.

"Damn. Matched set. I can get used to this."

"Don't. I'm on a fixed income."

"I'm not," he said.

He slipped off my satin underwear, parting my legs to put that amazing tongue of his to work.

I grabbed a handful of curls, soft and luscious. Just like the rest of him. The familiar fantasy I'd had since losing him emerged: the two of us naked on a beach at night, making love. Moving as one with moonlight rippling around us on the ocean's surface. We'd—pleasure claimed me, a rage of color taking hold. Reds, purples, electric pinks—I arched, ecstasy waving over me like a hot ocean, radiating vibrations from my core, across my face, down my legs. My fingers tangled in Sebastian's hair, then lost all strength, flopping away as I lay boneless. My heart pounded in my chest as I lay recovering.

I cracked my eyes open to see Sebastian remove his pants and slip on protection.

"Where have you been my whole life?" I exhaled, basking in the afterglow as he crawled on top of me.

"Right here, baby. Better get used to it." Sebastian entered with a deep thrust, releasing a throaty groan. Pleasure broke me in two, sending the room spinning. Slipping away, I grasped his solidness to anchor myself in the moment—our moment. His shoulders flexed like the Adonis he was. My fingers explored every inch of him until he took my nipple in his mouth, sucking while I—

Oh, my fucking God!

His thrusts sent fresh waves of ecstasy careening around my brain. Just when I thought our love making was winding down, he'd move me into a new position, then start again. Each round topping the last until we collapsed in a tangled, panting heap.

Holy shit.

Is this guy for real?

Yes.

And he's all mine.

Chapter 38

SEBASTIAN

My eyes opened to darkness, Barbara's naked body draped over mine. Her head snuggled against my shoulder. The amber glow from outside cast just enough light for me to see the room.

I'd been in this apartment before, when Tammy lived here. Brought her greens from the garden. Back then, the space was as beat up as the poor girl was herself. But no more. Fresh paint and a bed so solid it never creaked, despite the most epic lovemaking I'd ever had. Barbara flared a primal longing in me. One that seeped deep within my bones. All that pent-up frustration was worth the wait.

I tilted my head to watch her sleep. Skin so smooth it looked liquid. A hint of a smile creased her slumbering cheeks. *I like to think I had something to do with that.* But why was she here? Living on 6th Street? She must have had a blowup with her dad to justify a move to my neighborhood. Barbara wanted out of her dad's apartment, but a woman with her means had better options. I only lived here because of my mom. Well, that, and because it was home. Warts and all, I couldn't imagine myself living somewhere else. But hostilities with Mo had me wondering if it was time for that to change.

Barbara's remark about her underwear popped to mind. *Fixed income. Don't get used to it.* I'd been to where she grew up with her dad. He didn't seem to be a destitute man, standing kingly in his palace. He'd offered a fortune to keep me away from Barbara. He read the file, getting every detail of who I was. Or had been, before I went to law school, had a job...

Fuck me.

The lawsuit.

Glass shattered outside, as kids marauded at nothing-good-happens-o'clock. The soundtrack to the worst realization of my life. We weren't supposed to talk, let alone be together. As a couple.

No way some bullshit case against my racist employer would stop me from being with the woman I love.

There. I said it. *Love.*

I loved Barbara, and that meant more to me than some stupid job.

I wiggled out from under her and paced by the drawn shades.

I had to fix this.

If Xervo settled out of court—

"Come back to bed," a groggy Barbara mumbled, patting the spot I'd abandoned.

I padded across the room and slipped under the covers. Kissing her forehead, I wondered how I got so lucky, and what it meant for our future. Her dad and the whole Xervo mess chased sleep away. I lay barely breathing.

"I can hear you thinking, Mr. Kingsbury." Barbara's eyes were open and alert, blinking at me in the darkness.

"It's late. Let's talk tomorrow."

"Nope. Now." Barbara sat up, positioning her pillows against her headboard as if settling in for a good show. But where to start?

"You're serious?"

"I've got nowhere to be in the morning and something tells me you'll sleep better once you clear your mind."

She was right. Denying these inexplicable knowing moments prevented me from leaning into the magic. I needed more of that, more of her. Especially amidst the world's ugliness and work's madness. Fuck the world because they were out to fuck us, and not in the way I wanted. If we didn't look out for ourselves, who would? Who cared about the two naked people in this bed more than we did?

I hiked myself up to lean on the headboard, sighing. "The trial. How are we supposed to survive that and still be together? There's no ethical work-around."

"We both agree Xervo did us wrong."

"No argument."

"I can't drop the case, and I'd never ask you to leave a job for me. We could wait it out? It'll be over in a few weeks?"

I turned my head to her, the cloud storming across my face hidden by the shadowy bedroom. Probably for the best.

"I take it you don't like that idea?"

"Nope. I almost died. While I was getting pummeled, the only thing I regretted besides disappointing Mom was never seeing you again. So no, I'm not letting my asshole boss keep us apart."

"We could get suspended or disbarred..."

"No one is going to disbar us over this. At worst, we'd earn a reprimand."

"You act like that's nothing. Who'd hire us after that?" Barbara said.

Her agitation escalated, so I slid over and scooped her in, resting her head on my chest. "I'm not sure I'm cut out for corporate law."

"What?!" She pulled away, but I held tight.

"Stop for a second and listen."

Her tension faded, so I continued. "I love the law. But I'm sick of working for an asshole like Barr. There's got to be a way to be a lawyer and not work at a company that makes my skin crawl. No day passes without me wishing he'd let me go instead of you. That's not normal."

"To be jealous of an unemployed woman? Yeah, not normal."

"You've been on your own all these months. How's that been going?"

"Lonely. The freedom has been indescribable. Apart from my dwindling bank account, I'm great. But I don't get paid if we lose, so I literally can't afford to fail."

I debated asking the one question on my mind. Relocating from a Fifth Avenue luxury apartment to an Avenue C tenement was a mighty fall. And she'd done it in the blink of an eye, which seemed to be how she made all her decisions. She weighed options and plowed ahead, no matter how difficult.

I sat upright to face her. "Why are you broke? I thought your family had money?"

Barbara took her time answering, twisting the sheets. "We do. Tons of it, but I won't take a single penny. Not anymore. Not after what he did."

"I'm not following. What happened?"

I left her to reflect, staying quiet until she was ready. After a few minutes, her breath hitched as she began to cry. I squeezed her knee, a reminder that I was here and supported her. She sniffed, head bowed, before wiping her eyes with the back of her hand. I hated making her upset, but we had a lot of catching up to do.

"He sold me out. He knew I was getting laid off and not only did nothing, he encouraged it."

Of course.

I sighed. "His firm works for Barr. Sometimes it feels like they're the in-house counsel and I'm the consultant. I try keeping up, but I'm always two steps behind and reeling."

"So he hasn't involved you in the case at all?"

"They've got your dad's team working on it, and it's been mum. Barr drags me in to vent or threaten to shred evidence. I talk him back into the real world, then he storms off and we repeat it all the next day. You'd think his pricey lawyers would handle that."

Barbara hugged herself. The pain of having her family's company oppose her in court had to hurt. Even more than a blood brother leaving you lifeless in a park. I could get away from Mo, but the mighty Gregory Washington would always be her dad.

My conversation with him came roaring back. Despite my ignorance of his business dealings, he was convinced otherwise. I'd forgotten about his comment until now. The one about Xervo's pending VC investment. Regardless, dumping payroll and tanking your daughter's career were bloodless moves for a guy who supposedly loved his kid.

"What is it?" Barbara asked.

It seemed pointless to hide my visit.

"I went to your Fifth Avenue apartment. And met your dad."

"What? Why?"

"I expected to find you there and sweep you off your feet, but you'd already moved out. He accused me of being a bad influence, which I might be, but not in the way he suggested. He kept talking about some Xervo investment and accusing me of trying to derail everything."

She folded her arms. Were the room lighter, I'd likely see steam escaping from her ears.

"That has to be it. They were padding the financials in advance of VC financing. He didn't give a rat's ass that I was swept up in it. That's when I realized it must be business as usual for him. He sharks around town, devouring unsuspecting people and spitting out their bones." Barbara shivered. "He raised me to have principles, to not dishonor the 'great Washington name.' But look at what he does for a living? Once I understood, I couldn't stay. Or use the family money. Not anymore."

I didn't want to pile on, but as long as we were coming clean, I needed to, as well. Nothing I'd say would change her disillusionment in her dad, but she had to know. For the first time, I was glad not to have a father. One less person to disappoint me.

"I've never mentioned, but I have a juvenile record. Some petty thug stuff, some darker. It's all in the past and all sealed. Barbara, he knew. He waved a background report in my face and spouted everything about me but my underwear size. Fuck, he probably knows that, too. Then he..." I stopped before telling her about the bribe.

"Let me guess. He offered to buy you off?"

I swallowed hard. "Yeah."

"God damn it!" She threw her hands up before flipping up the sheets to stand. "How can he do this? He tries it every time I date someone he doesn't like! It's insane. Who does that?"

As pissed as she was, and as supportive as I wanted to be, naked Barbara paced the room, oblivious to how gorgeous she was. I mentioned my criminal record, and she ignored it. Had she heard me?

The streetlight haloed her curves as she moved about the room, breasts swaying... Her long legs disappearing and reappearing behind her foot board as she approached and receded from the window. I blinked carnal thoughts away.

"Did you hear what I said? About my record?"

"I already knew. It came out because of the beating. But I'm glad you told me. I wasn't sure what to believe, then the whole Mo nonsense..." she waved her arm. "It doesn't matter to me. That's in the past, right?"

It was about to be, but I didn't want to worry her. "Yeah, ancient history."

Liar.

"What are we going to do about my dad?" she asked.

"The two of you will work it out. You moved out. You're independent, doing your own thing."

"This is the first time I've had my own place. Before, I lived with other people and dipped into the family credit card whenever I wanted. There was always a safety net to catch me. Now that's gone. What if I can't do this adult thing on my own?"

When I started out, having a financial safety net wasn't an option. Once I turned 18, Mom was adamant I stand on my own two feet. It was hard, especially with my neighborhood reputation. No one wanted to hire me. Thought it was some ruse to launder money, but I got through it. The times I stumbled, Mom would be there to dust me off and tell me not to fuck up again. Eventually it stuck, and I made baby steps toward the person I'd become. Thinking of Barbara, it had to suck to learn self-sufficiency at our age and with smothering expectations of perfection.

"If you need help, let me know. I have savings."

"Thanks, but I really want to do this myself," Barbara said. "I'll be okay for a bit longer. A settlement from Xervo is a cushion I'm counting on. My Bergdorf concierge has left 20 messages. I don't have the heart to tell her the truth. That I'm shopping on Orchard Street now."

"Bergdorf concierge? I've no clue what to do with that. Sorry."

"Aargh!" she yelled, waving her arms. "It's just so frustrating! How did I let myself get tangled in this mess?"

"Counselor? If you're going to strut about naked, all hot and flustered, I'd prefer you do it in my lap."

She looked down at her body. Then at me, shaking her head. "Wish I could, but you rode me rough, cowboy. And you have to work in a few hours."

Barbara spun to the dresser at the foot of her bed. There was barely enough room to slide the drawer open, but she snatched a satin sleep shirt that fluttered down over her curves like liquid silver. Disappointment flickered across my brain.

She lay back down and hiked the covers up to her chin, grinding her jaw as she blinked at the ceiling.

I crept closer. "You know, I have something that works wonders to release tension."

She bristled, but I could feel her defenses melting as my hand inched under her nightshirt to caress her bottom.

"What is that?" She said, as I kissed the hollow between her collarbones.

I slid her on top of my lap. Neither of us got much sleep after that.

Chapter 39

SEBASTIAN

After reuniting with Barbara, work became a prison. We'd been together every day, always at my place. For ethical reasons, she told me nothing about her case during our stolen moments. Seven days of pure bliss. I hadn't been back to her bedroom since our epic night and ached for her when apart.

When I handed her a burner phone, she laughed. But it'd become our lifeblood. We'd text all day and into the evening if we didn't meet, keeping us bound at a time when contact could end our careers.

Don't leave a paper trail.

I'd be fine if we got caught, having been through worse. But Barbara? Her resume would take a bigger hit than it already had, and I refused to be the reason for her downfall. Again. Protecting her became the most important side hustle of my life.

Once this mess was settled, we'd rocket into our new life together. I'd yet to meet her brother up in Boston, and my mom wanted to drag us out to Pennsylvania to see her sister. We talked about returning to a beach for moonlit passion until our essential parts fell off. One day. Soon.

I rolled myself into my desk and refocused on the latest paperwork from Washington & Associates. The claimants were listed in a tiny column. I'd expected a bigger group to sign on, but seven was still an impressive number. I smiled, proud of all the hard work Barbara had done up to now. I spent my days wrangling Barr like a toddler. No matter the issue, he continually took the wrong path. The least human. His soul rot leaked everywhere. The longer I stayed, the more I feared catching his infection.

Part of me enjoyed the cat-and-mouse chase with Barbara. Danger thrilled; it always had. I'd too easily slipped back into habits I thought forgotten. But like comfortable shoes, they fit good as ever. Was Barr instinctively drawn to the darkness in me? Had he sensed a kindred spirit?

I'm not like Barr.

He's evil on purpose.

The choices I've made helped me survive.

I bucked the system for the right reasons.

My bare office stretched before me. I had three empty bookcases hauled away. No awards, no certificates of awesomeness. Everything I'd accomplished worth noting remained a secret, staying alive being chief among them. And turning my life around.

A transformation that dramatic proved Xervo could do it. But leadership had no plans to fulfill its potential. Be innovative and inclusive. Rake-in profits and have a thriving culture. The company didn't need to choose between revenue and people. I shared reams of data about the financial benefits of robust inclusion and belonging work. I suggested a second-chance program for system-involved individuals and brought Dante around to experience another way to live. Instead of support, Barr chided me for the unauthorized visit and demanded I check with the facilities team to be sure nothing was stolen.

Barr was spectacularly wrong about nearly everything. He and I hadn't seen eye to eye for so long, I almost enjoyed our arguments. They let me blow off steam and prevented me from doing something I'd regret.

I headed to his office, ignoring Yvonne's attempts to signal that it wasn't a good time.

I rapped on the open door with my knuckles.

"Got a minute?" I said, not waiting for an answer.

He looked up from the mound of paper on his desk, narrowing his eyes when he saw me. "What do you want?"

"Just your friendly reminder that it's not too late to settle."

He returned to his work. "Don't waste my time. They have no case."

"We both know they do. Washington & Associates advised you multiple times to end this, but you ignore the very people you hire to protect company interests."

He pretended to work, eyes on his shuffling pages. "I reject their advice—and yours—because you're gutless cowards running away with your tail between your legs at the first sign of trouble. Worthless, every one of you."

How I wanted to sucker punch him right now. Upside the head, leaving a fist shaped indent without breaking a sweat. That wouldn't help my cause. But I knew something that would. I slipped a hand in my pocket to finger my cellphone.

"No proof, no case," he said with a sing-song lilt. As if saying it made his words true.

"This company's actions speak volumes. You fired staff, then turned around and replaced them with new people." I stared into his face to see if any remorse surfaced but none did.

He sat back, surveying me. "Ever since you arrived, we've been butting heads. Why is that? Where do your loyalties lie?"

"With Xervo, of course. Isn't that why you hired me?"

Liar. You'd stab him now and feed his heart to Barbara.

"I hired you to do my bidding. You work for me, remember?"

"I work for Xervo, not you personally. While I report to you, I'm a licensed attorney with professional obligations to the company as a whole."

Did this guy not understand the burdens of a practicing lawyer? To him, I was a paper pusher. But I had to study and pass both the state bar exam and a character fitness review, sealed juvy record notwithstanding. If anyone needed a character test, Marshall Barr was candidate number one. He'd never pass. Problem was, I had. I took an oath to uphold the constitution and chanced losing my license by blindly following him down the unethical path. No job was worth disbarment.

Barbara flashed to mind. Our actions weren't exactly on the up and up, either. But our circumstances were different. I skirted the law for love. To dive into my woman and wrap her in my arms. And legs. Never for the weasel in front of me. And never to hurt people intentionally for profit.

Barr flushed red, looking like a sputtering tea kettle. "I never should have hired you. You looked good on paper, but you've been an annoying pain in my ass, fighting me at every turn."

"I thought I joined a solid company with strong values. Instead, I found a closed-minded organization with enough ethical violations to make a gangster blush."

"You're weak. Following idiotic rules and regulations gets us nowhere. Someone has to make the tough choices. You've got no stones."

"I've got stones. It's taken every ounce of strength not to pummel you for your illegal bullshit."

No more anger management. Stuff deep breathing and positive visualization. Not anymore. Barr was dirty enough to let others take the fall. But unlike last time, I wouldn't let myself get cornered in an alley while icy cuffs snapped over my wrists.

"Who the fuck do you think you are?" Barr blasted. "No one tells me how to run my company."

I slapped my palm on his desk with such force, he bounced in his chair. "You're a CEO not a crime boss. This behavior has to stop. It ends here."

"Is that a threat?" he said.

"A promise."

A smile crept across his face, exposing his tiny teeth. Like he'd never matured enough to deserve grown ones. He slithered his tongue over them before speaking. "If the handsome salary I pay you isn't good enough to keep you here, leave. Lawyers will line up around the block to work here. Hell, I might even quash this suit by hiring Washington back. One kind word, and she'll melt. They all do."

"You're disgusting."

"Yeah? Well, you're fired. For insubordination."

"I'm fired. You sure?"

"Absolutely. If you won't follow my direction, you don't deserve a paycheck."

"Good." I leaned my face so close, his sour breath turned my stomach. "Study my contract. Firing me for refusing to comply with illegal behavior triggers my parachute package."

I pulled my phone from my jacket pocket to show it's still recording.

"This conversation is uploading to the cloud. New York is a single-party consent state for recording." I tapped the red button to stop. "Don't waste both our time fighting my payout."

I righted myself in time to see his larynx bob as he swallowed. Quick as the slime he was, Barr bared his palms.

"Let's not be hasty."

"Too late. You fired me. I questioned, and you confirmed. We both know you'll never come clean with the board about why you forced me out, but I'd be happy to if you refuse to cut me loose. I'm sure you can dial up one of your patented lies to explain my generous compensation."

As my hand hit the doorknob, a delightful thought sprang to mind. "You make getting fired feel like a gift."

I slammed the door in his shocked face.

I couldn't help the extra bounce in my step, strolling home in the middle of the day. What I hadn't banked on was how quickly the neighborhood moms would mobilize. To them, my materializing mid-day didn't add up.

Mrs. Ferrante questioned me on the stairwell, not believing my lie about forgetting important work papers on my coffee table.

She ran across the hall to Mrs. Xie, who called her husband, who texted his sister, who worked with my mom at the DMV.

Not seven minutes after I kicked off my shoes, Mom was blasting me through my cellphone speaker.

The FBI should hire this crew.

"How could you let this happen?!" she yelled.

"The guy is the worst form of life. Better I leave than strangle him and get arrested for murder. Is that what you want?"

That comment calmed her down. "No. But what are you going to do? You need to work."

I hadn't gotten that far, thanks to the mom squad. In the past, I would have been on the phone with the job I turned down on the way home, on the off chance the person they hired didn't work out. But something stopped me. Watching Barbara succeed as a free agent proved there might be another career out there for me. One that nourished my soul instead of draining it. I needed time to think. And longer than seven minutes.

I laced my fingers behind my head as my mom's voice chattered from my phone on the kitchen counter.

"Sebastian, this is serious. Money doesn't grow on trees," she said.

"I'll figure it out. That's why I have savings."

"How much savings?"

"Enough." It was the first lie I'd told my mom since I was six. That time, I'd crawled on a chair to take cash out of the coffee can she hid on the top shelf in the kitchen cupboard. It was our rent money. But she went off to the movies and told me to eat leftovers instead of buying pizza. It was pizza night, and she knew it. I was good until that damn Gino's pizza rolls ad came on TV. It proved I was cosmically destined to have pizza. So, I took a few dollars and chowed down on two slices. When she noticed the can's label shifted, she beat me so hard I never lied to her again. Until now.

I had savings. I barely spent anything from my rising salary. And the stash from my last score meant I didn't have the loans that crippled most professionals for decades after graduation. I thought about buying an apartment uptown, like Mom nagged me to do. A showplace would prove that I'd "made it." But the more I saved, the more wrong it felt. This neighborhood was my home. I wasn't leaving it—and her—behind to live in a stuffy co-op with a bunch of strangers.

So savings accumulated. I'd stare at the figure in my bank account, wondering how that much money was mine. Until I stopped looking all together. Best I not track it. Knowing brought bad luck. It'd happened to nearly everyone I knew. Why would I be any different? By now, I likely had enough to buy a condo in a doorman building, but I only smelled trouble.

What did I need, anyway? Clothing for work, furniture basics, extra to have dinner out once in a while? And buy gardening supplies? So when the monthly emails arrived, I ignored them. They only linked to a dashboard to download my statements, but I never remembered the password.

Liar. It's your mom's birthday.

I sighed. I hated lying to her, and the longer we talked, the more likely it was she'd sniff me out. "I'm hanging up. Tell Mrs. Ferrante to mind her business."

I stripped to take a shower. I needed to wash every molecule of Barr off me. Hot streams of water penetrated my skin. I lathered my hair, vigorously scrubbing his slimy dealings away.

I was done with Xervo. Cut free from the twenty-ton anchor dragging me down. I'd been walking an ethical tightrope. It was a clear conflict of interest that would have landed me before a professional misconduct panel. And still could.

Funny thing was, I didn't care.

Back when I was in juvy, I'd spend hours plotting my escape. I swore to build a new life, away from all the people who'd betrayed me.

Once I started succeeding, I knew deep down I should move. I stalled, telling myself someone like me wouldn't hack it uptown. Besides, living here made me happy. In this neighborhood, I was King. I was Sebastian—a somebody. As annoying as it was to have my neighbors gossiping about my business, it came from a place of love. From personal investment in my success. They did it because they cared.

That devotion would be impossible to replicate anywhere else.

And I didn't want to try.

Barbara thrived here now. She'd made so many connections, it was breathtaking, weaving herself into the fabric as if she'd been here all along. I couldn't imagine she'd want to leave, so there was zero reason I had to, either.

Since childhood, I'd been sitting on the sidelines, afraid darker elements would claw me back. But in doing so, I'd missed out on so much goodness. Peers on the street eyed me warily.

Was I in or out?

One of us or one of them?

Until this moment in the shower, I wasn't sure. But now I knew. I was one of them. Of them in every way that mattered. Breathing the same air, walking the same streets. It was time for me to stop fearing who I was. Make peace with my past so I can drop the baggage and move on.

I shut off the water and swept the curtain aside, habitually reaching for my trusty hand towel, but stopping before making contact. The full-size set Barbara bought me hung unused. I had it for weeks, but never gave it another thought. My hand towel was too gross for her to contemplate touching. An unidentifiable shade of gray. Using it was a mindless habit I'd had since before I learned to shave. Mom and I shared one matching set. Mom had the bath towel and I took the hand towel and washcloth. It was all I ever needed. Good enough. Meanwhile, Barbara's bath sheet hung behind my bathroom door, looking big enough to hide a city bus. I was so busy defending my plot of ground, I failed to notice how small it was. I'd outgrown it, or rather, my notions of what it could be. Of what I could be if I only trusted myself.

God, how long had it been since I truly trusted my instincts?

Ignored the fear screaming in my ears and pushed forward, anyway?

Do the opposite of what I'd normally do.

My neck straightened.

Trust yourself.

Think bigger.

I balled the tatters of my hand towel and shot a perfect arc across the room into the wastebasket. It landed with a disgruntled thwack. I stepped out and wrapped soft terry around me like a cloak. It eagerly sucked the wetness off my body, as if impatient for me to get going. Or maybe that was me, finally ready to embrace the life I wanted.

Chapter 40

BARBARA

Sebastian and I sat eating at his little dining table. But he'd been doing more food swirling than ingesting since he shared the news about getting fired. Veins in his temples bulged as he relived the argument with our former boss.

"Am I a fool for going at Barr? I just couldn't take his crap anymore."

"Of course not. You lasted longer than I expected."

Sebastian looked up. "Yeah?"

"Definitely. I'm sure he deserved worse than whatever you said. You'll find a job fast. Don't worry."

He shrugged, a fork finally passing between his lips for the first time. The taste registered on his face. "This is delicious. You made this?"

"Your pantry is bare, Mr. Bachelor. Lucky for you, I brought my own ingredients."

His face softened. "You are an amazing woman. Have I told you this before?"

"Once or twice."

Sebastian leaned forward for a kiss, a delicious, peppery bite of our watercress salad lingering on his tongue. It was almost as tasty as him. Wavy hair, and the crown of his snake tattoo peeking out through the deep V of his T-shirt. The incredible design featured a cobra winding around his torso with two heads positioned across his chest. Covered at work, you'd never suspect a tender soul like his would have such a striking image inked beneath his suit.

"Tell me about the tattoo. Is that from your old life or new?"

He leaned back, his muscular forearms resting on the table. "Both. I got tattooed in my twenties as a gift to myself for passing the bar. This place, this neighborhood is home. And family, I'm sure you've noticed since moving here."

"I have, yes."

"I never wanted to forget where I came from. People look at me different, now. I wanted a reminder of my struggle so I'd never fall again."

He stood to remove his shirt, reaching for my hand. "I'll give you a tour."

I let him place my fingers on the warm nape of his back. His smooth skin firm to the touch, rich and inviting. I tore my attention away from his stellar physique to listen.

"The scales are bricks to represent the neighborhood. It starts with me and my mom at the bottom, winds around to when Dante ditched me on the wrong side of the wall..."

Vignettes appeared in windows within the graffiti-covered bricks, marking each milestone he honored. I circled his torso, tracing his life story with my fingers.

"I passed the bar, then went to work..."

"With a crown and scepter, I see."

"Hey, my name is Kingsbury."

"It suits you, my King." I raised my face to meet his. He pressed a tender kiss to my lips before directing my attention to his chest. As if I wasn't already distracted by his lean pecs.

"The two-headed cobra is both fierce and loving. Fierce, if you cross the people I love, tender for those who deserve it."

He looked me dead in the eye, saying more with a glance than words could ever express.

Sebastian's hands settled high on my waist, thumbs caressing the underside of my breasts and sending my desire skyrocketing. I'd never been with anyone like him, where my attraction to his mind was almost stronger than the physical embers sizzling between us.

Almost.

There was no denying the appealing package.

I kissed his chest, dwelling on a patch of bare skin. "You've left a blank spot in the snake... what goes here?"

"A special someone. The person who squeezes my heart like a fist and won't let go."

I looked up at his face. "How will you know? Isn't it risky to put someone on your skin?"

"What's life without risks?"

The second our lips touched, pleasure jolted my body to attention. Sebastian radiated everything I craved. To be heard, loved, and desired so much, the whole world and all its craziness slipped away when together. My heart threatened to explode as he devoured me, like the snake on his chest, consuming prey. Only I wanted to be absorbed, every inch of me melded into him. Our tongues explored with minds of their own as our hands did the same, his muscles twitching under my touch as he struggled to hold himself back. Forever the gentlemen, despite his street past. I dug my nails into his skin, clawing closer, signaling my permission to unleash the bad boy. Abandon rules and live for the moment.

"Please..." I whimpered, to which he answered with a sexy moan.

Permission granted, he cupped my bottom with his hands, hiking me up so my legs wrapped around his body. Heat seared me as his bare chest connected with my torso. Even my thin cotton top was an obstacle too far, and I imagined my shirt vaporizing so nothing lay between us.

My drapey T slid off my shoulder, leaving him free to nibble my collarbone as he walked us to his darkened bedroom. He deposited me on the bed, then we made quick work of our clothes. One flip left me dangerously straddling him where he sat.

The light filtering through his open door from the living room highlighted every contour of his body as we settled, grinding against each other. I moaned, my head dropping back as he suckled my breast to attention.

"The more I have you, the more I want," he spoke into my skin, the vibrations adding to the ones already creeping up my spine.

I slid off him to reach for a condom in his nightstand, sliding it on so I could follow, taking him deep within me.

Our sighs harmonized, the joy of contact a blissful relief as reality exceeded expectations. He shifted his hand between my legs, massaging me into a frenzy. We often made love, pacing ourselves and savoring each moment. Today was raw and needy, passionate and...

Hot waves of pleasure began at my core and shot out to my fingertips. Every hair follicle, pulsing and hissing with life like Sebastian's snake. He followed with a hard thrust and deep groan of his own. I collapsed onto his chest, forcing him flat onto the bed. My braids fanned around us like the first sun rays at dawn. That's what Sebastian was to me. Light. Hope. Love. A new beginning that I never wanted to end.

I brushed a tickle on my nose. My eyes fluttered open in the darkness to find Sebastian teasing me with the tip of one of my braids.

"Hey," he whispered.

I yawned and snuggled into the crook of his arm, tucking further under the covers.

"Why are you up?" I mumbled.

"Something popped to mind and can't sleep. It's about your case with Xervo."

The word "Xervo" knocked some sleepiness away, so I hiked up on an elbow to force myself awake. "What? What did I forget?" A yawn escaped as I spoke.

"You forgot yourself."

I flopped back down. "You leave me boneless, then expect me to be alert in the middle of the night? Can't this wait til morning?"

"You were their lead attorney for years. Now that I'm gone, it's occurred to me how improper it'd be for me to launch a case against them. They'll probably file an ethics complaint if they lose. Make such a fuss, the State will yank your law license. Or Barr will try some other dirty trick that'll cost you in the long run."

Dim light from the street filtered into Sebastian's bedroom, where worried eyes peered back at me. I loved that he was considering me and my career. It showed how much he cared.

My hand cupped his face, his stubble scratchy on my palms. "Sweetie... don't worry. While not ideal, it's the only way for my clients to get the justice they deserve."

"If you ask for a postponement—"

"No. What? I can't—"

"Listen. If you postpone, they'll have time to find another attorney..."

That got my attention.

"What you saying? Shit, Sebastian. Why did you wait until two days before the trial to drop this load on me?"

"It's late, I know. But I can't shake the notion that this case is risking your career. I'm thinking of the future—"

"So am I!" I hopped up, the chilly air erupting goosebumps on my skin. I searched the room for a shirt. No way I was having this debate buck naked, however quick. I would never abandon my clients, and it was unthinkable for him to suggest it. Even my 2 a.m. groggy brain puzzled that much.

I found my top and slipped it on. "Let me get this straight. You're so worried I'll thrash Xervo in court that you want me to quit? Tell me how that computes?"

He sat up straighter. "Say Xervo loses. They'll be bitter and Barr will seek revenge. On you. I wouldn't put it past him to start a vendetta that brings you down. If that happens, this whole case is a loss. Even if you win, you lose."

I swallowed the salty tears trickling down my throat, willing myself to remain calm. Showing emotion now would only confirm his point. That I was too weak to be successful on my own.

But this conversation insulted me to the core. Was he honestly convinced I should walk away from a case I'd sacrificed everything to win? My emotional and financial stake was impossible to verbalize. I would never abandon the people I rallied to an important cause. They believed in me and deserved a champion. Betraying that trust would haunt me far longer than anything Xervo did. That he brought it up at all was a gut punch from the last person I expected to doubt me.

Sebastian sat, legs folded in bed, white sheet stretched across his wide limbs. How could a man who accepted street justice deny me my day in court? After all the racism, wisecracks, and illegal firings, I earned an opportunity to hold them accountable. The fight was mine as much as my clients'. Why couldn't Sebastian see that? The two of us had been on the same page since I face planted in the sand. Why did he have so little faith in me now? Echoes of Joe rang loud, but I shook them off.

I slipped on my jeans without a word.

"Wait? You're leaving?" He asked.

I said nothing, zipping them as I headed for the bedroom door.

He popped up, his hand anchoring it shut just as mine reached the doorknob. "I'm trying to protect you. What happens after? Think of the consequences."

"You sound like my dad, treating me like a fragile porcelain doll, up on a shelf gathering dust while life passes her by."

"That's not fair."

"But ambushing me in the middle of the night two days before trial? That's fair?"

Quiet settled in, our heavy breathing the only thing passing between us.

"I'm sorry," he whispered.

"Me too." My words meaning something far different than his.

Sebastian nodded, regret sinking in. "Can I walk you home?"

"I want to be alone right now."

He released the door and stepped back, scratching his head.

"I only mentioned it because I love you."

"You can convince yourself otherwise, but deep down, you're acting from a place of fear. Or ignorance. I'm too sleepy and mad to decide which, and at this moment, I don't care. Either way, you're wrong. I organized this case on my own and will see it through. I am strong and capable enough to win. It's sad you can't see that."

My words resounded in the room as I made my way out, slamming his apartment door so hard I shuddered. Or perhaps the shakiness came from my profound disappointment in the man I loved.

Chapter 41

Barbara

I was sleep deprived the next morning, thanks to Sebastian's godly bedroom skills and 2 a.m. dumpster fire of a suggestion. Leave my case? What came over him? I'd ignored his texts and calls. Only my Aunt Evelyn's panic message jolted me out of final courtroom preparations. Months of work brought me to this point. The trial was tomorrow, and this urgent visit to my dad's frayed my last nerve.

Meet me at your father's apartment.

Was he sick? Or dying?

Or had he cooked up a desperate ploy to undermine me before court?

My mind flashed to Sebastian, but I blinked the image away. We'd get past our fight, but I still smarted from his lack of confidence in me. One man problem at a time...

As I entered the familiar elevator car at Dad's, a cacophony of memories pinged around my brain. Me in a school uniform, the green, blue and white plaid of the parochial academy I attended before going to the private school with the maroon uniforms. Me and Mom, holding hands. I'd look up into her deep brown eyes that smiled without words. She was the force of nature I tried to be, failing to fill her shoes after she died. I was away at college and returned home to a shell of a man where my father had been.

I braced my hand on the elevator's wood paneling, desperate to touch something that once lived.

"I miss you, Mom. I don't know what to do about Dad. I can't even recognize who he's become. If you were here, none of this would have happened."

Would my words reach her? Would she hear me? If I ever needed her love and protection, it was right now.

For this conversation.

The car passed the ninth floor, so I fished in my purse for a tissue to wipe my eyes and nose. I used the brass elevator button plate as a mirror, just as I had my whole life. I dabbed under my eye to prevent my mascara from smearing.

Salvageable.

I tugged my shirt neat and stared at my reflection.

I was me, but not. My braids were fun and looked well. People complemented me on them and Sebastian put them to great use in the bedroom. But I still felt like I was playing a role. Doing what others expected of me. Everything about my life was new, with important pieces yet to fall into place. When I pictured this conversation with Dad, it didn't happen with anxiety churning my gut raw. But here I was.

The elevator doors opened, and I walked to our apartment door. For the first time since grammar school, I had no key.

It's not home anymore.

I rang the doorbell, then heard footsteps approaching.

Aunt Evelyn flung it wide with a pained look on her face. Before I could enter, she slipped out, holding a gap ajar with her hand.

"You will have a lot of questions, but I ask that you let him finish. It's taken years for him to get to this point. So hear him out."

My blood drained. "What's going on?"

"Come." She guided us into the apartment. All appeared the same, except for the husk of a man at the far end of the living room, holding his head in both hands. He sat, not in his usual spot on the couch, but in a wingback chair by the darkened fireplace. Alone.

"Dad?" I crossed to him, sitting on the edge of the coffee table. But he didn't acknowledge me.

"Greg. Go ahead. It's time you told her." Outwardly calm, Evelyn stood behind the sofa, gripping the poor cushions for dear life.

She mistook my confused stare and creaked a stiff, reluctant smile.

This was absurd.

The yoke of emotional control we constrained ourselves with was so unnecessary. And for what? To save face? To look strong? What a farce.

Before I knew it, a laugh burst out of my mouth. Fresh, authentic, and so overdue! The outburst shocked my dad to attention and my aunt's expression warped in confusion.

But I couldn't stop. The rich laughter kept coming, doubling me over where I sat. "We're all so ridiculous! This formality?" Laughs rolled until my stomach ached and tears squeezed out of my eyes. "Why can't we let go of all this pompous shit and just be? Fuck! We're family! Oh my God, I forgot what a stick up my butt I used to have."

The two of them watched me like the curiosity I'd become until my laughs subsided. I dabbed my lingering tears away with my index finger, then pressed on my knees to standing. "I'm getting a glass of water. Want anything from the kitchen?"

I took three steps across the room and looked back. The two of them frozen in shock, not knowing what to do or say.

"If you want something, it's okay to ask." I said.

"Tea would be lovely, thank you," Evelyn said. "Greg? Do you need anything?"

He sat up straight. "I'd like a hug from my daughter."

My spirit soared. I crossed to him so fast I nearly knocked over a lamp. But I wouldn't have paused a second to pick it up. By the time I reached him, he was standing with his arms dangling limp at his sides.

I squeezed tight. It took a few moments, but eventually he bent his elbows to draw me in. No words exchanged between us, but I felt his sorrow. And regret.

His damp tears on my shoulder said he was sorry.

My tighter squeeze said it was okay, but it'd take time to regain trust.

His stroking my hair said he'd do what he could to make it right.

I squeezed his shoulders and stepped away. "I'll get that tea."

"Make it two," Dad said.

"Two teas, and why don't you open a bottle of Zinfandel for me. And don't skimp on the pour."

I navigated the kitchen as if I'd never left. Every item in its proper place, the same spots my mother kept them. My movements flowing like an ancient river etched in my consciousness. After retrieving the metal tray my parents got as a wedding present, I put two cups and saucers on it. My mom loved this set. It was a gift from her grandmother. White bone China with delicate pink flowers on vines rimming the lip. I grabbed the glass honey pot from the cupboard and added fresh lemon wedges to a serving dish. Next, I poured milk into a tiny cream pitcher. And tossed a few almond biscotti on the tray from the cookie jar. Reckless with no plate, their crumbs marring the otherwise pristine assembly.

But that's who I was now.

While I honored my past, I'm forging a future no longer bound by rigid family expectations. I'm tossing loose biscotti all over the damn place and it felt amazing.

When I entered the room holding both tray handles, I found the two of them chatting. My father kneeled to kindle a fire. He hadn't made one in ages, and the homey sight warmed me more than the flames ever could.

I set the tea down on the coffee table and handed Evelyn hers while Dad played Boy Scout, poking the tender blaze.

"Out with it," I said. "Why am I here?"

I raised the stem of my waiting wineglass and swirled twice to check out the legs before sipping.

My dad cleared his throat, still nursing his fire. "My role at the firm is not what you think."

He stopped, but I let the silence linger, urging him to continue. "After your mom died, my work quality slipped. I had trouble thinking clearly and managing the house, and you and your brother. It was too much for me. Following negotiations, I agreed to bring in other partners. Over the years, my majority stake was severely diluted."

"But it's still yours, right? You have the largest share of anyone?" I asked, tension rising in my chest. I didn't like where this was going.

"No. My stake is the smallest among the five partners. The other four vote as a block, stalling everything I try to do. Eventually, I stopped trying. I wanted my name off the company, but they refused. Instead, they give me additional salary compensation. In exchange, I agreed to step out of the day-to-day affairs of the business. Hiring, client development, operations—"

"There's nothing left!" My heart broke. Being pushed out of a thriving business you built from scratch was unfathomable. But suddenly the last decade made a lot more sense.

"I'm a figurehead. I schmooze at client functions, speak at conferences, and..."

He caught my aunt's watchful gaze, fishing for permission.

"Go on." Evelyn took a graceful seat on the couch, her ballet training still evident.

"What? Please." I asked.

My aunt urged him on with a raised teacup. I squatted next to him by the fire, flames reflecting in his watery eyes. I hadn't seen him this bereft since the funeral.

"They use me to deal with unsavory situations. If our clients wander into the unethical, they send me in to manage the mess. They started calling me 'the janitor.'"

My hand slapped over my mouth in shock. "Oh, Dad."

How awful for him. A proud Black man with his name on the door? Being called the janitor? It had to be humiliating for him to tell me.

"This explains so much."

He shrugged.

"Is that why you haven't been able to hire more Black attorneys?"

"Yes."

"Or Black employees?"

"Yes."

"Or women?"

"Yes."

"I asked about bringing you in many times, on your merits, but they refused every time. Since then, two other partners brought family in without a word of resistance. The picture has been clear to me for ages, but what choice did I have? I'm trapped in a prison with my name emblazoned across the door. They pay me well and I needed that when you and Brian were going to college. But this mess with Xervo…"

"Tell me." I urged.

"I can't. You're opposing counsel."

"Christ, Dad. Work with me." He couldn't start down the "coming clean" road and toss up a roadblock. Not after all we've been through.

He pressed his lips together, thinking before answering. "What I can say is that it's good you're not at Xervo anymore. Bad things are on the horizon. That's why I encouraged them to lay you off. Client privilege prevented me from warning you, but I did my best to get you safe."

I slipped onto my butt from my squat on the floor.

He got me fired… to protect me?

The news fit the man I'd known my whole life. But how did that match his behavior lately? Maybe it explained it all and I'd been too self-righteous to notice. I was so busy being angry at him, it never occurred to me that his motives were anything but nefarious. Being rejected by Xervo left wounds that were still healing. But I woke each morning elated to be free—of corporate work and family expectations. And as the case proceeded, I'd grown into a woman I loved. One relieved to have her father back.

As my mind rewrote the last few months, shame creeped in for not giving him the benefit of the doubt. But to be fair, he didn't seem to want it. Never once did he give me an inkling he deserved my continued loyalty. But he had it now and would forever more.

"Dad, you have an employment discrimination case. You've been marginalized at your own firm because of your race. Given less choice assignments and called a janitor for fuck's sake."

"That's the kindest of the terms they use…"

"My point exactly. This is actionable."

"I'm so close to retirement. It'd be easier if I just fade into—"

"No. We're not letting this go. You deserve compensation and your name off the door you paid for. If they're going to run around being scum bags, they can ruin their reputations. Not ours."

Dad smiled but it quickly faded. "I can't. Everyone will know how they treated me. How I let them treat me. I won't recover. Ever. How am I supposed to show my face in public after that?"

He rose from fire-tending to drop into his chair. Shaking his head, likely contemplating scenes of his future existence and not liking the early reviews. A year ago, I'd be there with him. Stuffing the nasty mess into a closet and barring the door with my back. But I'd changed. I was finally doing the job meant for me my whole life: holding corporations accountable. Who deserved justice more than my dad? Who endured outrageous indignity for so long?

I rose onto my knees, grasping his hands in each of mine to better face him. "We're going to make this right, I promise. But first, I have to kick Xervo's ass. It'll be a good warm-up for reclaiming your name and getting you a big enough settlement that you won't ever have to work again. Unless you want to, of course. Who knows? Maybe I'll start a firm and hire you myself!"

He laughed. Deep, yet exuberant, the vibrations reached the recesses of my heart. I used to lie awake at night listening to my parents whisper together in the evenings by this very fire. An eruption of his laughter, paired with a chorus of Mom's shushes. I'd bolt to my bedroom door, opening it wide to find out what was so funny. They'd say I'd understand when I was older and shoo me back to bed. It'd been so long since I heard him laugh, I'd forgotten how handsome he was when happy. Between mourning my mom's death and losing control of his firm, I realized how little he had to smile about in recent years. But that was about to change.

"Me work for you?" Dad said with a curious lilt, like the idea was just crazy enough to be outstanding.

"Tomorrow could be the beginning. A warm-up for Washington vs. Washington. We'll win, of course, then Leslie will write an article about our triumph."

My storyboard set his head bobbing with approval. I got it whenever he read my report card and liked what he saw. In grammar school, I'd pace our apartment, waiting for him to come home from work, pouncing the second he walked through the door. He usually arrived late, and by then, I'd worked myself into an absolute tizzy of anticipation. I waved my grades in his face before he dropped his keys or removed his coat. That's how desperately I needed his approval. His nods meant the world to me. And still did.

"I'll think about it."

"You do that." I polished off my wine and stood to head out.

"Stay. We can have an early dinner," Evelyn said.

"Next time. I have a big day tomorrow." I loved that there would be a next time. And a next, and a next. I kissed her cheek. "I can't wait for you both to meet Sebastian. He's amazing."

And he was, despite his middle-of-the-night nonsense. My afternoon with Dad showed what a gift forgiveness could be. My over-active outrage at Sebastian from the night before had already dissipated.

Dad cleared his throat, squirming uncomfortably in his chair. "About Mr. Kingsbury…"

"He told me, Dad. Don't hold his past against him. I think you'll love him and his feisty mother, Glenora. She reminds me a lot of Mom."

"That's saying something," he said.

"Yeah. It is."

Chapter 42

SEBASTIAN

"Sebastian!" Mo's mom pulled me into the same tight embrace I'd enjoyed since age seven. Her argument with my mom after Mo's beat down did nothing to dull her affection. Knowing that eased my nerves. A little. They'd been on edge since Barbara walked out this morning and hadn't let up. It prompted me to handle my outstanding business as she geared up to handle hers.

"Who's there?" Judge Peña hollered from the kitchen. He stood over Mo's son, who scribbled in a spiral notebook.

Homework.

A taskmaster, as always. And I knew what came next.

"Still a lawyer?" he hollered over.

"Yes, Judge." I pulled away from Mo's mom, her exasperation clear.

"Sorry. I've asked him a thousand times to stop," she whispered.

"Sebastian's a lawyer like me," the judge continued and slapped little Mo on the shoulder. "Keep at those books, young man, and you can be a lawyer, too. Make your papa proud."

I tried to smile, but being the focal point for the room's attention made my skin itch. "Mo home?"

"In the back. You know where."

I started toward Mo's bedroom, down the same long hall where his mom told us not to run as kids. Her collector set of Jesus plates lined the walls on both sides, each marking Stations of the Cross. She faithfully added one every year until the company went belly-up. Missing the last few, she substituted picture frames with each plate's photo.

Some things never change.

But a big one was about to.

In moments, I'd be done with my gangland debt. I'd be free from everything keeping me tied to a life I hadn't wanted for years, if ever. Standing in this hall, I realized I didn't just regret getting caught. I hated who I used to be. Someone soaked in machismo, more concerned about losing face than crushing someone else's. If I backed down, what would my boys say? It was all bullshit.

Weakness was going along. Weakness was acting with malice instead of being brave enough to walk away. Last night with Barbara, I pulled the same macho bullshit. But I didn't want to be that dumbass anymore. The guy pacing in an unlocked cage, too petrified to escape.

I looked back toward the living room. I marveled at this hallway as a kid. I'd never seen one that long outside of school. But at 8 feet, the narrow walls constricted the man I'd become. This life no longer fit.

I knocked on Maurice's closed door.

"Come," his voice said.

The moment I entered, Mo's eyes narrowed. He slammed his open dresser drawer. "You have a lot of nerve coming here. To my home where my kid—"

"Chill out." His anger spiked quicker than expected. "I only came to give you this."

I reached into my jacket for the cashier's check. Good as cash. The moment he took it, we were square. I extended my hand, but he looked at the white envelope with suspicion.

"What's that?"

"I'm paying you back."

"Beating your ass. Bro, that's free!" Mo barked a laugh while taking a seat on his bed, which squeaked its hearty amusement.

"Take the damn check, funny guy. It's all there. Every penny you paid for my school. We can go our separate ways."

"King..."

"No more King. No more titles. No obligation. On either side." I wiggled the paper in his face until his annoyance made him grab it.

Mo tore it open, discarding the envelope's gaping carcass on the bed with the same concern he showered on my bloody body in the garden. Instead of being grateful, he stared at the check with an expression I struggled to decode. Like he warred with himself. More than once, he held this money over my head, claiming I owed him. Maybe he didn't like the idea of setting me free. My beat down aside, being under Mo's protection meant something. To me and the neighborhood. Debts held power and repaying mine meant losing it. But I was ready to take my chances.

Instead, he did the last thing I expected. He tore the check in half.

"What the fuck!" I yelled.

"King..."

"Goddammit." I snatched the torn check back, the split separating the word hundred from thousand. Unusable. I'd have to go get another one.

I held the edges together like they'd magically reunite. "I'm getting another one and you will take it. I never should have accepted my cut in the first place."

"Will you shut up for a second? Damn motor mouth." He shifted closer, glancing at his closed bedroom door before speaking low. "There never was any money."

"What the fuck are you talking about?"

"There. Never. Was. Any. Money." Mo emphasized each word, but that didn't make them any easier to comprehend.

"Hold up, that can't be. I saw stacks of cash."

He sighed, hipping both hands and looking sideways to avoid meeting my gaze. "I cut the blow without a scale. I put too much in each bag and charged a fraction of what it was worth. I had barely enough to pay back the supplier. But I moved it so fast, he gave me more. By then, I gained a reputation. I led the crew and everyone said I'd arrived."

Mo made me do it.

I couldn't say no.

For once in his life, Dante told the truth. He'd lied so much, fact and fiction blurred. Especially when he accused someone I trusted of selling me out to the police.

"You trapped me in that alley on purpose," I said not asking. The facts screamed. But I still needed him to come clean.

"I had no money to give you. My best choice was to get you out of the way."

"So you got me locked up and took my place?"

"What choice did I have? Tell you I fucked up? Besides, you were bound to get cuffed. Way too honest. I just sped up the process. By the time you were out, I was rolling. No way I was giving that up. You wanted to get clean, remember? Way I see it, we both got what we wanted."

History rewrote itself, random pieces sliding into place to show a clear picture: Mo the rat. The first and likely only time Dante told the truth. Mo's betrayal burned deep. But one part of his story didn't add up.

"Wait. My cut paid for college and law school. Where'd that come from?"

Mo pressed his lips tight. But I wasn't leaving this apartment without the truth. What he said next would change the course of my life.

I crossed my arms.

"Shit. I promised I wouldn't tell."

"Who?"

"My uncle."

"What the fuck are you talking about?" I'd lost all patience with Mo's games.

"My money wasn't exactly liquid. When you came asking… I couldn't get coin from thin air. I had no choice."

"You borrowed money from the Judge?"

"No. He paid outright for your school. All of it." Mo shrugged a "my bad" like a kid who left his bike out in the rain. Something trivial and easily fixed. This didn't qualify. He screwed up a drug deal so royally, his uncle had to bail him out. His underworld nightmare became a gift beyond my wildest dreams. Drug money didn't bankroll my education. Breath left me, and I leaned on the wall to steady myself.

Mo poked a beefy finger in my chest. "You were the first and only recipient of the Judge Peña Scholarship Fund."

My mind went to the man in the kitchen with Mo's son. The same guy who'd tutored me for hours. Who believed in me enough to force me to do homework and study for tests when Mom was too exhausted from holding two jobs to keep her eyes open. He also warned me to stay clear of Mo's dealings after juvy, chasing me off the corner with the other moms. That same man punched my ticket to college.

Still a lawyer?

How many times had he asked that stupid question? Hundreds? Thousands? I'd laughed and smiled at the beginning. I made something of myself and appreciated the attention. But after years, it became agony. When I saw him coming down the street, or playing chess in the park after shooting baskets, I'd run the other way. Hell, I'd walk blocks in the wrong direction to avoid hearing those three words.

Meanwhile, shame shadowed me at school. I'd sit in lecture halls scanning my peers for signs of recognition. Evidence they saw my gang history tattooed on my face like Dante's tear. Even these days, I played the part of upstanding citizen, holding my head up, thinking myself better than Barr. But I was a professional crook who paid for school with drug money. Wrangling with that conflict left my insides tied in more knots than Mo's crew ever could.

But it was a lie.

I wasn't a criminal. Not anymore.

I should be relieved. But part of me was pissed as hell. At myself for being a clueless fuck, at Mo for foisting a lie on me for so long. Even now, I couldn't avoid the truth. All I'd done as a kid made my current life possible. My gang ties paved the road for the lawyer career I now enjoyed. Whether drug money or Judge Peña, my past life made my current one possible.

"Why would he pay all that money?"

"You had no father, and he had no son. No one to use his savings on."

"What about you? You're blood?"

"He couldn't exactly give money to the leader of the biggest illegal enterprise in lower Manhattan. He loves me, but them's the facts."

Mo reached an arm out and squeezed my shoulder. "The dumb fuck is super proud of you. Loves the idea that the kid he helped in that kitchen followed in his footsteps. I wasn't going to. You bring him honor and that means everything. Judge won't shut the fuck up about you. Drove me so nuts I—"

Our eyes met. The last piece falling into place. The reason my beat down almost left me dead.

"I thought it felt personal," I said.

"My own kid! He sat at the table after school saying that he wanted to grow up to be like Uncle Sebastian. I just... I had to do something."

Mo was a proud man and a leader. In his own way, Mo kept food on countless tables in this community while holding the rival hounds at bay. He even ran some legit businesses on the side that made food easier to find in an area no one else invested in. To have his son idolize another man strained his patience. Cruel as it was, I understood.

"Guess this makes us even, brother," I said.

"Yeah, it does."

We embraced, squeezing tight before thumping backs and bumping fists.

"No word to the Judge. Promise?" Mo pointed at me.

As I passed through the kitchen, the Judge looked up from his work with Jr. and smiled.

I hollered over to him, "I'm still a lawyer."

Chapter 43

Barbara

After leaving Dad's, an immense weight lifted. I wanted to call him over the last many months. Despite everything, I'd missed sharing my triumphs and hearing his sage advice. His absence left a void I only now acknowledged. But a new chapter was starting for both of us, and I couldn't wait to reconnect with Sebastian. I'd yet to reply to his texts, and he probably assumed the worst.

I shifted my grocery bags to unlock my building's front door. Hipping it open, the heavy metal slammed shut behind me as I mounted the stairs for my hike to the third floor.

Leaning over the rail, I checked for light under Nikki's door. We chatted in the evenings most days, she coming up or me going down. When living with Rebecca, I took the everyday female contact for granted. With Joe and Dad, I worked late so often, I seldom saw either at home. My challenging work schedule took priority, and I always presumed that's what success demanded. But life is too short to accept what is, as if it must always be. The people I loved deserved me to be more present, and I pledged to do better.

On the second floor, I passed through what I'd named "Nikki's Rainbows." The new glass sconces reflected off the freshly painted gray walls, creating a dazzling shower of reflection. A magic veil between the outside world and our apartments within cleansed me as I moved across the landing. I chuckled to myself, but crazier things were possible.

I'd come so far in such a short time. Who's to say I wasn't guided by powers beyond my understanding?

As I crested the top step, I found Glenora placing a white grocery bag on my doorknob. I didn't need to ask how she got in. Any apartment she buzzed would let her in. She was that beloved. Her giving nature reminded me of my mom. The mothering I'd missed for so long returned in a new form.

"Leaving me a present?" I said, jingling my keys.

"Oh, you're here. I found a sale on that over-priced dish soap you use. The blue kind? Two for six, so I picked you up a package."

She stood with her cheek outstretched, waiting for me to kiss her, which I gladly did.

"So sweet, thank you. Want to come in?" My bags crinkled as I one-armed them to unlock my apartment door.

"I have to get home and start dinner."

"I have plenty for both of us and would love the company, if you don't mind." I entered and left the door open for her to follow.

Glenora lived every moment on her own terms. If she stayed, it would be because she wanted to. She flipped the bolt closed behind her and hung her coat on one of the wall pegs I'd installed.

"What are we having?"

"I haven't decided yet." I smiled while emptying the contents of my grocery bags on the counter to take an inventory.

Glenora chuckled. "Figures."

"What do you mean?" Had she meant it as a compliment? Chock full of life lessons, I expected her to launch into one about food or planning ahead. Ever a mother, being around her made me long for my own.

How different would I be if Mom hadn't passed away? What mistakes could I have avoided? In my alternate future, would I have landed at Xervo, picked the wrong guy in Joe, and got tangled up with my dad? Perhaps not. But then, all those challenges led me to the happy life I had now. I might have walked the exact same journey to this very kitchen. After all, someone watched over me from above.

I looked up, through my ceiling to the heavens. My mom's presence filling the space powerfully, like she was trying to tell me something.

What, Mom? What is it?

"These veggies are beautiful." Glenora held one of the firm heads of broccoli with reverence. "These aren't from around here."

"There's an amazing market in the West Village near my dad's. I visited him this afternoon."

"Is that right?" She put the broccoli down, her attention shifting to me. "You saw your dad?"

"Yes."

"Hope it went okay."

"Better than okay. We cleared up some major misunderstandings on both sides. Turns out he tried to protect me from the whole Xervo mess. He knew I needed to leave before I did."

Glenora took a seat at my counter while I started prepping the veggies. Besides the broccoli, I bought red peppers, eggplant, onions, garlic, and tomatoes. I'd make a succotash of sorts to serve alongside the chicken breast waiting in the fridge. With ingredients like these, I couldn't go wrong. Which brought me back to her comment.

"What did you mean by 'figures'? About dinner?"

"You take the worst messes and turn them around in seconds. I've never seen anything like it."

"Hardly." Heat blushed up my cheeks, so I put my chef knife to good use on the onions. Accepting accolades made me uncomfortable. The extent of fear and doubt I choke down is laughable. If people found out, they'd lose all respect.

"Stop that and look at me," she said.

I set my blade down to meet her eyes. How far we'd come since that night she brought me a welcome casserole. And those bleak hours at the hospital. We expected to lose the man we loved. Even then, my heart loved Sebastian, though my brain refused to give in. My feelings for him rose quicker than any rational person would diagnose as possible. But there's nothing rational about love. Sebastian was part of me, and that included his mom.

"You can do anything you put your mind to. Whatever this gift is, bottle it because the rest of the world needs some. You're a strong, beautiful woman who turns every moment into a blessing..." Her voice choked, so she rested her hands on mine and patted them. "Your mom would be so proud."

Chills rippled through me. An echo from my past forcing its way into the present. She'd used the very phrase my mom said to me at bedtime. Every night when Mom tucked me in, she kissed my forehead and whispered, "You make every moment a blessing." Hearing those loving words once again meant everything. I knew without question that Mom was near. And she wanted me to accept Glenora's love.

I rounded the peninsula and tugged her into a tight embrace. We stayed that way for a long while. I didn't want to let go. Through her, I hugged my mom. Warm and petite, I even smelled mom's floral perfume—though Glenora wore none. At last, I pulled away.

"Excuse me," I sniffed. "I got so overwhelmed. Like Mom was here with us."

"She is. You loved her that much."

Unable to speak, I pulsed my head in agreement.

"Do you have a picture?"

I brought her the frame from my desk, a photo montage of my high school graduation, us baking in the kitchen, and me, Brian, and mom lying in bed reading a book. As I peeked over Glenora's shoulder, I burst full of so many memories no single one rose to the surface.

"She's lovely. And you are the spitting image of her."

I laughed the idea away. "Not by a long shot."

Glenora gave me her best, "oh come now" face. "You're stunning, but never mind that. Look at you two. Except for the hair, your faces are identical."

I inspected the images, doing my best to be objective. Our faces shared the same shape and eyebrows. My nose always favored Dad's, as did my stature. But side by side, it would be foolish to deny I held a striking resemblance to my mother.

She'd kept her hair short, while encouraging me to grow mine out, until I started getting extensions in middle school. Mom sighed over my class picture one year, and I could tell that she longed to make my Black face blend better with the others. All my friends sported long waves or braids flowing down their backs. I was thrilled at the time, but the closer I mirrored my classmates' appearances, the less I looked like my mother.

As a dutiful daughter, I did what she asked, never pausing to consider her motivations. But only one popped to mind. The woman I treasured more than anyone thought she wasn't good enough as she was. As nature made her. I hope she hadn't passed away harboring those doubts.

I set the picture in front of Glenora to check myself in the hall mirror. Since my failed wedding weekend, I'd struggled to define my identity. Who was I and what did I what to be? After so many months, I'd grown, embracing the woman I'd become. I loved my work, my man, and felt right in my skin for the first time—maybe ever.

I saw none of that in my reflection.

True, the braids were ethnically natural, but they weren't me either. My trademark mane rang just as false. Never since middle school had I stepped out into the world wearing nothing but my own hair. As my mother did.

I'd never get confused for Beyonce. But I wouldn't need to. I'd be me from head to toe. How awesome would it be to walk into that courtroom tomorrow and give them a mortal dose of unadulterated Barbara Washington?

I checked the time. It was still early enough for Nikki to work her magic.

"Glenora, don't kill me. But do you mind making dinner for us? I need Nikki to fix my hair for court, and it'll take every minute I can spare."

She took up the knife I abandoned on the cutting board. "Go on. I'll fix something and bring it over to the salon. Tell Nikki there'll be plenty for her, too."

Chapter 44

BARBARA

"You're serious?" Nikki stood unconvinced behind where I sat in the styling chair. Horror plastered on her face as we spoke to each other via the mirror.

She didn't hesitate to reopen the salon for my last-minute request. But her enthusiasm vanished the moment I told her what I wanted.

"You need to trust me."

"Gals ask me to remove their braids all the time. But a couple of days later, they come crying back for me to fix it. You're not that type, but I have to make sure you want to do this, and before such a big day."

How could I explain? It was because of court tomorrow that I needed this done tonight. But she was right about one thing. I'd never contemplated a more dramatic change. I found a cut online with a light fade on the sides and short curls on top. Rather than fearful, I fizzed with excitement.

No more extensions.

No more navigating braids.

No more hours in chairs and thousands of dollars a year.

I never considered removing my locks to go natural, but here I was on the brink. How would that freedom feel? I yearned to find out. Any hair disaster could be swapped back. Though, the mere thought of reverting sent sadness rolling through my mind like a fog, followed by a sharp pang of dread.

And surprise.

How long had I resented my hair? It flowed over my shoulders, but did it also cloak me with a false sense of security? The answer was clear. I'd come to rely on a magical mane, hoping to make the world forget I was Black. Fool them into treating me with the love and respect I deserved.

I squeezed my eyes shut, overcome with shame.

That's what I'd been doing all along.

Wishing to be white.

The truth exploded every fiber of my being, so hard, I expected my body to career across the room and smash against the opposite wall. I steadied myself on the armrests, bracing for the oncoming force. Harsh truths are always violent, angry at being ignored for so long. They smash and destroy while making their escape. But escape they must. Once gone, lightness is free to filter in, filling us until we emerge whole.

Seeing that photo of my mom through Glenora's eyes triggered my awakening. I'd forever be grateful for the thoughtfulness that brought her to my door.

Kismet.

But what else lies ahead?

I showed Nikki the picture on my phone. "I'm positive. Would this work for me?"

"Your natural hair is already longer. Are you sure about going this short?"

I couldn't imagine a better tribute to my mom than to mirror her elegance. The cut showcased mom's style, but with a modern twist she'd appreciate. Hell, she probably directed me to that hairstyle herself. And for good reason.

"I'm going to walk into that courtroom tomorrow and be seen. My eyes, my face, without any distractions. They wronged me and the others, but they will see me. All of me. I want them to know they got their butts whipped by a strong Black woman."

Nikki leaned into my ear. "They better watch out. Sit tight. I'll be right back."

My friend moved about her shop, donning her apron and tossing one over me, fastening the snaps behind my neck. She organized the rest of her supplies: the solution to break the keratin bonds of my extensions, another to de-tangle, and a third to moisturize. A deep cleanse would follow. But instead of holing myself away for a day or so until new extensions were attached, I'd have a natural cut. When I left the salon tonight, a heavy weight would be gone. Literally.

I hoped it'd suit me and that Sebastian would warm to the style as fast as he did my others. He's said countless times he loved the woman, not the hair. My latest impulse would put his pledge to the test. In contrast, Joe categorized hair changes as off limits. I discovered that after once debating getting a blunt, angled bob. He told me in no uncertain terms, no hair, no Joe.

Yet again, I ignored the sirens warning me about his superficial priorities. And it gained me nothing in the end. Miss Red Thong wore hair far shorter than what I toyed with back then. Another testament to his lameness and to the amazing man I now had in Sebastian. I replied to his text, apologized, and let him know I loved him and was with Nikki, working on a surprise.

Nikki's nimble fingers worked their magic. While she poked around my head, I reviewed my case files. The judge assigned to our trial had a reputation for siding with the employers. Anticipating his tendencies helped me to plan my approach.

Too often, employee disputes relied on the sympathy vote to win. But the law didn't care about emotion. Winning required impartial facts. When companies act wrongly, but shy of illegal, claims of mistreatment skidded on thin ice. My ice was so thick you could drive a semi-truck on it. I had data. I had witnesses. I had paper trails. Together, the evidence amounted to conclusive proof Xervo mistreated employees of color.

I'd never brimmed with such confidence going to court. In my heart, we'd already won. But they had lawyers, too. Good ones. I knew because I'd met most of them at Christmas parties. I flipped through my files from the beginning and searched for any details I might have overlooked.

An hour or so later, Glenora brought over dinner plates covered in foil. I nibbled on mine, but Nikki put hers aside. By then, her gloved hands were slathered in chemicals and oils. She bobbed in a trance-like rhythm while unbraiding my hair. My diligent braid cleaning regimen seemed to pay off, as Nikki found precious little scalp buildup. That made her detangling and combing easier. Nikki teased me about having the cleanest braids she'd ever seen, and like Glenora, said she expected nothing less.

Nikki and Glenora's compliments came at a good time. I'd need my A-game tomorrow, and when my hair was done, I'd be ready to drop in bed. I texted Sebastian that I'd see him in the morning. He'd be cheering me on from the back of the courtroom. As a former Xervo lawyer, his duty to them survived his unethical firing. That made him unavailable to testify without risking his career.

After my shampoo, Nikki turned me away from the mirror to prevent me from watching. Not that I wanted to. Tonight called for an unveiling. I'd always remember the moment I met myself. Three hours after we began my transformation, she squeezed my apron-covered arm.

"Done." She grasped her hands over her head, bending from side to side to stretch the stiffness out of her shoulders and back.

I searched her face for unspoken truth, not that Nikki was one to mince words. She spoke plainly and let the chips fall where they may. My hopes could be the latest casualty. "What do you think?"

"I'll admit it. When you dragged me over here tonight, I thought you were having a breakdown. But looking at you now, I can't imagine why you've styled your hair any other way."

I swallowed, relieved, but also unwilling to believe her. "You like it that much?"

"Love it, but it only matters what you think and how it makes you feel. Ready to see?" Nikki asked.

While excited to view the transformation, I was petrified in equal measure. My score tallied at 98% confident, and 2% convinced I'd hate it and burst into tears. Any blame for a hair disaster landed squarely on me. I dragged Nikki away from her quiet evening at home. With tonight's jury in, I prayed the verdict landed in my favor.

I sucked in as much air as I could hold and managed a controlled release. "Okay. Ready."

She swiveled the chair around, and my heart skipped. I leaned forward, touching my face, and my reflection responded. It was me, but it wasn't. As much as I sought myself in the mirror, my mother stared back. My body went cold, hot, and tingly at the same time. The resemblance left me speechless.

I fingered the tight curls at the nape of my neck, turning my head from side to side to check all angles.

Nikki retrieved a wide mirror and held it aloft with two hands so I could inspect the entire creation.

Short curls, maybe a half inch, cropped close to my head on the sides, fading into 3-inch curls on the top. Nearly a yard of hair—gone—making for a real unveiling. I'd hidden beneath it, shielding my true self from the world. The woman in the mirror oozed confidence. She seemed formidable. A person worth knowing, unafraid to grasp what she wanted. This haircut captured my essence and put it on display for everyone to see. I looked like me.

"So?" Nikki asked, eager for a review of her handiwork.

"It's perfect." I popped up to hug her.

She squeezed me tight. "I don't like to brag, but this looks fantastic. You have the bone structure to pull it off!"

Whether or not tomorrow's hearing came out my way, I'd already won. The experience helped me find a woman who'd eluded me my whole life. Me. That made Xervo firing me a blessing. It launched me to new heights, in work, in life—in love, and I would climb still farther.

Nikki lifted the edge of the foil covering her dinner plate, to fork a bite. She must be famished. I'd long since devoured mine. Now, I hungered for a more potent dish: justice.

Tomorrow couldn't come soon enough.

Chapter 45

SEBASTIAN

Dressing for court, an eerie silence clogged my apartment with foreboding. No bird tweets. No garbage trucks or shouts from the street below. The city paused in anticipation of our legal battle, and I prayed the outcome didn't disappoint.

Barbara fizzed with excitement when we spoke last night. Exhausted after her session with Nikki, she refused to come over. Or let me see her before morning, saying it would jinx everything. I almost snarked we weren't getting married, but the comment stuck in my throat.

We would marry. Not today, but one day soon. Our souls melded, completing the other. Yet we also stood accomplished and whole on our own. I only now realized that to be present for another person, you had to arrive fully assembled. Unshackling from the darkness of my past left me free to saunter into the future.

What would come next?

I'm still a lawyer.

But do I want to be?

Did I ever?

Or had my childhood fantasy expired?

My irritation grew the closer it came to court. Xervo's nonsense forced this trial, and it burned me that Barbara and her clients could lose. I adjusted my lucky tie, its silky green representing a payday. My black suit clung to my frame like armor. I dressed for battle, though the fight was no longer mine.

I'd kill to be by Barbara's side today, co-counsel fighting the bad guys. Helping the wronged get justice. Too many in this community fell prey to mistreatment, never getting a whiff of compensation.

And it's no wonder.

Justice was expensive, costing far more than any of my neighbors could afford. They weren't rich or well connected. Except for Mo, which is why his brand of business always boomed. Good people deserved fair treatment. It's why I became a lawyer.

The public defender assigned to me when I was a kid was kind, but useless. He oversaw too many cases to give any of them proper attention. I swore I'd have been better off representing myself. The facts didn't add up. We gave the cops zero reason to chase us that night. It was almost like they were waiting for me and Dante to walk by. I bolted out of habit, not knowing I had drugs planted in my pocket. Had they bothered to check the dime bag for fingerprints, they'd find Mo and Dante's—not mine.

I'd watched enough legal dramas on TV to learn a few things. The arrest felt like a set-up.

Because it was.

Studying law was a way to escape my upbringing. But being someone who'd seen jail from the inside made me vow never to go back—and keep as many people out as I could. Following the crowd into corporate law left me wasting my Robin Hood skills defending the sheriff. Barbara's fight reminded me the townspeople needed protecting.

By the time I arrived at the courthouse, small clusters of attendees crowded the hall outside our assigned room. I searched for Barbara, seeing the powder blue pantsuit she bought and—

Wow.

I almost didn't recognize her. She'd cut her hair clear down, leaving a curly top. I'd never met anyone so fearless, but then, that's how she approached everything. Bold and determined. Free of the long flowing hair from when I first saw her or the braids she'd worn lately, Barbara never looked more beautiful. Her warm eyes shined bright, angling to her striking cheekbones and plum lips, which glistened with gloss. As ever, her skin glowed.

Barbara owned the hall, wearing confidence like perfume. Passersby craned their heads back, wondering if she was "somebody."

That she was.

A special somebody.

She saw me standing off, waved me over.

I sank into Barbara's tight hug and million-dollar smile. So much was riding on this case. Not only for her clients, but for her. She'd worked for months without earning a penny. A loss today would leave her in a financial bind. But looking at her, you'd never know.

"Don't think I didn't see you standing over there giving me hungry tiger eyes." Barbara teased.

"Can't blame me. You came to court looking good enough to eat."

"You like?" She vogued into a dramatic profile, her diamond hoop earrings glinting in the sunlight from a nearby window.

"I love."

"I do too, but feared you'd hate it. I've had trouble with guys not wanting me to change my hair."

"I'm not most guys."

Her face softened as she took me in. "No. You're not. I'm continually realizing how much."

"I hope that's a good thing."

"It is."

"Lucky for you, because I have no intention of letting you get away, Ms. Washington."

"Oh, really?" Barbara leaned in. "Who says I'm going anywhere?"

Our lips met. Warm and inviting, this kiss said, "I don't give a fuck who's watching." It took all my willpower to resist pinning her arms overhead against the wall as I devoured her neck. She wisely drew back.

"Showtime."

"You ready?" I asked.

"Never more." She strode away, ushering her clients into the courtroom.

The clack of her heels demanded attention, and all heads turned to watch her enter. She sat at a brown wooden table at the front of the room, alongside her seven clients. Ironically, Portia sat closest to her. Barbara's former foe had become an ally in this fight.

I took a seat halfway back in an unoccupied row. With all the plaintiffs, I expected a bigger crowd, but the rows behind me were all empty.

Once the gallery settled, the bailiff began, "All rise. This court is now in session, the Honorable Judge, Walter Harlow, presiding."

A robed man entered, bald, white, and in his sixties. His rulings were tough, but fair. I reviewed his case history over the years and Harlow tended to favor employers. The only blessing was his rulings weren't as badly slanted as other jurists.

"Please be seated and come to order." The bailiff announced, and we all sat.

"Good morning. We will begin with opening statements," the Judge said.

Blood thumped in my ears in anticipation. But Barbara turned around, cool as anything, and gave me a sly wink.

Chapter 46

BARBARA

I pushed myself away from the table and rose, channeling my excited energy. I had this.

"Good morning. Today, we bring before you a travesty that is all too common in our workplaces. We think of ourselves as an evolved society, yet every day workers of color are systematically subjected to unfair treatment and unequal employment outcomes. This is what we will prove happened to my clients at Xervo.

"When they joined the company, they believed it to be an ethical workplace. What they endured proved otherwise. Today, we will present evidence showing Xervo and its leadership willfully committed de jure and de facto discrimination, exhibiting an intentional pattern of biased practices against employees of color.

"These illegal actions included disproportionate dismissals of high-performing workers—whose roles were subsequently replaced with non-minority workers—lower severance packages when controlled for employee grade and seniority, and retaliation against staff attempting to stop this wrongdoing."

I stopped to gather my breath. Stating the facts out loud in public made them infinitely more deplorable. I suppressed my outrage while Barr sat looking at his watch like he had someplace better to be. Perhaps it was an act for the jury. To his credit, the judge actively listened and scribbled notes. His worried expression spoke volumes about the merits of our case.

I paced over to stand before Barr's table. He slumped beside the assigned lawyer from my dad's firm, a young woman I'd never met.

How big of them to let estrogen through the door.

Barr's breath hitched when I caught his eye. I held his attention as I resumed, speaking loud and clear, so he had no choice but to hear every syllable.

"Today, we seek damages commensurate with two years' salary per claimant, inclusive of benefits, to compensate for lost wages and pain and suffering. We further seek punitive damages to discourage this practice in the future and compensate claimants for the lost career reputations that have contributed to many finding it difficult to find equivalent positions in the marketplace as workers of color."

Barr slammed his palm on the desk. "I will never bow to extort—"

The judge pounded his wooden gavel. "Ms. Lafferty! Ms. Lafferty, please control your client or I'll have him removed."

"Yes, Your Honor," Xervo's lawyer said.

I pulsed an eyebrow, smirking as I returned to my table.

Ms. Lafferty lifted her pad to hide their faces as she mumbled to Barr.

Better her than me.

Being in the same room with him for the first time in months made me wonder how I'd worked so long in his toxic shadow. His tantrums were no longer my worry, and that fact glowed like a warm fire within me. And I only just started.

I scanned my clients' faces as I sat. Their emotions ranged from elated to overcome. The prospect of reliving their injustice in public triggered last-minute jitters in the days leading up to trial. I tried to lessen the blow by practicing what to expect during intense mock trial sessions. But the real thing sparked powerful emotions, nonetheless.

Portia squeezed my knee under the table. "So far, so good."

"Counselor, your open, please?" The judge said.

Ms. Lafferty rose. "Before we begin, we wanted to restate our objection to this class preceding. These were employees at-will and were released with severance."

Judge Harlow rolled his eyes, beating me to it. "Your objection is noted. This proceeding will determine the case's merit. Please proceed with your open."

Ms. Lafferty sat. Giving her opening from a seated position screamed political theater. It was a risk, potentially being viewed as disrespectful.

"All Xervo workers are employees at-will. The company takes great pains to avoid reductions in force, but financial realities sometimes make this unavoidable. While we respect each of the claimants, appreciate their service, and genuinely understand their distress, this case is without merit. They were properly let go, received severance, and we wish them the best of luck finding future opportunities."

She leaned back, signaling her statement ended. The ball bounced to me.

"Ms. Washington, please call your first witness."

Portia would testify later. The rest I called, one by one, giving them a chance to share work histories in their own words. I had them read from annual reviews, which were each entered into evidence. No one had any indication they were in jeopardy before the firings happened. News that three of them were replaced by white people left five of our six jury members shaking their heads. The sixth woman seemed oddly fascinated by her cuticles.

Randall spoke next. I'd subpoenaed him to testify. We covered how Barr routinely disparaged Black people, including me. They objected to discussing my employment, but I won the point, showing how it demonstrated a pattern of discriminatory behavior. Randall also mentioned the special severance packages organized at Barr's request to "quietly make employees go away," most of whom were from minority communities. Ms. Lafferty attempted to trap Randall in a lie on cross, but it backfired. He simply shared how he was phased out with a deal of his own after attempting to advance inclusion and diversity programs via the human resources team. On redirect, I ensured he used the word "retaliation," a term with legal significance, crossing that off my to-do list.

Portia went next, both to share her own story, and to confirm the ongoing payments made to certain dismissed workers. Since we left, we'd learned that Chen was among these. Elizabeth declined to testify, so I respected her wishes and skipped subpoenaing her.

When we broke for lunch, I saw my dad sitting in the last row. His eyes were wet and glassy as he struggled to suppress emotion. Some of these stories might be hitting close to home. I called him over and he navigated against the flow of bodies heading out to hit the bathrooms and grab food.

"Everything okay?" I low talked.

Instead of answering, he wrapped me in a hug. "You made me so proud today. You're doing a great job."

"Thanks." I pulled away, but he gathered me back in. Tight. It was so unlike him to be this demonstrative, and in public.

"What's wrong?"

"Seeing you... with your hair? It's like watching your mother. I can feel her. My Lena is close."

I forgot he hadn't seen my cut. His reaction mirrored mine back in the salon. I choked a sob of my own, as my insides swirled with a mix of grief, love, and hearty appreciation for my parents. Together, they'd prepared me for the life I now lived. If not for them and their frustratingly high expectations, I could very well have floundered.

I kissed my dad's cheek. "Mom's here. I feel her, too."

Dad reached into his wallet and pulled out a photograph, creased white from years of refolding. He handed it to me.

A chill sent goosebumps flushing my skin to attention. "When was this taken?"

"The day we went to get our wedding license at the clerk's office. It was in this very building. She wore a powder-blue pantsuit and sparkly pumps with rhinestones. She wanted to be Cinderella for a day. Have you never seen this?"

I hadn't. The picture quivered in my trembling hand. No way it was a coincidence. Me, wearing the same-colored pantsuit as my mom, with the same blinged-out shoes? At the same stone building my mother smiled in decades earlier in the identical clothing?

I refocused on the grainy picture. The two of them looked so happy. Him in his brown suit, her in a blue one. The start of a loving future cut short. One day, I'd get a marriage license of my own. I'd commit to a special someone and have a memorable day. No vision emerged for what that ceremony would be, but I knew who I wanted it to be with. But that fairytale was for another day. I had to get my mind right for this afternoon's proceeding.

Yvonne would go next, then Xervo's HR director. After that, Lafferty would take the floor to present Xervo's case.

I debated calling Barr to testify but decided against it. He'd lie so convincingly, he could very well sway the jury. If Lafferty had any smarts, she'd call him herself. But part of me doubted whether she had the guts. Barr was such a lying skunk, putting him on the stand was essentially suborning perjury. I'd have presented so much damning evidence by then, he'd have no choice but to lie.

"Barbara," Sebastian jogged in from the hall, waving a manila envelope. Worry creased his forehead. He swept the room for eavesdroppers before he spoke, stopping where I stood with Dad.

It was the first time they'd been together since their exchange at his apartment.

Sebastian's eyes darted between us, asking permission to speak in his presence.

"It's okay," I said. "We're good."

The two men fidgeted, looking beyond uncomfortable. Neither spoke. I'd have to fix this relationship, and soon.

Sebastian handed me the envelope. "Xervo filed an ethics complaint against me with the State Bar Association. They're accusing me of acting unethically when I was an employee."

"Did you?" Dad asked, his mistrust ratcheting up the tension.

I rested my palm on Dad's arm, a soothing gesture I copied from my mom. His muscles relaxed. It must be hard for him to re-enter my life after all these months. He'd missed a lot and I didn't have time to rehash it now.

"Dad, please..."

Sebastian bristled. "Unless you consider refusing to break the law unethical, I've done nothing wrong. It's utter bullshit to have this arrive during recess."

I scanned the complaint, and it looked flimsy. They accused Sebastian of working surreptitiously for me on behalf of the case while still employed by Xervo. He hadn't, of course. If they found out about us, it'd look bad on the surface. Sebastian had nothing to do with my case. I legally obtained every file through discovery. Barr's insult wasn't lost on me. His veiled suggestion that I couldn't assemble a winning case without a man's help.

"Put me on the stand. I want to testify. They're accusing me of dirty tricks but fired me for trying to stop theirs." Sebastian clenched his fists with purpose.

I loved him for wanting to support the cause. But highlighting his role as General Counsel would expose me to improper accusations of my own. It was too risky. Though my heart yearned to give Sebastian an opportunity to clear his name.

When on the island, Sebastian shared how thrilling it was to land a job as General Counsel. He'd long wanted the power to put a positive imprint on a company. Xervo was his chance. Ironically, he made a better General Counsel than I would have been. While he focused on improving people's lives, my attention had been trained on the next ladder rung.

I squandered countless opportunities to help others while at Xervo. Taking this case helped me make amends and prove how much I'd changed. I couldn't jeopardize it all, even for the man I loved.

"Sweetie. I can't. You know that."

Sebastian paced away, then swirled to gesture at the witness chair with the envelope he held. "I'm not scared of that weasel, but he should be scared of me."

"No one thinks you're scared, least of all me. But we've got to be smart about this. Come here."

He pouted over and gave me a hug, pressing his cheek to my forehead.

"I love how passionate you are," I said.

"They screwed my girl. I want them to pay." The moment the word "screwed" left his lips, he blushed tomato red and snapped his head toward my dad in horror. "I'm so sorry sir, I—"

Dad chuckled as Sebastian released me and stepped away like we'd been caught necking on the couch. "I've heard way worse than 'screwed,' son. Anyone that protective of my daughter is okay by me."

"Nice to have you on our side."

"I've always been on my daughter's side. You? Well, my bet is you'll grow on me."

Sebastian extended his hand to shake. "I look forward to it."

In a blink, my two hotheads started a new chapter. They made an unlikely pair: the aristocrat and the reformed gang leader. Both strong willed. Both mine. I wondered how Sebastian would take to having an elder man in his life? It'd be a different experience for him. And for his mom. Me and my brother were so indoctrinated into toeing the family line, I wondered how my dad would fare grappling with a fearless soul like Sebastian? I guess we'd all find out.

Sebastian kissed the side of my head, then popped out to get some air before court resumed. It left the perfect opportunity to revisit my dad's future.

"You know, you haven't said anything about your own employment case. Made any decisions?"

"I'm considering it. The only thing keeping me from leaving was my name on the door. Suing them for damages is a huge step." He rubbed his bald head while thinking.

"We Washingtons are nothing if not bold. Come on," I said, nudging shoulders. "We both know they don't deserve you."

"I'll think about it. I didn't realize I'd raised such a relentless bulldog."

"Yes, you did," I said.

He squeezed my hand. "Take a few minutes for yourself. Act Two starts soon."

Promptly at one o'clock, court reconvened. I called Yvonne to testify. Dignified in a dark skirt suit and white ruffled blouse, her fearful eyes darted to Barr as she passed, trembling like a terrified mouse. He answered by grinding his jaw and crossing his arms. Unlike the rest of us, Yvonne still worked at Xervo. But from the looks of my former frat-boy boss, she wouldn't for much longer. Yvonne's pre-trial prep confirmed Barr's pattern of discrimination pre-dated Xervo.

I gave her a moment to settle in her seat before asking her to state her name for the record. Her attention fixed on Barr, so I moved my body to block her line of sight. No way she'd speak freely and honestly about her boss with him shooting daggers at her.

"Ms. Jones, can you tell us what you do at Xervo?" I asked.

Yvonne's voice quivered as she spoke. "I am the Executive Assistant to our CEO, Mr. Marshall Barr. I also sit in the reception area and greet visitors."

"You've worked for Mr. Barr for years, is that right?"

"Yes, nearly twenty. We were a lot younger then. Both of us." She smiled in a way one does when you have a crush, but it vanished as quickly as it arrived.

I turned to look at him.

Is that why she stayed? Trying to win the affections of a man who reviled all she stood for as a Black woman? My stomach lurched at the thought, but I knew it happened all the time. We seek affection from people unwilling to grant us the respect we deserved. I did it myself with Joe.

Barr played with his watch again. He had no concern about Yvonne's testimony. He had her wrapped around his finger.

We'd see about that.

"In the time you've worked with Mr. Barr, have you ever heard him speak disparagingly about marginalized people, and by that, I mean those from Black, Latino, Asian, LGBTQIA+, or other under-represented backgrounds?"

It was a direct question, but she ignored it. She twisted the cuff of her blouse, staring at her lap. I couldn't get her to visually engage.

This wasn't going as I'd planned.

Moments before, I held sympathy for her. But if Yvonne chose to protect that rat of a man, she'd earn no mercy from me. "Your Honor, please instruct the witness to answer the question."

"You will answer, Ms. Jones." Judge Harlow said.

"I can't recall."

I can't recall?

"Is that so?"

"Yes." Yvonne pinched her lips tight.

I swirled on my heel to find Barr practically laughing.

He'd gotten to her. Threatened her or promised her something in exchange for silence. Yes, she worked for him, but what about her duty to the truth? To us?

"Your Honor. In light of this witness' reluctant honesty, I'd request she be declared a hostile witness."

"So declared. Ms. Jones, you are under oath and ordered to truthfully answer the questions put to you. Is that clear?"

"Yes, sir," Yvonne whispered.

"Please proceed with your questioning, Ms. Washington."

I squared my shoulders toward the witness chair. "Did you previously declare in pre-trial prep that you were afraid of Mr. Barr and the power he held over your career?"

The question, and its coercive implications, settled the room to attention. The longer I let it stew, the more restless sounds emerged from the gallery as we all awaited an answer. Real court was slow. It wasn't like the television, where witnesses eagerly spilled the beans. I readied to prompt the judge when she finally spoke.

"Yes. I did say that. I do feel that." She said into her lap.

"Has anyone threatened you, or asked you to give false testimony today?"

"Yes."

"Do you see that person in court today? Can you point them out for us?"

I cleared the way for Yvonne to aim a finger at Barr, his attention finally focused on the trial.

"Let the record show Ms. Jones pointed to Xervo CEO, Marshall Barr. Now Ms. Jones, I'm going to ask you the question again: have you ever witnessed Mr. Barr speaking badly about marginalized people?"

"Yes. About others and about me. He's implied Black people are less intelligent. He's also told me in the past to turn down my jungle music. Oh, he also said to do what he says, or I'd be gone. And that I'd never find another job because 'no one wants to be stuck with an old Black hag.'"

Two jurors gasped, earning them a stern glance from the judge.

"Is that why you stayed so long?"

"Yes, and because he said he'd tell my next employer I was late and stole from coworkers."

Outraged murmurs filled the room. I finally understood Sebastian's desire to punch walls. But I'd do Barr one better and get him where it hurt.

"Ms. Jones, did Mr. Barr ever discuss his business decisions with you? About the company layoffs from five months ago?"

"Just once. He said I should feel special. I was going to be the only Black person left."

Chapter 47

SEBASTIAN

By the time Barbara finished with Yvonne and the HR Director, Xervo was ground to pulp. The company defense was paltry, and how could it not be? Barbara had the goods: documents, witnesses, injured parties. Barr didn't have a leg to stand on. His lawyer knew it, and so did he. Best to save on billable hours and wrap up quickly. That's what I'd do.

When Ms. Lafferty stood next, I expected her to rest their case. Instead, she announced her next witness. "We call Barbara Washington to the stand."

Barbara's confident face froze in shock. "Your Honor, I didn't see my name on the witness list."

"Ms. Washington has information critical to our case that has just come to light. We have the right to mount a vigorous defense." It was Lafferty's turn to take the upper hand.

"How will I cross?" Barbara asked.

"You should have planned for this, Counselor. They are well within their rights."

I turned in my seat to find her stunned dad, looking as worried for his daughter as I was. With his firm representing Xervo, he couldn't help. My conflict of interest left me equally powerless.

Barbara whispered to her clients, who huddled around her. When finished, they each bent heads in silent prayer.

"Ms. Portia Robinson will do my cross."

Portia? My confidence imploded. It was Barbara's turn to get stuck in an alley, and I had no way to help. Their case would unravel if not handled properly, but they had no choice. My nerves screamed as Barbara calmly walked to the stand and took a seat.

Ms. Lafferty reveled in her sneaky legal maneuver. It was her turn to grill the woman who'd been mopping the floor with her all day.

"Is it true that you are in a relationship with our former General Counsel, Mr. Kingsbury?"

Barbara tensed, her eyes steeling. I was 25-feet away and easily read the "don't fuck with me" in her expression.

"Yes," Barbara said.

"Isn't that convenient?"

"Actually, it's been the most inconvenient thing in my life." Barbara folded her hands in her lap, tilting up her chin to maintain eye contact with her questioner.

Good. Barbara was back in command.

"You expect us to believe that you didn't take advantage of Mr. Kingsbury to gain access to private Xervo information? Information you needed to mount this proceeding?"

Barbara's brow furrowed. "This case took months to prepare. I received all documents properly through discovery, handling all aspects of the case on my own."

"Xervo gave you the highest seat of legal power at its company, yet you show no loyalty?" Lafferty said.

"As much loyalty as they showed me when letting me go two weeks after I received a standing ovation at an all-company meeting."

Lafferty leaned in, both hands on the edge of the witness box. "Let's be honest, this whole proceeding is a warped fantasy to get revenge on Xervo?"

"You're mistaken. This case seeks fair treatment and respect for my clients as workers of color."

"Is that right?" Lafferty strolled across the room to retrieve a short stack of photographs from a folder. She laid them out, one by one, in front of Barbara.

"These were taken of you and Mr. Kingsbury. Can you please describe for the record what they show?"

Barbara looked down, then immediately squeezed her eyes shut. Struggling to compose herself, she took a cleansing breath.

"Please answer the question, Ms. Washington."

"It shows me cradling Seb—Mr. Kingsbury the evening he was badly beaten in a community garden."

Fuck me. Must be stills from YouTube.

I could see it in Barbara's eyes. She was back there. Holding me, thinking I'd never survive. She'd rolled over in bed to trace my scars countless times since then, tears sliding down her face, reliving the worry of losing me forever. I'd kiss her tenderly and tell her not by a long shot.

Where the hell were they going with this?

"He was critically injured. Is that right?" Lafferty asked.

"Yes. What are you implying? That I did it?"

"Did you? Lover's quarrel?"

"He was jumped in a park! I called an ambulance. Any reasonable person would have done the same thing."

"So you saved his life?"

"I made a phone call. If I hadn't, others surely would—"

"But you were the one to dial 911, ensuring medical attention arrived as quickly as possible. Would you say he was grateful?"

"Of course."

"In your debt?"

Damn. Lafferty boxed her in.

Barbara realized too late where the questions headed. Her face sank. "I never thought of it that way."

"But you admit it'd be natural, under the circumstances, to feel obligated to the person who saved you from dying?"

Barbara's lips pressed tight. She'd walked into a slanderous line of questioning and getting out of it would take a masterstroke.

I glanced over at her clients, who sat erect in their chairs. Though not lawyers, it was plain that Barbara was rattled.

"Please answer the question. Do you agree that it would be natural for Mr. Kingsbury to feel indebted to you for saving his life?" Lafferty said.

"I made a phone call. Nothing more."

"Don't be modest, Ms. Washington. You also stayed at the hospital for hours, orchestrating his care and sitting by his bedside."

She strode to her desk to retrieve papers. "These are statements from Mr. Kingsbury's insurance company, indicating you were acting on his behalf. I'd like them entered into evidence."

"So entered." The judge said.

Barbara's face echoed the panic from that night in the garden. Her tear-stained face, pleading with me to hold on, was all I remembered before waking up groggy and in pain. Her testimony had become equally tragic. Xervo's slimy shock tactic accomplished a timely score, pushing Barbara off her game. Her fear could very well be the last image the jury got unless she recovered.

"I supported a former colleague in a very serious situation."

"It's the nature of that support I'm questioning, Ms. Washington. Much of this case depends on the hiring data submitted into evidence. Him being in your debt provides a powerful motive to doctor those files and undermine Xervo's case."

"Was there a question in there?" Barbara's eyes flashed defiance.

"I'll rephrase. Did you coerce Mr. Kingsbury to falsify data as repayment for your medical assistance?"

"No!"

"Did you conspire with Mr. Kingsbury to falsify data as retribution against Xervo for getting passed over for a promotion, and later, dismissed?"

"No, what a ludicrous suggestion. The data we received was stored in digital archives. Mr. Kingsbury had no access to any of it. Neither did I, even when employed as acting General Counsel. Barr was renowned for his secrecy. He doled out information in an eyedropper, rarely giving enough for anyone on the legal team to do our jobs properly. I was banned from using company financial systems and was unable to pull my own original reports. All requests funneled through Mr. Barr's admin. He controlled the flow of information. He controlled our hiring practices. He controlled everything."

"You're shifting blame when it more rightly lies with you for whipping up conspiracy theories. Isn't that right?" Lafferty said.

"Barr ruled Xervo like a tyrant. Trusting no one and managing all decisions himself. Now that wrongdoing has been exposed, he can't dodge accountability, misdirecting accountability to the only Black leader who's ever worked on his executive team. The board approved my hire, but he opposed me at every turn. If anyone has a vendetta, it's Mr. Barr against me. Not because of my qualifications, not because of my education, stellar work, or track record of success. The board wanted to promote me, but Barr refused. He didn't want me at Xervo because of the color of my skin."

All the blood drained from Lafferty's already translucent complexion. She just got smoked by her last witness. She thought putting Barbara on the stand and showing her bloody pictures was genius. Barbara's testimony was so brutal, it'd leave Lafferty with scars.

Barr's lawyer stood, mouth agape, likely lost in thought until the Judge cleared his throat. "Counselor? Your next question?"

Dazed, she looked from him to Barbara, then back.

"I've nothing else for this witness." Lafferty backpedaled a few steps before pivoting to return to her seat. Attendees sat in stunned silence as the magnitude of Barbara's words crackled in the air.

He didn't want me at Xervo because of the color of my skin.

Barbara summarized her entire case in a singular moment of naked truth. Ugly and raw, but undeniably true.

I sat back, crossing my arms with pride.

She'd won.

Barbara turned in her seat to face the judge, barely suppressing her joy. "I have no further questions for this witness."

Forty minutes later, I stood on the sidewalk in front of the courthouse while Barbara swapped hugs with elated clients. Her hard work and persistence had paid off. From the looks of the jury during their closing arguments, Barbara's clients would soon have justice.

There was no telling what the award would be, even if they won. But unless the amount made Xervo sweat, they'd continue business as usual. Any employer monitoring the proceedings would likewise take a low award as a green light to avoid needed change.

Every person in that room knew those workers got screwed. The jury and judge's reactions throughout the day made it plain they held no sympathies for Xervo's position. Hopefully that disgust would translate into a financial windfall for Barbara and the others.

Barbara sauntered over as her adoring fans disbursed. "The waiting is the worst."

I curled my arms around her waist. "If only I could think of a way to pass the time? Apparently, I'm highly impressionable and can't withstand your seductive charms."

Her body shifted so close I could smell her perfume of victory. "I'm banking on it."

I dropped my lips to hers, my heartbeat echoing in my ears. Wet and wild, all barriers keeping us apart had vanished. We both knew it. This was our first kiss of freedom. My hands explored her curves like we were the only people in the world instead of eager lovers on a crowded Manhattan sidewalk. My mouth traced the contours of her face until I nibbled my way to her earlobe.

"Come with me."

I dragged her back toward the building, up an elevator, then navigated a maze of hallways until we reached a locked office.

"What's this?" She asked.

"Thought we might want a private space to wait for the verdict. My friend rents space here and is out of town." I lifted the ring of keys and jiggled them for effect.

"Mr. Kingsbury! Will I be safe with you?"

"Not in the slightest." I opened the door and yanked her through, slamming it shut behind us and drawing the shade down over the smoked-glass window. I strolled to a wall of shelves, pressed a button, and a Murphy bed descended into place. Every faux knick-knack, fixed in place, went along for the ride.

"You have got to be kidding me! A bed!"

Not waiting for a response, I tossed my suit jacket and tie on the desk, while Barbara kicked off her sparkly pumps. I was on her in an instant, her blue suit abandoned with mine, along with a haphazard pile of shirts, pants, and panties.

As we stood bare facing each other, memories of our adventures in her four-poster jolted my friend to attention. His movement did not go unnoticed.

Barbara curled her fingers around him and squeezed, sending a flood of desire raging through me.

I devoured her mouth, my throaty moan mixing with hers. Her skin, a luscious ocean of silk I wanted to drown in. I backed us onto the bed, dropping on top of her until her ample breasts pressed into my chest.

"You, my dear, are a temptress. You seduced me, took advantage of my weakness for your beauty. You are guilty as hell, and it's time you pay for your crimes."

"Should I be afraid?" She purred.

"Very."

"Are you ready to announce your punishment?"

Fuck yes.

Barbara laid back and took me whole, every inch, meeting me thrust for thrust. Pleasure flowed to and from every extremity, rising, throbbing for release.

But not yet.

I had other plans.

I withdrew to drink her wetness. Every drop, salty and sweet and divine beyond measure. She writhed against my mouth, the pleasure a torment. Her nails tangled in my hair, her mounting desire flaming mine.

"Sebastian...I..." Barbara sucked rush of air as her body tensed. Limbs frozen as a flush rippled her skin, her nipples peaking into chocolate drops. I devoured each on the way to her mouth, her arms limp on the bed.

Her recovery wouldn't last. I knew she needed more.

We rolled on our sides and I entered her from behind, pulling her close while attending to her spot. Thrust after thrust, we joined and receded, each nanosecond of separation an agony.

"Who's your king?" I whispered in her ear.

"You are... You're my king." Breathless, her answer barely audible.

"And who's my queen?"

"I am."

"You better fucking believe it."

We flipped to facing. I was so desperate for Barbara, I ached. From my legs to my hands, wet in her passion, to my mind, a blind rage of longing, begging for release. I couldn't hold it much—

Ecstasy. It knocked me senseless, dragging me along in an undertow of bliss as Barbara surfed one of her own. I forgot where she ended and I began. We were one, fused into a tangled pile of spent limbs, basking in our joy until a lover's sleep claimed us.

Chapter 48

BARBARA

My first solo jury win became the cherry on a magical day. And I almost missed it. Drunk on post-passion sleep, six verdict calls got muffled under a pile of abandoned clothes. After frantic, sloppy dressing, the smirks tossed our way as we entered the packed courtroom made the judgment even sweeter. That, and Barr's furious face. It progressed from a pale pink to deep maroon by the time the judge finished announcing general and punitive damages, then adding attorney costs as well.

All told, the number shocked me. Even with no award cap on discrimination cases, the sizable amount would make heads turn. This judgment would enable us to put this mess behind and start fresh. And while happy to prevail, a pocket of sadness remained in my heart that bringing the case was even necessary. If not for Barr's blind bigotry, we might still be working there. Instead, we'd spent months fighting for rights granted at birth, but too often denied.

Next, I'd help Dad get his due, forging a new legacy for our family name. The world would recognize us as THE lawyers that made racist employers pay. I'd found my calling and the life meant for me all along. I'd studied, and worked, and sacrificed, but trained for the wrong event. Instead of seeking validation from overlords who thought me inferior, I'd excel on my own. Going forward, I'd crave their low expectations like air. Every time an adversary underestimated my abilities would make winning that much sweeter.

My company logo would be a heaping pile of ash, their remains after I smoked them in court.

I gathered my belongings from the table as Yvonne approached. I owed her, big time.

"Thanks for your testimony. Sorry it was so tough." I paused from stuffing folders into my briefcase.

"I wasn't sure who I wanted to win. Does that make me awful?"

"No. It makes you human. But you deserve better. If you stay there, don't let him treat you that way. No more nasty comments about jungle music."

She grimaced. "Hearing it said out loud today... He's treated me so horribly for so long."

"If he gives you any trouble, give me a call." I grasped her hand and squeezed tight. Hopefully, some of my hard-won determination would sink in. She needed to make a choice that brought her happiness. And respect. I knew better than anyone, sometimes you had to leave to find it.

Looking back, I was just like Yvonne. Afraid to speak and doubting my worth. And because I couldn't recognize it, no one else did. Or not the leaders in charge. I wrongly assumed their low regard was my problem to fix. If I only shouldered more work, crammed more nights and weekends, Barr would see my value. And once that happened, I'd have arrived. If these many months taught me anything, it was that people denying my worth were smallminded and wrong. Because they were incapable of more, didn't mean I should accept less.

I'd been so paralyzed by fear and Impostor Syndrome, it never occurred to me to make my own opportunity. My dad had, so the concept shouldn't have been so foreign. But I saw it as a binary choice. Build a large firm from nothing, or go the corporate route, working my way up to command teams around the globe.

Becoming an entrepreneur that sipped coffee at 10 a.m. in a cafe? Where was the status in that? Where were the junkets forcing me to rub elbows with people I couldn't stand to advance my career? Gone—and thank goodness. While forming a huge company wasn't for me, coming and going as I pleased and answering to myself suited me just fine.

I cleared the courtroom doorway and saw Sebastian chatting with my dad. Two of the men I loved most. Yet, it was my lover who made my heart stop and race at the same time.

Sebastian embodied everything I ever craved in a man and never knew I needed. He was unbelievably strong and unwavering in his loyalty. Fierce when called for, but tender underneath. His were the hazel eyes I wanted to wake up to in the morning. And now nothing stopped us from being together, forever.

Chapter 49

BARBARA

It took two months to settle the paperwork and disburse funds. After all was finished, Sebastian and I decided to take a vacation. I left him in charge and was not entirely surprised when he booked a fare-saver adventure to the same wedding resort where we met. Mid-week, with no weddings happening, we quickly became first-name favorites of the friendly staff.

As evening settled in on our third day, I dressed in our cabana, wearing the white maxi-dress he'd bought me earlier in the day. He wore white linen pants and a cotton shirt, leaving the top buttons open to his deliciously tan skin and newly healed tattoo. Sebastian added a tropical scene with the two of us laughing in a convertible to the spot that had once been blank.

I headed for the door, but he took my hand to stop me. "I have something for you to wear tonight."

Images of a ring box flashed to mind, but I blinked them away.

From behind his back, he pulled out a clear plastic container holding a red calla lily. We'd seen them all over the island, learning how they represented courage and determination. Tears choked my throat as he slipped the corsage onto my wrist.

I smiled my appreciation. Using my free hand to fan my face dry.

"You are the love of my life." Sebastian lifted my fingers to his lips.

"And you are mine."

He pulled me close for a kiss. Warm and familiar, yet lusty and exciting. But then, every moment together was a gift from Heaven. He'd refused to make love to me since we'd arrived. His teasing sent me into a deeper heat than I thought myself capable.

Tonight felt like the night.

Hand in hand, we strolled the lighted walkway to the smooth sand at the ocean's edge. Waves rolled in and receded at their own lazy pace. My dress fluttered in the briny breeze dancing my skin to attention. The sky paused in a dusky moment of indecision. Inky blue up high, where a single star twinkled brightly. Below, the day's last peachy burst of light faded into the horizon.

"Does this spot look familiar?" Sebastian asked.

Sand. Sky. Ocean. It looked like every other area along the beachfront. I swiveled my head to search for a landmark, but the only thing behind us was a row of lounge chairs.

With a man slumbering in one.

Your next mister right could be anywhere. Even here on this island.

Rebecca's prophetic words hit like a thunderclap.

"You remember," Sebastian said.

"This is where I was sitting. The day I was supposed to get married."

He took my hands in each of his. My heart raced as I relived our weekend together, all lightness and adventure. I remembered the thrill of kissing Sebastian. The laughter of riding in the convertible, wind whipping the hair I no longer needed to feel whole. He brought me back from the darkness. Showed me life had more to give, if only I had the courage to claim it. After those two days, I believed in myself again. It was the greatest gift I've ever received.

"The day I first saw you, I thought I'd never seen anyone so beautiful, and so lost. I wanted to rush over and take your sorrows away. That day you stole my heart and haven't once let it go. You're strong and gorgeous, giving and brilliant. You deserve to be loved with every ounce of the passion you dedicate to others."

I pulsed with life, every cell tingling as he spoke.

How had I gotten so lucky?

"I have one more thing for you to wear tonight. Reach into my breast pocket."

He wore a wide grin as I slipped my hand in and pulled out a diamond ring.

I gasped. "You didn't!"

He took it from my shaking hand and knelt. In the torchlight, I saw it better. An emerald-cut diamond flanked by two round emeralds. I'd mentioned it once in passing, and he'd not only listened—he remembered. He slid on the gold ring I'd wear for the rest of my life. It was everything, and I feared dying of happiness.

"Be my wife. Together, there's nothing we can't do. Make love to me. Make babies with me. And yes, dig potatoes with me."

I laughed at that, tears streaming. He knew I hated digging in that damn garden.

"You're my everything. And I want to be with you always." His happy tears dazzled, reflecting the nearby flames. His wavy hair fluttered in the tropical air, soft and touchable.

My Sebastian.

My husband-to-be.

"Don't leave me hanging!" He joked.

"Yes! Of course, of course! I'll marry you!"

He jumped to his feet, snatching me in his arms, twirling me around. We kissed. We laughed. We admired the ring together, chattering "I love yous," before starting the cycle all over again.

We'd be together always. We'd build a happy, full, and meaningful life. Full of love and purpose and adventure.

He raised our hands in a champion move over our heads as we walked up the beach and a chorus of cheers erupted. Startled, I squinted to make out the faces in the crowd gathered ahead. Our friends and family stood toasting us with champagne flutes under a canopy of white lights.

My dad, brother, and Aunt Evelyn.

Sebastian's mom, Nikki, and Ramon.

Leslie, Rebecca, and Kyle.

Mo and Judge Peña.

And Portia, who had quickly become a close friend in my new life. How thoughtful of Sebastian to include her.

"How?" I asked, genuinely shocked.

Sebastian shrugged. "I flew them in. They're here to celebrate our love."

"It's perfect. Thank you."

Sebastian kissed me hard and the chorus of cheers grew louder.

Ramon tossed in a "You go, girl," among a smattering of whistles.

As we approached our families hand-in-hand, torches fluttered in the wind, but never extinguished. Just like our love. A passion for the ages, our love would endure until our very last breath.

Wow, everyone! Thanks for spending your reading time with Barbara and Sebastian. Writing this book changed me forever, and I hope you loved it too. Next up in Book 4: Leslie and Evaristo in **What We Give Away**!

Leslie is an award-winning journalist who charges head-first into NYC's most dangerous stories. Her only fear: getting too close to the only man she's ever loved. In What We Give Away, Leslie dives deep into her biggest story yet: herself! She exposes a huge cultural lie and gets a second chance at love! Don't miss Barbara's bestie on a bold journey of her own. **Pre-order it now.**

Plus, don't forget to **get your free prequel copy of The Breakup**. It's the story of Barbara's broken engagement to Joe, and you won't want to miss it. Learn more on the Free Prequel page.

Want more? **Turn the page to read chapter one of Love, Only Better**, Bold Journeys Book 1. It's the beginning of the two-book story arc of Rebecca and Kyle. Can you say juicy?

Turn the Page to Read Chapter 1 of

Love, Only Better

Bold Journeys Book One

It's Rebecca's turn...

Love Only Better: Chapter One

It wasn't as if the words were unexpected. Hell, Rebecca said them to herself a thousand times over. Only, this was different. Hearing someone else say them—someone she loved. Someone who shared her life and her bed for three years—somehow made them true. And to have Ethan say them. For him to let them free that way. Now, they were alive to reverberate through the universe and rebound on her in unforgiving ways. And he'd no longer be around to save her.

Frigid. Ice queen.

Who calls someone they love an ice queen? Rebecca wondered.

That's the ticket. Ethan didn't love her. Had he ever? Or was she just a bad lay; a notch on his belt. Not even a trophy. A third-place yellow ribbon no one wanted, abandoned in the bottom of a drawer.

A wisp of spiderweb dangling from her headboard above fluttered in time with her cleansing breaths. Dust covered. Abandoned. Even the stupid spider hadn't stuck around.

Frigid. Ice queen.

She flipped up her covers to snatch a tissue from across the room, wiping her eyes and nose before tossing it into the wastebasket under her old desk. The desk in name only. Even bac k in high school, she did her homework on her bed. The desk chair, like now, was a glorified staging area for clothes somewhere between clean and dirty.

Did she still have it?

She yanked the center drawer open, pawing the time capsule within. Old lipstick, diaries, hair elastics, the wallet-sized card reproduction of her university diploma, tarot cards, and there it was: her third-place ribbon. She won it at summer camp for archery. She'd never held a bow before then, or since. But there it was; evidence that she was once good enough at something to warrant recognition.

The silky cord slid between her fingers until hitting the tassel knot.

So fitting. Third place. Rebecca was third place in her own life, too. She was certainly last place to Ethan. He was probably off finding himself a blue-ribbon sex machine worthy of His Majesty. Even at this hour. New York City never sleeps, after all.

Growing up in the belly of Manhattan, the buzz of life at all hours was as natural as air. The humming streetlights, the shadows, everything held a pulse. Teeming.

Except for her. Rebecca was the one spot of lifelessness in the whole city.

Frigid. Ice queen.

She dropped the ribbon in the drawer and slammed it shut, then quickly froze. Alert, she listened for sounds of stirring. Barbara, her roommate and best friend, was fast asleep in the next room. A lawyer with a big day in court ahead.

Rebecca released her breath, then strode back to bed, flopping on top of her navy down comforter and making herself a burrito with its folded edges. It was as close as she would get to an embrace for who knows how long.

Wiggling for her night table, she switched off the light. Shadows formed at familiar angles on her ceiling. The ceiling she'd pondered for twenty-eight years. Framed pictures of Salvador Dali and Kandinsky hung over her low, long dresser, once filled with frilly pink play clothes, now stuffed with T-shirts and leggings in mismatched shades of black. Her collection of discount designer shoes spilled out of the closet, distractions for the shortcomings of her noir wardrobe.

Her eyes drifted closed.

Ethan's contorted, red face jolted her awake.

Would she ever sleep again?

Would she ever love again?

Would anyone ever love her?

Was she even worthy of being loved?

She wasn't sure.

On cue, her nemesis, the mourning dove, made a fluttery landing on the air-conditioning unit blocking half of her window. The distinctive coo was maddening. Was that how Ethan felt when she was unable to climax in bed? A fury of frustration without an outlet?

Rebecca abandoned covers and leaped to battle stations. The vinyl shade creaked its objection as she bent it up to spy on the enemy. The pink towel she put out to dull the air-conditioner drips from upstairs had become a bird magnet. Twigs, leaves, tinsel? Where did they find tinsel in June?

"Shoo! Shoo!" Rebecca whisper screamed, banging on the glass with her fist.

The dusty bird settled in.

"Go on. *Go.*"

"Becca! Are you fucking kidding? It's 4:00 a.m.!" Barbara shouted through the wall.

"Sorry!" Rebecca hollered back, watching the bird tuck its wings for sleep. There was a beat of silence.

"Shit," Barbara muttered. Rebecca heard her feet hit the floor and storm down the parquet hallway, a staple of 1950s' NYC apartments. The bathroom door closed.

Rebecca dropped the shade and collapsed into the cup of her papasan chair under the window, drawing a branded fleece blanket over her. It was one of the many freebies she got working in advertising; this one was from her hotel client.

After the flush and wash, Barbara exited then walked through Rebecca's perennially open bedroom door and switched the light on.

Her hand shielded her eyes from the sudden brightness.

Barbara stood in a pink satin Victoria Secret nightie, a matching sleep mask holding up her long, dark locks—a top-shelf weave and proudly not hers—flowing over ebony shoulders.

"What the hell are you doing up?"

"I'm so sorry—"

"Jesus, what happened?"

"What do you mean?"

"You look like a clown on acid."

Rebecca crawled out of the saucer and stood in front of the mirror.

"Yeah, not my best look."

Black mascara streaked down her face from the blotchy eyes she had been rubbing for hours.

"Where's Ethan? I thought he was staying over?"

"Gone."

"Gone home?"

"No. Just gone. We're done. Well, actually, he was done with me."

"Wow. I'm so sorry. But... not as sorry as you should be for waking me up..." Barbara said, launching herself to Rebecca's bed and sliding her sleep mask down over her eyes.

"That's it? That's all the consoling I get? I have a blowout with my boyfriend who calls me a 'frigid ice queen' and leaves, and..."

"He didn't," Barbara said, lifting up on her elbow and raising her mask.

"Oh yes he did."

"You're not an ice queen. You know that."

"Counselor, the evidence is overwhelming."

"He's a jackass. I've always thought so."

"Oh, he's not that bad..."

Barbara raised an eyebrow.

"Come on!"

"I won't lie to you and say I'm disappointed he's gone."

"But... I am," Rebecca whispered.

"All I mean is he didn't treat you right. You can absolutely do better."

Barbara patted the bed next to her. Rebecca folded her arms and looked away.

"You CAN do better. Ethan will regret losing you, and you'll look back and NOT regret losing him."

Rebecca pouted her bottom lip.

"Suit yourself. I must sleep more, though." Barbara left the bed, popped a squeaky kiss on Rebecca's forehead.

"Leave that damn bird alone, will you?" she said before leaving.

"You left the light on!" Rebecca called after her, but Barbara's bedroom door closed with a click.

Sighing, Rebecca crawled out of the chair and crossed the room to switch off the light. Dawn's blueness was already invading. She looked at her bed, but instead returned to sit under her fleece blanket, gathering it about her.

Maybe she could sleep if she was out of bed, away from his smell. She'd have to change the sheets later. She wanted to change everything; beginning with herself.

To keep reading, **buy your copy of Love, Only Better at this web link** or visit: paulettestout.com/buy-books.

Post a Review

If this book meant anything to you, please take a moment to leave a review. Like you might skip an empty restaurant, the same applies to books! Thanks for helping to fill my restaurant! :)

paulettestout.com/review

Acknowledgements

As my writing journey continues, there are a growing list of people whose support means the world. Thank you for believing in me.

To my amazing sensitivity readers, Dr. Shirley Knowles and Michelle Quarles, who collaborated with me for over a year to bring truth and authenticity to Barbara's journey. Our work together changed me for the better. Your insight and humor brought raw honesty to Barbara's experience as a Black woman and I'll be forever grateful.

To sensitivity reader Melany Barrett, for giving your fresh eye to the story, sharing your own experiences as a Black woman.

To my sister, Roxanne Media, for our frank conversations about navigating the world as woman of color. Your love, honesty, and selfless dedication to caring for our family gives me space to create and I'm eternally grateful.

To my editor, Miranda Darrow, for once again wrangling my many distracting tangents. I'm a willful writer, and so value your tough—but reasoned—suggestions.

To my talented cover designer, Rena Violet of Covers by Violet, whose breathtaking creativity never ceases to amaze.

To beta reader, Karen Branstein, for her honest input and eagle eye for typos.

To my critique partner, Kelly Ralston, for your unwavering support. Thanks for patiently listening to the many ramblings of this, often distressed, creator.

To my dear friends Amy D 'Alessio and Maureen Jones for being steady, loving forces in my life and inspiring me to create.

To Laura Henry, your love and positivity for my writing means more to me than you'll ever know.

To the members of the Women's Fiction – Indie Author Support Group, you have become true friends and collaborators in all things literary, and I'm very grateful.

To the members of WFWA and Every Damn Day Writers Group, who provide my daily dose of writer friendship when I'm typing alone in a room. Thank you for your giving support.

To Lainey Cameron and Charlotte Dune, who created a Thursday community online that has blossomed into many valuable friendships.

To my children, Max and Veronika, whose love, support—and patience are both boundless. Thank you for making my writing journey feel magical.

Last and first, to Markus, my husband, the fairytale endings I write are inspired by the amazing life we've built together. Thank you for making me better.

Thank you all, and to my amazing readers, for supporting my author journey!

About the Author

Paulette Stout is the fearless author of fast-paced contemporary women's fiction tackling social issues often ignored. With Paulette's books, readers get bingeable prose, relatable characters, and compelling stories that make you both feel and think.

Her 10 book award recognitions span her titles—Love, Only Better and What We Never Say—adding to her three media industry awards, including a MediaWeek All-Star.

Raised by a single dad in Manhattan, you can now find Paulette rearranging words into pleasing patterns while wearing grammar t-shirts at her home in Acton, Massachusetts.

Connect with Paulette on her website at paulettestout.com, on Instagram, Facebook or TikTok @paulettestoutauthor and on Twitter/X @StoutContent.